D0648575

SOLDIER IN THE RAIN

WILLIAM GOLDMAN

SOLDIER IN THE RAIN

NEW YORK

ATHENEUM

PUBLISHERS

1960

ASBURY PARK PUBLIC LIBRARY
ASBURY PARK, NEW JERSEY

Copyright © 1960 by William Goldman. All rights reserved
Library of Congress catalog card number 60–9580
Published simultaneously in Canada by Longmans, Green & Company
Manufactured in the United States of America by H. Wolff, New York
Designed by Harry Ford

FIRST EDITION

Lines from "Danny Boy" copyright 1913 by Boosey and Company
Used by permission

FOR

JAMES

GIFT
7/27/71
9554

SOLDIER IN THE RAIN

I.

It was four o'clock and things at last were quiet in the Transient Company, so Sergeant Clay decided to pay a visit on Master Sergeant Slaughter. Walking out of the supply room, he locked the door carefully behind him, then took a few steps into the sunshine. He stopped, suddenly perspiring. Even though it was four o'clock in the afternoon and even though it was not yet the middle of April, it was hot. The southern sun burned down, unhampered by clouds, scorching the dusty ground. Clay wiped his forehead with the back of his hand and adjusted his fatigue cap until the visor was approximately on a level with his nose. Then, tilting his head back so he could see, he moved slowly toward the orderly room.

Walking around the back, he came upon half a dozen new recruits—each in his first week of military service—hiding in the shadow of the overhanging roof. They started guiltily at his appearance and hurried out into the sun, bending over to search for cigarette butts.

"Rest," Clay said. "Take it slow."

They looked at him, hesitating a moment before moving back to stand again in the shadow.

"Thank you," one of them said.

Clay grinned. "Made in the shade," he muttered. "Definitely made in the shade." He paused and looked at them. They were staring out past him and, turning, he followed their gaze.

The Transient Company was located directly adjacent to the post stockade, and now, in the center of the barbed-wire enclosure, Clay saw Sergeant First Class Priest putting a bunch of prisoners through calisthenics. The prisoners were running wearily in place while Priest stood at ease in front of them, yelling out the cadence. "Double time!" Priest roared. "Faster, goddamit! Double time!"

"Poor bastards," Clay said, and he walked on by the recruits and rounded the corner of the orderly room. As soon as he was out of sight, he bent down low and began creeping forward, moving rapidly beneath Captain Magee's window. When he was safely past, he stood up straight and walked slowly to the window directly behind the first sergeant's desk.

"Hey, Billy," he whispered. "I'm going up on Main Post to see Slaughter awhile. Okay?"

Master Sergeant Booth looked out the window at him. "Okay," he said.

"Bye-bye, Billy," Clay said. He waved once. Again he crept under Captain Magee's window, again stood up when he was safely past. Then, slowly, shoving his hands into his pockets, he sauntered back to where the recruits were hiding. He rounded the corner and stopped.

They were gone.

Momentarily puzzled, Clay looked around. Probably were hiding someplace else by now. Maybe in back of the mess hall. Or behind one of the barracks. Or . . .

The recruits were stretched in the dust along the outside of the stockade fence, doing push-ups along with the prisoners. Sergeant First Class Priest leaned against the fence, staring from one group to the other, counting cadence. "Up, down, up, down, up . . ."

Clay ran over toward the stockade. "What the hell's going on?" he shouted.

Sfc. Priest faced him through the fence. "Just teaching your boys how to soldier," he said.

"Yeah?" Clay said. "When did you learn?" He walked in among the recruits. "Get out of here back to your barracks." The recruits stood, brushing the dust from their fatigues. They nodded toward Clay and hurried away.

"Big hero," Priest said.

Clay stared at him. "Go beat your prisoners," he muttered.

Priest put his mouth up next to the fence. He spat once and walked away.

Clay watched him a moment, watched as Priest strode through the stockade compound and out of it, finally disappearing inside the back door of MP Headquarters. When Priest was gone, Clay hurried to the company parking lot.

His car, a thirteen-year-old 1940 Ford convertible, was waiting for him, the top down. Clay approached it, opened the door, stepped inside and sat. Uttering a cry of pain, he jumped up. The red leather seats were burning. He got out of the car and rubbed his hands across his butt, patting it tenderly where it had been singed by the leather. Then he pounded his fists onto the car seat, trying to cool it. Dust rose. He touched the seat with his finger. It was still hot. He pounded it some more, harder, but suddenly he was bathed in sweat, so he stopped, contenting himself with waving his cap across the leather, trying to create a small breeze.

Looking up, he realized that several of the prisoners were watching him from behind the barbed-wire enclosure, pointing at him and laughing.

"Hey, stupid," one of them called.

"What?" Clay called back.

"He knows his name, all right, all right," another prisoner yelled.

Clay ignored this.

"It won't hurt him none," a third yelled. "Can't you see he's a lard ass?"

"Knock it off down there," a guard warned, walking over.

The prisoners quieted.

"The aw-dassity of them convicts," Clay muttered, glancing out from under his cap, checking to see if they were still watching him. They were. Slowly, with great dignity, he re-entered his car and lowered himself down onto the still-blazing red leather. "Owww," he whispered, moving around, turning the ignition key. "Owww," he said again, as he shifted into reverse and backed out onto the company street. Doffing his cap, he waved good-bye to the criminal element, and the car moved forward toward C Road. Clay turned left and drove past the Transient Company, past the Stockade, past MP Headquarters, heading for the Main Post of Camp Scott, which was two miles away.

Camp Scott was one of the biggest Army posts in the country. More than seventy-five square miles of land, it seemed to stretch endlessly, always flat, always hot. There were a few hills over on the eastern side, near the bivouac area, but otherwise, the essential quality of the post was flatness. Everything was flat: the ground, the few square-cut hedges, the clay-colored barracks, hundreds of them, set flush against the clay-colored ground. When the Korean War started in June of 1950, Camp Scott had become a major center for basic training. Now, almost three years later, with the war still dragging on, the post was busier than ever.

Off to his right Clay saw a company in dumb show, practicing the bayonet. Two hundred fatigue-clad men stood in a huge circle, parrying gracelessly with imaginary adversaries, lunging forward, then returning to the on-guard position, then lunging forward again. They practiced the movement over and over, and from that distance, through the hot, wet air, Clay heard the faint cry of "Kill . . . kill . . . kill. . . ." Then silence. Then, again, ". . . kill . . . kill. . . ." A final whispered ". . . kill. . . ."

To his left, another company of trainees was running into its barracks with a roar, a field first sergeant standing out in the center of the street, yelling after them, "Knock the goddam doors down, knock the goddam doors down," while the men pushed and shoved, elbowing one another, forcing themselves inside, out of sight, out of mind, out of the everlasting sun. "Too slow, too slow," the field first sergeant yelled. "Get out here and do it again."

Clay drove on. He felt cooler now; the red leather seats no longer burned. He reached up with one hand and adjusted his fatigue cap, pushing it farther back on his head. Boy, but there were an awful lot of trainees on post! How many? He closed one eye. Twenty thousand? Twenty-five? It was something like that. And one way or another they all came through the Transient Company, waiting a day or two, processing and pulling details, then getting shipped to their various companies for basic training. How many sheets had he given out? Twenty-five thousand men in the past four months, seventy-five thousand the past year. Two sheets to a man. How many was that? Twice seventy-five was . . . ? A hundred and fifty? Yes. A hundred and fifty. He himself had given out a hundred and fifty thousand sheets in twelve months. Now, if he'd been in business for himself, at a dollar profit a sheet, how much was that? A hundred and fifty thousand dollars a year. He would have made that much. And in ten years he would have made a million. More than a million. In less than ten years he'd have made his pile.

"Woweeoboy," he said out loud. "I should have gone into the sheet business."

Clay braked the car suddenly. He was at a cross street and a company was marching by, back from the ranges. A road guard stood in front of him, blocking his way. The corporal in charge of the company was singing, "I got a girl who lives in the West," and the company echoed, "I got a girl who lives in the West." Then the corporal again: "She's got mountains on her chest." And the echo: "She's got mountains on her chest."

Clay lit a cigarette and inhaled deeply, waiting for the company to pass. Not moving had made him a target for the sun again, and he rubbed his perspiring forehead with his sleeve. The company drummer was marching by now, striking rhythmically at the center of his drum. And from the distant ranges, Clay could hear the intermittent report of M-1 rifles, sounding like a child's popgun. The company was almost gone and the corporal's voice was softer: "I don't know but I've been told." Then the company: "I don't know but I've been told." "Eskimo girls are mighty cold," the corporal sang, and the company echoed, "Mighty cold," and the road guards pulled away. Clay raised the clutch, pressed down on the gas pedal and moved forward.

A moment later he was in Main Post. There was grass here, and ahead he could see the great stretch of carefully tended lawn that made up the Parade Ground. Beyond that was the nine-hole golf course and, set between the two, the Officers' Club. Traffic was snarled in front of the Main PX, so Clay had to wait again before he could drive by. From the sidewalk, two girls waved to him. "Hi, Eustis," they called, and he waved back, giving them the smile. Traffic cleared and he turned right onto Third Street, cruising past Divisional Headquarters, past the Service Club.

Finally, he slowed.

A small sign set in from the sidewalk said *Information and Education Headquarters,* and in back of it was a square gray wooden building. Clay drove into the driveway and stopped. Getting out, he walked to the rear of the car and pulled the canvas top with both hands, tugging, pushing, finally forcing it up and over so that it covered the car. Then, adjusting his fatigue cap until the visor was approximately on a level with his nose, he entered the building quietly, tiptoeing along the corridor until he reached Slaughter's door. Silently he turned the knob and got down on all fours. Throwing the door open, he commenced to crawl forward, groaning terribly, gasping for breath. Grabbing Slaughter by the foot, Clay forced himself up into a kneeling position.

"Tell . . . Colonel . . . Custer," he whispered, his face contorted with pain. "Tell . . . him . . . the . . . Little

Big Horn . . . is . . . a . . . tr—" He fell over backward and lay still.

Master Sergeant Slaughter applauded warmly. "Moving," he said. "Undeniably moving."

"Thank you, thank you," Clay said, clambering up on top of Slaughter's desk, crossing his legs. "Howdy, Maxwell."

"Good afternoon, Eustis," Slaughter answered, staring contemplatively at the large framed photograph of Maude Adams that served as the only decoration on an otherwise blank wall. Finally he turned in his mammoth leather swivel chair to face Clay. "I've got news," he began.

"Me, too," Clay interrupted. "Hey, Maxwell, you know what? I been doing some thinking and you know what I figured out?"

"What?" Slaughter asked quietly.

"I figured out that you and me, we ought to go into the sheet business."

Sergeant Slaughter returned his gaze to Maude Adams.

"Hey, no kidding," Clay went on. "Do you realize that all we got to do is sell a hundred and fifty thousand sheets a year and zingo, we're millionaires? How about that? Isn't that something? What do you think?"

"I think it's easily the finest idea you've had all week, this being Tuesday."

"What's wrong with it? I think it's sensational. Hell, everybody uses sheets."

"Eustis," Slaughter said. "Where are we going to get the money to buy them?"

"We don't need money," Clay said, leaning forward. "I can steal 'em. I bet I could steal two sheets out of every laundry package and no one would know."

"Please, Eustis," Slaughter began. "I told you I had news. Of considerable interest, I think. So—"

"Hell," Clay went on. "I could hock four from each

package. Easy. Maybe even six. Maybe . . ."

He stopped as Slaughter arose from his swivel chair, crossing the room to his soft-drink machine. Slowly raising his right hand, he dealt it a solid blow just above the coin-return slot. After a moment, the machine belched once, *Awwk,* dropped a cup, paused, then filled the cup with grape-ade. Gently removing the cup, Slaughter returned to his swivel chair and began to sip.

The soft-drink machine stood as a monument to Master Sergeant Slaughter's ingenuity—he was the only soldier on post, officer or enlisted man, to have one of his very own. Major General Simmons had a Coke machine in his office and so did Colonel Rafferty, but Slaughter was the only man able to exercise freedom of choice. By simply dialing the selecto-bar, he could choose Coke, root beer, ginger ale, cherry soda, lemon-lime, or grape. Grape was his particular favorite.

In his own way, Master Sergeant Slaughter was a celebrity, known throughout the post by both officers and enlisted men. Part of this was due to his recognizability—he stood not quite five feet ten and weighed well over two hundred fifty pounds. In a sitting position, he resembled an overweight Buddha. He knew all the influential people on post, his contacts being both secret and endless. He read a great deal, spoke excellent English, devoured butter brickle ice cream by the quart and worked the Sunday *New York Times* crossword puzzle in ink. All in all, Sergeant Clay thought him to be the smartest man he had ever known.

"Okay," Clay said, when Slaughter had finished his grape. "You don't want to go into the sheet business, we'll find something else." He shrugged. "What's your news?"

"They're closing the post," Master Sergeant Slaughter said.

* * *

Sergeant Clay allowed his fatigue cap to slip down over his face. Then, carefully, he blew it back into position. It was one of his best tricks and he did it only at moments of importance. "What post?" he said finally.

"This post."

"When?"

"Soon."

"Bull."

Slaughter shook his head. "No," he answered quietly. "It isn't."

"How'd you find out?"

"An acquaintance of mine works in the Pentagon. He just called me. The official announcement won't be for a while yet. Perhaps not for a month. But it will come, Eustis. Rest assured."

"Well, ain't that something," Clay muttered. He jumped down from the desk top and contemplated the soft-drink machine, his right hand half raised. Then, shaking his head, he reached into his pocket and took out a nickel. Selecting a Coke, he inserted the nickel and waited while the cup filled. Then he drained it in two swallows. "How can they do it?" he said finally, his voice growing louder. "How can they do such a thing? Ain't we still fighting in Korea?"

"Not much any more," Slaughter said. "It's mostly truce talks now."

Clay hopped back onto the desk and crossed his legs. "Maxwell?" he asked. "How should I feel about it?"

"Well, I can tell you how I feel about it," Slaughter answered. "I'm not happy."

"Why not?"

"Because basically, Eustis, I'm a conservative. I resist change. Any change. I like it here. I've got a nice job. I've got a nice office. I'm thinking of having it air-conditioned."

"Air-conditioned!"

Slaughter nodded. "Perhaps in a month or so. An acquaintance of mine is getting an extra unit."

"That's wonderful. I'm real proud of you, Maxwell."

Slaughter nodded again. "Thank you."

Clay leaned forward. "Hey, what about this post stuff? Are you sure? They're really gonna close it?"

"They really are, Eustis. They're going to kill it. The powers that be. They're going to sit back and watch it die."

"Now ain't that just like the stupid Army!" Clay exploded, yanking his cap down over his face. "Ain't that just typical? Here they are, fighting a war and they're gonna close up just about the biggest post they got while the shooting's still going on. What are they gonna do with all them trainees out there?"

"Oh, they'll finish up," Slaughter answered, sitting deeper in his swivel chair. "They'll finish up and more lads will come in and for a while I imagine everything will appear unchanged. This is a huge post, Eustis. It's three times the size of Manhattan Island. It takes a lot to kill it. But slowly, perhaps in one month, perhaps in two, it will start to die. First a barracks will get boarded up. Then a company. Then a battalion. The post will grow suddenly quiet. Less shouting, less beating of drums. And then, in six months or so . . ." Slaughter spread his hands out wide. "Nothing."

"You mean we're gonna all get shipped out in the next six months?"

Slaughter nodded.

Clay slid off the desk and began pacing around the room, fiddling nervously with his fatigue cap. Finally he stopped. "Hey," he blurted out. "Hey, Maxwell. How about you and me getting sent someplace together? Huh? I mean, we're a team. You can't go breaking up a team."

"Where would you like to go, Eustis?"

Clay shrugged. "Someplace cool."

Slaughter nodded. "That shouldn't be too difficult. I think I can manage that."

"Well, hell," Clay said, grinning suddenly. "Then who cares? Let's go celebrate the closing. Let's go tip a few. Let's really tie one on. Let's do that, huh?"

Slaughter shook his head. "It's Tuesday," he answered.

"Aw, come on, Maxwell. Couldn't you break your rule? Just this once?"

"I'm sorry, Eustis. I'm a creature of habit. I can't."

"Well, I can," Clay said. "And I'm gonna." Turning, he sauntered toward the door. "Bye-bye, Maxwell. See you around."

"Until that time, Eustis," Slaughter answered. "Until that time."

Outside, Clay paused a moment on the steps, then moved slowly toward his car. Grabbing the top, he yanked at it, pulling it down into the open area behind the back seat. Perspiring slightly, he began to drive to the Transient Company. He made it through Main Post without difficulty, but up ahead he saw that C Road was jammed. It was nearing the end of the training day, and the companies were marching back from the ranges. The hot, wet air was filled with singing and yelling and the beating of drums. Dust rose from thousands of boots. Above the dust, the black layer of soot from the coal-burning stoves of all the barracks was settling, the dust and soot meeting in mid-air, C Road disappearing in the haze. Clay coughed, wiped his forehead, then turned sharply to the right, speeding past the parade ground, the Officers' Club, the golf course, heading for the bivouac area. When he reached it, he turned left and drove quickly along the deserted road for two miles before turning left again, heading directly into the setting sun, to approach C Road from the rear.

Ahead of him was the MP station. Clay stared. Sfc. Priest

was standing on the front steps, his arms crossed on his chest. Clay started driving by, but then, suddenly, he braked. "Woweeoboy," he said out loud. "Here's where I make a little pile," and he turned into the MP driveway. Getting out of his car, he hurried around to Sfc. Priest. When he stood in front of the other man, he nodded. Sfc. Priest nodded back.

Then they stared at each other.

Sergeant First Class Priest was easily the least-liked non-com on the post. Clay had managed to stay clear of him until six months before, when Priest had refused Clay a permit to drive his red convertible on post, saying that the car was unsafe, falling apart and a danger to pedestrians. Since Clay had paid well over one hundred dollars for it, he protested vigorously, but all to no avail. They had a running battle on the telephone for a week, but it is doubtful that Clay ever would have received a permit had not Master Sergeant Slaughter had a talk with Priest, the specifics of which Clay never discovered. The results of the conversation were quick and sure, however; the next day, Clay had his permit.

"Hot, ain't it?" Clay said casually, rubbing his foot in the dust at the bottom of the steps.

"Who says so?" Priest returned, glaring down. He was a big man, tending slightly to flesh, with small eyes and a stiff black crew-cut.

"Nobody says so," Clay muttered. "But my sweat keeps telling me it's kind of warm out."

"This ain't warm," Priest said. "Hell. This ain't even luke."

"Maybe you're right," Clay agreed. There was a pause.

"I like it hot," Priest said then. "The hotter it is, the better I like it. I like to sweat. It makes me feel good."

"Oh, who don't?" Clay nodded. "There's nothing like a good sweat to make a body feel alive." He started jumping up and down. "Think I'll work me up a little sweat right now."

Priest watched him. "What the hell are you doing here, Clay? You and that junk heap of yours. What are you coming to see me for?"

"No reason, Priest. It's just that I was on my way back to the company and I couldn't make no time, on account of all them *thousands and thousands* of trainees marching in my way. I mean, look out there. The roads is clogged."

Sfc. Priest looked. Then he nodded.

"I mean, did you ever see so many trainees in all your life?" Clay went on. "Just listen to all that noise." He stopped, and the rhythmic marching grew louder. There was less singing now, and the voices of the field firsts filtered in to them. "Pick up the step! Pick up the step! Road guards out! Road guards in! Pick up the damn step!"

Clay stared at the faceless, helmeted men moving by. "There's thousands of 'em, Priest. Wouldn't you say that? Thousands. Maybe more."

"So what?"

"Nothin'." Clay shrugged. "Except that it's a nice feeling. Just knowing that you're standing right smack in the middle of maybe the biggest training post in the whole world. It gives you a real feeling of security, don't it?"

"No."

"Well, it does me. No kidding. Sometimes I just lie awake in bed thinking about what a great place this is to be, and how wouldn't it be a shame if they ever closed it."

"Closed it?"

"Yeah. Sure. You know. Closed it up. This post right here. So that there wouldn't be nothin' at all. Just weeds. And the wind blowing by. Nothin' else. No people. Just the weeds and the wind."

"You're nuts," Priest said.

"Oh, sure," Clay agreed. "I probably am. I doubt they'll ever close it. Not this post. Maybe Indiantown Gap, sure. Or maybe Breckinridge. But not Camp Scott. They'll never close this one. What do you think, Priest? Do you think they'll ever close it?"

"Naw."

Clay extended his right hand. "For how much?" he said.

Sfc. Priest took a step up the stairs. "What are you talking about?"

Clay shrugged. "Nothin'. It's just that I got a feeling. Like a voice in the night comes to me and says, 'Eustis, pack your duffel bag. We're moving out.' That's all. I just got this feeling, see? And I wonder if I'm right."

"You're nuts," Sfc. Priest said.

"Twenty bucks," Clay answered, raising his right hand higher. "Twenty bucks says they announce it inside a month."

"You're on," Priest said, reaching out.

Clay pulled back. "Well now, wait a minute," he began.

"Put your money where your mouth is."

"That makes it a matter of honor," Clay muttered. "Twenty bucks it is."

They shook hands.

"You are one stupid bastard, Clay. You know that?"

"Probably," Clay agreed. "And you're a smart one, aren't you, Priest?"

"I get along."

"And I guess I better be," Clay said, readjusting his cap. He turned and hurried back to his car, muttering "Woweeoboy, woweeoboy," over and over. Backing onto C Road, he drove past the stockade to the Transient Company. Jumping out of the car, he doffed his cap to the jeering prisoners behind the barbed-wire fence, stuffed his hands into his pockets and sauntered slowly across the company grounds to his barracks.

The first floor was filled with recruits, some writing letters, some playing cards, some lying quietly on their bunks. "Hi, Sergeant Clay," a bunch of them called.

"Gentlemen," he nodded, hurrying up the stairs to the second floor. It too was filled with recruits, and again some of them called his name, "Hi, Sergeant Clay," "Afternoon, Sergeant Clay," and again he nodded, this time adding a left-handed salute.

He unlocked the door to his cadre room, stepped inside and closed the door behind him. Quickly unbuttoning his fatigue jacket, Clay flopped full length on his bed. It was terribly hot, and he wriggled out of his pants, kicking them off onto the floor. Bending his legs, he pulled at his laces and pried his boots off, using the foot of the bed for a lever. Then he rolled around on the sheets, drying himself. Sheets were one of his great extravagances—he always kept an extra supply in his foot locker and changed them at least once a day. Pulling his T-shirt over his head, he dropped it to the floor and lay still now, clad only in his socks and his blue silk underwear. The underwear was elegantly decorated with the outlines of butterflies, the gift of a buxom *Fräulein* named Hilde whom he had befriended during his occupation tour in Germany. Bending his legs a second time, he yanked off his socks and dropped them onto the floor. His body was wet again, so he rolled around on the sheets until he was dry.

Then, slowly, he reached out to his bed table and picked up the large leather picture frame and placed it on his stomach. "Hey, Donald," he said softly, staring at the color photograph of the beautiful golden retriever lying asleep in the shadow of a tree. "Hey, Donald, guess what? We're shipping out. You and me and Maxwell. We're going someplace cool."

Carefully putting the picture frame back on the table, Clay stood and took off his underwear and tucked a towel around his waist. "They're closing the post," he sang suddenly. "It'll look like a ghost." Not bad. At least for a starter. He looked at his sheets. They were soaked through, so he decided to change them. Pulling the dirty ones from the bed, he dumped them onto the floor, then opened his foot locker and lifted out two clean sheets and a pillowcase, spreading them across his mattress. "They're closing the post down," he sang. "It'll look like a ghost town." There. That was much better. Two double rhymes. Fantastic.

Singing his song over and over, Sergeant Clay went down for his shower.

Fifteen minutes later he was back in his room. Taking another pair of blue silk underwear, he put it on and opened his wall locker, studying his wardrobe, closing first one eye, then the other. Finally he began to dress. He chose a pair of brown gabardine slacks and a flowery yellow sports shirt that hung loosely outside his trousers. Sitting on his bed, he donned short black nylon socks and black loafers. He spent a few minutes combing his hair, making sure that his cowlick fell casually down across his forehead. "Rooty, tooty, tooty," he sang out loud. "Dee toot, dee toot, dee toot." Of all his compositions, it was his favorite song. It had no tune and he had never bothered inventing words, but the rhythm was strong and he always sang it whenever he was particularly happy. "Rooty tooty tooty," he sang. Into his right rear pants pocket went his wallet; his handkerchief went into the left rear. Into his shirt pocket went a pencil, a piece of paper, cigarettes and matches. "Dee toot, dee toot, dee toot." Reaching into his foot locker, he displaced a pile of handkerchiefs, revealing an enormous number of contraceptives. He took three and put them into his right front pants pocket.

Finished, he walked to his wall mirror and looked at himself.

Had it not been for his smile, Sergeant Clay would have been extremely handsome. His eyes were very large, blue and shining; his nose was straight and regular, his teeth even and white. His complexion was perfectly clear and his mouth, at least in repose, nice enough. But when he smiled his face seemed almost to double in width. It was an enormous smile, a practically perpetual smile. And no one can be handsome when he smiles all the time.

Clay turned from the mirror. Touching the top of the picture frame with one hand, he walked from the room, locking the door behind him. Then he hurried down the stairs, waved to the recruits and left the barracks.

Passing the orderly room, he glanced at his watch. Six twenty. He was on schedule. The night was pleasantly warm, so he slowed, ambling toward his car. The seats were cool now and he shifted into reverse, backing out of the parking lot, moving along the company street until he came to C Road. Then he turned left and sped along the quiet thoroughfare. The road was deserted, the evening quiet; there were no trainees in sight. Only the brightly lit barracks on either side of the road showed any signs of life. Relaxing, sitting deeper in the red leather seat, he sped contentedly toward Main Post.

It was six thirty when he reached the Officers' Club.

Sergeant Clay parked his convertible and walked across the lawn to the main entrance. The Officers' Club at Camp Scott was one of the larger buildings on post. A square brick structure, solidly built, it gave a feeling of permanence, of stability. On the outside, scattered green vines struggled to make up the losses forced down by the midday sun. From inside the building, Clay could hear soft music coming from a juke box. It was a pleasant place, cool and green, with the vast parade ground stretching out in front. Settling himself at a patio table near the entrance, he took the folded sheet of paper from his shirt pocket and smoothed it out before him. Reaching for the yellow stub of pencil, he licked the blunt point and, at the top of the paper, wrote the date. Beneath that, he made a list of numbers, from one to fifty. Then, settling himself in the canvas-backed chair, he waited.

In a few minutes, the first girl arrived.

Her name was Mary Jane and she was a town girl, from Hastingsville, very tall, with stringy black hair. As she passed by, she smiled. "Hello, Eustis," she said.

"Howdy, Mary Jane," he answered, smiling back, staring at her. She was wearing a thin blue summer dress. She was flat-chested and her calf muscles bulged and her legs needed shaving. Clay shook his head.

Then, licking the point of his pencil stub, he printed the letter *D* in the space opposite the first number.

Clay lit a cigarette and waited. Another girl appeared at the far end of the walk, accompanied by a young officer he did not know. She was another townie, and she worked in the Main PX during the day. She was wearing a low-cut green peasant blouse and her large breasts vibrated as she moved.

She smiled at him. "Hi, Eustis," she giggled.

He nodded to her. "Howdy, Emma." She had broad hips and thick legs and there was a noticeable tire of flesh around her middle. He thought for a moment, staring after her, watching her breasts bounce. "Good boobs," he said half aloud, and wrote *C—* in the space opposite the second number.

Now, at the bottom of the walk, he saw Janey Rafferty, accompanied by her father, a colonel, who was executive officer on the post. Janey was almost fifteen, with light blonde hair and long, beautifully shaped legs. She skipped on ahead of her father, who strode stiffly behind her. When she passed Clay, she glanced over and winked, mouthing the word "Eustis." He grinned back at her. She was very pretty, but from the waist up she was built like a boy. Clay shook his head. Young girls were always tough. He felt certain that any day now she was going to blossom; he just knew it. But could you take that into consideration? He shook his head again, closing his eyes, trying to make up his mind.

It was at this point that Private First Class Meltzer arrived, on the run.

Pfc. Meltzer was editor of the Camp Scott weekly newspaper, and he was always running. Tall, very thin, he had curly brown hair, a quick smile, and a face that was only now recovering from the ravages of adolescence. As he hurried up to Clay, he had on dark gray slacks, a blue cotton-cord jacket, a white button-down shirt, and a black knit tie, all carefully tailored and pressed. Yet somehow they gave the impression of being secondhand or belonging to somebody else. The shirt collar hung loosely at his neck, the trousers barely cleared his ankles, the knit tie was pulled way over to one side. Meltzer was relatively new on post and Clay did not know him well. Slaughter did, though; Meltzer's office was down the hall from Slaughter's in the I. & E. building, and they both lived in the same barracks at Headquarters Company.

"Hi, Sarge," Meltzer said, stopping in front of Clay's table.

"Howdy, Meltzer," Clay answered, glancing up, then returning his gaze to the far end of the walk.

"Maxwell Slaughter told me you'd be here," Meltzer went on hurriedly, "so I just ran over. He said you wanted to celebrate."

Clay nodded. Two more girls were going by and he wrote *D—* and *F* on the sheet of paper.

"What do you want to do?" Meltzer asked. "We better get started. I'd like to get to bed early. Let's go. Come on. What do you say?"

"In a sec," Clay answered. Another girl was walking by. This one was short and hairy and fat and flat-chested, and she had a mustache. Clay sighed and wrote *INC.* on the paper. Pfc. Meltzer walked around the table, staring thoughtfully down at the list of numbers and letters. Another girl appeared. She was over six feet tall, very skinny, and her teeth were bad. Clay shook his head and wrote *INC.* again.

"What are you doing?" Meltzer asked him.

Clay looked up. "Grading women," he replied.

"What's that?"

"Game."

"I never heard of it."

"That's on account of I made it up."

"How do you play?"

"Well," Clay began. "It's like this. First you got to get a pencil and a piece of paper. Then you get to station yourself someplace advantageous. Like here. Where there's lots of women walking by." He shrugged. "Then you just grade 'em. That's all there is to it."

"But how do you do that? I mean, how do you score?"

"Oh," Clay nodded. "Just like in high school. A, B, C, D, F, and Incomplete. A is for gorgeous. B is for nice. C is average. D is bad. F is for just awful. And if they're monsters, then you give 'em Incomplete. That's my biggest category, Incomplete. I'm a tough grader."

"That sounds like a great game," Meltzer said, and he whipped a pencil from his inside coat pocket and a slip of paper from his wallet. "Where are they?" he asked. "Where are they?"

"They'll be along," Clay answered, his eyes fixed on the end of the walk. "And this here's a particular good spot. 'Cause you're so close. The closer, the better." They were sitting no more than five feet from the walk. Their table was round and white, and from the center rose a large green umbrella. The entire area was elevated, providing a view of the parade ground. A soft wind had risen in the last half hour, and above them the sky was flooded with stars.

"Here comes one," Meltzer said excitedly. Clay nodded. She was of middle height and trimly built, but her legs were thick and short and her complexion was terrible.

"Bad pimples," Clay muttered softly.

The girl looked at him. "Evening, Eustis," she said.

"Howdy, Louise," he answered. "Nice night."

"Ummm," she nodded. "Beautiful," and she disappeared inside the Officers' Club.

Meltzer grabbed Clay by the arm. "What did you give her? What? What?"

Clay held up his paper. "D," he said. "How about you?"

"B," Meltzer answered.

"B!" Clay exploded. "You gave her a B! Are you blind?"

"I thought she had a nice figure."

"You see them pimples?" Clay asked. "You happen to notice them glistening there in the moonlight?"

"I didn't think they were so bad."

"Not so bad? Not . . ." he stopped, lowering his voice. "You see, Meltzer, this here is a game of skill. It takes practice. And you got to have standards. That's the most important thing of all. Standards. So . . ."

"I'll call them as I see them," Meltzer said.

Clay pulled his chair away and lit a cigarette.

"This is a terrific game, Sarge. It really is. Look. Here comes another one."

She was walking slowly, holding hands with a young officer. She wore a white blouse buttoned to the neck and a blue pleated skirt that swirled around her legs as she moved. She was short and broad in the hips, but her breasts were better than average and her complexion was clear. She waved to Clay. "Hi, Eustis."

"Howdy, Martha," he answered, waving back. He was about to write C+ on his paper when Meltzer grabbed him again, this time by the shoulder.

"A-minus," Meltzer said.

Clay stood up and walked to the next table and sat down.

"What's the matter?" Meltzer called.

"You play at your table," Clay told him, "and I'll play at mine." He stared down the walk and saw Ellie lumbering toward them. Ellie was an Incomplete. King glanced at Meltzer. "Try her on for size," he said.

Ellie strode by without a word.

"Don't you know her?"

Clay nodded. "Maxwell fixed me up with her once. Blind date. We didn't hit it off so good."

Pfc. Meltzer hesitated, his pencil an inch above the paper. "I just hate to give her a low grade," he muttered. "It doesn't seem nice. I mean, how would you feel if a couple of girls sat around and graded you?"

"You'll never be any good at this," Clay said, folding up his paper and sticking it back in his shirt pocket. "Let's go celebrate."

"Wait a while. There's some more girls coming."

"I thought you was in a hurry."

"Oh, I am. I always like to get to bed early."

"Let's go, then."

"Ten more," Meltzer said. "Just let me grade ten more. You can play too."

"Thanks," Clay mumbled. "I'll just watch." He lit a cigarette and sat back in the chair, his hands behind his head, staring up at the stars. Two girls appeared at the far end of the walk. "Don't tell me what you grade 'em," he called over to Meltzer. "Please."

Meltzer nodded, staring at the pair. He waited. A cluster of three came up the walk. Then two more. The wind blew softly by.

"How do you want to celebrate?" Meltzer asked then, his eyes still on the far end of the walk.

"Oh, I figured we'd just sort of go into Hastingsville and maybe pick up a couple of girls and get 'em drunk and then take 'em out in the car and see what happens. How's that sound?"

"I couldn't do that," Meltzer replied, grading the eighth girl.

"Why not?"

"I'm engaged. It wouldn't be right."

"Okay," Clay said. "Then we'll just drive into Hastingsville and have a few drinks and then go to a cathouse. That suit you any better?"

"I wouldn't feel right doing that, either," Pfc. Meltzer said. The ninth and tenth girls were coming up the walk, laughing to themselves.

"Hi, Eustis," they called.

"Howdy," Clay replied.

"What else?" Meltzer asked.

Clay shrugged. They stood and started down the walk toward the parking lot, Clay ambling slowly, his hands in his pockets, Pfc. Meltzer dashing on ahead.

"There must be something," Meltzer said, turning around, walking backward.

"Well. I suppose we could go to the post library and pretend we was MPs."

"What for?"

"To scare the fairies. They always sit around in the library. They get pretty sweaty when an MP comes around." They were standing by the red convertible now. Clay opened the door and got in; Pfc. Meltzer vaulted over the door into the seat.

"I don't want to do that either," Meltzer said. "It doesn't seem nice. I mean, how would you feel if you were a fairy and somebody did that to you?"

"Sweaty," Clay said.

"Don't you have any other ideas?"

"Yeah," Clay answered, and he turned on the ignition. The red car shot forward. "Let's get drunk . . ."

"I don't have much of a liquor capacity," Pfc. Meltzer said, talking very slowly, his eyes half closed. It was an hour later, and they were sitting at a bar in Hastingsville. "At school, they used to call me 'Two-brew'."

"Do tell," Clay answered. He finished his beer and signaled the bartender for another.

"No more for me, thank you," Pfc. Meltzer mumbled. He placed his elbows heavily on the wooden bar and dropped his chin in his hands. "You sure drink a lot, don't you?"

"Four beers ain't a lot," Clay said. "Four beers ain't nothing."

"The reason I don't have much of a liquor capacity," Meltzer confided, leaning toward Clay, talking softly, pausing after each word, "is that I don't drink much. You see, drinking is just like anything else. It takes practice. The more you drink, the more it takes you to get drunk. Did you know that?"

"Nope."

"Well, it's the truth, Clay old boy. That's an absolute scientific fact. It's why alcoholics drink so much. Because they've had all that practice." He paused. "This has been a terrific celebration."

"Oh, yes," Clay said. "It sure has." He drained half of the glass of beer and set it back on the bar. It made a wet circle and he stared at it.

"The reason I never had much practice drinking," Meltzer went on, "is that I was always in training. For track. I used to run an hour every day. Run, run, run. That's what I liked to do. Do you like to run?"

"Nope."

"Well, you should. There's nothing quite so enjoyable as running around and around and around. It really makes you feel alive. Did you know that?"

Clay squinted into the mirror over the bar.

"I'm a terrific runner," Meltzer mumbled, nodding his head. "I can just fly."

"Where'd you go to school, anyway?"

"Yale. It's a terrific school. But I'm not a typical Yaley. No sir, boy. I'm sort of an offbeat Yaley, you know what I mean?"

"I guess."

"They've got the most terrific track there. At Yale. Every afternoon I used to go up into old Payne Whitney and run and run and run. Around and around and around. That's what I like to do. Do you like to run?"

"How about a cup of coffee?" Clay asked.

"Oh, I don't drink coffee much, Clay old boy. Caffeine. It cuts down your wind. For running. I'm a terrific runner, I can—"

"What say I drive you back to post?" Clay cut in.

"I can run the mile in four minutes," Pfc. Meltzer finished. He leaned closer and lowered his voice confidingly. "But don't tell anybody."

Clay looked at him. "Bull," he said.

"It's the truth. At least, I think it is."

"But nobody ever done that."

Pfc. Meltzer put his finger to his lips. "Shhh," he whispered. "Don't talk so loud. I don't want anybody to find out. About me being able to run the mile in four minutes. They'd make me run for the post track team. And I wouldn't like that. In college I never ran on the college track team. I only ran by myself. In old Payne Whitney. Around and around and around."

Sergeant Clay sipped his beer. Four minutes. He looked

closely at Meltzer. It was possible. Meltzer had the build for it; he was skinny enough and his legs were long. "You really can do that, huh?"

"Oh, I think so," Meltzer announced. "Yes, I definitely think so. Of course, I've never been timed, but I feel confident."

Clay nodded. Four minutes. Four minutes in the Rose Bowl. That's a hundred thousand seats. At five bucks a seat. That made five hundred thousand dollars. Minus expenses. "Hey, Meltzer," he said. "How much you figure it would cost to rent the Rose Bowl?"

"I don't know. A lot. Maybe twenty-five thousand dollars."

Clay whistled. Subtract that from five hundred thousand and what was left? He lifted his glass and dipped his finger in the beer ring, doing the subtraction on the bar.

"Hey, Meltzer," he asked casually. "You got a manager?"

"What would I want a manager for?"

Well, you'd have to give Meltzer a split. Maybe half. That was fair. Now, you figure half of what was left would still be close to a quarter of a million. So you run in the Rose Bowl four times and you've got it made. Clay drained his glass and set it on the bar. "Come on," he said, grabbing Meltzer by the arm. "Let's get started."

"Where are we going?" Meltzer asked.

"To get rich," Clay answered. "To make our pile." He pulled Meltzer through the bar and they hurried across the street to the red convertible. Then they started the drive through Hastingsville.

Hastingsville was an army town. It began to flourish when Camp Scott was young, and now that the post was closing, Hastingsville would certainly die. There was one main street, brightly lit by neon signs, filled with saloons and souvenir shops and military stores. At the far end of the main street stood the one permanent structure, a medium-sized, squat building with Gothic pillars which served as police station, fire department and city hall. There were a few grocery stores on the side streets, plus half a dozen garages, and beyond these a series of small wooden houses, each with its own wooden porch and wooden fence. Quiet in the daytime, Hastingsville came alive at night— the sidewalks on the main street were lined with old men and old women, sitting stiffly in wooden folding chairs, gossiping, muttering, watching the soldiers walk by.

Sergeant Clay drove quickly through Hastingsville, away from the neon, into the moonlit night. When he was a safe distance from town, he pulled over to the side of the deserted road. "Okay now, buddy," he said. "Here we go." He pushed Pfc. Meltzer out of the car.

"What are we going to do, Clay old boy?"

"I'm going to leave you here," Clay said. "And then I'm going to clock a mile on the speedometer. Then I'll stop and turn around and switch off the lights. When you see the lights go off, you start running. I'll be waiting down there, timing you. Okay?"

"Well, I don't know," Meltzer began.

"Just give it a try," Clay said. "And remember. When the lights go off, you start. I'll turn 'em right back on again so you'll be able to see the finish line." He reached out and shook Meltzer's hand. "Give it all you got." Waving, he drove down the straight, quiet road. In a mile, he stopped and turned the car around. Staring at his watch, he waited until the second hand reached the top.

Then he switched off the light.

The seconds began ticking by. Clay switched the headlights back on again. Nervously, he lit a cigarette. Half a minute. He got out of the car and walked around it. Seventy-five seconds. He threw the cigarette away and lit another. Two minutes. Flicking on the car radio, he fought through the static until he heard a few notes of hillbilly music. He turned to another station. More hillbilly music. Clay flicked the radio off. Three minutes. One minute to go. Of course, these weren't ideal running conditions. The track at the Rose Bowl was probably a lot better and besides, Meltzer was wearing white buckskin shoes. So maybe if he did it in four minutes and a little more, it would amount to the same thing. Twenty seconds to go now. Fifteen. Clay peered into the night, his hands above his eyes. The smoke from the cigarette made him blink so he threw it away. He glanced down at his watch.

Four minutes.

He waited. Four minutes and ten seconds. Four minutes and twenty seconds. He lit another cigarette and inhaled deeply. Four minutes and forty seconds. Five minutes. He turned the ignition key and let the motor run. Then after seven minutes of waiting, he began driving cautiously back down the wrong side of the road. No Meltzer. He picked up speed. Maybe something had gone wrong. Maybe he'd slipped and broke a leg. Or maybe a heart attack. Still no Meltzer.

Finally Clay saw him. He was walking slowly in the middle of the road, his hands in his pockets. Clay pulled alongside. "What happened?" he asked.

"I threw up," Meltzer said, and he pointed. "Back there."

"Hop in," Clay muttered. "I'll drive you back to the post."

"Oh, I feel much better now," Meltzer told him, jogging up and down. "I think we ought to try it again."

"I don't," Clay said. "This time you're liable to die on me."

Meltzer shook his head. "This time we'll do it differently. You drive alongside me. And give me encouragement.

You know, cheer me on and like that."

"Why?"

"My fiancée does it for me. It makes me run faster. Whenever she cheers me on, I go just like the wind."

"You do, huh?"

Meltzer nodded. "Absolutely. And it's fun that way. For everybody. You'll like it. My fiancée does."

"What's her name?"

"Myrtle, and she—"

"Figured," Clay mumbled.

"She goes to Smith," Meltzer finished. "She's a terrific girl." He took a deep breath and got down into starting position. Clay pulled around him to the right side of the road. "Come on," Meltzer called. "Hurry up. I feel like flying."

Clay jockeyed the car back and forth until the mileage gauge rested on an even tenth. Then he looked at his watch. "Twenty seconds," he said. "Ten."

"Remember to cheer just as loud as you can," Meltzer said.

Clay nodded. "Five. Four. Get set. *Go!*" and with that Pfc. Meltzer took off.

From the beginning, it was evident that Pfc. Meltzer could run. His arms churning, his head bent forward, he raced along the road in giant strides. Clay drove slowly alongside, the steering wheel in one hand, the watch in the other. "Go, Meltzer," he yelled. "Go on, Jerry boy!"

"That's right," Meltzer called back. "That's right."

"You can do it, Jerry boy. Pick 'em up and lay 'em down. Chew 'em up and spit 'em out. Fly, man, fly!"

"That's right," Meltzer called. "Louder."

They moved along the highway in the direction of Hastingsville. Off in the distance, Clay could see the neon signs blinking; red, then blue, then red again. "Woweeoboy," he shouted. "Make way for the fastest man alive. You got 'em,

Jerry boy. You got 'em now!"

"I got 'em," Meltzer answered. "That's right."

"Move!" Clay shouted. "Move out smartly, Jerry boy. Let 'em know you're coming. Make way out there. Make way."

"You tell 'em," Meltzer said. "That's right."

"You're taking off, Jerry boy. You're taking off. You're flying." He glanced down at the mileage gauge, then out at Meltzer, then back at the mileage gauge. Half a mile! Quickly he brought the watch up close to his face and looked at it. Two minutes! Half a mile in two minutes! "You got 'em," Clay screamed. "Two minutes for the half. You got 'em, Jerry boy."

"I got 'em," Meltzer said, his voice not quite so loud. But he had not slowed. He was still running with the same effortless strides.

Clay bounced both hands on the steering wheel. Then he glanced into the rear-view mirror. He groaned. Back down the road, a car was coming. If the goddam car got in the way . . . But it looked a long way back, the headlights just small bright specks in his rear-view mirror. "Faster!" he cried. "Faster!" Maybe Meltzer could do it. Maybe he could. How many seats in the Rose Bowl? A hundred thousand. And maybe they could tour to Soldier's Field in Chicago. That was even bigger. Even bigger! "Go on, Jerry boy! Fly!" Slaughter would have to know right away. Clay glanced into the rear-view mirror. The car was coming up on them, the headlights growing in size, bigger now, much brighter. But Maxwell was doing the puzzle. Tonight was Tuesday, and that was when the Sunday *New York Times* came, so Maxwell was doing the crossword. Could he bother him? Yes. Sure. This once he could. Maxwell would understand. Hell, Maxwell was his partner so he'd understand. "You chew 'em up!" Clay called. "You got 'em now, Jerry boy." Pfc. Meltzer merely nodded, his pace slowing slightly. And the car behind them was coming like a streak! The headlights blazed into the rear-view mirror. "Hey!" Clay cried. The headlights were blinding, brighter, brighter. "Hey! Look out where you're—"

There was a crash.

The night exploded and the red convertible skidded along the highway, spinning around. Clay gripped the wheel as the car completed a circle and came to rest on the side of the road, facing Hastingsville. Turning off the ignition, he sat back in the seat and put his head in his hands, his eyes shut tight. Had it been his fault? Maybe. Maybe it had. He turned around and stared. The other car was resting in the ditch on the opposite side of the road. No one moved in the other car.

"Woweeoboy," Clay muttered. "Woweeoboy."

"I think they're dead." It was Pfc. Meltzer, and he was leaning against the hood of the car, staring through the windshield at Clay.

Clay nodded.

"Are you hurt?"

Clay shook his head.

"I think they are," Meltzer went on. "They aren't moving. I think they're dead."

"Stop saying that."

"And you want to know what else?"

"What else?"

"I don't feel so good, either," Meltzer mumbled. Then he wrapped his arms around his stomach and staggered over to the side of the road.

Slowly, Sergeant Clay got out and walked around his convertible. The back fender was bashed in and the left tail light was up over the handle of the trunk, but other than that, the car was much the same as before. Then, taking small steps, he moved hesitantly to the middle of the road, breathing deeply. Up ahead he could see people streaming down the highway toward him. Citizens of Hastingsville. He took another deep breath. A third.

Finally, he shoved his hands into his pockets and approached the other car. It was in bad shape. The grille was gone and the hood jutted out over the windshield. Clay shuddered. He walked slowly around the car, peering through the windows. Two people were in the front seat; a man behind the wheel, and, sprawled across him, a girl. Closing his eyes briefly, nodding his head, Clay opened the right front door of the car.

The light went on suddenly, flooding the car, and at that moment Clay smelled the most beautiful, the most extraordinary, the most absolutely exquisite smell of his entire life.

Alcohol!

"Hey, Meltzer," he called over his shoulder. "They're plastered."

The girl moved into a sitting position and blinked several times. Then she smiled. "Hi, Eustis," she said.

"Howdy, Bobby Jo," Clay replied. "What's new?"

"Nothin' much."

"You okay?"

She nodded. "Fine."

"How's your friend?" Clay asked. "He okay too?"

She elbowed the boy several times. He turned his head toward the light. Clay groaned. It was Corporal Lenahan. Corporal Lenahan was an MP.

"Hey, sweetie," Bobby Jo said. "You okay?"

He nodded. "Fine, sugar. What happened?"

"Somebody been in a accident," Bobby Jo said. "I think it was us."

Corporal Lenahan managed to open the door and stagger out of the car. He gaped at it for a while. "You're right, sugar," he said thickly. "You sure as hell are right." Using the car for support, he made his way around the back and up along the side until he stood near Clay. Slumping against the car, he began to giggle. "Let's not tell a soul about this," he whispered, putting his finger to his lips. "Shhh. Let's keep it quiet."

Clay glanced down the road. The people were closer now, less than a hundred yards away. "That's going to be tough, Lenahan," he answered.

Corporal Lenahan shrugged. "Just trying to make it easy on you," he said, grabbing Clay's shoulder, blinking, staring up into Clay's face. "Oh, for chrissakes," he muttered. "It's you."

"Evening, Lenahan."

"You're in trouble, Clay, you know that? I was just trying to make it easy on you. It was your fault."

"My fault?" Clay said, backing away. Corporal Lenahan groped for the car and leaned against it.

"You're goddam right."

"I don't quite see it that way," Clay said. "I mean, it appears like you was the one who hit me. And from behind. Not to mention the fact that somebody around here stinks like a brewery."

"That don't matter," Lenahan said. "That don't matter at all. Hell, man. You was stopped dead on the highway."

The first townie was on them then. He was an old man, wrinkled and thin, and he had no teeth. "Anybody kilt?" he asked.

"Nope," Clay told him.

The toothless man shook his head. "Figgered sure someone been kilt from the sound. That was some sound. *Boom!*"

"Sorry," Clay muttered.

The toothless man shrugged and leaned against the side of the car to wait. Other people hurried up, a dozen or more, gathering quietly in clumps around the two cars, jabbering among themselves. Clay watched them.

"Nobody kilt," the toothless man called out.

"We thought sure someone been kilt from the sound," a woman answered. "That was some sound, all right."

"Yeah," Clay said. "*Boom!*"

He walked quickly away from them, searching for Pfc. Meltzer. He looked in his car but Meltzer was not there. He looked closely at all the people standing around. No Meltzer. Finally he walked off the road into the ditch.

Pfc. Meltzer was lying on the ground.

"Upsy-daisy," Clay said, starting to lift him.

"Put me back," Meltzer whispered. "I don't feel so good."

"Me either," Clay told him. "But the cops is going to be coming soon and they're gonna want to see the both of us."

"It's my stomach," Meltzer explained. "It keeps throwing up."

"Sure," Clay said, starting to lead him out of the ditch. "Sure."

"I think it was all that running," Meltzer went on. "What do you think?"

"Possible." Clay nodded, and by that time they were back onto the road and the Hastingsville police chief was standing by the red convertible.

"Anybody hurt?" the chief asked.

"Nope," Clay answered.

"And it's a living miracle, too, chief," the toothless man said, suddenly stepping between the two of them. "I was sitting there and I thought the sky exploded. You never heard anything like it."

The police chief nodded.

"You gonna take 'em all to jail, chief?" the toothless

man went on. "You gonna do that?"

The police chief nodded again.

"*Zowee!*" the toothless man shouted, turning to the others. "Let's go!" And with that, he began running back toward town.

News of the accident had preceded them, and by the time they got to the police station it was jammed. And so was the city hall. And so was the fire department. They were all the same room, a gigantic, low-ceilinged rectangle, perhaps fifty feet long, with a large unlit potbellied stove standing in the center. Six dark brown fans hung from the ceiling, the blades turning slowly, uselessly, stirring up the hot stale air. Twenty old men and women stood muttering quietly, clustered around the potbellied stove, while an equal number were spread across the room, leaning against the walls, waiting.

The toothless man was the first one inside. "Nobody kilt," he said loudly, and hurried to the potbellied stove.

Sergeant Clay came next, followed by Pfc. Meltzer. Blinking, Clay looked around the room, reaching for his handkerchief to mop his face.

"That there's one of the drivers," the toothless man said, indicating Clay. "Seems he was stopped on the highway."

Clay shook his head, continuing to mop his face. Pfc. Meltzer leaned against him. By this time, Pfc. Meltzer was a light green. "I've got to get to bed soon," he whispered. "I don't feel so good."

Clay nodded. "You look fine, Jerry. Never seen you looking any better." He thrust his hands into his pockets and started to walk around in a small circle.

Meltzer followed him. "Are we in trouble, Eustis?"

"Shouldn't be," Clay muttered. "They hit us. We was moving and they hit us from behind. And besides, Lenahan's stoned. So it shouldn't be bad."

"But he's an MP," Meltzer whispered. "Didn't you say that?"

"Don't remind me," Clay said. "Don't remind me."

Corporal Lenahan and Bobby Jo came in with the police chief. Lenahan was slightly more sober now, but he still walked unsteadily, waving his arms in the air as he spoke. "We were driving along," he said. "And they were stopped dead on the highway. It was their fault."

Clay walked over. "That's a damn lie," he said.

"Easy, son," the police chief said. "Just take it easy."

Clay winked at Bobby Jo. "How you feel?" he asked.

She smiled back at him. "I feel fine, Eustis." Then she lowered her voice. "But I ain't allowed to talk to you. My sweetie said for me to keep quiet."

Clay nodded and went back to Meltzer. "She's a good girl," he whispered. "She'll be on our side."

Meltzer looked at Bobby Jo. She had short brown hair and bright eyes and her complexion was perfect. "B?" he said.

"Just about. And she's a very intelligent girl. Very intelligent and very friendly."

The police chief came over. "Let me see your driver's license, son," he said.

Clay reached into his pocket for his wallet and handed it over. The police chief riffled through it. Then he stopped.

"Looks to me like your license has expired," he said.

Clay grabbed his wallet back and stared at the license. *Expires December 31, 1952,* it said. Four months ago. He grinned at the police chief. "Just recently," he said. "Just a couple days overdue is all."

The police chief walked away. Clay stood still, shaking his head. Then he put his hands into his pockets and started walking in a small circle. The room was growing hotter as more and more people pushed their way through the doorway. Clay looked at them. They glanced away, then back at him. Again he shook his head, listening as the news made a circuit of the room. "Expired . . . expired . . ." from one person to the next, very quietly, "expired . . ."

The toothless man walked up to him. "Hey, is it true?" he wanted to know.

Clay nodded.

"It's true," the toothless man called out, moving across the room, spreading the news. "True . . ." the townspeople whispered, "true . . . true . . ." They were all watching him now, quietly, while the toothless man moved back and forth, talking, gesturing like a cheerleader.

Clay hunched his shoulders and stared at the floor. Pfc. Meltzer stood beside him. They waited, listening to the sounds of the room, the whispering, the coughing, the shuffling feet. Then, suddenly, the sounds stopped and, for the first time, the slow, dry whirring of the fans became audible. Clay looked up.

Sergeant First Class Priest was standing in the doorway.

In full uniform, Sfc. Priest was an awesome sight. He was over six feet tall and his jet black hair stood straight up like stiff brush bristles, so that the hard bone of his scalp was visible. His black boots were brilliantly shined and his uniform perfectly pressed. His chest was lined with medals and they caught the light, glistening, as he stood solidly in the doorway, filling it, grinning horribly, staring around the room.

He stepped forward and approached the police chief, and there followed a brief, whispered conversation. Then Priest walked across the room toward Clay and Meltzer. Meltzer moved backward until he stood directly behind Clay. Sfc. Priest stopped.

"Hello, you little fart," he said.

Clay nodded. "Howdy, Priest. How are things?"

"I'll tell you how they are. You know what I got in my hands? I got the bloody end of the stick in my hands and you know where it's going? It's going up, Clay. Up yours."

"Now, let's take it easy," Clay said. "There's just been a little misunderstanding is all. A little accident. I'm sorry it happened to be one of your boys, but if they can't hold their liquor, then—"

"You and your goddam bets," Priest cut in. "You and your goddam voice in the night. 'A voice in the night comes to me and says they're closing the camp.'" He held up a gloved fist. "I got your voice in the night, Clay. Right here. The news about the closing is all over post."

"Oh," Clay said.

"You're going in the stockade, Clay. You know that?"

"That bet was a joke," Clay began. "You didn't actually expect I was going to go through with it. It was just a little joke, Priest. I thought it might be fun if . . ."

Sfc. Priest walked back to the police chief. "He's drunk, chief. Drunk as a lord. And he's got no license to drive. And he was stopped on the highway. And—"

"Now just a damn minute," Clay interrupted, walking over. "In the first place—"

"Easy, Sergeant," the police chief said. "Rest easy."

"Look at 'em go!" the toothless man yelled from beside the potbellied stove. "*Zowee!*" For the first time, the room grew noisy, people talking among themselves while ten more men and women crowded in through the doorway.

"Knock off that noise!" the police chief yelled. The room quieted. "All right now, Sergeant," he said softly. "Suppose you tell us what happened."

Clay nodded. "I'm not drunk," he said, wiping the perspiration from his forehead with the back of his hand. "That's the first thing. I am dead sober. Now, he's not," and he indicated Lenahan. "You tell 'em, Bobby Jo. Is he plastered or isn't he?"

"Hi, Eustis," Bobby Jo said, and she waved to him.

"Hi," Clay said.

"That stupid son of a bitch was stopped dead on the highway," Lenahan called out. "It was all his fault."

The police chief raised his hands. "Go on," he said to Clay.

"Okay." Clay nodded nervously. Priest was staring at him, watching him and grinning. The room grew hotter than ever. "Okay. I'm not drunk. And I wasn't stopped on the highway. I was slowly moving forward."

"How fast?"

Clay squinted. "I don't know exactly. Maybe ten, maybe fifteen miles an hour."

"That's a goddam lie!" Lenahan shouted. "He was stopped dead."

"It's the truth!" Clay cried. "And I can prove it!"

"Go ahead," the police chief said.

"Well—" Clay began. Then he stopped, pulling at his ear. "This may sound a little strange, maybe, but it's the god's truth, because I know I was going that fast because my friend here was running and I was timing him and he just done half a mile in two minutes, and in order for me to keep up with him which I was doing I would have to be going that fast and I was and I rest my case."

"Who were you timing?"

"Him." Clay indicated Meltzer.

"What were you timing him for?"

"A business agreement we was thinking of entering into."

"You," the police chief said, pointing to Meltzer. "Why were you running?"

"Me, sir?" Meltzer answered. "I like to run. I run all the

time, sir."

"See?" Priest said, and he winked toward Lenahan. "Both of them drunk as lords."

"Come over here," the chief said.

Pfc. Meltzer hesitated. Trembling, very pale now, he marched over to the police chief and stood stiffly at attention.

"Who are you?" the chief asked.

"Sir," Pfc. Meltzer said, saluting sharply, "Pfc. Meltzer reports, sir."

"At ease, Private Meltz," the police chief said.

"No, sir. Meltzer."

"All right, Meltz. What happened?"

Pfc. Meltzer saluted again. "No, sir. You've got it wrong. My name is Meltzer."

"Don't try being funny, son. Just go on."

"Begging your pardon, sir. I'm not trying to be funny. But my name isn't Meltz, sir. It's Meltzer."

"What the hell is that man talking about?" the chief said.

"He's a little scared, Chief," Clay answered. "Let me explain." He looked at the police chief. Then he looked at Pfc. Meltzer. Meltzer was standing at attention, his arm locked in saluting position. Quickly, Clay looked away, but it was too late. In a moment he was giggling. Desperately, he tried holding his breath. The next thing he knew he was hiccuping. "I'm sorry," he managed to say. "I'm sorry."

"Drunk," the police chief said. "Obviously intoxicated."

A murmur went up in the room, punctuated only by a single intermittent hiccuping sound. "He's plastered, all right," the toothless man said. "He can't hardly stand up straight."

"This man's got a long record of drunkenness," Sfc. Priest cut in. "Clay's known as one of the biggest lushes on post. A general all-around troublemaker."

"The way I see it," the chief said, "these two men were drinking and for some reason or other they stopped suddenly on the highway and the corporal here unavoidably struck them."

"We was not stopped!" Clay cried. "We was running the four-minute mile and we would have made it, too, if that lunkhead could hold his liquor."

"Who you calling a lunkhead?" Corporal Lenahan yelled.

"I'm innocent," Clay went on. "You got to believe me." He ran over to Bobby Jo. "Tell 'em," he pleaded. "Tell 'em what happened."

"Hi, Eustis," Bobby Jo said.

"We'll keep him in custody overnight," Sfc. Priest said. "And tomorrow we'll start setting up the court martial."

The police chief nodded.

"I'm being railroaded," Clay said. "Meltzer, say something."

Pfc. Meltzer gestured helplessly.

"Nobody's going to railroad me," Clay cried. "Chief. Chief, what about him? What about Lenahan? He hit me from behind. And if I'm drunk, what do you call him?"

Corporal Lenahan stood still, blinking. Sfc. Priest crossed quickly to him and they whispered to each other for a minute.

"Chief," Sfc. Priest said then. "Corporal Lenahan here has something to say. Say it, Lenahan."

"I wasn't driving," Lenahan mumbled. "She was," and he pointed to Bobby Jo. "Isn't that right?"

"Whatever you say, sweetie," Bobby Jo smiled.

"Were you driving, miss?" the police chief asked.

"Did my honey say I was driving?"

"Yes."

"Then I was driving, all right."

"Tell the chief the rest, sugar," Lenahan whispered.

"The rest?" Bobby Jo blinked.

"Yeah. About how you saw them parked in the middle of the road. Not moving."

"Oh, my, yes," Bobby Jo said. "They was parked in the middle of the road. Not moving."

"He's a goner now," the toothless man yelled. "They'll put him in the pokey for sure!" The people near the pot-bellied stove crowded closer together, and those around the walls moved slowly into the center of the room. Clay turned, watching as the ring closed on him. Again the noise began and now there was no stopping it. Clay grabbed Meltzer and tried shaking him, but Meltzer only sagged, staring out, his eyes half closed. The noise increased; everyone was talking now. Clay listened as the words leaped out at him, "Jail . . . jail . . . jail . . ." and he tensed, looking around, but there was no opening in the ring, no place to run. Priest and the police chief were talking hurriedly and Priest was smiling and Lenahan was whispering to Bobby Jo. Clay just stood there, sweating terribly, with Pfc. Meltzer leaning against him, using him for support. The police chief nodded to Priest, who nodded back, smiling. Then Priest nodded to Lenahan and Lenahan nodded back. Finally Priest walked across the room. Clay waited.

A blue tent sailed in through the doorway.

Priest grabbed Clay. The noise in the room was unbearable, and Clay tried to twist free, but Priest held him tight.

"What's going on here?" somebody roared.

The noise lessened.

"Somebody better tell me what's going on here!" the voice roared again. Clay looked up.

"Oh, Maxwell," he said. "I'm mighty glad to see you."

"Who are you?" the police chief asked.

"Never mind who I am. Just tell me what's going on."

The chief stared. "I'm sorry," he said then. "I didn't recognize you in your pajamas, Sergeant Slaughter."

Slaughter nodded once. He walked over to Clay. "What is all this?" he said.

"They're railroading me, Maxwell," Clay whispered. "Priest is railroading me."

"That man is in a good deal of trouble, Sergeant Slaughter," the chief said.

"He's a fine American lad and a crackerjack soldier," Slaughter answered.

"Nevertheless—" the chief began.

"Who's that fat guy in the pajamas?" the toothless man called out, and immediately the crowd echoed the question and the noise returned.

"Let's have it quiet!" the police chief yelled, walking up and down, shaking his head. "A good deal of trouble," he repeated.

"Name it."

"Well, first of all, he was driving a vehicle without a license."

"That true, Eustis?"

"It had only recently expired," Clay answered.

"What else?"

"It appears he was drunk."

"That true, Eustis?"

"I only had four beers, Maxwell. Honest to God."

"I can vouch for the lad's honesty," Slaughter said. "He's not drunk. What else?"

"Well," the chief went on, "he claims he was clocking what's-his-name over there in the four-minute mile."

"Jesus!" Slaughter said. He turned to Clay. "You had to do this on a Tuesday, didn't you? You couldn't wait until tomorrow."

"I'm sorry about the puzzle, Maxwell. But I didn't mean for this to—"

"The four-minute mile," Slaughter interrupted. "How much were we going to make out of it?"

"Millions," Clay said, stepping forward. "Maybe more. We—"

"Where?"

"The Rose Bowl," Clay whispered. "In the Rose Bowl. I figure we can rent—"

"Later," Slaughter cut in.

"I want to know who that fat guy is," the toothless man said again. "And what's he doing wearing pajamas?"

"I told you for the last time," the police chief said.

Slaughter turned back to the chief. "Again, I vouch for the lad's honesty. He's a fine boy. A fine, delicate, sensitive boy. I believe his story. In fact, I promise you what he says is true." He turned on Clay. "Jesus Christ, Eustis!" he exploded. "The Rose Bowl!"

"Shhh," Clay whispered. "I'll tell you about it later. I—"

"You finished yet, Slaughter?" Sfc. Priest said, stepping forward. " 'Cause when you are, we're taking your little friend with us."

Master Sergeant Slaughter spread his arms out wide. "I'm just asking a few questions, James. You don't mind that, do you?" There was no answer. "Do you?" Slaughter repeated, staring at the other man and smiling blandly.

"No," Priest snapped after a long pause. "Take your time."

"Thank you, James," Slaughter said.

"At any rate," the chief finished, "there was a collision and—"

"Who was the other driver?" Slaughter asked.

"This young lady," the chief answered, indicating Bobby Jo.

"It's a lie," Clay said. "Bobby Jo wasn't driving. It was that lunkhead Lenahan."

"Who you calling a lunkhead?" Corporal Lenahan wanted to know.

"Hello, there," Slaughter said softly, walking up to Bobby Jo.

"Hi, fatty," she answered.

"He's fat, all right," the toothless man shouted. "*Zowee!*"

"I guess I'd better be saying good-bye to you, Bobby Jo," Slaughter began, his voice very low. He smiled gently, and wiped the perspiration from his face.

"Where you going, fatty?" she asked.

"Oh, I'm not going anywhere, Bobby Jo," Slaughter answered. "It's you that's taking the trip. It's you that's going away, Bobby Jo. Not me."

"I'm not going no place, fatty," she said.

"Oh, yes, you are," Slaughter replied, his voice even softer now. "Yes you are, Bobby Jo. You're going to the Pit."

"Pit?" She took a step backward.

"It's a terrible place, I'm told," Slaughter whispered. "Deep and black and filthy and full of rats with yellow teeth. And the walls are lined with slime, Bobby Jo."

"What are you talking about, fatty?" she said, taking another step backward.

"Oh, it's terrible," Slaughter whispered. "Just terrible. It horrifies me even to think about it. I get the shivers, Bobby Jo. Whenever I think of them lowering you into the Pit it makes my heart sad."

"You ain't sending me into no Pit," Bobby Jo said.

"Of course not," Slaughter nodded. "Not me. Him," and he pointed to the chief of police. "He's going to do it to you. And do you know why?"

Bobby Jo stopped. "Why?"

"For lying!" Slaughter thundered, his voice suddenly

filling the room. "That's what they do with liars in this state." He began whispering again. "They put them in the Pit. I can hear the rats screaming now as they see you being lowered down. Such a pretty little girl. With such tender pink flesh. Rats love pink flesh, Bobby Jo. And they'll gnaw at you slowly, to make you last. They'll gnaw at your pink, tender flesh and you'll scream, but no one will hear you. Down you go. The rats see you. Lower. They start that screaming. Lower. Lower. You can see their eyes now. Yellow eyes. Lower. You're almost on the ground now, Bobby Jo, and the rats are about to start gnawing on your pink, tender—"

"Don't let 'em do it!" Bobby Jo yelled, and she ran to the police chief. "Don't put me in no Pit!"

"What pit?" the chief asked.

"The girl's gone loony," the toothless man shouted.

Bobby Jo clambered up on top of the police chief's desk. The crowd moved forward again, and the noise began.

"Stop her before she jumps off," the toothless man warned. "She's trying to kill herself."

"I wasn't driving!" Bobby Jo shouted from atop the desk, waving her arms in the air. "I wasn't driving. I don't even know how to. I ain't old enough." She paused. "I'm only fourteen."

"Fourteen?" Clay said. "Fourteen?"

"He was driving," Bobby Jo went on, pointing to Lenahan. "Not me. So don't put me into no Pit."

The crowd slowly started heading for the door. "What a night," the toothless man said. "Zowee!" Slaughter walked over to the police chief.

"Listen, everybody! Listen!" Bobby Jo shouted, still standing on the desk. "I want everybody to know something. I want everybody to know that I'm a good girl and I never done nothin' wrong."

"Fourteen," Clay said again. "The aw-dassity."

"May we leave now?" Slaughter asked.

The police chief shrugged.

"And let's just forget about the license business," Slaughter went on. "A simple oversight. Of no consequence whatsoever."

The police chief shrugged again.

"All right with you, James?" Slaughter said.

Priest glared at him a moment. "Get the hell out of here," he muttered.

"Good night, James," Master Sergeant Slaughter said. "Come along, Eustis." He made his way toward the door. Clay followed close behind, dragging Pfc. Meltzer along by the hand.

"Thank you, Maxwell," Clay began, when they were outside. "Thank you very much."

Slaughter nodded.

"I feel sick," Pfc. Meltzer mumbled. "In my stomach."

"The Rose Bowl," Slaughter said.

"You don't understand," Clay began, following Slaughter into the night. "You see, it's got a hundred thousand seats, and if we sell them at five bucks a seat we'll—"

"We'll have enough to go into the sheet business, won't we, Eustis?"

"Yeah," Clay said, excitedly. "Yeah, that's right." The three of them moved slowly through the darkness, Slaughter in front, Clay one step behind, dragging Meltzer. The night was very cool. "That's right, we will. And from there—"

"From there, who knows, Eustis?" Master Sergeant Slaughter said. "From there who knows?"

This happened on the evening of the fourteenth of April.

The post was closed on the tenth of October.

Which left a few days in between.

II.

Randy Scott was in big trouble.

Tied hand and foot, he lay unconscious in one corner of the deserted mine shaft. Beside him was a square wooden table with a candle burning on top. The flickering yellow flame cast weird shadows on the wall, highlighting the many cuts and bruises which dotted Randy's bloody face. On the far side of the mine shaft another candle burned, outlining three hunched figures, all wearing six-guns, who were drilling small holes in the wall of the mine, then filling the holes with sticks of dynamite.

"Wake up, Randy," Clay muttered, chewing down harder on his popcorn. "Wake up."

Randy Scott stirred. Slowly, he first opened one eye, then the other. He blinked. Again. Three times. Then he shook his head from side to side, in obvious pain.

"He's hurt bad," Clay whispered. "He's lost a lot of blood."

Pfc. Meltzer nodded. "He'll get out of it all right."

"Yeah?" Clay said. "Well, he better get a move on. They're gonna blow the mine up inside of two minutes."

"Shut up down there," a flat, nasal voice said from a row behind them.

Clay took a fresh handful of popcorn.

Randy was awake now. Gritting his teeth, he pulled on the ropes that held his hands. There was no give. He pulled again, harder, and the cords in his neck stood out taut. The ropes held. Randy sagged momentarily, closing his eyes. Again he shook his head, but now his face reflected defeat as well as pain. He looked across at the three shadowy figures who were still jamming sticks of dynamite into the mine wall. Randy's eyes narrowed and his jaw jutted out even further and his lips formed a thin straight line.

"The candle," Clay said. "Use the candle."

Randy nodded and slowly, painfully, brought his legs up under his body. Then, forcing himself, he pushed forward into a kneeling position. Had the other men heard him? He stopped. Watching. They had not. Crawling silently to the table, he turned until his hands were over the candle flame.

"He's gonna do it," Clay cried. "Just like I told him."

"Will ya shut up down there," the nasal voice said again. Clay finished his popcorn, crumpled the bag and dropped it on the floor.

The flame licked at the ropes. Randy gritted his teeth, pushing his hands down farther, closer to the flame.

"That must hurt something awful," Clay whispered.

Pfc. Meltzer nodded.

"Stay with it, Randy," Clay said. "You can do it. You can do it."

"Will ya for Christ's sake shut the hell up down there," the nasal voice said.

The ropes parted. Silently, Randy rubbed his bruised wrists, restoring circulation. Then, catlike, he bent down and untied his feet. Finally he stood, holding onto the wall for support. Bending his legs twice, he took a deep breath. At last he was ready. Picking up a rock, he took aim. The rock sailed through the air. Randy's aim was true. The distant candle toppled and went out. The three men turned, reaching for their six-guns. With a backward flick of his hand, Randy knocked his own candle over. The mine shaft was plunged into darkness. Then Randy charged.

"We're home free!" Clay yelled. "There's only three of 'em."

The mine shaft was filled with sounds. Punches and grunts, bodies falling. Then shots. Four in quick succession. A pause. Two more. Another pause. One final shot. A candle flame flickered on. Again the mine shaft was covered by a film of yellow light.

"Whew," Clay said.

Randy Scott held the candle. At his feet lay the three men. Dead. Randy nodded.

"The bastards shot each other, Meltzer. How about that?"

"Pretty stupid," Meltzer answered.

Randy climbed slowly out of the mine shaft. Above, the sky was filled with stars. The sound of hoofbeats. A posse rode into view, led by a girl. She stared at Randy's bloody face. He smiled. The girl dismounted.

"Don't kiss her, Randy," Clay said.

Randy kissed her.

Clay stood up. "Let's get out of here," he muttered, and he started jigging up the aisle, Pfc. Meltzer a step behind. They walked through the lobby of Theater Four and outside. On the sidewalk, Clay stopped and lit a cigarette. "What a great pitcher," he said, throwing an uppercut. "Woweeoboy!"

Meltzer shrugged and looked around. "Where's Maxwell?" he asked.

"He's watching the Joanie Crawford over at Theater Two. He'll meet us at the NCO Club soon as it's done." They started walking along the sidwalk.

"You sure I can get in, Eustis?"

"Course you can get in. No sweat." He whirled and threw a combination of punches, a left to the head, right to the body, right to the head. "Boy, that Randy Scott. He is the toughest man in the movies."

"Alan Ladd," Meltzer said.

Clay stopped. "You must be kidding."

"Alan Ladd has never lost a fight. He is undefeated, untied and unscored on."

"Yeah, but who's he ever fought? Nobody. A bunch of nobodies."

"Nevertheless," Meltzer answered, "he is undefeated. Randy Scott wouldn't stand a chance."

"There just ain't no point in arguing," Clay said. "You're wrong." He plunged his hands into his pockets and they walked in silence for a while. It was a cool night, and the ground was still damp as a result of the afternoon rain. They turned right and walked across the parking lot of the NCO Club. As they approached, the sound of the juke box began, softly at first, growing louder.

Clay walked inside and flashed his membership card to the corporal at the door. The corporal nodded and looked at Meltzer.

"Who's he?"

"Pfc. Meltzer," Clay answered. "Pfc. Meltzer is the editor of the post newspaper and he is thinking of doing a series of articles about the club. I said I'd show him around."

"Okay," the corporal said. "Sure."

They walked past him. "See?" Clay whispered. "No sweat. Here we are."

The white NCO Club at Camp Scott was an enormous rectangular building divided into two large rooms. The front room, in turn, was divided into three areas: the restaurant area, which consisted of a juke box together with a series of aluminum chairs and tables; the television area, which consisted of a television set with aluminum chairs lined up in rows in front of it; and the letter-writing area, which consisted of aluminum tables and chairs plus a candy-bar machine. The entire room was brightly lit from above by rows of long fluorescent tubes.

The back room was the bar.

Near the doorway was the bar itself, running the width of the room. In the center was a large dance floor. Surrounding that, filling the remainder of the room, were tables and chairs. It was very dark, except for an enormous juke box near the dance floor, which flickered continually, giving off a rich red glow.

Clay and Meltzer paused in the doorway of the bar,

blinking, getting accustomed to the darkness.

"Stinks, huh?" Clay said.

Meltzer nodded.

Clay shrugged. "Anyway, the liquor's cheap. What do you want?"

"Milk?"

"Please," Clay said.

"Well, I don't know, Eustis. Ever since the accident I've been back on the wagon."

"There is those that doubt you was ever off. How 'bout a Coke?"

"Okay."

Clay walked up to the bar. "Beer and a coke," he called. A moment later, the bartender brought over two glasses. Clay paid him. "Kind of quiet tonight," he said.

The bartender nodded. "Everybody's writing letters."

Clay picked up the glasses and walked back to Meltzer. They moved forward and took a table at a corner of the dance floor away from the juke box. "Maxwell likes to sit here," Clay explained. "It's got the best view."

"Where is he?" Meltzer asked.

"He'll be along. He probably stayed to watch the previews tonight again. Maxwell's very big on previews."

Pfc. Meltzer looked around the dark room. "Is it always so empty here, Eustis?"

Clay shook his head. "It's on account of the post closing. They made it official today. So everyone's off writing letters."

"But I thought everybody knew about that."

"Everybody did know. But today they made it official." He drank half his beer. Pfc. Meltzer continued to stare around the room. The juke box changed records and a saxophone solo started. Two couples stood up and began to dance. Clay tapped his foot in time with the saxophone. Then there was a commotion at the doorway behind him and he knew that Slaughter had arrived.

"My stein, please," Slaughter said. "To the top." The bartender nodded and reached up to a shelf over the cash register. Bringing down an enormous round glass, he filled it and handed it to Slaughter. Slaughter drained his stein and handed it back. The bartender refilled it. Then Slaughter paid him and walked over to the table.

"I'm sorry to be so late," he began, easing himself down into his chair. "But I received some information which—"

"Randy Scott or Alan Ladd?" Clay said.

Slaughter looked at him. "Randy Scott or Alan Ladd what?"

"You know. Who's tougher?"

"Definitely Randy Scott," Slaughter answered.

"There," Clay said to Meltzer. "See?"

Meltzer nodded. "What's your information?" he asked.

"Eustis here is getting discharged," Slaughter answered. "That's my information."

Clay stared across the table. "What are you talking about?"

Slaughter took a large swallow of beer. "As I was leaving the theater just now I ran into an acquaintance who works at Personnel. We got to chatting about this and that and he happened to say that your papers had come through for processing. Your enlistment is practically up, Eustis. Did you know that?"

"Everybody knows how much time he has," Meltzer said. "I've got exactly a hundred and one days. Everybody knows—"

"You sure, Maxwell?"

Slaughter nodded.

"How could you forget?" Meltzer went on. "How could you possibly forget?"

Clay shook his head. "I don't know. It was six years ago. I was a teen-age juvenile at the time. Now hush up and let me think. What's the date?"

"April 28, 1953."

"Well, then, lemmesee—1953, subtract six years is . . ." He threw his arms into the air with a shout. "Hey, Maxwell!" he cried. "Hey, Maxwell! You're right. You're right. My time is up!" Jumping to his feet, he raced to the bar and bought half a dozen beers. Hurrying back, he set them on the table. "On me," he said. "All you can drink is on me tonight. We're gonna celebrate. We're gonna really tie one on." Grabbing a beer, he chug-a-lugged it. Grinning, he wiped his mouth with the back of his hand. "Go on," he said. "Start. Them beers is getting warm."

Slaughter leaned forward, looking up at him. "Are you going to re-enlist, Eustis? Or are you getting out?"

Clay grabbed another glass and raised it high. "I would like to propose a toast!" he shouted, and all the people in the room turned to look at him. "To me. To Eustis Clay, who ain't gonna be a soldier no more!" He looked down at Slaughter. "You drink to that, Maxwell?"

Master Sergeant Slaughter nodded. "I'll drink to that, Eustis," he answered slowly. "I'll drink to that." He raised his glass.

They drank.

There was something strange inside his mouth. Clay could feel it. Something very strange. With a groan, he rolled over onto his back. The bed creaked. Instinctively, his hands went to his swollen belly and pressed down. His stomach was bad. But not as bad as his mouth. There was definitely something very strange lurking inside. Lifting his right hand, he dropped it beside his lips. It crept along his face, waiting a chance. Quickly, it reached inside and pulled.

Clay shouted and let go of his tongue. That was it. Someone had done something strange to his tongue. But what? And how? Maybe someone had stolen it. No. That couldn't be. Hadn't he just pulled it with his own hand? He groaned again. Louder. Now he knew. It wasn't his tongue at all. It was his head. His head was spinning. His head . . .

He sat up quickly, blinking. The room was leaning at a peculiar angle so he pushed against the wall with one hand until it was level. Then he raised both hands to his head and squeezed it. His stomach hurt. Stumbling to his feet, he managed to reach the wall and lean against it, massaging his stomach gently. Lying down was out. No good. But leaning against the wall wasn't much better. Groping for his toilet-article kit, he grabbed his towel and felt his way toward the door. Kicking it open, he stepped outside.

The barracks was quiet. Except for occasional scattered coughing, there was no sound. Holding tight to the wooden banister, Clay crept down the steps to the latrine. The latrine was divided into thirds—showers, toilets and sinks—and he stood, staring from one to the other, undecided on which to use first. The sinks were nearest, so he turned on the cold water spigot and bent down, his mouth wide open. He took a huge swallow. Good. Another swallow. Better. Closing his eyes, he drank until he could feel his stomach swelling. Then he stood and inspected his face in the mirror. There was no doubt about it. He did not look well.

Three recruits walked in, putting on their fatigues, getting ready for KP. They saw him and stopped. "Morning, Sarge," one of them said.

"Morning," Clay said.

"You okay, Sarge?"

"I guess," he said, starting toward the shower room. He stopped. "Matter of fact," he went on, turning to face them again, "I never been better. A civilian. I'm a civilian. I'm getting out." Grinning to himself, he entered the shower room and turned on the water. Slinging his towel over a hook, he stepped under the shower, closing his eyes as the warm water cascaded down. "I'm getting out," he sang suddenly. "Let's give a shout. 'Cause I'm getting out." That wasn't bad. He nodded and sang it again. "I'm a civilian," he sang. What rhymed with civilian? Million? No. Billion. That was even better. "I'll make a billion as a civilian. Let's give a shout 'cause I'm getting out." The water pounded at the base of his neck and he took a deep breath. His head had stopped hurting. Even his stomach was a little better. He turned off the water and, whistling, dried himself and walked up the steps to his room.

Propping his pillow against the wall, he flopped down and reached out for the picture frame. "Hey, Donald," he said. "Hey, Donald, I'm getting out. Isn't that something? I'm getting a discharge and I'm gonna make a billion dollars and you ain't gonna eat nothin' but steak ever again." He stared at the picture a moment longer, then replaced it on his desk. His stomach was rumbling like crazy. He sat up straight. "I'm getting out," he sang softly. "Let's give a shout. I'll make a billion 'cause—" He stopped suddenly.

How?

How was he going to make a billion? Good question. Clay scratched his head. Then, reaching onto the floor, he took his yellow pencil from his shirt pocket. Adjusting his pillow, he licked the end of the stub. Just what exactly was he going to do? He closed his eyes and thought for a moment. Work. That was one answer. He could go to work. Nodding, he wrote the letters *W-o-r-k* on the wall alongside his bed. Underneath, in smaller letters, he wrote *J-o-b*, hesitated, then added a question mark. He stared at the words for a long time. Finally he shook his head. There had to be something better than work. But what? What else was there?

He closed his eyes again and the answer suddenly flashed across his mind.

School.

That was it! He could go to school. Excited now, he wrote *S-c-h-o-o-l* on the wall in large letters. It made sense. You could earn a hell of a lot more money with a college diploma than without. College. Football games. Girls. Happily, he began to write *C-o-l-l-e-g-e* under *School. C-o-l* . . . How did you spell "college"? With a *d* or a *j*? He shook his head. It didn't matter. *C-o-l* was enough. He knew what it meant. Clay stared at the letters. How long did college take? Couple of years, at least. And how much did it cost? He shrugged. That didn't matter either; he had the money coming from the government. Still, there were a few things he wasn't sure about. But Meltzer had gone to college. Meltzer would know. So all he had to do was go and ask him. Singing his song to himself, Clay began to struggle into his clothes.

Twenty minutes later he pulled the red convertible into the parking lot of Headquarters Company. He got out and glanced around. The post looked dead. Ahead of him, the squat gray barracks seemed to be pressing deeper into the dust. Above, the sky was dark and gray. Gray was the color. Everything looked gray beneath that gray sky. Pulling his fatigue jacket tightly around him, he headed for the first barracks. Meltzer lived there, on the second floor, just a few beds away from Maxwell's room. Opening the front door, Clay stepped inside and walked upstairs.

Pfc. Meltzer lay sprawled on his face, clad only in his cotton drawers. Clay bent down and touched him on the shoulder. "Meltzer," he whispered.

Pfc. Meltzer rolled over.

Clay shook him. "Hey, Jerry," he said. "Hey, Jerry, wake up." He shook him again, harder.

Pfc. Meltzer shot out of bed, eyes wide. "Voof," he said.

"Shhh," Clay whispered. "It's me. Eustis."

"Whazzrong?"

"Nothing. Everything's fine. I just thought we might have a little talk."

"What time is it?"

Clay looked at his watch. "Nearly four thirty."

"Four thirty! In the morning?"

Clay nodded. "I didn't mean to bother you or anything. It's just that I thought we might have a little talk. You know." He shrugged. "A talk." He smiled nervously. "Forget it. You go on back to sleep."

"No," Meltzer said. "It's okay. I better go put some water on my face." Turning, he walked down the stairs to the latrine, Clay following a step behind. Filling a sink with cold water, Meltzer plunged his head into it, exhaling. He raised his head, opened his mouth and took a deep breath. Then he submerged again. When he had done this several times, he rubbed his face briskly. "I'm not much in the mornings," he explained. "It takes me a while to get going." He began slapping his face sharply, first one cheek, then the other. Finally, he nodded. "All right, Eustis. What's up?"

Clay took off his fatigue cap and flipped it around his index finger. "Well," he began. "Like I said. I just wanted to have a little talk."

"What about?"

"School," Clay blurted suddenly. "College. Tell me about Yale, Meltzer."

"Yale? What for?"

Clay shrugged. "I don't know. I was just thinking about maybe going there, that's all."

"Oh," Meltzer said.

" 'Cause as you well know, I am leaving the service presently, and I figured it might be a smart thing to go to school before I took me a job."

"Oh," Meltzer said again.

"And you seemed to like Yale well enough."

Meltzer nodded. "We can't talk in here," he said. "Let's go someplace." They left the latrine, tiptoeing through the quiet barracks and outside. Meltzer sat on the bottom back step, Clay right beside him. They stared east for a while, looking at the upper edge of the rising sun on the horizon.

"Going to be hot," Meltzer said quietly.

Clay nodded. "What about this Yale?" he asked.

"Well, gee, Eustis, I don't know exactly what to say." He shook his head. "I'm not so sure you'd like it. I mean, it's not pretty to look at or anything. And the buildings are old."

"But it's a good school, ain't it?"

"Yes. It's very good."

Clay nodded. "That's what I thought. I don't see much point in going to a college if it ain't good."

Meltzer reached down, nervously picking up a handful of dust, letting it trickle slowly through his fingers. "You finished high school, didn't you, Eustis?"

"Oh, sure."

"How was your record?"

"Terrific. I only got caught once. And that wasn't my fault. See, we was stealing toilet paper out of the girls' locker room and this buddy of mine got stuck in the—"

"I meant your scholastic record, Eustis. You know. Grades."

"Crappy," Clay muttered. "But then, I never studied too much."

Meltzer nodded. "Yale's pretty hard, Eustis. There's a lot of work."

"Well, I figure I can do a little better now. After all, I ain't a teenager any more. So I don't guess the work would bother me that much."

Meltzer looked out at the sun again. "I'm still not so sure you'd like it, Eustis."

"I don't see why I shouldn't. There's a lot of parties, ain't there?"

"Yes, but—"

"And I can take easy courses so the work won't bother me. But what I want to know is, how about the girls? Them Yale coeds, Jerry. Are they nice?"

"There aren't any, Eustis. It's a boys' school."

"No girls?"

Meltzer shook his head.

"Well, how in the hell can you have a school without girls? What do you do there?"

"You study, and you—"

"How about that other place?"

"Harvard?"

Clay nodded.

"They haven't got any girls either. Not really. Unless you want to count Radcliffe. But they're pretty ugly."

Clay stood up. "No girls," he muttered. "The awdassity."

"Why don't you go to a state school, Eustis? They've got girls."

Clay shook his head. "No point to that, Jerry," he said quietly. "I joined up to get out of state. So there's no sense in going back." He shrugged. "I don't know. Half-hour ago this seemed like a red-hot idea. But maybe not."

"I didn't mean to discourage you, Eustis."

Clay stepped down into the dust. "It wasn't nothing you said." He kicked at the ground with his toe, watching as the dust rose. Then he looked at Meltzer. "I'm sorry for getting you up, Jerry. I apologize."

"It's all right, Eustis. I don't mind. If there's anything else . . ."

"See you," Clay said, and he waved once, then turned the corner of the barracks. He walked slowly, kicking at the ground, watching the dust rise. The sun was already hot on the back of his neck. No girls and all that studying. How bad was his high-school record? He opened the door to his car. Bad. Really bad. He slammed the door. But hell. He hadn't studied. And besides, he didn't like it much. Still, his record was bad. Backing the car around, he drove toward C Road.

The post was coming to life. There were other cars out now, and in the distance he could see some trainees standing on their barracks steps. Then reveille sounded on the loudspeakers all over the post and the recruits poured out, filling the company streets. Poor bastards, Clay thought. Poor, poor bastards. He drove past MP headquarters. Beyond, the prisoners were walking slowly around inside the stockade compound. Clay pulled into the company parking lot and stepped out of the convertible.

Some of the prisoners hooted at him from behind the fence. "When you gonna join us?" one of them yelled.

"Never," he yelled back. "I'm a civilian. I'm getting out."

They quieted, staring at him as he walked into the mess hall. Private Cronkite, the third assistant cook, was racing frantically around the cooking area. Half a dozen KPs stood off to one side, watching him.

"Hey, Cronkite," Clay said. "Hey, guess what?"

"Don't bug me now, man," Private Cronkite said. "I just screwed up the pancake batter."

"I'm getting out," Clay went on. "I'm gonna be a civilian."

Private Cronkite cursed softly to himself, shaking his head.

"What's for breakfast?" Clay asked.

"Come on, man," Cronkite answered. "Later."

"Something smells funny," Clay said. Picking up the morning paper from Capital City, he walked over to a table and sat down, thumbing through page after page until he came to the comics section. Then he rested his chin in his hands and read intently for a few minutes. Licking his thumb, he turned to the sports section. "Woweeoboy!" he said out loud, staring at the headline.

The Kentucky Derby!

Native Dancer was running in the Kentucky Derby. On Saturday. This coming Saturday. "Hey, how far is it to Louisville," he shouted over his shoulder.

"Three, four hundred miles," one of the KPs answered.

Four hundred miles. Eight hours. He could get a three-day pass and leave early, leave Thursday noon, tomorrow, and get to Louisville by tomorrow night. For the evening. To celebrate. To celebrate his getting out. Louisville was wild on Derby weekend. Mint juleps and parties and women from all over the country.

He sniffed. "That smell's getting worse," he said, turning. Private Cronkite was bending over an enormous bowl of batter, holding his nose.

"I think it's gonna explode," Private Cronkite said. He whirled on the KPs. "Well, don't just stand there. Open the windows!"

Clay got up from the table and walked to the door. "See you, Cronkite."

Private Cronkite muttered something in reply.

The sun was already strong when Clay approached his barracks. Inside, the recruits were standing bunched by the doors, awaiting the whistle for breakfast. Clay moved through them, nodding, and on up the stairs, undressing as he went. With a little luck, he could get an hour's nap before he had to start the day. And the first thing to do was see Captain Magee and get that three-day pass. He opened the door to his room and walked inside. Then he would invite Maxwell to the Derby. Clay lay back on his bed, kicking his pants to the floor. He rolled toward the wall and was about to shut his eyes when he saw the words. *S-c-h-o-o-l, C-o-l, W-o-r-k, J-o-b?* Work? What kind of work? Well, what was the best way to make a lot of money fast? He thought a moment. Oil. That was the answer. Go wildcatting for oil. Find some big oil field and zingo, you're made overnight. But what did an oil field look like? He shrugged. Maybe uranium was better. Go wildcatting for uranium. Less competition. What did uranium look like? Green? Was it green? And was it hard or soft? Probably hard and green, like a jewel. Slaughter would know. Slaughter would be his partner. Together, why together they could . . . But first Captain Magee. And then Native Dancer. And then a mint julep. And then all those women, lined up in a row, wearing mink coats. Nothing else. Just mink coats. Hundreds of them. No. More than that. Thousands. Hundreds of thousands. Millions. Billions. Trillions. What came after trillions? He shrugged once more and closed his eyes. Slaughter would know.

It was late in the morning before Captain Magee made his appearance in the orderly room, and when he did, Clay was waiting for him, paper in hand.

"What's the poop, Sergeant?" the Captain said.

Clay moved forward, handing over the paper. Captain Magee took it from him and walked into his office, reading it. "What is it?" he asked, sitting at his desk.

"Three-day pass request, sir. For this weekend."

Captain Magee looked like a carrot, conical and red. He stared up at his supply sergeant. "I don't know," he began.

"I'm celebrating, sir. I'm going up to Louisville for the Derby."

"I don't know," Captain Magee said again. "Colonel Ellison is coming down sometime this week. He told me so himself. Casual inspection. I think I'll need you on the job."

"But I'm celebrating, Captain. I'm getting discharged, so I'm going up to Louisville. You just got to sign. I'll have the supply room looking perfect. You can trust me."

"You getting out of the service, Clay?"

"Yessir."

"Well." Magee shrugged. "In that case." He picked up his pen and signed the form. "Four thirty, Clay. Four thirty tomorrow. No earlier. You understand."

Clay nodded. "Yessir," and took the form from the captain.

"Congratulations, Sergeant. You're making a wise move."

Clay saluted and left the office. Dropping the form into Master Sergeant Booth's lap, he crawled up on top of Booth's desk. "Type this up for me, boy. I'm off to the races."

Master Sergeant Booth was a quiet, scholarly-looking man, thin, with graying hair. He pushed his rimless glasses farther down onto his nose and peered over them at Clay. "You really getting out?"

"Yup."

"Smart." Booth nodded. "Real smart."

Clay grinned. "You expecting any bodies this morning, Billy?"

Booth shook his head. "Maybe this afternoon."

"Okay," Clay climbed off the desk. "Well, if you need me, I'll be up at Maxwell's a while." And, pulling his fatigue cap down until the visor was approximately on a level with his nose, he tilted his head back, shoved his hands into his pockets and left the orderly room, moving slowly in the direction of the parking lot. "Rooty, tooty, tooty," he sang out loud, waving to the prisoners in the compound, bowing, getting into his car. "Dee toot, dee toot, dee toot." It had turned into a beautiful day; the troops on the road moved briskly, swinging their arms; the company at the bayonet field seemed more adept than usual, changing quickly from one position to another. How much should he offer Slaughter? A partnership was fifty-fifty, but he needed Slaughter for the brain work. He himself would be the idea man, but brain work was needed from that point on. 51-49? Maybe 60-40. That might appeal to Maxwell.

Main Post was busy, but there was a parking place in front of the PX, so he took it and hopped out of the car. Pushing his fatigue cap flat on his head, he walked inside. "Morning, Eustis," Clara said. Clara was the cashier, tall and bony with bad teeth. INC., he thought automatically, then smiled at her. "Just stopped by to tell you the news, Clara. I'm getting discharged."

"Really, Eustis?"

"Yup." He nodded and moved to the hosiery counter.

"Morning, Eustis."

"Howdy, Helen." C-plus. "I'm getting discharged, Helen." He moved forward.

"Morning, Eustis."

"Howdy, Susie." D. "I'm getting out." He continued on, from one counter to the next, circling the store. When he was finished, he walked to the entrance. "Bye, now," he called.

"Bye, Eustis," they all answered, waving to him. "Bye-bye."

Getting back into his car, he drove to the I. & E. building, parking in the driveway. Quietly, he entered the building and moved along the corridor to Slaughter's office. Throwing the door open, he raced around the desk and dropped to his knees at Slaughter's feet.

"But dammit, Isabella, you just got to believe me. It ain't flat. It's round."

Slaughter smiled. "Civilian Clay," he said.

Clay got up and closed the door. "Hey, Maxwell, you want to hear something? Listen," and he started to sing. "Let's give a shout, 'cause I'm getting out. I'll make a billion when I'm a civilian."

"Very catchy," Slaughter nodded. "You're particularly talented this morning."

"Thank you, thank you." Clay bowed low, then crawled up atop Slaughter's desk, crossing his legs. "Hey, Maxwell," he said then, leaning forward. "What color is uranium?"

Slaughter looked at him. "You going wildcatting?"

Clay nodded. "There's millions in uranium, Maxwell. You know that? The world is very short on uranium. All we got to do is find us a patch of it and lay a claim and then just sit back and light see-gars."

"We?"

"Yup. You and me. I'm the idea man. You do the brain work."

"Wonderful," Slaughter said. "A brilliant idea. Now, I'll tell you what. You go out and buy a pair of burros, and while you're gone, I'll fill out my leave request. By the time you're back, I'll be packed and ready. Then we'll ride the burros into Hastingsville and start looking. Hastingsville has always struck me as a likely uranium site. There's an empty lot behind City Hall I suspect is just crawling with uranium."

"You finished?"

Slaughter nodded.

"Well, then, I just want to say one thing. I'm serious, Maxwell. I mean it."

"Exactly what do you mean?"

"Well." Clay fiddled with his fatigue cap. "I'm getting

out. And your enlistment must be up sometime. So I'll wait around for you. And then we'll be partners. 50-50."

"Eustis," Slaughter began.

"51-49. You get the 51."

"Eustis," Slaughter said again.

"Okay. 60-40. That's fair. You couldn't ask for more than that. You—"

"Please, Eustis. I'm very touched. And I'm serious, too. Very touched. But no."

"Well, why not? Come on, Maxwell. You're too smart to stay in the stupid Army, anyway. Let's get out now. You and me together. Hell, there ain't nothing we can't do. So why not?"

Master Sergeant Slaughter rested his head in his hands. "It's a funny thing," he muttered. "You're not the first one to say that to me. Far from it. Every month or so I hear it. Usually from some college-boy private. 'Get out, Slaughter. You're too smart to stay in the stupid Army. Get out now.' It's very complimentary."

"Well, why don't you?"

"You want a serious answer?"

"Yup."

Master Sergeant Slaughter sat back in his swivel chair, his hands crossed in his lap. "You're my dearest friend, Eustis. You know that, don't you? I genuinely admire you, and I have genuine admiration for very few men. And that's complimentary, too."

Clay nodded.

"Looking at you, of course, one might wonder why. Seriously. Look at you. Sitting there. With that stupid smile on your face."

"That's part of my charm."

"Yes," Slaughter said. "Yes, it is. And you've always had it. I've known you for six years now, since your first month in the Army, and you had it then. I remember you so clearly. Basic training. I was your first sergeant, and I remember that stupid smile. Every morning when you walked into the orderly room for sick call. You had diarrhea. You had diarrhea every day the first three weeks of training. Every damn day. The doctors gave you medicine. It didn't work. Nothing worked. You had the worst case of diarrhea in medical history. So you never trained. Just sat in the barracks all day, holding your stomach."

"It was very painful," Clay muttered. "Hurt something awful."

"And then I caught you that afternoon, drinking from that bottle of mineral oil. I remember that as plain as plain. There you were, holding that gigantic bottle of mineral oil, swilling it down."

"I never figured you could walk so quiet," Clay said. "Otherwise you never would have caught me."

"And I stared at you then, Eustis, and I thought to myself, this boy is so stupid that he's smart. And you looked at me, still with that goddam bottle of mineral oil in your hands. And you smiled. And you put your finger to your lips. And you said, 'Let's keep this a secret, okay, Sarge?' And right then, right at that moment, I knew. I said it to myself. 'This boy isn't stupid,' I said. 'He's indestructible.' "

Clay giggled.

"And you are, Eustis. You are indestructible. But I'm not."

"So what?"

"So what?" Slaughter smiled. "Just this—" and he pointed toward the window—"the world's outside that window, Eustis, and it scares me. It's awfully big out there."

Clay clambered down from the desk and approached the soft-drink machine. "Hell," he muttered, selecting a root beer. "Hell, Maxwell." He drained the cup in two swallows and got back up on the desk. "You're not making any sense a-tall."

"Oh yes I am," Slaughter answered. "You forget. I wasn't born a soldier, Eustis. I was a civilian once myself. For years. For many unpleasant years."

"It'd be different now, Maxwell. You'll see."

Slaughter shook his head. "I doubt it. And even if it were different, I doubt that I'd believe it. The memories are still very strong."

"What memories?"

"Childhood. Growing up. Fat boy on the block. I was always fat, Eustis. Fat baby, fat child. It used to worry me terribly. And the only way I knew to calm myself was eating. So I'd eat. Fattest boy in grammar school. Fattest boy in high school. But I thought, if only I could go to college, everything would be different. I couldn't afford it, so I went to work. Shoe clerk. File clerk. Grocery clerk. Years and years. And then finally I had enough money. So I picked up my books again and off I went to college." Slaughter sighed. "Three years. At the good old U. of Illinois. In good old Champaign. I was a good student. Studied all the time. Used to sit in the end zone for the football games. Saw Tommy Harmon play once. But college wasn't any better than grammar school. Or high school. Or being a file clerk."

"You coulda always gone on a diet, Maxwell. You still could."

"Oh, I did, Eustis. Continually. Once I lost over sixty pounds. But nothing changed. Nothing changed at all. Not until the blessed war."

"Come on, Maxwell," Clay said, leaning forward again. "Come on. Please. I'm asking you. Get out. I'll wait."

Slaughter shook his head. "I'm sorry, Eustis. But I've made my bed. I like the Army. It's my home. But not yours.

So go and make your millions and I'll wish you joy."

Clay pushed himself off the desk. "Maybe you'll change your mind. Think about it."

"I do, Eustis. All the time. But there's not a chance."

Clay shook his head, walking slowly to the door. "Hey," he said then. "You wanna go to the Kentucky Derby?"

"When is it?"

"This Saturday. I'm driving up tomorrow noon. Come on. We'll have a ball. Get drunk on mint juleps. Women. Native Dancer's running. He's a cinch. We'll probably make a little money on the side."

"I think not," Slaughter said. "You go. I'll busy myself around here."

"Suit yourself." He opened the door. "See you, Maxwell."

"Until that time."

Clay closed the door and walked back to his car. It was too bad about Maxwell. But maybe he'd change his mind. Doubtful, though. Very doubtful. "I'm off to the Derby," he sang suddenly. What rhymed with Derby? Herby. He drove out of the I. & E. building. But he didn't know anybody named Herby. No good. "I'm off to Louisville," he sang. That was worse. Nothing rhymed with Louisville. Races. That was it. "I'm off to the races, kicking off my traces, and going places." Three rhymes. Sitting deeper in the seat, he closed one eye and sang it again. Maybe he should be a songwriter. Not a bad idea. Not a bad idea a-tall. He drove quickly down C Road. "I'm off to the races, going places, kicking off my traces, off to see new faces, changing bases . . . Cases." He could use that, too. But how? It had to make sense. That was the thing about song words. They had to make sense to be any good. Cases. Hmm. He was still pondering the problem when he pulled into the company parking lot and sauntered toward the mess hall for lunch.

The afternoon went very quickly. He had to clean the supply room, get it looking neat, phony up a few forms. He swept the floor twice and carefully stacked the blankets and sheets into large, even piles. He was about to start rearranging the rakes and shovels when suddenly sixty new recruits were standing in line outside. Maybe they were the last; there was no way of telling. But they needed sheets and blankets and pillowcases and forms had to be filled out and it took a while. By the time they had gone to their barracks, the afternoon was nearly over. Clay swept the supply room again, taking care of the corners and under his desk and along the counter. Finished, he glanced around the room. It looked clean. Nodding, he locked the outside door, stopped briefly in the day room for a candy bar, and headed for his barracks.

He was tired. He had been up for a long time, and last night had been a toughie, so he undressed slowly, dropping his clothes onto the floor. Spreading clean sheets across his mattress, he lay down, singing his horse-racing song over and over. "We're going to the Derby, Donald," he said out loud. "To make our pile." He thought a moment. Should he pack now? No. Tomorrow. It would give him something to do. Besides, his clothes would be less wrinkled that way. He yawned. The room was pleasantly warm. A new song. That was what he needed. Something commercial. Horse-racing songs weren't commercial. He reached for a Baby Ruth and dropped the wrapper on the floor. Love songs. Those were the best kind. Good old plain old love songs. Why wouldn't Slaughter get out? It was a damn shame. He would have a hell of a time prospecting for uranium alone. There'd be no one to talk to. And he'd have to read up on uranium. And who wanted to do that? Not him. "Not me," he said out loud. That college idea. It was no good. He shook his head. Who needed college anyway? You could make money without going to college. He picked up his pencil stub and carefully erased the words *S-c-h-o-o-l* and *C-o-l* from his wall. *W-o-r-k* and *J-o-b?* were left. What kind of work? Songwriting. Love songs. I love you. I love your . . . Your what? Eyes? No. Every song said that. Mouth? That was good. I love your mouth, I love your teeth, I love whatever's underneath. Not bad. It rhymed okay. But did it make sense? No. He shook his head. The room was getting warmer and his tongue felt dry. I love your mouth. Maybe the stock market would be the place. Wall Street. Stocks and bonds. Dark suits and top hats and canes. I love your nose, the way it goes, round and round just like a hose. That rhymed, too. But it wasn't romantic. Love songs had to be romantic. And sincere. Or maybe gambling. You could make a pile gambling and not have to pay any taxes either. Maybe he could make a pile on Saturday. Bet a long shot. Watch it come in. But what about Native Dancer? Maybe he could dope Native Dancer. He would have to check on it when he got to Louisville. How did you dope a horse? Aspirin? Maybe. But it would have to be a lot. Hundreds of aspirin pills. No good. Too hard to swallow. He felt hot now and his head began to ache slightly, persistently. Sleep. That was what he needed. A good night's sleep. I love your mouth. No. Give me your mouth. Better. Yeah. Give me your mouth. Give me . . . What else? He nodded. Give me your boobs. That was sincere. He rolled over toward the wall, staring at the two words, *W-o-rk, J-o-b?* Sweating, he closed his eyes. What rhymed with boobs? Something. It would come to him in time . . .

He awoke sharply. It was dark out and he lay still, blinking. Why was he awake? He listened. No noise. He felt all right. What was it? He stared at the ceiling. Now his head hurt him. He rubbed his eyes. Sleep. Back to sleep. Work? Job? He could be a songwriter or he could be a Wall

Street man or he could be a gambler or he could be an explorer. His head throbbed. He could be a songwriter or a Wall Street Man or an explorer or anything. Anything. Anything in the whole wide world. Standing on top of the world, looking down, owning it all, every bit of it, millions and billions of everything, and he owned it all. He owned Wall Street and he owned Native Dancer and he owned the world and it came to him then, came to him suddenly, with such terrifying force, such totally unexpected surprise that he sat up straight, rigid, unable to breathe. For a moment he froze, jackknifed. Then he fell back, groping, fumbling for his pillow, finally grabbing it, forcing a corner of it into his mouth, biting until his jaws ached, trying to stifle the sound . . .

It took him exactly fifty-four minutes to re-enlist the next morning. Clay clocked it himself, staring dully at his watch as he left the company, staring at it again on his return. Walking into the supply room, he looked around. It was beautifully clean. He seated himself at his desk and stared out past the counter to the splash of yellow sunlight beyond the door. Every so often a breeze stirred the dust, spinning it around, but otherwise there was nothing. Nothing at all. Nothing to do but stare.

Booth came in later in the morning. Clay glanced up at him.

"You okay?" Booth asked.

Clay nodded.

"Going to the Derby?"

Clay nodded.

"Noon?"

Again, the nod.

"I'll cover for you."

"Thank you, Billy," Clay muttered.

Booth turned. "You sure you're okay?"

A final nod.

Booth was gone.

Clay stared at his watch. Almost eleven. His neck was stiff. He twisted in his chair. A slight breeze outside. Dust blew past the doorway. He watched it. Five after eleven. Quarter after. The sun grew brighter and he was sweating, and he blinked as his eyes began to water. A shower would make him feel better. Run some hot water on his neck. Loosen it up. Pack and then shower and then go. While the recruits were at lunch. Just pack up and shower and go.

He picked up his pass in the orderly room at ten of twelve. Then he walked slowly to his barracks. It was empty. Dragging his feet, he took the stairs one at a time, his boots banging into the wood, making a soft, hollow sound in the still barracks. He unlocked his door and dragged his suitcase down from on top of his wall locker. Undressing, he left his clothes on the floor and started to pack. He took the picture frame and carefully placed it inside the suitcase, padding the edges with blue silk underwear, socks and T-shirts. He opened his wall locker. One jacket would be enough. One jacket and two pairs of pants and a couple of shirts. He packed them quickly, closed his suitcase and left it in the middle of the floor.

Kicking his clothes into a haphazard pile, he pulled the sheets from his bed and dropped them on top, leaving the mattress bare. Do it good. Air it a couple of days. Grabbing a towel, he left the room and went down to the latrine. He turned on the water, testing it, waiting for it to get warm. Then he stepped under and closed his eyes, letting the water sting against his neck, loosening the muscles. That was better. That was much better.

He thought for a moment that he heard voices, but he paid no attention. Cronkite must have screwed up lunch, too, the recruits were back so soon. Cronkite wasn't much of a cook. What was he? A draftee? Saxophone player? That was it. Cronkite had been a saxophone player before he was drafted, so naturally they made him a cook. Typical. Typical and stupid. Goddam stupid Army! Stupid! Stupid! Stu . . . He stopped. No point. No point in going on like that. Not any more. He moved his head from one side to the other, massaging his neck. In a little he would be all right. Sure. In a little he would be fine. Clay closed his eyes again.

When he opened them, he was horrified to see Captain Magee standing in the doorway. Captain Magee gaped and stepped aside, and another man appeared. The Colonel. Colonel Ellison. Automatically, Clay snapped to attention and saluted.

Automatically, the Colonel returned the salute. Then he dropped his right arm and looked away. "Tell that man to cover himself," he muttered.

"Cover yourself, Clay, cover yourself," Captain Magee said.

Clay turned around and faced the wall. "Yessir." When he looked back, they were gone. He relaxed. That was close. Did the Captain know he was taking off early? No. How could he? He was just making a casual inspection of the barracks, so how could . . .

Casual inspection of the barracks! His room! Unlocked! Open! "No!" Clay cried, and he bolted out of the shower room and up the stairs. Running inside his room, he stopped, staring around. "No," he cried again. From an officer's point of view, it did not look good. Frantically, he grabbed an armful of sheets from the floor. Where? The foot locker? No. That was jammed full. The wall locker? He opened it. Yes. There was some room. Dumping the sheets, he grabbed some clothes and stuffed them on top of the sheets. Then some more clothes. Then shoes and boots and dirty laundry.

And then Captain Magee was standing in the doorway, pale, his mouth open.

"This your room, Clay?" Captain Magee said.

Clay nodded. "Yessir." He backed up, trying to close the wall locker. Now the Colonel was standing in the room, watching him. Why hadn't he taken a towel? He was dripping on the floor as the Colonel approached, shaking his head.

"Messy," the Colonel said.

"Yessir," Clay said.

The Colonel turned to Captain Magee. "Will you tell that man to cover himself?"

"Cover yourself, Clay. Cover yourself."

Clay turned and faced the wall. Glancing over his shoulder, he saw the Colonel run a finger across his window sill. Black. The finger came away black. Clay stared at the wall. The Colonel was behind him now. Then there was a terrible sound. His wall locker was opening. There was a clump. That would be his shoes falling out. A louder clump. That would be his boots. A softer sound. Dirty laundry. Clay stayed at attention, his eyes shut.

"Messy," the Colonel repeated, walking away.

"Clay," Captain Magee said.

"Yessir?"

"Come see me, Clay. When you're done with your shower. Will you do that?"

Clay nodded. They were gone. He waited. Then, stepping over the pile on the floor, he moved slowly to the stairs. At the bottom, he paused a moment before driving his right fist into the wall. He thought he heard a knuckle pop and it stung a little. But it didn't really start to hurt till later.

* * *

It was not yet six o'clock when Master Sergeant Slaughter walked into the NCO Club. Nodding to the corporal at the door, he moved through the large front room, which was empty except for a quartet of uniformed WACs eating hamburgers next to the juke box. Continuing on, he stopped at the entrance to the back room. It was empty, too, and quiet, and he waited a moment, getting accustomed to the darkness. The bartender was talking softly to two men seated at the bar. A young couple was holding hands at a table close to the dance floor. Slaughter looked around. At the farthest corner table sat Eustis Clay, facing the wall.

Slaughter approached the bar. "My stein, please," he said, and he waited while the bartender reached up and brought it down from the shelf over the cash register, then filled it to the top with beer. Holding the glass in both hands, Slaughter stared at it a moment before bringing it carefully to his lips and draining it. "Again, please," he said, and after the bartender had refilled it, Slaughter paid him. Cupping his stein gently in his right hand, his fingers around the stem, he skirted the dance floor, making his way among the tables. When he stood directly behind Clay, he stopped.

"Good evening, Eustis," he said.

Sergeant Clay did not reply.

"It comes as something of a surprise seeing you here," Slaughter went on. "I thought you'd be in Louisville by now. I—"

"Go away," Clay said.

Slaughter reached down and picked up Clay's glass, sniffing it. "Ahh, boilermakers," he said. "Ambrosia. Nectar. The choice of gentlemen the world over."

Clay turned slowly. "Goddamit, Maxwell," he muttered. "Please, go away."

Slaughter set the drink down. "All requests dutifully honored," he said, and turning, he walked back across the room until he came to his table, situated between the entrance and the dance floor. He sat down. A waitress had just come on duty so he signaled to her, and while she was walking over, he finished his beer. She took the stein from him and retreated back to the bar.

The club was slowly starting to fill. Half a dozen men stood at the bar, and three couples were seated at the other side of the dance floor. Someone put a nickel in the juke box and Frank Sinatra started singing of lost loves and long lonely walks in the fog. A boy and girl began to dance, slowly, their bodies close together, swaying back and forth. The waitress returned with his beer. Slaughter paid her. A young master sergeant walked up behind him and whispered something in his ear. Slaughter shook his head. "Impossible," he said. "Not nearly enough." The young master sergeant nodded and walked away. Slaughter sipped his beer. Two tall, thin WACs moved to the juke box and stood, their faces reflecting red in the red glow of the machine. Slaughter shook his head. Frank Sinatra was gone now and Doris Day was singing in his place, singing of lost loves and long lonely walks in the fog.

Slaughter finished his beer and signaled for the waitress. An old, gray-haired corporal bent down behind him and whispered something in his ear. "All right," Slaughter nodded. "As a special favor." The corporal thanked him and hurried away. The waitress came and took his stein, bringing it back full a moment later. Slaughter paid her, tipped her, held her by the arm. "Send a double boilermaker to the gentleman in the far corner," he said. "And here's a little something extra for your trouble." He gave her some money and she thanked him, hurrying back to the bar.

The two thin WACs began to dance together in front of the juke box, smiling, concentrating on each other. Frank Sinatra was back again, in a happier mood, and Slaughter listened a moment, watching as the waitress carried the double boilermaker the length of the room and set it down on Clay's table. The club was growing smoky and someone dropped a glass of beer, the sound of shattering glass momentarily cutting through the room, followed by a grumbled curse. Sergeant Clay was trying to stand now. Both hands flat on the table, he pushed himself to his feet. Picking up his drink, he began to move toward the dance floor, holding on to passing chairs with his free hand. Slaughter watched him. Clay reached the juke box and rested a moment, leaning against it, and several girls called out to him, "Hi, Eustis, hi," but he did not answer. He pushed away from the juke box and crossed the dance floor slowly, with great difficulty, weaving, taking tiny steps, his eyes focused on the bare yellow light bulb over the entrance door. When he reached Slaughter's table he stopped and leaned over, resting his free hand flat on the table top for support.

"I come over to thank you," Clay said. "For the drink."

"You're quite welcome, Eustis. You needn't have bothered."

"An' also because I been rude." He spoke very slowly, pausing between words. "Unnecessarily."

"I understand," Slaughter said.

"No, you don't. No, you don't understand."

"What happened to Louisville?"

"Pimplebrain Magee restricted me to post. That's what happened."

"Had he cause?"

Clay shrugged.

"It's been a difficult day for you, Eustis. Why don't you sit down?"

"Nope. I just come over to thank you is all." He turned around, squinting. "Which way did I come from?"

"North by northeast, approximately. But it's a long

journey, Eustis. Why not sit down a moment and gather strength?"

Clay fell into a chair, spilling part of his drink. "Sloppy bastard," he muttered, licking his hand tenderly. "That's what Pimplebrain called me."

"Did he really?"

Clay nodded.

"Then he must have seen your room."

Clay nodded again, continuing to lick his right hand.

"Hurt your hand?" Slaughter asked.

Clay shrugged.

"Accident?"

Clay shrugged again.

"Supply room or barracks?"

"Barracks!" Clay said savagely. "Army barracks!"

Slaughter nodded and sipped his beer. Clay closed his eyes briefly, then forced them open. Holding his drink in both hands, he brought it carefully to his lips and took a long swallow. Another. Finally he shook his head and set the glass back on the table. The juke box stopped and for a moment there was quiet. The new record began. Fiddles and harps and the song from *Moulin Rouge.* Half a dozen couples appeared on the dance floor. Clay watched them, moving his head slowly, one side to the other, in time with the music. From the bar came a burst of laughter, building, building, then slowly dying. Clay slumped deeper in his chair, his legs sprawled out into the aisle. The Club was half full now and Slaughter sipped his beer, waiting. Another burst of laughter from the bar. The fiddles and harps reached a crescendo. The record ended. Quiet. Then a saxophone and a trumpet began battling, blaring out one against the other, growing louder and louder. A fat, tightly corseted girl raced onto the dance floor, swinging her hips obscenely. Reaching out for her partner, she brought him close, her body pressing flat against his. Clay looked at her. She was already starting to perspire and her legs were thick. Her calf muscles bulged as she moved. Shuddering, he turned to Slaughter.

"I re-enlisted this morning," Clay said.

"I know," Slaughter answered quietly.

"Yup," Clay nodded. "I filled my own vacancy. Isn't that something?"

Slaughter did not reply.

"Lost money on the deal," Clay went on. "Leave pay. Travel pay. But I had to get it over with."

"Well," Slaughter said, "it's done now."

"Yes," Clay said. "It sure is." He took another long swallow. Then he reached across the table and grabbed Slaughter's arm. "Why did I do it, Maxwell? Why did I do it? I honest-to-god don't know. I knew this morning. I barrel-assed up there like a shot. But I don't know now."

"It's done, Eustis. Forget about it."

"Maybe it's because I'm stupid," Clay went on, his voice growing louder. "I think maybe that's it. On account of I am so goddam stupid I belong here. Right here in the goddam stupid Army with all the other goddam stupes. Maybe that's it."

"Maybe."

"Goddam stupid Army!" Clay said, half shouting.

"Easy, Eustis," Slaughter said. "Take it easy. Have another drink." He raised his arm for the waitress. Clay slumped down onto the table top, mumbling. Slaughter paid the waitress when she returned and pushed the glass across the table, setting it directly in front of Clay's nose. Clay stared at it cross-eyed.

"I'm down, Maxwell," he whispered. "I'm really down."

"I know."

"It's just that it's such a measly life. Such a goddam

measly life. Look at that," and he pointed to the fat girl. Her face was streaked now, and dark perspiration stains spread around her armpits, soiling her blouse. "I'm gonna end up marrying something like that some day," Clay said. "She's measly enough."

"Courage," Slaughter said.

"It stinks, Maxwell. The whole goddam measly life stinks."

"It's not so bad."

"Yes it is."

"It's not so bad, Eustis. Take my word for it."

"What's good about it? Name just one good thing."

"Well," Slaughter began, "after twenty years, you can retire."

"Retire! On what they give you? You're crazy. They just give you enough to starve on. They're not so stupid after all. No. It's us that's stupid. The lousy Army outsmarts us every time."

"You can retire," Slaughter said again.

"Yeah? On what?"

Master Sergeant Slaughter looked from one side to the other. Then he turned and looked behind him. Finally, he leaned forward across the table. "I know a place," he whispered. "Believe me. I know a place where you can live like a king."

"Where?"

Slaughter took a large swallow of beer and set his glass down, toying with the wet rings on the table. Clay cupped his chin in his hands, waiting. Slaughter looked across at him. Very softly, he began to speak.

"In the Pacific," he began. "In the Pacific there's a place. I saw it once, during the war. A little island. Lush and tropical. Thick with green foliage. A long white beach shining in the sun. Blue waters rolling in. Specks of white foam dancing on the sand. Overhead nothing but blue sky, stretching on and on. That's my place, Eustis. That's where I'm going when I retire. To my own little island in the sunshine."

"You are?"

"Absolutely. And the people are friendly. Kind and generous and round. All the girls are slim and round. With such skin. And bright eyes. And smiles to melt your heart. Long legs and flat stomachs and firm round breasts tilted up."

Up?"

Slaughter nodded. "Up."

"What do they wear?"

Slaughter spread his hands on the table. "Nothing. Absolutely nothing."

Clay stared at him. "Where'd you say this was?"

"In the Pacific."

"And you seen it?"

"Yes. One time only. But that was enough. Oh, Eustis, it's a paradise beyond dreaming. And I'm going back there. I'm going back there and live like a king."

"It sounds beautiful, Maxwell. Just beautiful."

"And it is."

"Maybe . . ." He stopped and shook his head. "That's fine for you. But what about me? I tell you I'll end up married to some fat, sweaty girl and die a miserable death. I can see it, Maxwell. I know it's coming. I mean it. I'm washed up, Maxwell. You know it's the truth."

"I tell you what," Slaughter whispered, leaning forward. "Does my island appeal to you?"

"Oh, yes."

"Why, then, we'll share it."

"You mean that? You really mean that?"

"Certainly. I'll go there first and get things ready. Then, when your twenty years are up, you'll come. Picture the scene, Eustis. You, standing up in some small craft. Me, waiting on the beach. The craft pulls you through the blue breakers. I wave. I am surrounded by maidens, dozens of them. In the background is the chief, arms crossed. Flowers nestle in the maidens' hair. White flowers in dark hair. A gentle breeze. The waves soften. The winds caress. The maidens dash into the shining blue water, calling your name. I'll have taught them. 'Eustis,' they cry. 'Eustis.' The sun stands still. The sky is perfectly blue. You leap from your boat. The maidens fling themselves into your arms. Flowers in your hair. Kisses on your cheek. I walk into the water. We meet. 'Welcome, friend,' I say. 'Welcome home.' The maidens begin to sing a native song. The chief makes you an offering, some gift of great loveliness. The girls lead us along the beach. The sun goes down. Soft fires on the beach. We have just finished a sumptuous meal and I retire. I bid you good night. You are alone, now. Alone with the maidens. They are dancing in the moonlight, dancing and smiling at you. They move slowly, in rhythm to some exquisite distant music. Closer. They come closer. You can see adoration in their eyes. Adoration and desire. The air is rich with perfume. Still closer. You can reach out and touch them. 'Eustis,' they whisper. 'Eustis Clay.' They begin to caress you, gently, lovingly. You close your eyes." Slaughter paused.

"That's the most beautiful thing I ever heard," Clay mumbled. "In my whole life."

"It's yours, Eustis. Yours and mine. To share."

Clay licked his lips. "Them dancing girls," he whispered. "That music. Closer and closer."

"Every evening, Eustis. Every night."

"To us," Clay said, raising his glass. "To our island! To—" He stopped abruptly. Then he slammed his glass down, slopping his drink across the table top. "No," he said. "No."

"Why no?"

"Because it's ridiculous, that's why. That's fifteen years away. You'll be old and I'll be old, too, except I'll be dead and in the ground." He slammed his bruised hand against the table, then drew it back quickly, muttering to himself. Gently, he massaged his fingers, shaking his head. "I'm going back to my table," he said. He tried to stand, but he lost his balance and fell back into the chair. "I can't even do that," he muttered. "I can't even do that."

"You don't want to wait?" Slaughter asked.

Clay said nothing.

"Well then, you don't have to. I'll share it with you tonight, Eustis. Close your eyes. Close them. Are they closed?"

Clay nodded.

"All right. Now, first you must listen for the music."

The saxophone-trumpet record was blaring again, and Clay shook his head.

"Not that," Slaughter said. "Don't listen to that. Strike it from your mind. This is soft music. Gentle, quiet music. Coming from a great distance. Can you hear it?"

"Nope."

Slaughter sighed.

"I hear that juke box, Maxwell, and that's all."

"Then try a color instead. Blue. Blue for the water and the sky. Do you see it? Deep blue for the water. Light blue for the sky. Top and bottom."

Clay pressed his finger tips against his eyelids. "I don't see nothin' but nothin'."

"Give it time, Eustis. Deep blue for the water, light blue for the sky. Deep blue for the water, light blue for the sky. Now wait. A speck of white. It's the beach, Eustis, coming alive. Stretching along the water. White as snow. And beyond that, green. Green foliage, lush and deep. And then there—there—running down the beach—the maidens. Aren't they round? And aren't they beautiful? And—"

"Up!" Clay cried. "They do point up!"

"Of course. And see how they run. To meet you, Eustis. See? Arms out wide."

"And they got flowers in their hair," Clay whispered, sitting back. "And they're calling my name. And . . ." he folded his arms, dropping his chin onto his chest. "Hey, Maxwell," he said then. "Look what they're doing now . . ."

III.

The girl strolling up the walk toward the Officers' Club had yellow teeth, an underslung jaw, and was built like a boy. Pfc. Meltzer watched her a moment, shook his head, and wrote *INC.* on the paper in front of him. "I wonder what I'd grade Emmy?" he said.

"Hi, Eustis," the girl said.

Clay smiled at her. "Howdy, Paula." He turned to Meltzer. "Who's Emmy?"

"Emmy's my fiancée," Meltzer answered.

Clay nodded and glanced down to the end of the walk. It was early Saturday afternoon, work was finished for the week, and they were sitting quietly at their separate tables, the large green umbrellas shielding them from the sun. A soft wind blew in from the parade ground.

"I thought you told me her name was Myrtle," Clay said then, taking a cigarette from the pocket of his red-and-blue sports shirt. He picked up his book of matches from the table and lit the cigarette with one hand, blowing the match out gently, watching the smoke rise.

Another girl appeared at the end of the walk, accompanied by a first lieutenant. The girl was short and stocky, but she had a nice smile. "Hi, Eustis," she waved.

"Howdy, Tessa," he smiled, waving back. "Beautiful day."

She nodded, and he watched her disappear into the Officers' Club. He wrote *C—* on his sheet and turned to Meltzer. "What did you give her?"

"C," Meltzer said. "Because of her smile."

Clay grinned. "You're getting better all the time, Jerry. No doubt about that. You're really improving. Couple more sessions and you'll make the first team."

"Thank you," Meltzer said, stretching. He looked at

Clay. "It is Myrtle. But I call her Emmy. I mean, you just can't go around calling somebody Myrtle. That would be a terrible thing to do. Don't you think so?"

"I guess."

"Myrtle's such a crummy name, don't you think? I do. It makes you sound like you're eighty years old." He paused. "Anyway, I wonder what I'd grade her."

"You got a picture of her?"

Meltzer shook his head. "I don't believe in that. That's jerky stuff. Carrying pictures around."

"Well, what does she look like?"

Meltzer squinted. "That's hard to say. She's got a terrific personality. She's very clever and all. And she laughs a lot. She's got a terrific laugh."

"I don't quite see her yet," Clay muttered.

"Well, I guess she isn't exactly what you'd call beautiful. I mean, you wouldn't stop to turn around when she walks by. But she's really got personality. I don't know exactly how to describe her. It's tough to describe somebody when you really know them well."

"What color is she?" Clay asked. "You could start with that."

Meltzer laughed. The door to the Officers' Club opened and a captain stepped out. "She's a wonderful athlete," Meltzer went on. "She can beat me at golf. And she plays tennis. And she swims. And she's tall, taller than average. Maybe five foot six. And she's slender. Not thin, but slender, if you know what I mean. And—" He stopped suddenly as the captain stepped between them, staring first at one, then the other.

"Okay, okay," the captain said sharply. "What's the story?"

Neither of them answered.

"What's the story?" the captain repeated. "What are you doing here?"

Clay gaped up at him, trying to cover the grading sheet with his hands.

"You!" the captain said to Clay. "What's going on?"

Clay was unable to reply.

Meltzer stood suddenly. "I'm Pfc. Meltzer, Captain," he began. "Editor of the post newspaper. This is my layout man. We're thinking of doing a series of articles on the Officers' Club, so we came down here to look it over." He held up his grading sheet. "Just taking notes, Captain. That's all. Shorthand. Want to make everything just as accurate as we can."

"Oh," the captain said. He took a step backward. "Would you like to come inside and look around?"

"No thanks, Captain. Maybe later. Right now we're mostly interested in the architecture and the landscaping. That kind of thing."

The captain nodded. "Sure." He took another step away from them. "Well, anytime you want to come inside, just do it. All right?"

"Thanks for your co-operation, Captain," Meltzer answered. "Much appreciated."

The captain disappeared back inside the Officers' Club.

Meltzer waited a moment until he was gone. Then he grabbed Clay by the shoulders. "Eustis!" he cried. "Eustis! He believed me!"

Clay nodded.

"He really believed me," Meltzer went on, shaking Clay back and forth. "How about that?" He let go of Clay and started jumping around the table. "And I did it all myself."

"I was took by surprise," Clay mumbled. "The awdassity of that man. Butting in like that. Who does he think he is? Asking us what we was doing."

"Woweeoboy," Meltzer said, sitting down again. "Wait till I write that to Emmy."

"You're really improving," Clay said. "You stick with

me and Maxwell and there's no telling how far you can go."

"Me," Meltzer whispered. "Talking like that. And to a captain. I can't believe it."

Clay stood. "Well, he may not in a few minutes. We better get out of here. I had enough architecture."

Meltzer bounded on ahead of him as they moved toward the parking lot. "Let's eat," he yelled over his shoulder. "I'm hungry."

"Okay by me."

"Where? The Footlong?"

"Where else is there?" Clay answered.

"Footlong *ho!*" Meltzer cried, vaulting over the door into the front seat. In a moment he was singing. "Bulldog, bulldog, bow, wow, wow. Eli Yale. Bulldog, bulldog . . ."

Humming along, Clay started to drive.

The Footlong was a hot-dog stand on the road to Hastingsville. A small, square wooden shack, it stood in the center of a large graveled lot which was usually jammed with cars from the post. Originally it had been called "Footlong Frankfurters," but the lower half of the sign had blown away years ago, and Paulie had never bothered to replace it. Paulie owned the Footlong and was its sole employee. He was a small, pudgy man who always talked about the weather. He wore dark pants and a white T-shirt and a white apron, and he tied the apron below the bottom of his potbelly, so that the flab jiggled freely as he moved back and forth behind the counter.

Clay parked at the rear of the lot, instinctively brushing away the flies that always buzzed over the area like a dark cloud. He and Meltzer got out and walked past the lined-up cars to the stand. "Afternoon, Sergeant Clay," Paulie said. "How many?"

"Howdy, Paulie," Clay answered. He consulted with

Meltzer a moment. "We want four footlongs and two bags of potato chips and four Cokes."

Paulie nodded. "The usual?"

"The usual."

Paulie laid out four twelve-inch buns and inserted four footlongs. Then he piled them high with ketchup, mustard, pickle relish, chopped onions, sauerkraut, salt and tomato wedges. Wrapping them in wax paper, he set them on the counter, along with the rest of the order. "I hear it snowed last night in Denver, Colorado," he said.

"That so, Paulie?"

"That's what I hear." He looked around. "Where's Mr. Slaughter today?"

"He had to go into Capital City on business," Clay answered, taking out his wallet. It was the last weekend of the month, and he stared sadly at the two one-dollar bills nestling together.

"I'll pay," Meltzer volunteered.

"No," Clay began. "I can—"

"Don't be silly, Eustis," Meltzer said, and he handed a ten-dollar bill across the counter. Paulie gave him change and they started picking up their food.

"I'll pay you back," Clay said.

"Don't be silly," Meltzer repeated. "I won't accept it."

Clay balanced the Cokes in his hands and tucked the bags of potato chips in his pockets. "Thank you, Jerry," he said.

"You're welcome, Eustis."

"See you tomorrow, Sergeant Clay," Paulie called. He mopped his neck and chin with his handkerchief. "And it was a hundred and six in Death Valley."

"Tomorrow it is," Clay answered, and they turned, threading their way slowly back to the red convertible. "Hey, Jerry," Clay said, as they walked along, "tell you what." He blew at a fly that had landed on his nose. "I'll buy you dessert. A beer at the NCO. Maxwell won't be back for a while, so we'll have a beer or two. Sort of even us up for lunch. By that time Maxwell'll be back and we'll do something."

"Beer in the afternoon?" Meltzer said. "I don't know."

"Be good for you. You want to make the first team, don't you? You can't stop now."

"Okay, Eustis. If you say so."

Clay nodded. "I definitely say so." They reached the convertible and, fighting off the flies, balanced the Cokes on the dashboard, unwrapped their footlongs and started to eat.

"Taste all right?" Paulie called from the counter.

Clay raised his right hand, touching his thumb to his index finger.

"Why is Maxwell in Capital City?" Meltzer mumbled, his mouth full of frankfurter.

"Huh?"

"I said, why is Maxwell in Capital City?" Meltzer repeated, louder.

"Business," Clay mumbled, taking another bite.

"What?"

Clay gestured with his thumb. "Business."

"Oh." Meltzer nodded, stuffing more footlong into his mouth, washing it down with a swallow of Coke. "What kind?"

"Secret."

"I can't understand you when your mouth is full, Eustis."

"Same here," Clay said. He shielded the footlong with his hand as the flies bunched for an attack.

"What kind?" Meltzer asked again.

"Secret," Clay repeated.

"What is it?"

Clay looked around. No other car was close. "Maxwell thinks he's losing his hair," he whispered. "He goes into

Capital City once a month to see a hair doctor."

Meltzer reached out for his second footlong. "Did you say something about a hair doctor?"

"Shh," Clay said, putting his finger to his lips. "Maxwell is very sensitive."

"But you can't grow back hair. It's impossible."

Clay nodded. "Maxwell's found some witch doctor in Capital City. Five bucks a throw. It don't do no good, but it makes him feel better."

Meltzer shook his head. "Boy, Maxwell sure takes care of himself."

"Course he does," Clay said. "He's got to."

Meltzer looked at him. "What do you mean, he's got to?"

"Nothin'. But maybe you noticed that Maxwell's a trifle on the heavy side."

"Well, is he sick? Is there something the matter with his blood pressure? Or his heart? Is anything—"

"Course not," Clay said. "Maxwell just takes things slow and easy, that's all."

"A hair doctor," Meltzer muttered. "Isn't that ridiculous?"

They finished their footlongs. Then, quickly, while the flies were regrouping, Clay gathered up the wax paper and the cups and sauntered over to a large empty wastebasket. Raising his hands high, he dropped the bundle, and as it hit the basket, he made the sound of a bomb exploding. "*Bonkokasplatt!*" He was good at making sounds. Always had been. Natural gift. He hurried back to the car.

"Hey, Jerry," he said. "Hey. Listen to this. Ready? Here goes. *Bonkokasplatt!!*"

"Terrific," Meltzer said. "A bomb exploding."

"Right. Now guess this." He made another sound.

"Mortar shell?"

"Right again. Now here's some machine-gun fire." He closed his eyes and made the sound.

"That's wonderful, Eustis."

"Thank you. Thank you. Now wait. Listen. I can put 'em all together." He closed his eyes again and took a deep breath. "*Bonkokasplatt! Pkew. Pkew. Pkew. Bonkokasplatt! Eeeerewpong. Pkew. Pkew. Rrrmpow. Eeeerewpkong. Bonkoskasplatt! Pkew. Pkew. Bonko—*"

"Eustis," Meltzer began.

"*—kasplatt! Pkew. Pk—*"

"Eustis," Meltzer said again. "People are watching us."

Clay opened his eyes and looked around.

"Everything all right?" Paulie called from behind the counter.

Clay flushed. "Fine," he mumbled, starting the car, backing out onto the highway.

"Those were terrific sounds, Eustis," Meltzer said. "Just about the best I've ever heard."

Clay nodded, muttering to himself.

"Maybe you'll end up as a sound man someday, Eustis. Ever think of that? For television or radio?"

Clay looked at him. "You really think so?"

"Maybe."

Clay brightened. "Hey, Jerry," he said suddenly. "Listen to this," and he closed one eye, starting to make the sounds again, only much louder, much more realistically, until Pfc. Meltzer shouted "Bravo!" and broke into wild applause.

The NCO Club was jammed. The corporal at the door recognized Meltzer, waving him through, and they hurried across the crowded front room toward the bar. It was even more crowded, and they stood a moment in the doorway, getting accustomed to the darkness.

"Why so many people?" Meltzer asked.

"End of the month," Clay told him. "Everybody's busted and there ain't no place any cheaper than here."

They started moving along the bar, looking for a spot. All the stools were taken, and men were standing three deep behind them.

"Hey," Meltzer said, pointing. "There's a stool."

Clay shook his head. "Let's find someplace else."

"There isn't anyplace else."

"Well, let's wait, then."

"What's wrong?"

Clay dropped his voice. "I don't want to sit next to him." Meltzer looked.

Sergeant First Class Priest was sitting on the adjoining stool, talking to Corporal Lenahan.

"Don't be dumb," Meltzer said, and he edged his way onto the stool. Clay pushed in beside him, and they ordered beer. The noise was terrible; the juke box blared through the packed room, forcing the voices up, and the two sounds met in useless battle.

"Gee, what a terrific place," Meltzer shouted. "Real folksy."

"When I feel like thinking deep," Clay answered, "I come here."

The bartender brought their beers, and Meltzer raised his glass. "To your health, Eustis," he said, and, closing his eyes, he drained the glass in two swallows.

"There's no law says you got to drink it that fast, Jerry."

"I don't taste it so much that way," Meltzer said. He paused, shaking his head. "You sure I'm going to get to like it?"

"Absolutely."

"Then let's have another, Eustis. I'm on my way. First team, here I come."

Clay signaled for the bartender.

"How about that captain at the Officers' Club," Meltzer shouted. "Wasn't that something?"

"Absolutely."

The bartender brought the beers and Clay paid him.

Meltzer picked up his glass, staring at the liquid. "This stuff really goes through me," he said. "I have to go to the latrine already." He laughed. "How about that captain? You know, three months ago I probably would have fainted."

"You're a cinch for rookie of the year," Clay said.

"And you weren't much help, either."

"He took me by surprise," Clay mumbled.

"Not me, boy. I rose to the occasion." Meltzer drank his second beer quickly. "This stuff really goes through me," he said. "I'm off for the latrine."

"That's impossible," Clay said.

Meltzer inched down off the stool. "Save my seat. I've got to hurry." He pushed through the crowd as Clay fought his way up onto the stool.

Ordering another beer, he looked after Meltzer, who was rounding the corner of the bar, running for the men's room. Clay shook his head. It just wasn't possible. Beer couldn't go through anybody that fast. Meltzer still had a lot to learn. But he was coming strong. It was too bad he was getting out so soon. How long did he have yet? Seventy days? Maybe eighty? Clay couldn't remember. But Meltzer kept a chart on his desk in the newspaper office with the days marked off. Lots of the draftees did that, though. Most of them, maybe. How many days did he have left? Eighteen hundred? More? Clay shrugged. What difference did it make? He sipped his beer. Still, it was a shame Meltzer was getting out so soon. But that was the trouble with buddying up to draftees. You had no one to blame but yourself. He shrugged again. Maybe there was something to that sound-man business. Work on the TV. Make a pile. Probably have his own program after a while. Make a few sounds, sing a few songs. Balance a broom or two. He was even better at balancing brooms than he was at making sounds. How about putting them all together? Sing a song, make some sounds, and all the time you're balancing two brooms, one on each little finger. Fantastic! It'd be a cinch to be popular. A little something for everybody. Maybe he could make up a song about sounds. It would be tough, though. What rhymed with *Bonkokasplatt?* He would have to work on it. And he'd probably need an agent. All the big stars had agents. Slaughter. Slaughter would make a terrific agent. Sure. Slaughter could handle him and they'd both make a pile. The record changed on the juke box, the voices lowered, and that was when Priest spoke to him.

"How's the Jew-lover?" Priest said.

Clay whirled in his seat. "What did you say?"

"I just asked how the Jew-lover was, that's all," Priest repeated.

"What the hell are you talking about?"

"Nothing."

"Then what did you say that for?"

Priest shrugged. "If the shoe fits . . ."

Clay stood up suddenly. "You know what, Priest? You make me sick. Why aren't you out eating babies or something?"

Priest got off his stool, looking down at Clay. "You want to watch what you're saying, Clay. For your own good."

Clay turned abruptly and pushed his way out of the crowd. On the fringe, he turned and stared back. Priest was talking with Lenahan, both of them laughing. Clay started walking slowly toward the men's room. What a thing to say! What a stupid, dumb, moronic thing to say! Calling him a Jew-lover. Hell, he didn't even know any Jews. He wasn't a Jew and Slaughter wasn't a Jew and Meltzer . . .

Meltzer?

No. Ridiculous. Clay stopped beside the men's room door and leaned against the wall. Absolutely ridiculous. Meltzer couldn't be. Clay closed his eyes. Well, what did he know about Meltzer? Not much. He was from New York and there were a lot of Jews in New York. But that didn't mean anything. Hell, President Roosevelt was from New York and he wasn't any Jew. And how about Mayor LaGuardia? And besides, Meltzer didn't even look like one. Clay opened one eye.

What did they look like? Well, they had big noses and black curly hair and they were rich and they had horns. No. They didn't have horns. That was just something somebody had told him once. So they were rich, with big noses and black curly hair. And Meltzer's hair wasn't black. Clay opened his other eye. But it was curly. And Meltzer had money. Didn't he pay for lunch with a ten-dollar bill? And how could anyone have ten dollars left at the end of the month of a Pfc.'s pay?

"What are you doing here, Eustis?"

Clay turned, smiling suddenly. "I just felt like leaving, Jerry. Figured I'd wait for you here. It was too noisy at the bar." His hair was dark brown when you looked at it closely. So Meltzer was rich and he had dark brown curly hair.

"What do you want to do now?"

Clay moved quickly to one side, peering at Meltzer's profile. "Oh, I don't know," he said casually. "Maxwell ought to be back soon. We could go wait for him." That was a good idea. Maxwell would know.

"Suits me," Meltzer said, moving through the front room to the entrance of the club.

Clay hurried alongside, staring at his profile. Finally, he closed one eye and squinted.

"What are you doing?" Meltzer asked, facing him.

"Nothing," Clay laughed. He shook his head. When you examined it closely, Meltzer's nose was not small. Not small at all. Hey, that rhymed!

"I think I'll write to Emmy and tell her about what happened at the Officers' Club," Meltzer said.

"I think I'll just wait for Maxwell," Clay said.

They walked outside and down the steps to Clay's car. Getting in, they drove quickly along the road toward Headquarters Company. Parking in the company lot, Clay walked behind Meltzer, following him into the barracks and up to the second floor. Meltzer opened his foot locker, took out a pen and a pad of paper, fell onto his bed and started to write. Clay watched him a moment, staring, then turned and walked away in the direction of Slaughter's cadre room.

He knocked at the door. There was no answer. It was probably too early for Maxwell to be back. With a shrug, he tried the door. It was open. "Maxwell?" he said. "Maxwell?"

"Come in, Eustis," was the soft reply.

Clay pushed the door open. Master Sergeant Slaughter was sitting on the side of his bed, clad only in his underwear. He held a hand mirror close to his face and was examining his hairline.

"You're back early," Clay began. "And am I glad! I got something to talk about."

"I'm getting bald, Eustis," Slaughter said in a half whisper. "The doctor told me so. 'Slaughter,' he told me, 'you're getting bald.' And there's nothing anyone can do about it." He ran his hand through his hair and then brought his palm down in front of his face, counting the hairs. "Six, seven, eight," he muttered. "Eight hairs just fell out." He ran his hand through his hair again, and again he counted. "Six that time. Eustis, what am I going to do?"

"You could stop running your hand through your hair, Maxwell. That might help."

Slaughter shook his head. "This morning," he said, "twenty-three hairs on my pillow. It's only a matter of time." He dropped the mirror onto his bed table. "Jesus. That's all I needed."

Clay walked up and stood over Slaughter, peering down. "Looks mighty thin from up here, Maxwell," he said.

Slaughter nodded. "Thank you. Thank you very much."

"Come on now, Maxwell," Clay laughed. "I was just joking. You look the same as always. Now you know you never been exactly bushy up top."

Slaughter lit a cigarette. "I want," he said, "to change the subject."

Quickly, Clay went to the door and looked out. Pfc. Meltzer was still on his bed, writing. Clay closed the door and hurried back to Slaughter. "I got something to tell you," he whispered. "Something I maybe just found out."

"How much are we going to make on it?"

"No. No. Nothing like that. But listen. A little while ago in the NCO Club. You know what happened? Priest said Meltzer was a Jew."

"Did he now, Eustis?"

"Yup." Clay nodded, waiting.

Slaughter said nothing.

"Go on," Clay said, finally.

"I didn't think you'd asked me a question."

"Well, I didn't exactly. But go on anyway. Tell me."

"About Jews?" Master Sergeant Slaughter rearranged his many pillows and lay back. "Very strange people," he said then. "Very strange. They exist almost totally on a diet of matzos and gefüllte fish." He paused. "All right, Eustis. Now you tell me."

Clay sat on the edge of Slaughter's bed and started talking very softly. "Well," he began. "I done some dee-ductions. If that's what you mean."

"I assumed you had," Slaughter nodded.

"Now first of all, he's got curly hair," Clay went on. "And it's dark brown. And his nose ain't exactly tiny. And besides that, he's rich. He bought me lunch today and he paid with a ten-dollar bill. I figure that's important."

"You do?"

"Yup. And I also figured you'd take it from there."

Slaughter blew a smoke ring, and Clay watched it soar upward, grow larger, fainter, until it disappeared.

"That was a good one, Maxwell," he said. "That was a beauty."

"What difference would it make, Eustis? About Jerry? One way or the other?"

Clay thought a moment. Then he shrugged. "I don't know. But it's sure the kind of thing we ought to find out about. Don't you think so?"

"Definitely," Slaughter agreed. "So why don't you ask him? That might be an excellent way of learning the truth."

Clay shook his head. "I couldn't do that," he answered.

Slaughter blew another smoke ring, waiting until Clay was finished watching it. "Well, Eustis. I can't think of anything better."

"There is one thing," Clay whispered. "Only I'm not so sure about it."

"Why don't you tell me?"

Clay dropped his voice even further. "Maxwell," he said. "Do you think Jews have horns?"

"What a lovely idea, Eustis."

"Do you think they do?"

"It would certainly make your detective work a great deal simpler. All you'd have to do is go examine his head."

Clay pulled at his lower lip. "The only thing is, I'm not so sure it's true. I know somebody told me once. Swore up and down that—"

"Priest?"

"No. Somebody else. I can't remember."

"Strange we haven't noticed them before."

"I think they're very small," Clay explained. "So that you wouldn't see them unless you looked real close." He snapped his fingers and stood up. "You wait here. I'm gonna check." Opening the door, he shoved his hands into his pockets and strolled down the center aisle to Meltzer's bunk. Walking up behind Meltzer, he bent down.

Meltzer turned. "Almost finished," he said.

Clay nodded, not moving.

"Well?" Meltzer asked.

Clay grinned. "Nothin'," he mumbled, and he hurried back up the aisle to Slaughter's room. "I couldn't see nothin'," he whispered, closing the door.

"Damn," Slaughter said.

"I might have been able to, but he turned his head."

"Well," Slaughter shrugged, "we'll just have to think of something else."

"Can you feel them, do you think?"

"If they're there."

"Then how about you grabbing him by the arms and pinning him down and I'll feel his head?"

"That may be just a trifle crude, Eustis."

"I guess." Clay thought for a moment, pulling at his lip. "Hey. Hey, how about telling him he needs a haircut and then bribing the barber to cut all his hair off?"

"Possible," Slaughter mused. "But Jerry might get angry. And besides, he'd be able to tell what the barber was doing."

"We could wait until he was sleepy."

"Ahh," Slaughter nodded. "Now there you have it. We'll wait until he's particularly tired and then we'll carry him to a barber shop. Do you know any barbers we can bribe?"

"Don't you?"

"As a matter of fact, yes. But I think there are too many possible slip-ups involved. You'll have to think of something better. Remember, Eustis. You're the idea man."

"I'm thinkin' awful hard," Clay said, and he closed his eyes.

There was a knock at the door. "Okay for me to come in?" Meltzer asked.

"Certainly, Jerry," Slaughter answered.

Pfc. Meltzer closed the door behind him. "Did Eustis tell you what happened between me and the captain?"

"No."

"Well, listen. We were sitting in front of the Officers' Club—"

"You got something stuck on your head," Clay interrupted. He stood up next to Meltzer. "Don't move. I'll get it."

Pfc. Meltzer reached down for Slaughter's hand mirror and looked at himself. "I don't see anything."

"It's gone," Clay mumbled. "Feather or something."

"Anyway, we were sitting in front of the Officers' Club and . . ." He stopped again. "What are you smiling at?" he asked Slaughter.

"Nothing, Jerry. I'm sorry. Please go on."

"Well, anyway, we were sitting there and this captain—"

"Maxwell's losing his hair," Clay said. "He's all upset."

"Are you, Maxwell?"

Slaughter nodded. "My doctor discharged me today. He told me there was nothing more he could do. 'Slaughter,' he told me, 'there's nothing more I can do. You're going bald.' "

"That's a shame, Maxwell."

"I wonder if I'm getting bald," Clay said. "Hey, Jerry. Hey, feel my head to see if I'm getting bald."

"What are you talking about, feel your head?"

Clay shrugged. "I just wondered if I was getting bald. I thought maybe you could feel my head. To see. And then I'd feel your head to see if you was getting bald. That way we'd both know."

"What is all this head business?" Meltzer asked.

"No head business," Clay muttered. "It's just that I sort of thought it might be nice to know if—"

"There's nothing wrong with getting bald, Eustis. My father's bald, and it doesn't bother him any."

"Hey, Jerry," Clay said quickly. "You got a picture of your father?"

"Not here. I told you I don't believe in that jerky picture stuff."

"Damn," Clay said.

"Enough!" Slaughter announced, rising from his bed of pillows. "I want a drink."

"The NCO's mobbed," Meltzer said.

"We'll go to the Service Club, then. And mingle with the privates."

"Don't you want to hear about the captain?"

"Very much, Jerry. But go get ready. Tell me on the way up."

"Okay," Meltzer said. "But I still don't get all this head business." He left the room.

Slaughter closed the door and waited a moment. "Eustis," he said, "sometimes you're impossible."

"Why? We want to find out, don't we? If only he had a picture of his old man. Then we'd know for sure."

"Maybe you could get Jerry to write for one."

"I don't know about that."

"Well, then, why don't you write the letter yourself? Copy Jerry's penmanship. It might take some practice, of course, but—"

"Yeah," Clay interrupted. "Hey, that's it. I'll spend a

couple of days practicing. And then you tell me what to write. And we'll send it off. Maxwell," he cried, clapping Slaughter on the back, "you and me together. We can do anything."

The Service Club was a large wooden structure located near the I. & E. building on Third Street. Painted a dull yellow inside and out, it served as a home away from home for the trainees on post. There were many rooms, each named for its particular function. There was the letter-writing room, the ping-pong room, the television room and the get-acquainted room where, on Saturday nights, the officers' wives held forth, directing ice-breaking games for the trainees and any girls from Hastingsville who happened to be nearby. There was also a cafeteria and a beer bar. The beer bar was long and rectangular, brightly lit, filled with square, linoleum-topped tables. At one end of the room stood the juke box, and beyond it a small, empty room used for dancing.

Slaughter, Meltzer and Clay walked into the beer bar, where Clay selected a table halfway between the counter and the dancing room. Slaughter and Meltzer sat down, Clay standing over them, staring at the top of Meltzer's head.

"Now cut that out," Meltzer told him.

Clay turned away. "Lemme get the first round," he said, and he hurried off to the counter, returning a moment later with three glasses of beer. Sitting with his back against the wall, he surveyed the room. "Not much here," he muttered.

The large room was empty, except for a few scattered trainees who sat quietly, talking softly, drinking beer. The juke box was silent.

"Why is it so quiet?" Meltzer asked.

"I imagine most of the lads are on pass," Slaughter told him. "Those that could get away. The rest . . ." He shrugged. "It's still early. They'll come in later."

"What a jerky place," Meltzer said. "The 'get-acquainted room.' Boy, is that scary. It's right out—"

"I got acquainted there with a major's wife one time," Clay remembered. "She was a little old, but full of fight."

"Bull," Meltzer said.

Clay raised his right hand. "So help me."

"Anyway," Meltzer finished, "I still say it's right out of 1984."

"Huh?" Clay said.

"It's a book, Eustis," Slaughter explained. "An excellent novel."

Clay stared around the room.

"It sure scared me," Meltzer said. "I read it while I was in basic training. It hit home. I used to read it after lights out, sitting on the second-floor landing underneath the fire light. I never was so scared by a book in all—"

"Contact!" Clay said.

"What?"

Clay pointed. "The second from the end." Meltzer looked.

Five girls were walking into the room. They stopped at the bar a moment, giggling to themselves, bunched together. Ordering Cokes, they hurried to a table across the room.

"The second from the end," Clay said again, a smile fixed on his face. He was staring at a tall brunette with long, curling hair. She wore a white skirt and blouse, with a pearl necklace and pearl earrings. She sat down. Clay still stared at her. She glanced around the room, then caught Clay's eye. Quickly she looked away.

"That's from Capital City," Clay said, watching her.

"How do you know that?"

Clay shrugged. "I got a instinct."

"Trust Eustis, Jerry," Slaughter said. "He knows."

The girl looked at Clay again, and again quickly away.

She whispered something to the quartet around her, and they giggled.

"I'm making points," Clay mumbled, looking at her.

"What's he doing?" Meltzer asked.

"Making points," Slaughter sighed.

Clay rested his chin in his hands and continued to stare. She was looking back at him, more and more frequently now, for longer periods of time.

"I'm almost home," Clay said.

"You're embarrassing that girl, Eustis."

"Hush," Clay whispered. "I'm concentrating." Slowly his smile broadened.

"She's smiling back at him!" Meltzer said.

Clay stood. "If you gentlemen will excuse me, I have a engagement." He took two steps, then turned to Slaughter. "Juke box, ho," he said, and he shoved his hands into his pockets casually, sauntering away. When he reached the juke box, he squinted, starting to read the titles.

"What's going to happen now, Maxwell?"

"The lady will join him at the juke box," Slaughter replied. "It's only a matter of time."

"I'll believe it when I see it," Meltzer said.

The five girls were talking rapidly to one another, and occasionally their giggling drifted across the room. They talked and talked and then the brunette stretched. Clay waited at the juke box, his hands in his pockets. The brunette stretched again.

"My God, Maxwell," Meltzer said. "She's getting up." He watched as she stood by the table a moment. Then she started to walk. "She's only going for a Coke, Maxwell. That's all." The girl approached the counter and leaned against it. Clay still read the song titles. "She's a B-plus," Meltzer said. "She's really pretty." The girl counted her change, slowly turning. Finally she began to walk back to her table. Clay did not move. Slaughter watched idly, sipping his beer. The girl put the Coke bottle on the table.

"I told you," Meltzer whispered. "She just wanted another Coke. She . . ." He stopped.

Change in hand, the girl sauntered across the room to the juke box. Crossing her arms in front of her, she started reading the titles.

Clay dropped a dime onto the floor. For a moment they both looked at it. Then Clay bent to pick it up, muttering something, smiling. The girl smiled back at him. Clay stood again, closer to her now, and together they read the titles on the juke-box machine.

"Poor child," Slaughter said softly.

"I don't believe it," Meltzer exclaimed. "How did he know she was going to the juke box?"

"She wasn't. But if Eustis had gone to the men's room, then by God, she would have gone to the men's room." He finished his beer and walked to the bar for another.

"She's talking to him," Meltzer said, pointing, when Slaughter returned.

"Of course," Slaughter nodded. "And now the next step is the smile. Just wait." Clay was speaking quickly now, moving his hands, laughing, his blue eyes wide and bright. Every so often he brushed his hair back, only to have it fall loosely across his forehead. "That boy is sometimes so charming it makes me sick," Slaughter said.

"I don't get it, Maxwell. I could never do anything like that."

Slaughter sighed. "This may come as something of a shock to you, Jerry. But among certain classes of women, Eustis is one of the more successful studs now operating."

"Which classes?"

"The lower classes. Mentally, I mean. That boy is positive murder on moronic women. Plus any with mother complexes. Somehow he brings out the instinct. It's frightening. Judging from his actions here, I would guess this girl to be in the latter category."

Clay's hands were clasped behind his back. Shyly he scuffed at the floor with one shoe, his head down, his shoulders hunched together. Then, very slowly, he raised his head, a gigantic, open smile on his face.

"Game, set and match," Slaughter said.

"That's sickening," Meltzer mumbled.

"Of course it is," Slaughter agreed. "I don't begin to understand its appeal. But it's very basic. Eustis knows it somehow, though. He divines it, I think. Right now, for example, you've got to realize that he's lying like a madman. Sometimes he's a refugee. Or an orphan." Slaughter shrugged. "Of course, Eustis is an orphan, but still . . . Since Korea, he's usually been a spy. An officer on a secret mission. Being parachuted behind enemy lines the day after tomorrow. Standard English thriller material."

"Look, Maxwell," Meltzer said. "Look. They're going dancing."

Hand in hand, Clay and the girl walked into the back room, momentarily disappearing from sight. The music started, slow and sad. They appeared again, moving easily, their bodies close together. The girl's eyes were closed. Clay raised one hand and touched his thumb to his index finger, grinning at Slaughter.

"He likes to keep me posted," Slaughter explained.

Meltzer grabbed his beer glass and drained it. "Boy," he said. "I'd like to see him get away with that on a Smith girl."

"So would he," Slaughter answered. "So would he."

"She must be a real mental midget. You know that, Maxwell?"

"Very likely. We'll find out."

"How?"

"He'll bring her over just before the kill. Eustis always introduces me. It makes him feel better if I chat with them a while. It's sort of a pasteurizing process."

Meltzer shook his head, staring into the next room, watching as Clay and the girl drifted slowly into view, turned, then disappeared. "I don't understand him sometimes," Meltzer said.

"You should try, Jerry. I mean that. Understanding Eustis is one of the great joys in life. Watching his mind operate. The thoughts that boy has." Slaughter shook his head. "I marvel."

The room was slowly starting to fill, trainees drifting in quietly, two or three at a time, their faces still lined with dust from the morning's activities.

"You can never get really clean in basic," Meltzer said. "No matter how hard you try."

Slaughter nodded.

Meltzer turned to him suddenly. "What was all that head business, Maxwell? Why was he acting like that?"

"Don't you have any idea?"

"Maybe."

"I was going to apologize about it, Jerry. I'll try and explain." Clay danced into view again, pointing his index finger toward the girl's head, winking.

"Go on, Maxwell."

Slaughter sat back and breathed deeply. "You see, for Eustis, the shortest distance between two points is a parabola. He is engaged in a running con game with the world, and since the world has most of the advantages, he feels he has to be devious in order to come out on top. It's his way. And once you know that, he's a lot easier to predict. He goes 'round about,' like the Boyg said."

"I don't get you."

Slaughter took a long drink of beer, slowly setting the

glass back on the table. "This afternoon Priest told him you were a Jew."

Meltzer nodded, said nothing.

"He was finding out. In his own way."

"Didn't he know?"

"Evidently not."

"Is he upset?"

Slaughter shook his head. "I don't think so. Nothing really upsets Eustis. He just gets a trifle confused from time to time."

"Well, why didn't he just ask me?"

"He couldn't possibly have done that. Remember? The parabola?"

Meltzer shook his head. "What was he looking at my head for? Horns?"

Slaughter nodded.

Meltzer burst out laughing. "I'm sorry," he said. "I shouldn't laugh. But that's so terrible I can't stand it."

"It does show a certain lack of education," Slaughter agreed.

"What should I do about it, Maxwell?"

"Nothing. At least not now. Look—" and he pointed—"we have visitors."

Meltzer turned and saw Clay walking slowly toward them, one arm draped around the brunette's shoulders. "He's still smiling at her," Meltzer whispered.

"Never change a winning game," Slaughter answered, as they stood.

Clay stopped on the other side of the table, his arm still around the girl's shoulder. "Candy," he said, "I'd like you to meet a couple of friends of mine. This here is Major Slaughter. And this is Lieutenant Meltzer. Gentlemen, I'd like you to meet Candy Simpson."

"Charmed, Miss Simpson," Slaughter said.

"Captain Eustis was just telling me about you, Major," Candy said, her voice heavily southern. "While we were in there dancing. All about the jump and—"

"Jump?" Meltzer said.

"The parachute jump," Clay replied quickly, pushing Candy down into a chair. "The one we're taking. Behind enemy lines. To help speed up the truce talks."

"I don't think it was wise of you talking about it, Captain," Slaughter said.

"Oh, I won't tell a soul, Major Slaughter. I promise. On my word of honor."

"I don't doubt you, Miss Simpson," Slaughter said. "But in our line of business, discretion is the better part of valor, as they say."

"I know, Major. I understand." She smiled at Clay. "You all lead such thrilling existences. Captain Eustis told me about some of what you've done. It's so exciting. Just to look at Captain Eustis, you'd never think it."

"The captain has done some miraculous things," Slaughter agreed. "Some of them defy the imagination. Why, I can remember once—"

"Candy is from Capital City," Clay interrupted, nodding at Meltzer.

"What brings you to Camp Scott, Miss Simpson?" Slaughter asked.

Candy giggled and turned, waving to the quartet of girls across the room. "Why, we heard about the post being shut up. So me and some of my girl friends drove on down to look at it. We've never been here before."

"I'm taking Candy on a tour of the post," Clay said. "All the little nooks and crannies. We're not gonna miss a thing." He stood up.

"What do you do in Capital City, Miss Simpson?"

"Nothing, Major Slaughter. Nothing exciting, anyway.

Me and my girl friends, we just finished high school. We're going to Capital City College in the fall."

"We may as well get a move on," Clay said.

"Why, I think college can be very exciting, Miss Simpson. In a way, I envy you."

"Did you like college, Major Slaughter?"

"Not much, Miss Simpson, but—"

"We gotta be going," Clay said.

"—Lieutenant Meltzer here—"

"See you later," Clay said.

"—went to Yale and had a very pleasant time of it."

"Yale?" Candy asked.

Meltzer nodded.

"We're off to take in the post," Clay said.

"Yale!"

Meltzer nodded again.

"A Yale man!" Candy exclaimed, staring at Meltzer. "I had a cousin once who went out with a Yale man."

"Class of Fifty-one," Meltzer told her.

"My cousin went to the Yale Senior Prom."

"Let's get a move on," Clay said. "We gotta be going, yes, sir."

"Did you ever go to the Yale Senior Prom, Lieutenant?"

Meltzer nodded.

"What was it like?"

Meltzer shrugged.

"What the hell's going on here?" Clay said.

"Tell me about it, Lieutenant."

"It was just like any other dance, Candy," Meltzer began, leaning forward across the table, smiling at her. "Soft lights. Soft music." He took her hand. "Would you dance with me, Candy? Now? Before the big jump?"

"Why, I'd love to, Lieutenant," she whispered. "I've never danced with a Yale man before."

"Now just a damn minute," Clay said. "Hold the . . ." He stopped as they glided past him, moving toward the juke box. Then he spun around and stared at Slaughter. "What happened?" he said.

"You've just been rabbit-punched by the Ivy League, Eustis, that's all. Now sit down. And please, close your mouth."

Clay sat down. "I'll kill him," he said.

Slaughter sipped his beer.

Clay looked into the other room, watching as the two bodies began to turn, slowly spinning out of sight. He pounded his fist on the table. "I'll kill him," he said. "The aw-dassity. And him just a lousy lieutenant. I'll kill him. I'll cut him in little pieces. I'll blast him to smithereens. I'll—"

"You better not," Slaughter said quietly. "People might accuse you of prejudice. Jerry's a Jew."

"Yeah, well I don't care if he's a goddam Eskimo, I'm still gonna . . ." He stopped, looking at Slaughter. "How do you know that?"

"He told me."

Clay stared back into the other room. As Meltzer moved into view, he held up his right hand and touched his thumb to his index finger.

"No kidding, Maxwell?"

"So it seems, Eustis."

Clay shook his head. Meltzer disappeared again. Slaughter finished his beer.

"I'll poison his gefüllte fish," Clay said suddenly. He sat up straight. "Hey. Hey, that's just what I'll do. I'll go out to some river and catch me a gefüllte fish and I'll poison it and send it to him all wrapped up. Like a present. How about that, Maxwell?"

"Brilliant, Eustis. Typically brilliant."

"Lemme see. I'll need a fishing net and some bait and

some secret poison. Like them pygmies use in the jungle pitchers. And a hypodermic needle. And what else?"

"You might take some gloves along. You wouldn't want to leave any fingerprints."

Clay nodded, closing one eye. Gloves, poison, bait and a fishing net. But what did gefüllte fish like to eat? Worms. Probably worms. Get up early in the morning, dig up a couple of big fat worms, and take off.

"Hey, Maxwell," he said. "You know any pygmies?"

"None intimately, Eustis."

"Damn." Clay shook his head. "Hey, Maxwell," he repeated, tugging at Slaughter's shirtsleeve.

"What, Eustis?"

"I didn't really believe any of that horn business."

"That so?"

"I was just fooling around with that. You believe me?"

"Of course."

"Hell, nobody got horns."

"Only cuckolds," Slaughter answered quietly.

Clay turned to him. "What's that?"

Master Sergeant Slaughter sat back in his chair. "It's a crossword-puzzle word, Eustis. Of very little value. But if you'll buy me another beer, I'll be only too delighted to tell you what it means . . ."

IV.

The long line of recruits stood sweating in the sunshine. Seventy-five men, they waited in front of the open door of the supply room of the Transient Company, shifting from one foot to the other, talking discontentedly among themselves, perspiration pouring from their faces, spotting their clothes. As the wait continued, the talk grew louder, and a few of them began walking, two paces out of line, two paces back. A great pile of green duffel bags lay off in the dust to one side. The grumbling increased in volume as the sun poured down, and they stared now, as one man, through the open door.

Inside, the supply room was steaming. Sergeant Clay raced around, gathering bundles of sheets, carrying them back to the long counter that stretched across a third of the room. He was wearing fatigue pants and a T-shirt and the sweat dripped from his forehead into his eyes, stinging, and his fingers were wet. He wiped a wet arm across a wet forehead and checked the counter. The forms were ready, the sheets were ready, the pillowcases, the blankets. Blankets! He shook his head, blinking as the perspiration attacked his eyes again. Then, nodding, he walked from the supply room into the comparative coolness of the sun.

"All right, at ease!" he shouted, and the line of men stopped moving. "Now hear this," Clay went on. "When you go inside, grab yourself a pillow slip and two sheets and two blankets and sign the form at the end of the counter, and then get out, and I don't want no talking." The grumbling began again. "Okay, go," he said, and he hurried back into the supply room, standing behind the counter, watching as the men filed by.

The heat inside was worse now than before, with the recruits shuffling through, and he watched them carefully, checking to see that they took what they were supposed to take, signed where they were supposed to sign. Reaching into his pants pocket, he brought out a soggy handkerchief and wiped it across his eyes. It did no good. Counting the men as they passed—thirty, thirty-three, forty—he sagged against the counter and leaned down, cupping his wet chin in his wet hands. As soon as they were gone, he decided, he would slip out and pay a visit to Slaughter. It was about that time. Fifty. Fifty-five, sixty. Just stuff the forms into his desk and close up the supply room and take off. Seventy, seventy-two, seventy-four.

As the last man walked out, Clay pulled on his fatigue jacket and picked up his fatigue cap, hurrying to the door. He locked it, then proceeded with caution toward the orderly room. Creeping beneath Captain Magee's window, he rounded the corner, stood up straight and moved slowly to the window behind Booth's desk.

"I'm off to see Maxwell," he whispered.

Booth turned a sweating face toward the window and nodded.

Clay waved good-bye and, adjusting his fatigue cap until the visor was approximately on a level with his nose, walked toward the parking lot. The top of the red convertible was down, and he did not bother pulling it back. It was just too hot. A group of prisoners stood in the compound, but this time they did not yell at him. Instead they stared sullenly, acknowledging his wave only by nodding.

Backing out of the parking lot, Clay turned left on C Road, starting the drive up to Main Post. It was still early afternoon and as he drove along everything was quiet. The post baked silently under the sun. He drove around a company of trainees, but today there was no singing; just the dead sound of boots treading on the hard, dusty ground. To his right, the bayonet field was full, but he heard nothing;

the mimed gestures were slower today, more painful, unaccompanied by sound.

Clay sped on. Ahead was Main Post, and he drove through it quickly, turning when he came to Slaughter's street. Parking in the I. & E. driveway, he got out of the car and, not bothering to readjust his fatigue cap, walked inside. He moved noisily down the corridor to Slaughter's office and threw the door open without ceremony.

Then he stopped dead.

It was beautiful. Clay stood in the doorway and closed his eyes, leaning against the door frame. He took a deep breath. Another. Shutting the door, he crossed to Slaughter's desk, sitting down on top of it.

Shaking his head, he stared at Master Sergeant Slaughter's window, and at the air conditioner nestling inside.

"Like it?" Slaughter asked.

Clay nodded.

"I do, too. It adds a note of modern elegance, don't you think?"

"When did you get it? Why didn't you tell me?"

"I was just about to call. A gentleman came during the noon hour and installed it."

Clay clambered down from the desk and walked over to the air conditioner. He bent down closer to it. The air blew refreshingly in at him. Unbuttoning his fatigue jacket, he raised his T-shirt and allowed the cool air to dry the skin on his stomach. Then, turning, he repeated the process on his back.

"Boy," he said. "Woweeoboy!"

"It's yours as much as mine, of course," Slaughter said. "Any time you want to use it. Stand there all you want to. Any time."

"Thank you, Maxwell," Clay said. He glanced at the soft-drink machine, dialed a Coke, and inserted his nickel.

Draining the cup quickly, he dropped it in the wastebasket, made the sound of a bazooka, *Ttthhhhooooooom*, and walked back to the air conditioner. Sitting underneath it, he smiled happily as the cool air floated across his scalp. "I ain't never gonna move again," he muttered. "They can bury me right here."

"Hot in the supply room?" Slaughter asked.

"It's a inferno," Clay answered. "That's what it is. It is so hot I thought I was just gonna drool away and disappear. You never seen anyplace so hot in your life."

"Bad ventilation, I suppose."

Clay nodded.

"I'm full of sympathy, Eustis."

"This is heaven," Clay whispered, and he closed his eyes.

"It must be terrible working under such intolerable conditions," Slaughter said. "It seems a crime that a man of your stature has to do it."

Clay opened one eye, cocking his head. Maxwell was acting funny. "What do you mean?"

"Oh, nothing, Eustis. Nothing at all." He opened his arms expansively. "It's just that when a dear friend of mine suffers discomfort, it moves me. I begin to think, Oh, if only there were some way I could help him. If only I could somehow bring him out of his misery into the light." Slaughter was staring across the room. Clay followed his gaze.

It was then that he first saw the fan.

A giant fan, lying in the corner. An enormous fan, glittering gray, lying there. A beautiful fan, a gigantic fan, a . . .

"What's that?" Clay asked, casually.

"What's what?"

"That." He pointed with a flick of his hand.

"Oh, that," Slaughter said. "It's a fan."

"Yours?"

Slaughter smiled. "It recently came into my possession, yes."

Clay closed his eyes. "Your cup's really runnin' over, Maxwell. First a air conditioner, now that thing."

"I've been very fortunate," Slaughter agreed.

Then neither of them spoke for a while.

"What do you plan on doing with it?" Clay asked finally.

"The fan?" Slaughter smiled again. "It's a funny thing you ask, Eustis. Because I'm not exactly sure in my own mind what I'm going to do with it. As a matter of fact, I was pondering that particular question when you walked in."

"I suppose you ain't really got much use for it no more," Clay said, "now that you got this," and he indicated the air conditioner.

"Well, now, Eustis, I'm not sure. A man can always use an extra fan in weather like this. I might put it in my room back at the company."

"You already got two in your room back at the company."

Slaughter nodded. "True," he said. "But in weather like this, who can be sure? I read in the paper that it's going to get hotter, Eustis. From now on, the paper said. Hotter and hotter right through the summer. After all, this is still only June. July and August are yet to be heard from." He sighed. "I imagine the paint will be peeling from the walls before too much longer." He sighed again. "I don't like hot weather myself, being, as I am, a trifle overweight. But you, Eustis. How do you feel about hot weather?"

Clay shrugged. "I don't mind it none. Matter of fact, I kind of like it sometimes. I come from a long family of hot-weather lovers. I ever tell you that?"

Slaughter shook his head. "You're the fortunate one, Eustis. You, not me. Why, if our positions were reversed, I know that I would do whatever was in my power to secure such a beautiful piece of workmanship." He pointed to the fan.

Clay stared at it. "Looks kinda lopsided," he said.

Slaughter shrugged.

"I doubt it even works," Clay went on.

"You might plug it in and see," Slaughter said. "Just as an experiment. There's a socket right over there."

Clay got to his feet and brushed himself off. Then, slowly, he crossed the room, staring down at the fan. "Lord knows it ain't brand new," he muttered. "Look how it's been scratched." He got to his knees and lifted it. It was heavy. Very heavy. That was good. And sturdy. Like a rock. "It's terribly lopsided," he said.

"Probably it doesn't even work, Eustis. But why not plug it in just the same?"

Clay plugged it in. For a moment, there was nothing. Then the great blades began to move, slowly at first, then faster and faster, and the room was filled with the whirring of the blades beating the air. Now the blades were invisible, and Clay, crouching, pushed his face forward until it was only inches away from the sound. He closed his eyes. For the second time that afternoon, he was cool. Of course, the fan was not the air conditioner, and there was no use in thinking that it was. But still, he was cool. Wonderfully cool. Beautifully cool. And it would fit perfectly on his desk. And there was a socket in the wall close beside. So if he sat in his desk chair, no matter how hot the day, he would be cool and relaxed and comfortable. That was the way he felt now, relaxed and comfortable, and it was with considerable reluctance that he reached out and unplugged the fan. The whirring sound softened, the blades became visible again, moving slower and slower, circling around and around. Then they stopped.

Clay turned. "Seems to work okay," he said, and he walked back to the air conditioner.

Slaughter nodded. "I thought it did." He smiled at Clay. "You don't mind if I do some work now, do you? You can stay if you like. But I'm rather busy this afternoon."

"Me, too," Clay said. "I've got to be getting back to the company. There might be some more bodies coming in later." He shook his head. "Boy, if they're serious about closing this post, they're sure going about it bass-ackwards."

"Oh, they're serious, all right," Slaughter answered. "Have you been by the 54th recently?"

Clay shook his head.

"Half a dozen companies are boarded up already, Eustis. Just sitting there, empty and rotting. They're hollowing out the post. But slowly. The body's still moving, even though the heart has stopped beating."

"Yeah," Clay said. "Maybe so. But I got to be going." He took a step toward the door. Snapping his fingers suddenly, he turned. "Hey, Maxwell," he began. "I knew there was something I meant to say. And you know what? I been thinking. I been thinking that it might be a nice thing if I could do you a favor. Hell, you're always doing things for me, and I never get a chance to do nothing for you. And it's about my turn, don't you think?"

"Eustis," Slaughter said, "I am genuinely touched."

"You see," Clay went on, lowering his voice, "just yesterday I got in a whole new supply of drawers, cotton. The newest style the Army got. With elastic tops."

"Drawers, cotton, you say? With real elastic?"

"Absolutely. You'd love 'em. Why, they'd take inches off your middle."

"Inches? How marvelous."

"And they're so thin and light you won't think you're wearing nothing at all. They make you feel like you was walking on air. And they don't stick to you no matter how hot and sweaty you get. Oh, they're beautiful, Maxwell. No doubt about that."

"They sound it, Eustis. They really do."

"How 'bout if I bring you up half a dozen?"

"Wonderful," Slaughter said. "Eustis, you've made my day. You really have. You've brought a little sunshine—"

"In exchange, of course," Clay cut in.

"Exchange? For what?"

"You know damn well for what, Maxwell. Now, is it a deal? Okay? I'll bring 'em right up."

"You drive a hard bargain," Slaughter said. "Let me see. Six beautiful new pairs of drawers, cotton, with elastic tops, for that thing, that relic, that secondhand, lopsided, scratched gray fan? Is that what you're offering?"

"Yeah," Clay said. "That's what I'm offering. On account of you done so many things for me. That grubby old fan ain't worth a thing anyway. Is it a deal, Maxwell? Huh? What do you say? How about it? Okay?"

"Don't," Master Sergeant Slaughter said, "be ridiculous."

"You mean no deal?"

"Something like that."

Clay nodded. "Think it over, Maxwell. I gotta shove off." He put his hand on the doorknob. "See you around."

"Until that time, Eustis."

The door closed. Slaughter sat back in his swivel chair, watching the door. Folding his hands in his lap, he waited.

"Eight pairs of drawers, cotton," Clay said, sticking his head back through the door.

"You're letting the hot air in," Slaughter told him.

Clay hesitated a moment, then walked into the room again, closing the door, leaning against it.

"Is eight your final offer?"

Clay adjusted his fatigue cap, pushing it down over his

eyes. Tilting his head back, he peered at Slaughter. "Yup," he said.

"I must have time to think," Slaughter said, getting up from his desk, striking the soft-drink machine just above the coin-return slot. The machine belched once, *Awwk.* Slaughter took the cup of grape and returned to his swivel chair.

"Well?" Clay said.

"Perhaps if you had said twelve pairs of drawers, cotton," Slaughter mused. "Perhaps then."

"Okay," Clay answered. "I'll give you twelve. On account of us being friends. But that is it. The end. Final." Casually, confidently, he walked over to the soft-drink machine. Taking a nickel from his pocket, he stared at it, then put it back. Raising his right hand, he hesitated a moment before swinging down at the general area above the coin-return slot.

The sound of the blow filled the room briefly.

The machine did not belch. Clay uttered a cry of pain. Feverishly, he began shaking his hand back and forth, blowing on it.

"Hurt?" Slaughter asked.

"It's damn near broke off at the wrist," Clay said. "Look. It's swole already. Them machines is dangerous, Maxwell." He shook his hand, faster than before.

Slaughter looked at him sadly. "You're absolutely right," he agreed. "Perhaps I should put up a sign. *Nickels preferred.* How would that be? I might even—"

"First things first," Clay interrupted. "Twelve of them new cottons."

"Plus six mattresses," Slaughter said.

"Mattresses!"

Slaughter nodded. "I am in dire need of mattresses. Twelve drawers, cotton, and six mattresses."

"Okay," Clay said. "Fine. Is it a deal?"

Slaughter looked at him. "Is what a deal?"

"Dammit, Maxwell!" Clay said, climbing on the desk, sitting cross-legged. "I want that fan. I need it. Now—"

"Of course you do," Slaughter agreed. "I understand your position perfectly. It's only the question of terms that separates you from it."

"Lemme have the fan, Maxwell. Come on. I'll give you the cottons and I'll give you the mattresses so . . ."

Master Sergeant Slaughter leaned back in his swivel chair. "Did you happen to notice," he began softly, "on your arrival this afternoon? Did you happen to notice the ghastly state this building was in?"

"No."

"Well, take my word for it, Eustis. It is. The grass needs cutting and the floors need waxing and the windows need cleaning." He threw his hands in the air. "It's a disgrace. I am filled with chagrin whenever I leave the building."

"Twelve drawers and maybe a couple of mattresses and we'll—"

"Bodies," Master Sergeant Slaughter announced. "I must have bodies." He pounded his fist on the desk. "I must have bodies, and quickly."

"What are you talking about?"

"You know perfectly well what I'm talking about. Why, you told me with your own lips how jammed the Transient Company is at this moment. Hundreds of recruits down there, Eustis. Hundreds of bodies. I want some of them. Tomorrow!"

"Okay," King whispered. "I'll try to sneak you up a couple in my car."

"A couple," Slaughter said. "To cut the grass and clean the windows and wax the floors. In this heat. Do you think me cruel, Eustis?"

"Six, then. I can fit six in my car. I'll have 'em up here

tomorrow morning. Now—"

"Sixteen," Slaughter said, his voice suddenly loud. "Sixteen bodies."

"I can't do it, Maxwell. You know I can't do it."

"Sixteen bodies and twelve drawers, cotton, and six mattresses," Slaughter said.

"No."

"Seventeen bodies and twelve drawers, cotton, and eight mattresses."

"Maxwell—"

"Twenty bodies and twelve drawers, cotton, and eight mattresses." He cupped his hand around his ear. "Do I hear more? Going once. Going twice—"

"Stop!" Clay cried. "Stop. Okay."

"Sold!" Slaughter said, standing up, grabbing Clay by the hand. "You're a hard man, Eustis. You drive a hard bargain."

Clay mumbled something and remained where he was, sitting cross-legged on the desk, his chin in his hands.

"The fan is yours," Slaughter said, moving to the corner, picking it up. "Here. May you enjoy it in good health."

Clay took the fan and set it down on the desk. He looked up at Slaughter. "You won't tell nobody?"

"All transactions in strictest confidence," Slaughter answered. "Rest assured. Besides, who would I tell? You really got the best of me that time, Eustis. I'm proud of you."

"Yeah," Clay muttered, getting off the desk. "Sure. And if you was to give away nothin', it would still cost plenty."

Slaughter smiled. "Have the bodies here tomorrow morning at nine," he said. "Sharp."

"Okay," Clay said. "I'll get 'em up here somehow." He walked to the door.

"And it's a beautiful fan, Eustis. Practically new. You

have no cause for embarrassment. To tell the truth, I had originally planned on getting a great deal more for it. But you outthought me, Eustis. You brought me to my knees."

Clay turned. "You just saying that, Maxwell?"

Slaughter raised his right hand. "Honor bright."

"Well," Clay said, grinning suddenly. "Ain't that something?" And with a flourish of his fatigue cap, he closed the door behind him. Once in the corridor, the hot air hit him and, gripping the fan tighter, he hurried down the hall and outside. Opening his car, he placed the fan gently on the front seat beside him and, glancing at it continually, holding it steady with one hand, he began the drive back to the Transient Company.

As he opened the door to the supply room, the rush of stale, burning air forced him back a step. Bracing, he ducked his head and drove through it. Immediately, he began to perspire, but he did not slow. Circling the long counter, he raced to his desk and, grabbing the cord, plugged the fan into the wall socket. The blades started to turn. He watched them. Soon they were invisible, and the whirring sound began.

Setting the fan in the middle of his desk, he sat down in front of it and leaned forward, slowly removing his cap, closing his eyes. As the perspiration dried, a smile came over his face. He inched still closer, putting his nose right up next to the invisible blades, and listened to the sound. *Whirr*, it went. *Whirr*. Already he was relaxed. He could feel his hair blowing wildly as the cool air massaged his scalp. The sound seemed louder. Happily, he began to imitate it.

"Whirr," Clay said. "Whirr, you bastard. Whirr. Go on, you gray beauty. You thing, you. Go on and whirr. *Whirrrr* . . ."

"Everything all right, Eustis?"

Clay stopped suddenly, grinning up at Master Sergeant

Booth. "Lookee, Billy," he said, and he lifted the whirling fan, holding it high. "Ain't it a beauty?"

Booth's eyes narrowed. "You just buy that, Eustis?" he asked. "PX having a sale on fans?"

Clay put the fan down hurriedly and walked around his desk until he stood in front of it. "Not exactly," he answered.

"Where did you get it from?"

"Why don't we just say I found it."

"All right, Eustis. You found it. You didn't happen to find it from Slaughter, did you?"

"Maybe." Clay shrugged. "Maybe not."

"Let's have it, Eustis," Booth said quickly. "How much did you find it for?"

Clay opened his arms wide. "Why, Maxwell just up and give it to me."

"What did you up and give him?"

"A few little odds and ends," Clay admitted. "A couple didos."

"Such as?"

Clay lowered his voice. "Well, to tell you the truth, Billy, there is something you ought to know. Like I made a promise to Maxwell that we could send him a couple recruits tomorrow morning to tidy up the I. & E. Building."

"Okay," Booth said. "He can have a couple."

"I figured you wouldn't mind none. I'll take care of transporting 'em myself. It won't cause you no bother a-tall. I'll get the truck and—"

"Truck!" Master Sergeants Booth said. "What truck?"

"For the recruits," Clay explained. "To get 'em up there."

"How many?" Booth asked.

Clay did not reply.

"How many, Eustis?"

Still no answer.

"Ten? Twelve? Fifteen?"

"More," Clay said. "But you're getting warm."

"Twenty?"

Clay nodded.

Booth shook his head.

"Maxwell's a hard man in a haggle," Clay muttered. "He's awful tough."

"You didn't give him anything else?"

"Course not."

"Okay." Booth shrugged. "But it's your baby. If Magee catches you, I don't know a thing about it."

"Thank you, Billy," Clay said.

"Twenty men," Booth muttered. "Jesus." He turned and left the supply room.

Sergeant Clay moved around to the front of his desk and sat back in his chair, listening to the afternoon whirr by.

When retreat had finally blown, he picked up his fan and locked the supply room. Stopping briefly in the Day Room for two candy bars, he proceeded to his barracks. Carefully stepping over the recruits who were writing letters on the stairs, he unlocked the door to his room and closed it behind him. "Lookee, Donald," he said out loud. He plugged in the fan and set it on the edge of his bed table. He undressed quickly until he was wearing only his blue silk underwear. Then he took some clean sheets from his foot locker and remade his bed. Finally he lay down, turning his body toward the fan. The truck. How was he going to get the truck? From Tozzi. He would have to get it from Master Sergeant Tozzi of the motor pool. But what would Tozzi want? Underwear? Why not? Tozzi would probably be satisfied with underwear. Six pair. With elastic tops. What was Tozzi's waistline? Thirty-eight. Maybe forty. And six pair was too many. Three. That would probably be enough. Three would be plenty.

There was a knock at the door.

Clay sat up in bed. "Yeah?" he said.

"It's me, Eustis. Jerry."

"Come on in," Clay said. Pfc. Meltzer opened the door. "Make yourself comfortable."

Meltzer closed the door behind him. "Wow," he said, looking around. "What a pigpen!"

Clay grunted. "You're talking about my home."

"Well, you still might give it a sweep every once in a while, Eustis. What a slop pile! I bet you could grow potatoes on the floor."

Clay pushed his face toward the fan.

"Hey," Meltzer said, picking up the picture frame from the table. "Who's this?"

"That's my dog," Clay told him. "That's my Donald."

Meltzer looked down at the color photograph. "Irish setter?"

Clay shook his head. "Golden retriever."

"Is he smart?"

Clay nodded.

"What can he do?"

"Do?" Clay snorted. "Nothin'."

"I thought you said he was smart."

"He is. He's a genius. But he don't do no tricks."

"What's so smart about him, then?"

"He loves me," Clay said quietly. "That's all."

"Oh," Meltzer said, and he put the picture back on the table. "Anyway, he's very pretty."

"Thank you, Jerry." Clay reached over for a candy bar and held it out. "Want one?"

"No thanks. I've had supper." He looked at Clay. "Let's do something. Let's go to the flicks. There's a Bob Mitchum at Theater Two. What do you say?"

"Naw. Why don't you get Maxwell?"

"I can't. He wants to see that Joanie Crawford picture again. Sometimes I don't know what's the matter with him. He saw it twice already."

"That ain't nothin' for Maxwell. He seen *Mildred Pierce* eight times."

"Let's go catch the Bob Mitchum," Meltzer said. "I saw the previews last week. It's got a million fights in it." He began sparring in the hot room. "Pow! Smash!" He stopped. "Hey, you know what you ought to do? You ought to rent this room out as a Turkish bath. No kidding. Of course, you'd have to clean it up some first."

"I'm comfortable," Clay said, and he pointed to the fan.

"Well, I'm not. So come on. Let's go see Bob Mitchum." He began sparring again. "Pow!"

"I can't tonight, Jerry. I'm just not gonna move until tomorrow." He pushed himself up on his elbows, sticking his head close to the fan.

"Okay," Meltzer said. "I just thought I'd run down and see."

"We'll do something tomorrow night sure. All right?"

"Okay," Meltzer repeated. "So long, Eustis." And he closed the door.

Clay reached for a candy bar and, dropping the wrapper on the floor, quickly devoured it. Then he lay back. Outside it was growing dark, black ugly clouds forming on the horizon. Clay smiled as the cool air swept over his dry body. The whirring sound filled the room. He shut his eyes. "Man, oh man, what a fan. Bigger than a frying pan." No. That stunk. How about that Turkish bath idea? If you put six chairs in the room and cemented up the window . . . Where could he get cement? Somewhere. Shouldn't be too tough. But would it be worth it? How much could you charge for a

Turkish bath? Two bits. Maybe fifty cents. And you could only do it when the recruits weren't snooping around. That didn't leave enough time. Maybe the recruits could be around, though. Maybe they liked Turkish baths. He would have to ask a few of them tomorrow. He could have four sittings a night. Four times six was . . . twenty-four. And twenty-four times fifty cents times seven days a week was . . . Twenty-four times seven times fifty cents times fifty-two times . . .

He heard only the whirring of the blades, growing louder, louder, beautifully louder, and then he was asleep.

He awoke early the next morning, showered and dressed and combed his hair. Unplugging his fan, he carried it with him down the steps, carried it carefully, holding it in his arms, pressing it against his chest. Walking into the mess hall, he selected a seat close to a socket, plugged the fan in, and got his breakfast. He ate in cool comfort, and when he was finished he took the fan with him to the supply room. Installing it in the middle of his desk, he sat back and closed his eyes, waiting for the day to begin.

After most of the recruits had eaten and were slowly walking back to their barracks, Clay left his desk and hurried to the orderly room. There was no one inside, so he sat down atop Booth's desk, crossed his legs, picked up the telephone and asked the operator for the battalion motor pool. In a moment there was a voice on the other end.

"Motor pool."

"Lemme speak to Tozzi," Clay said.

"Okay," the voice said, and then several people were yelling. "Tozzi. Tozzi. Tozzi. Phone."

Master Sergeant Tozzi had been in charge of the battalion motor pool for as long as anyone could remember. A short, potbellied man, he had curly salt-and-pepper hair, and even though he had been in the Army for twenty-five years, he still spoke with a heavy Italian accent. Clay could hear the phone being picked up again.

" 'Allo," Master Sergeant Tozzi said.

"Angelo," Clay began, his voice low. "This is me. Eustis."

" 'Allo," Master Sergeant Tozzi said again.

"You got a spare truck down there? I got to make a couple trips up to Main Post."

"Shu."

"Can I borrow it?"

"Shu."

"Thanks, Angelo. I'll be down in a while."

"Fo' how much?" Master Sergeant Tozzi said.

"I'm kinda low right now," Clay told him. "But I think I can manage a couple pairs of drawers, cotton. Brand new. With elastic tops. Okay?"

"Shu," Master Sergeant Tozzi said.

"Thanks, Angelo," Clay said. "I'll be down."

"Goo'bye," Master Sergeant Tozzi said.

Clay hung up the phone and stretched. Through the window he saw Booth walking into the company street, so he hurried out of the orderly room and joined him. "Morning, Billy," Clay said. "Sleep good?"

Booth nodded.

"Do me a favor, will you, Billy? Get the troops out here pretty quick. I'll grab my twenty and hide 'em in the supply room. Tozzi's gonna give me a truck."

"Truck," Booth muttered, and he shook his head.

"It might be kinda tough explaining all this to Magee," Clay went on. "You know what I mean? So you wouldn't mind getting started now, would you?"

Booth nodded and pulled his whistle from his pocket.

"Can I blow it today?" Clay asked.

Booth handed the whistle to Clay. Clay stuck it in his

mouth and inhaled deeply. Then he blew. The high-pitched sound cut through the still morning air. Clay blew again, louder, and the first recruits came bolting through the barracks doors. There was a pause. Then the rest of them came, streaming out, racing into the company street, buttoning their pants, adjusting their caps, blousing their boots. Clay and Booth moved to the now-deserted barracks steps. From the street the recruits watched them, whispering, looking around. Gradually they quieted.

"At ease," Booth shouted, and the company obeyed. Booth turned to Clay. "Take your boys," he said, "and get out of here fast."

"Thank you, Billy," Clay answered, and he jumped off the steps, running to the end of the line of recruits closest to the supply room. He counted off twenty men. "Ten-*hut!*" he shouted. The twenty men came to attention. "Right *hace!* Forward *harch!*" and he led them off to the supply room.

When he had them safe inside, he put them at ease. "Okay," he told them. "Now listen. You just wait right here. Don't move. You got that?" They indicated that they had. Clay walked to a pile of underwear and removed three, size thirty-eight. "Now I'm going. But I'll be back in a couple minutes. So when you hear a truck horn honking outside, I want you to run out and get in the back. And no talking. No noise. Okay?" They nodded and he left them, closing the door of the supply room.

Walking quickly to C Road, he turned right, away from Main Post. He tucked the underwear under his arm and began to whistle. The battalion motor pool was one block down, and he reached it inside five minutes.

Master Sergeant Tozzi was standing outside the small office. To his left was a large truck with a half-open canvas top.

"Morning, Angelo," Clay said, stopping beside him.

Master Sergeant Tozzi doffed his cap.

"Here," Clay said, and he handed him the underwear.

Tozzi took the three pairs and held them to the sun, examining them for holes. Then he pulled the elastic on each pair, watching carefully as it snapped back into shape. Finally he turned to Clay and nodded.

Clay grinned and stepped up onto the running board of the truck. "I'll bring it back later," he said, opening the door and getting inside. "So long, Angelo." He turned on the ignition and put his foot on the gas pedal. The motor coughed. He pressed down harder. The motor coughed louder. Shaking his head, Clay checked to see that he was in neutral. Then he made a third try. The motor coughed.

Clay got out of the truck. Master Sergeant Tozzi was standing below, looking up at him, his hands behind his back.

"I think something's wrong," Clay said, pointing to the truck.

Smiling broadly, Master Sergeant Tozzi nodded in agreement.

"What is it?"

"Eetsa gotta no gas," Master Sergeant Tozzi said.

Clay stared at him a moment. "Angelo, old buddy," he began, finally.

Master Sergeant Tozzi left him and walked around a corner of the office building and disappeared. In a moment he was back, carrying a large red can. "Here'sa gas," he said.

Clay reached out for it.

Master Sergeant Tozzi pulled it away, set it down, standing in front of it. "Feel jak widda zip," he said then, miming a zipper with his hands.

"I'm clean out of field jackets," Clay answered. "Honest."

"Feel jak widda zip," Master Sergeant Tozzi repeated. "For my small boy."

Clay raised his right hand. "I'm out of field jackets, Angelo," he said. "It's the truth. I might be able to somehow get ahold of a pair of fatigue pants, but . . ."

Master Sergeant Tozzi shook his head. "No feel jak widda zip, no gas inna truck. Okay?"

"I can't, Angelo. Don't you believe me? I—"

"Goo'bye," Master Sergeant Tozzi said, and he picked up the gasoline can and started to walk away.

"Angelo!" Clay called.

Master Sergeant Tozzi stopped. "Okay?" he asked, his back still turned.

"Okay," Clay muttered, "but you're a no-good—"

"Atsa right," Tozzi nodded. "And you my friend." He began pouring the gasoline into the truck. "Small feel jak," he said, over his shoulder. "For my small boy." He dropped the gasoline can onto the ground. "Eetsa go now."

Clay got back into the cab. "Thanks," he muttered. He turned on the ignition and the motor started.

Master Sergeant Tozzi waved good-bye.

Clay drove away. Turning left at the motor pool entrance, he sped back up C Road to the Transient Company, shaking his head. He was behind schedule. He looked at his watch. Way behind schedule. He spun the truck into the Headquarters Company street, then braked, suddenly, staring out.

Captain Magee's Chevvy was in the parking lot.

That was bad. That was very bad. Nervously, he honked the horn. Again. Clay waited. In a moment, the men appeared, moving quickly toward the truck. He counted them. They were all there. When they had climbed inside the back, he jammed the truck into first and headed for C Road, turning left, safe at last, driving toward Main Post.

Slaughter was awaiting their arrival on the front steps of the I. & E. Building. "Eustis," he called. "A good, good morning."

Clay nodded and walked around to the back of the truck. "Okay," he said, "everybody out. Fall in." The men alighted quietly. "Forward *harch*," Clay called. "Column left, *harch*. *Hut*, two three four." By this time they were moving rapidly in the direction of the steps, closer and closer to Slaughter. When they were almost on top of him, Clay shouted, "Squad, *halt!*" and the group stopped, staring nervously up at Slaughter.

"Gentlemen," Slaughter said. "Gentlemen, at ease." The group relaxed. "In the back," Slaughter told them, "in the back you will find some excellent utensils. The windows are to be washed. The grass is to be cut. The floors are to be waxed and polished. Is that clear?" They nodded. "You're a fine-looking group of lads and I'm sure you can do a marvelous job. Are there any questions?" There were none. "Then I suggest you begin, gentlemen. Around that way." The group filed off.

"You lemme know when they're done," Clay said. "I'll pick 'em up."

"Of course, Eustis," Slaughter answered, walking toward the truck. "And now for the mattresses."

"Mattresses?"

"Naturally. Where are they?"

"I didn't bring 'em up."

"You jest," Slaughter answered, his voice rising.

"I couldn't, Maxwell. Captain Magee got there early and—"

"I need those mattresses," Slaughter said. "Now. Immediately. An interested party is coming this morning."

"Lemme bring 'em when I pick up the bodies, Maxwell. This damn truck ain't exactly loaded with gas."

"Ahh," Slaughter said. "Then you've seen Angelo today."

Clay nodded.

"Give him my very best, will you? But later. First, the mattresses. I'm sorry to put you to all this bother, Eustis. But it must be."

Clay took off his cap and wiped his face. "Six, wasn't it?"

"I believe the number was eight. And Eustis. Please. Make them good ones. As thick as possible. Tufted. Unstained. Reasonably clean."

"Depends what's in stock," Clay answered, and he climbed back into the truck. "Be back soon." He started the motor.

"And bring the underwear," Slaughter called. "I'm very anxious to see it." He slapped at his middle. "Inches," he said. "Marvelous."

Clay backed out onto the street and began the drive through Main Post. He made good time, gunning the truck, racing down C Road to the Transient Company.

Turning into the company street, he pulled the truck in close behind the supply room and got out, softly shutting the door. Then he crept around the corner of the supply room. Pulling his cap down over his face, lengthening his stride, he stayed close to the building, in the shadow. The supply room door loomed up ahead of him, and with a burst of speed he jumped through it, shoving his cap onto the back of his head.

Then he hurried to the far corner of the room to the main mattress pile. Grabbing two, he slid them across the concrete floor to a position close by the entrance. He returned to the pile and grabbed two more. The heat was terrible, and his fatigue jacket already clung to his body. Dropping the second pair of mattresses onto the first, he paused, wiping his face. It was too hot to work, too hot to move. What he needed was a little cooling off. Happily, he turned toward his desk and had taken several steps before he realized it.

The fan was not there.

Not there? Clay scratched his head. Had he left it on

the desk? No. Where, then? Beside his desk, out of sight. He nodded and hurried behind the long counter, walking slowly around his desk. No fan. "Funny," he said out loud, and sat down in his chair to think. If it wasn't by his desk, where was it? Where had he left it? He shook his head. Where had he been? Two places besides the supply room. The mess hall and the barracks. Probably it was in the barracks, but just to save a trip, he decided to visit the mess hall first. Pulling his cap down over his face, he walked out into the sunshine.

The mess hall was deserted except for a few recruits finishing KP. Clay closed the door behind him and began a systematic search. First he looked on the table where he had eaten. Then he looked on all the other tables. Then he looked under all the other tables. Finally he glanced into the cooking area. Nothing. No fan. He left the mess hall and, half running now, made his way toward his barracks.

It, too, was deserted. Taking the steps three at a time, Clay unlocked the door to his room. The heat inside was stifling but he plunged ahead. The room was as he had left it. He picked up the pile of sheets from the floor and looked under it. He picked up the pile of clothes from the floor and looked under that. He moved his bed. He opened his foot locker. He opened his wall locker. He lifted his mattress. Nothing. No fan.

Panicking now, he stood in the middle of the room, turning around and around. "Gone," he said out loud. "Gone." Some son of a bitch had stolen it. He drove through the heat out of the room, hurriedly locking the door behind him. He raced down the steps out of the barracks, running at full speed, making a slow curving turn into the company street, bolting along it until he reached the orderly room.

"Billy!" he cried, throwing the door open. "Billy! Some son—" He stopped abruptly, panting. Master Sergeant Booth was shaking his head. Clay turned, slowly. Then he could hear the sound. The beautiful whirring sound. Growing louder.

Captain Magee was sitting in his office, and the fan was sitting on his desk.

"What's the poop out there?" Magee called. "What's all the noise about?"

Clay plunged inside Magee's office. "Sir," he said, "that fan. That—"

"New this morning," Captain Magee said happily. "And let me tell you it's a beauty. You think you've felt strong fans before, but take a look at this." He turned the fan so that it blew on Clay.

Clay closed his eyes.

"Now if that's not a fan, then I'd like to know what is," Captain Magee said.

Clay nodded in agreement.

"Most men mind the heat more than me," Magee went on. "But even so, I'd like to see the man jack who minded a little extra comfort now and then." He turned the fan back around and stuck his face up close to the blades. "That's comfort for you," he said, staring through the invisible blades at Clay.

"Yessir," Clay said. "Excuse me, sir," and he walked out of the office into the main part of the orderly room. Moving from Magee's sight, he gestured frantically toward Booth. Booth shook his head and shrugged. Clay clenched his fists. Booth shook his head again. Clay grabbed his fatigue cap and twisted it in his hands. Then he threw it to the floor and jumped up and down on top of it.

"Who fell down out there?" Captain Magee called.

"No one, Captain," Booth answered. "It's all right."

Clay raised his right foot and kicked his hat toward the door. Then he walked over and picked it up and jammed it fiercely down onto his head. Raising his right fist, he shook it toward the ceiling, and on that gesture, he opened the door and walked outside. "The aw-dassity!" he shouted. His fatigue cap was squeezing his temple, so he jerked it off and reset it. Then, kicking at the dust, his hands in his pockets, his head bent low, he started to walk.

His initial reaction was a desire for revenge, and with that in mind, he made his way toward the company parking lot. When he reached Magee's Chevvy, he stopped and looked around. It was safe. He could not be seen from the orderly room. Using his index finger, he printed a dirty word in the dust on the Captain's hood. Then, standing on tiptoe, he wrote an enormous swearword on the roof. Now, when the General flew over the Captain's car, he would blow a gasket. Chew Magee up, down, right, left, through the middle and consecutive. Once the General saw it, Magee was through, washed up, *finish*— He stopped and shook his head. What would the General be doing flying over the Captain's car? And even if he did, why would he look down? No good. It wouldn't work. His index finger was black with dust and, guiltily looking around, he wiped it on his fatigue pants.

What else could he do? Well, he might let the air out of the tires. Or loosen the front door so it would fall off when you touched it. Or maybe a bomb. Yeah, a bomb. Stick it in the motor. But how did you make a bomb? Maybe Tozzi would know. Tozzi knew everything else about cars. So he could get Tozzi to make the bomb and then he himself would take it and connect it to the wire in the motor so that when you touched the ignition key, *boom!* To smithereens! Clay wiped the sweat from his forehead. But would Tozzi be able to keep his mouth shut? What if Tozzi squealed? Then Priest would be after him. Priest would like that. To gun him down in the dust. Shoot him in the belly and watch him wriggle around with the dust rising. He could hear

Priest's laugh as he crawled forward, reaching out, digging into the dust, trying to get away. Priest was tromping down on his hands, laughing louder, louder.

Clay walked away from the car, shaking his head. This was getting him no place. Maybe Slaughter would know what to do. Slaughter! The mattresses! Clay shrugged. The mattresses would just have to wait. Maxwell would understand. He leaned against the side of the supply room and dropped his chin onto his chest. Revenge was wrong. That was the mistake. He could have his revenge later. The important thing now was to get the fan back. But how?

Well, he could always steal it back. "Yeah," he said out loud. Then, a moment later, "Nope." What would be the good of stealing it? He would never be able to use it in the supply room again. He would have to keep it hidden. So what was the use? Unless he stole it and then disguised it. Yeah! Made it look like something else? Like what? Maybe a box. No. Why would he have a box on his desk? How could he explain it? No good. But what about a radio? He snapped his fingers. That was it. A radio. He could disguise the fan as a huge radio. Bigger than huge. Enormous. That was more like it. The biggest goddam radio you ever saw.

MAGEE: (pointing) What's the poop here? What's that?

CLAY: Radio, sir.

MAGEE: That's the biggest goddam radio I ever saw.

CLAY: Yessir.

MAGEE: How come it only makes that whirring sound?

CLAY: It's not working so good, sir.

MAGEE: Carry on, Sergeant.

Clay nodded sharply. "Woweeoboy!" he said, starting to walk toward the supply room. He stopped. But what if the

Captain decided to steal the radio? He would, too. If he'd steal a fan, he'd steal a radio. And then naturally he'd try to fix it. He'd look inside. He'd see the fan. He'd . . .

Clay leaned against the supply room again, rubbing his chin on his chest. The radio was out. So was stealing. The fan was too big to disguise anyway. What else was there? Maybe he could trade for the fan? No. He wasn't any good at trading with officers. Slaughter was. Slaughter knew how. But he didn't. Clay shrugged his shoulders. There was only one thing left to do.

He would have to lie.

Master Sergeant Booth was standing in the doorway when Captain Magee looked up from his fishing magazine.

"What's the poop, Booth?" Captain Magee asked.

"Sir," Booth replied, "The supply sergeant requests permission to speak to you."

"Clay?"

"Yes, sir."

"What about?"

"He says it's on a personal matter, Captain. Should I show him in?"

"Sure, sure." He closed the magazine, dropping it in his top desk drawer. Moving the fan to the front of his desk, Captain Magee sat deeper in his chair, waiting. Then Sergeant Clay was in the room, standing rigidly at attention. "At ease," Magee muttered. Clay clasped his hands behind his back. "Go on, Clay. Talk. What is it?"

"Sir," Clay said softly, "it's about the fan."

"What fan?"

"The one on your desk, sir. That one." He pointed.

Captain Magee put his hands around the base of the fan, protectingly. "What about it?"

"I need it, sir."

"Why?"

"For my health, Captain," Clay whispered, and he looked at the floor . . .

There was a long pause.

"This is very embarrassin' for me," Clay went on finally, his voice very low. "I didn't really want for no one to know about it. But that fan, Captain. I need that fan on account of it was doctor's orders for me to have it. To help my disease."

"Disease? What disease?"

"Scabosis," Clay whispered, still staring down.

"Scabosis?"

"Somethin' like that, sir."

"Well, what in hell kind of disease is scabosis? I never heard of it."

"It's very rare," Clay assured him. He glanced up quickly at the Captain, then hurried on. "You see, I ain't been feelin' up to snuff lately, so this morning I went up to see the doctor and he gave me this examination. And then after that, a couple of tests. That's when he told me about my disease. It's on account of me spending so much time in the heat, Captain. I been sweating too much. Overworking my sweat glands, he said. So what was happening was that they was beginning to get tired. And when that happens, you get scabosis."

"Go on, Clay."

"Well, you see, sir, when the sweat glands can't throw out no more sweat they sort of go crazy and you get a rash. And then you get scabs on top of the rash. That's why they call it scabosis. But when you got a fan working you over, you don't sweat so much and it sorta gives the sweat glands a chance to get their strength back, so to speak. And that's why I need that fan." He paused, dropping his chin onto his chest.

Captain Magee shook his head. "Clay," he said, "do you honestly expect me to believe that?"

Clay blinked. "Yessir," he answered. "Yes, sir, I certainly do." He began shifting his weight from one foot to the other.

"What was the name of your doctor, Clay?"

"Name?" Clay grinned. "I can't remember, Captain. It was something like uh . . . now, what was it?" He snapped his fingers. "Seems to have slipped my mind, sir. But I know I'll think of it." He started inching toward the door. "And as soon as I do, I'll let you know. And I'm sorry to have bothered you, and . . ."

"You're not excused, Clay," Captain Magee said. "So come back here."

Clay grinned again, twisting his fatigue cap in his hands. "I just didn't want to bother you no more," he answered.

"Now, what's the phone number of the infirmary?" Captain Magee asked.

"Two-nine-two," Clay said quickly. "It's two-nine-two."

"Sergeant Booth," Captain Magee called. "Get me the phone number of the infirmary."

There was a pause. Then Booth's voice came from the outer room. "Two-nine-two, Captain," he said.

"Thank you, Billy," Clay said softly.

Captain Magee picked up the phone. "Two-nine-two," he said. He waited, his face close to the fan. As soon as he heard the receiver being picked up, he began to talk. "This is Captain Magee of the Transient Company. Let me speak to a doctor."

"I'm a doctor," the voice on the other end said.

"Well, I'm calling about one of my men, Doctor. Who says he visited you this morning."

"One moment, Captain. I'll have to get my files." There was a pause. Then Captain Magee heard the sound of a heavy blow, followed by a loud, belching noise. *Awwk.* Then the receiver was being picked up. "Damn file drawer was stuck," came the explanation. "The heat."

"Of course," Captain Magee said, turning his head from one side to the other in front of the whirring blades.

"Now what was it you wanted, Captain?"

"Some information about one of my men. Sergeant Clay. First name . . . um . . . What's your correct first name, Clay?"

"Eustis, sir."

"Yes. Sergeant Eustis Clay."

"Ah, of course. Sergeant Eustis Clay. I remember him well."

"You do?"

"He was up here this morning. Fine lad."

"Yes, Doctor . . . ?"

"Schmidt," came the reply.

"Well, Dr. Sch—"

"Major Schmidt."

"Well, Major Schmidt—"

"That was him," Clay said excitedly. "I knew I'd remember. His name was Major Schmidt."

Captain Magee waved him into silence. "Now, the reason I'm calling, Major, is this. Just what's the poop on him? I'd like to know."

"Very complex," the Major answered. "Very complex indeed."

"I understand that, Major. Because Clay just explained it to me and there were a few things I wasn't so sure about. So if . . ."

"What did he tell you, Captain? In your own words."

"I thought you might tell me, Major."

"Glad to, Captain. But it's very complex. Takes a long time. And I'm busy today. Now if you'll just tell me what it is you don't understand, why, we'll clear it up in no time. So start!"

"Well," Captain Magee began. "He told me he had scabosis, and—"

"That's just the layman's term," the Major interrupted, chuckling.

"Yes, well, he said he had it and—"

"Oh, he does, he does."

"And that it started because he was perspiring too much. His sweat glands were overtired. That a rash was forming and after that, scabs. And that he needed a fan to control the amount of perspiration."

"Is that all, Captain?"

"Yes. More or less."

"Well, no wonder you're confused. These layman's explanations are always getting us into trouble. That's approximately what I told him, Captain. But it leaves a great deal unexplained. Actually, it isn't the sweat glands per se. The lad's real difficulty lies in the central epidermal layer. You follow me?"

"Sure, Major."

"Now, in our constant war against disease, the central epidermal layer acts as what you might call a buffer. A shield. Between the internal epidermal and the external epidermal. Now the internal epidermal gets along pretty well by itself. He's an independent cuss. But the external epidermal. He's the fellow that needs help. You still with me, Captain?"

"Of course, of course."

"Well," and the Major chuckled again, "in Clay's case, it's just the reverse. His external epidermal is fine. Just fine. But there's trouble aplenty with the internal epidermal. And that's where the central epidermal comes in. What we've got to do is strengthen that internal epidermal, give it a chance to catch up with itself. Of course, there's only one difficulty with that."

"What?"

"It can't be done," the Major said. "It's impossible." He paused. "And that's the main trouble. So what we've got to do is overstrengthen the central epidermal so that it can start pulling some of the chores of the internal epidermal and that way, you see, the internal epidermal gets back to normal. It's sort of a backward way of going about it, but it's all we can do."

"But the fan, Major. What does he need the fan for?"

"Oh, the fan's a very valuable little dingus, Captain. I don't know if you understand quite how valuable it is. It means a great deal to Clay. I can promise you that." He paused. "You know about perspiration, don't you, Captain? You know what it is."

"Sure," Magee said. "It's sweat."

"Oh, it's a little more than that, Captain. It's a saline fluid, you see. S-a-l-i-n-e. Six letters. And it comes from the central epidermal. Now you get the whole picture, don't you?"

"No," Captain Magee said. "I don't."

"Well, Jesus, Captain! Use your head! If the central epidermal is working all day making sweat, how the hell is it going to get overstrengthened? I mean, you tell me, Captain. We've got to rest that central epidermal. Rest it like crazy. That's our job. Now you're with me, aren't you?"

Captain Magee nodded. "You mean he needs the fan."

"Absolutely. I'd hate to see what would happen to that boy if he didn't have it. First a rash. Then scabs. You should see those scabs, Captain. Big as a silver dollar. Big and purple. And they're not just ordinary scabs, Captain. You bet they're not. They're creeping."

"Creeping scabs," Captain Magee said.

"Makes me shudder just to think about it, I can tell you. And such a fine lad, too. He's the supply sergeant, isn't he?"

"Yes."

"You're a lucky commander, Captain. The boy is devoted to you. He was telling me about it this morning."

"Was he?"

"Yes indeedy. But I guess all your men are. We hear a lot of fine things about the Transient Company, Captain. I can tell you."

"I guess we do our job all right," Captain Magee said.

"Well, if that's all you'll be needing, Captain, I've got an operation coming up in a little while."

"I'm sorry to have bothered you, Major Schmidt."

"Don't give it a thought, Captain Magee. Not a thought." He paused. "Oh, yes. If you see that supply man of yours, tell him to get up here right away. He may have forgotten. There are some more tests."

"I'll send him right up, Major."

"Well, good-bye, then, Captain. Up the Navy."

"Good-bye, Major." Magee hung up. Then he sat back in his chair, shaking his head. "You've got scabosis, all right," he muttered to Clay. "But of course, that's just the layman's term."

"I guess," Clay said.

"Take the fan, Clay. It's yours." Clay nodded and stepped forward and unplugged it. "Oh, yes, Clay. The Major needs you for more tests. You forget?"

"No, sir. I knew the Major wanted to see me." He picked the fan from the desk and cradled it in his arms. "Thank you, sir," and he turned and left the office. Outside, he and Master Sergeant Booth nodded pleasantly to each other, and then he hurried through the front door of the orderly room into the sunshine. "Woweeoboy," he cried. "Woweeoboy!"

Running to the supply room, he closed the door, looking around. Where was a good place to hide the fan while he was gone delivering the mattresses? He would have to camouflage it. But where? He decided on the pile of blankets in the far corner. Lifting up half the pile, he placed the fan inside and pulled the blankets over it. It looked bulky. Grabbing some entrenching tools, he crisscrossed them on top and took a backward step, inspecting it. He nodded. It looked fine.

Then he grabbed up two more mattresses and carried them across the room and dropped them on the other four. Running back, he lifted the last two mattresses and lugged them across the room. Now the underwear. He went to the pile and selected twelve pairs. Tossing the underwear on top of the mattresses, he paused, breathing deeply. It would be fastest if he carried the whole thing in one load. Just shoulder it and around the side of the building and dump it all in the back of the truck out of sight. But could he lift them all? He stared down. Eight mattresses was a lot of mattresses, even if they were thin. He shrugged. He would just have to try.

Dripping with perspiration, he squatted and shoved his arms under the mattresses. Then he started to lift. They were heavy. He grunted. Now they were off the floor. He began to rise. Could he make it? Taking a deep breath, he forced his legs straight and, staggering under the load, lurched into the supply-room door, pushing it open.

He had taken no more than two steps into the sunshine before he realized his error. He should have made four trips. Two mattresses were light and easy to carry, and, more than that, you could glance out the door and see if the way was clear. When you carried all eight at once, you could not glance out the door to see if the way was clear. And now, as he staggered forward, Clay realized that the way was not clear.

Because Captain Magee was standing in front of him.

"What the hell are you doing with those mattresses, Clay?" Captain Magee said.

Clay took a step backward, trying to maintain his balance. "Mattresses, sir? What mattresses?"

Captain Magee did not reply.

"Oh, these mattresses," Clay hurried on, staggering sideways a step. He smiled. What was he doing with the mattresses? It was a good question. "Just airing them, sir," he answered quickly. "They gets awful musty if you don't air 'em every so often." He staggered backward another step, then lurched forward, then backward again.

"Good idea, Clay," Magee said. "Damn good idea."

Clay's knees started to buckle. "Thank you, sir."

"But what about the dust, Clay? Do you think it's smart? Airing the mattresses in the dust? If only we had some grass around here, then—"

"Oh, the dust don't hurt 'em none, Captain." He forced his legs straight again. "It comes right off when you beat 'em. First air 'em, then beat 'em. They come out fine." He began reeling backward, finally coming in contact with the supply-room wall.

"Need any help, there, Clay?"

"Oh no, sir. Thanks just the same. I'm used to this. Do anything often enough and you get used to it. I'll—"

"How far are you going to carry them?"

"Just over there, sir," Clay said, nodding. "Behind that barracks. It's nice and flat back there." Pushing off the supply-room wall, he began a half-stagger in the direction of the barracks. His arms ached terribly from the strain, but he tensed them, moving steadily away.

"See you later, Clay," Captain Magee called.

"Yes, sir," he shouted back. Rounding the corner of the barracks, he fell against a wall, out of sight. Dropping the mattresses, he massaged his arms a moment, then crept to the corner of the barracks. Captain Magee was getting into his Chevvy. Clay waited. The door closed. The motor started. The car shifted into reverse.

Clay returned to the mattresses and grabbed one, pulling it away from the pile. The Captain's car was at the corner of C Road. Clay stood over the mattress, holding onto it with both hands. The Captain was driving up C Road toward Main Post. Clay glanced in that direction. Captain Magee was looking out at him from the car window. They both waved.

Then the Captain was gone. Clay flopped onto the mattress and lay still, breathing deeply. He rolled around on it then, relaxing. Finally, with a sigh, he stood up and dragged it back to the pile. He re-counted the underwear. It was all there. Bending down, he shoved his arms under the pile and, inhaling, began to lift. His entire body was soaked, and sweat streamed down his forehead into his eyes. He blinked several times, slowly forcing his legs straight. Balancing the pile as best he could, he lurched forward, starting toward the truck. When he reached it he dropped the mattresses again and rested a moment, wiping his face. His fatigue jacket stuck to his skin and he pulled at it, flapping his arms in the air, trying to restore the circulation. Bending down, he grabbed two mattresses and threw them into the back of the truck, out of sight. Then two more. Then the last four in one load. He took a step back and looked. The mattresses were hidden. He could drive up to Main Post in complete safety. Nodding to himself, he rolled the underwear into a ball, tossed it into the cab of the truck and climbed in after it. In a moment, he was on C Road, heading toward Main Post.

Ten minutes later he parked the truck in the rear of the I. & E. Building and hurried up the back steps. Edging past the recruits who were buffing the waxed corridor, he approached Slaughter's office. He knocked once, walked inside and saluted.

"Morning, Major Schmidt," he said.

"If it isn't scabby Sergeant Clay," Slaughter replied. "Do come in."

Clay closed the door. Walking to the window, he flopped down beneath the air conditioner. Clay took off his fatigue cap. "I'm dying of the heat, Maxwell," he said. Pushing his face up against the air conditioner, he closed his eyes.

"Warm out, is it?"

"Yup."

"But you're feeling all right otherwise?"

"Yup."

"And how's your disease? Scabosis, isn't it?"

Clay nodded.

"Jesus Christ, Eustis!" Slaughter roared. "How the hell can you make up a name like that?"

"The bastard didn't believe me," Clay muttered.

"Of course not. Scabosis! My God. Only a cretin—"

"I thought it was pretty good, Maxwell. It come to me all of a sudden. Like a flash. And—"

"You're continually doing this to yourself, Eustis," Slaughter interrupted. "And you've got to stop. You've got to learn. Swim in your own waters, for God's sake. You're over your head. Even I have limits."

"There's nothin' you can't do, Maxwell. Face it."

Slaughter sighed. "I'll fail you someday, Eustis," he said. "You'll see." He paused, shaking his head. "I trust you brought the mattresses."

Clay nodded. "In the back of the truck. The underwear's up in the cab."

"The underwear. Marvelous." Slaughter sat down in his swivel chair. "Would you mind putting your hands over your ears a moment?" Clay put his hands over his ears, while Slaughter gave a number to the telephone operator. Slaughter nodded, and Clay dropped his hands. "I always think it best to keep my dealings private. You understand?"

Clay nodded. "Who are you talking to?" he asked.

Slaughter shook his index finger and spoke tersely into the phone. "The merchandise is available in the back of a truck." He paused. "Yes. Parked right here." He looked at Clay. "Can you wait for a few minutes?"

Clay glanced up from the floor. " 'Course. You're givin' me a examination."

"You'd best come right over," Slaughter said into the phone. "Now." He waited. "Nothing. Think nothing of it. Good-bye." He hung up. Smiling happily, he stood. "I'm off for the drawers, cotton," he announced, and he left the room.

Clay closed his eyes, relaxing on the floor under the air conditioner. He listened as it purred softly, covering him with cool air. Already his skin was dry and his arms no longer ached. He exhaled deeply. It had been a busy morning. Too busy. It was just too hot for so much activity. But now it was almost over. What else was there? Just Tozzi and that was all. Feel jak widda zip and he was finished with his obligations. Then he could rest. Rest and relax in front of the fan until they shut the post out from under him. He just didn't care what they did, not so long as he could sit in front of that fan and listen to it whirr. "Rooty tooty tooty," he sang, half aloud, cushioning his head on his arms.

Slaughter burst through the door. "Eustis," he said, "look! I'm beautiful."

Clay glanced up. Master Sergeant Slaughter was standing over him, clad from the waist down in his new drawers, cotton. Clay pushed himself into a sitting position.

"What do you think, Eustis?"

Clay cocked his head to one side. The elastic top was stretched taut, struggling desperately to contain Slaughter's stomach. "Turn around once, Maxwell," Clay said. "Slow."

"My middle has vanished," Slaughter said happily, commencing to turn. "I'm positively sylphlike."

"Little snug in the back, maybe."

"Nonsense," Slaughter said. "You know, Eustis, I feel like a new man. All men are vain, one way or another. I happen to be a secret narcissist."

"You're putting a terrible strain on that elastic," Clay said.

"Nonsense," Slaughter repeated. "It is obviously of the very highest quality." He started putting on his pants. "You have made my day for me, Eustis. And I thank you."

"Glad to oblige."

"Have a drink," Slaughter said, striking the soft-drink machine. *Awwk.* When the cup was full, he handed it to Clay. "What a marvelous morning," he went on. "You have your fan. I have my underwear. Look, look," and he bent down in the general vicinity of his feet. "I can practically touch my toes."

There was a muffled sound, *ping*, and Slaughter stood up quickly. "Goddamit," he said.

"Elastic snap?"

"No," Slaughter answered, and, taking hold of his trouser tops, he walked around his desk and sat down. "Don't be absurd."

"You oughtn't to bend down like that, Maxwell."

"I'll bend down if I want to," Slaughter said, cupping his face in his hands, staring down at his stomach.

"It's not my fault," Clay went on. "That underwear is brand new. But if you're—"

"The underwear is fine," Slaughter interrupted.

"I heard it snap, Maxwell. It went *ping*. I heard it with my own—"

"The subject is closed," Slaughter said. He pulled up his pants with both hands and sat deeper in his swivel chair. "What happened back at the company?"

"Magee hocked my fan. He just up and took it, so—"

"So you told him you had scabosis."

Clay nodded.

Slaughter shook his head. "I can picture the whole scene vividly. It's horrible."

"You disappointed in me?"

"Vaguely."

"I'm sorry." Clay stood slowly and stretched. "I just couldn't think of nothin' better right off." He buttoned his fatigue jacket. "Anyway, it worked out fine. You got to admit that."

Slaughter nodded.

Clay walked to the door. "I guess I'll be getting back to the company now. Thank you, Major."

"Nonsense. I enjoyed it."

Clay slapped his cap onto his head. "Oh-ree-vor," he said, and he walked into the corridor. "See you later, Maxwell."

"Until that time, Eustis."

Clay closed the door and sauntered along the hall and outside. Walking down the steps over to the truck, he looked in the back. The mattresses were gone. Shaking his head, shrugging, he got in and started the drive back to the Transient Company.

Ten minutes later, he pulled the truck up behind the supply room and got out. The sun was hotter than ever, and he knew the supply room would be burning. Slapping his hands together with each step, he ambled along, singing, "Rooty tooty tooty, dee toot, dee toot," over and over.

Pausing at the supply room door, he took a deep breath and plunged inside, racing across to the pile of blankets. He threw aside the entrenching tools, lifted half the blankets and gently removed the fan. Spinning the blades once with his finger, he ran to his desk, set the fan down carefully and then plugged it in. As the blades started to turn, Clay sat down and leaned forward. "Ahhh," he said out loud. "Ahhh."

Somewhere he heard a door slam. Clay closed one eye for a moment and listened. Footsteps. He could hear boots in the dust. And muffled voices. Coming closer. Hurriedly grabbing some papers from his top desk drawer, he slapped them down in front of him and started to read. They were laundry slips, but he read them anyway, starting at the top with towels. He had got no farther than washcloths when Captain Magee walked in, stopping by the door.

"Good thing you're back," Magee said.

Clay put down the laundry slips. "Yessir." Magee stared around the supply room. "Anything wrong, Captain? Anything I can do for you?"

"Yes," Captain Magee said. "Tell the Sergeant everything you know."

Clay stared.

Sfc. Priest was standing in the doorway.

"Come on in, Sergeant," Captain Magee said.

Priest took two steps forward.

"This is my supply man," Magee went on. "He'll give you the rest of the poop."

"Yes, sir," Priest nodded.

Captain Magee started for the door. Then he stopped, turning to Clay. "How's the scabosis?" he asked.

"How's the what?" Priest wanted to know.

"Scabosis," Captain Magee told him, and he shrugged. "Of course, that's just the layman's term."

Sfc. Priest smiled.

"What's going on?" Clay said, standing. "What's he doing here?"

"I called him here, Sergeant."

"Why?"

"You know those mattresses you were airing?"

Clay nodded.

"Some son of a bitch stole them," Captain Magee said. Then he walked out of the supply room.

Clay slumped back in his chair. Priest's smile broadened. Taking out a notebook, he walked around the counter, standing over Clay.

"Howdy, Priest," Clay began. "Nice day, huh? A little warm, maybe, but there's those that like it that way. Course, there's those that don't, but—"

"That's right, you little bastard," Priest said, looking down. "Squirm."

"Just being friendly is all," Clay said, staring straight ahead, out the door. "What the hell are you doing here, anyway?"

"I'm on duty, birdbrain. The Captain called us about the theft. That's what."

"Yeah. But why you?"

Sfc. Priest laughed and slapped Clay hard on the back. "I volunteered. Just the minute I heard there was trouble in the Transient Company, I volunteered."

"You wasted yourself a trip," Clay said, pushing his face close to the fan.

Sfc. Priest opened his notebook. "Tell me what happened."

Clay shrugged. "Well, I took me some mattresses out for airing. They gets awful musty bein' stuck in here. And now I guess they're gone. That's all."

"Where were you at the time, birdbrain?"

"Up on Main Post," Clay muttered, sighting through the fan, one eye closed.

"Doing what?"

"Things."

"What things?"

"Nothin' much." He smiled. "Now, listen to me a sec, Priest. The way—"

"You listen to me, birdbrain," Priest cut in, bending down, his face close to Clay's. "There's one thing I know."

"What's that?"

"You didn't air no mattresses."

Clay said nothing.

"The day you air mattresses when it's this hot out is the day you can roll me up and hock me for an oyster. You hear what I'm saying, Clay? You understand me? So what I figure is that somebody did steal those mattresses. And that somebody is you. So the Captain made a mistake and it's up to me to set him straight. Now, what were you doing up on Main Post? Seeing Slaughter? Is that it?"

"I think you got something there, Priest," Clay began. "About it all being a mistake, I mean. I just been doin' some thinking. It just come to me. The whole thing is a mistake. Now, I'll tell you what I think happened. I think that somebody spotted those mattresses lying out there in the dust and thought to himself, Those mattresses oughtn't to be here—those mattresses ought to be back in the supply room. And so he picked 'em up and carried 'em back and set 'em down on that pile over there."

"Don't make too much sense," Priest said.

"Oh, sure it does," Clay went on. "I bet all we got to do is just count that pile of mattresses and check it with my records and we'd see it would tally up. It was just some thoughtful recruit thinking he was doing someone a favor. You know how thoughtful them recruits are, don't you, Priest?"

Sfc. Priest stood and started walking toward the mattress pile. "Let's count 'em," he said.

Clay bolted from his chair and ran in front of him. "Oh, that's such hot work, Priest. Counting all them heavy mattresses in this horrible heat. I wouldn't think of putting you to all that trouble. Don't you see? You could just sort of take my word for it. You could just say that we counted 'em and that they all was present. You could just sort of tell that to the Captain."

"Why should I?"

"Underwear?" Clay said. "With elastic tops? All you want?"

Priest did not reply. Instead, he walked back to Clay's desk and sat down.

Clay looked around the supply room. "Tool kit?" he whispered. "Almost new. With six screwdrivers and a complete set of pliers?"

Sfc. Priest was silent.

"Two field jackets and a pick and shovel?"

Silence.

"Ten old copies of *Esquire?* Plus five bodies a day for a week to help mow the dirt around the MP building?"

No answer.

"Fifteen bodies a day and an old car radio plus the pick and shovel and the tool kit."

"How about this?" Priest said, and he pointed to the fan.

"Oh, that," Clay laughed. "Hell, I'd just be cheating you. That's just a lousy old decrepit thing that's fit to bust any day."

Sfc. Priest leaned forward until his face was close to the whirring blades. "Gives off a good breeze," he said. "Looks almost new."

"Just a repaint job is all. They fool you sometimes. I tell you, it's no good."

"I want it."

"Well, it ain't for sale!" Clay shouted. "So forget it. Now, let me show you the tool kit."

"I want the fan," Sfc. Priest repeated.

"No." Clay hurried to the desk. "No. Listen, Priest. This tool kit is brand . . ."

Sfc. Priest stood and walked around the counter.

"Where are you going?"

"To inspect the scene of the crime," he answered, and he was out of the door.

Clay grabbed his fatigue cap and tore after him. "I'll give you all my underwear," he said, walking a half step in front of Priest. "It's the best the Army got and it's new. It's—"

"Where exactly did you air these mattresses?" Priest interrupted. "Captain said it was in back of the barracks. This one?"

Clay nodded.

Priest knelt down and examined the dust. "Right about here, wasn't it?"

"Yeah."

"Here's where they were, all right," Priest said, pointing at the dust. "All eight mattresses. You can see the outlines if you look close. Now wait. Here's footprints coming up to the mattresses. Two sets." He stared up at Clay. "Two men stole 'em. That settles it." He stood and started walking toward the orderly room.

"Priest!" Clay called.

"I'm ordering a complete investigation," Priest answered, not stopping.

Clay watched him move away. Then he dropped his chin onto his chest. How much trouble was he in? He closed one eye. Too much. But the fan. He couldn't give that up. Not the fan. Anything but the fan. But what if Magee found out about Major Schmidt? That would be bad. That would be very bad. Disastrous. Or would it? Supposing the Captain did find out. What could he do? Supposing he knew about everything. Just exactly what could he do?

"Court-martial," Clay said out loud. "Court-martial." He broke into a run. "Priest," he yelled. "Okay. Okay. But stop."

Sfc. Priest stopped.

Clay ran up to him. "It's yours," he muttered. "Take it and get out of here."

Sfc. Priest slapped him on the back. "Birdbrain," he said, and he walked into the orderly room, Clay close behind.

Captain Magee was waiting inside. "Well?" he said.

Priest consulted his notebook. "All settled, sir," he began. "We counted the mattresses in the supply room. They're all there. So what I figure is that someone saw them airing and thought it was a mistake and took them back to the supply room." He closed his notebook. "Investigation completed."

Captain Magee shook his head. "Thank you, Sergeant," he said. Sfc. Priest saluted, did an about-face, and left the orderly room. Captain Magee stroked his chin for a time. Clay moved to a window and pressed his nose against the pane, staring out.

"Doesn't make too much sense," Captain Magee said finally. "Not when you think about it. What do you say, Sergeant?"

Clay did not reply.

"What do you say, Sergeant?" Captain Magee repeated.

"Yessir," Clay muttered softly, still staring out the window.

"What do you mean, 'yessir'? 'Yessir' it makes sense or 'yessir' it doesn't make sense?"

"We counted the mattresses," Clay answered, his voice very low. "They were all there. It was probably some recruit. Probably thought he was being helpful."

Captain Magee nodded, looking at Clay. "What's the matter with you, Sergeant? You're talking funny. Don't you feel well?"

Clay continued to stare out the window. There it was.

He could see it now. The fan. Sfc. Priest was walking up to MP headquarters, carrying the fan. He swaggered along, swinging the fan in one hand. But that was no way to carry it. You could hurt it that way. Didn't he care? You should hold a fan with both hands. Close to your body. Protect it. Clay closed his eyes.

"You don't look good," Captain Magee said. "How's the disease?"

Clay opened his eyes. How was the disease? Where had the fan gone? He would have to explain it somehow. He thought for a moment. It was easy. If he wasn't sick, he wouldn't need the fan. No disease. No fan. As simple as that.

"No scabosis," Clay whispered. "I ain't got it."

"You haven't got it!" Captain Magee stepped forward. "What the hell's the poop here? The whole company's gone nuts this morning. A little while ago you had it. Now you don't."

"Major Schmidt said he'd made a mistake. He wants his fan back."

"Oh, he does," Captain Magee answered. "Well, I don't know about you, but I'm getting to the bottom of this." He hurried into his office and picked up the phone. "What the hell was that number again?"

"Two-nine-two," Clay muttered, walking into the office, sagging against the wall. What if Maxwell wasn't there? He shrugged. What did it matter now?

"Hello, Major Schmidt," the Captain said then. "This is Captain Magee again."

"Ah, yes, Captain. How nice to hear from you."

"I'm calling about my supply sergeant again, Major. And what I want to know is, what's the poop?"

"Which poop do you mean?" the Major answered.

"Well, Jesus, Major, you've got to admit it's kind of

strange. A little while ago this man was practically dying of scabosis. Now he says he hasn't got it. He said you made a mistake."

"Oh, that poop." There was a pause. "What the man says is quite correct, Captain. We thought he had scabosis. It looked for sure like it was scabosis. We up here were positive. But then we gave him the blood-urinalysis and—"

"What's that?"

"Take a little blood. Take a little urine. Shake 'em up good. See what color it turns."

"Oh."

"Yes. Well, we gave it to Clay and it didn't turn color. That clinched it. The man doesn't have scabosis. As a matter of fact, all he needs to do is bathe a little more often. You might tell him that."

"The Major says for you to bathe a little more often," Captain Magee said.

Clay nodded.

"Anything else, now, Captain? I've got that operation in a few minutes. Stomach job. And we're running low on anesthetic. I think it's going to be a bitch."

"Well, Major, as a matter of fact, as long as I've got you on the phone, there is one thing."

"What's the poop, Captain?"

"Well, it's my big toe. On my right foot. It hurts. It looked like a corn. But it's too small to be a corn. And when I walk—"

"Know exactly what you mean, Captain," the Major said. "You say it looks like a corn. Except that it's too small."

"Yes."

"We call those semi-corns. Pesky little things, aren't they?"

"Yes, they are. Is there something I can do for it?"

"Certainly. Certainly. Just soak it in tomato juice for two hours."

"Tomato juice?"

"Yes, indeedy. Get yourself a couple of those big cans of tomato juice. Pour 'em in the tub. Stick your foot in. That's all there is to it."

"Just plain tomato juice, Major? Any special temperature?"

"Jesus Christ, man! You're not going to drink it! Of course, any temperature."

"Thank you, Major."

"Good-bye, Captain."

Magee hung up. "Damn fine medical man," he said. "Doesn't beat around the bush."

Clay nodded.

"All right, Sergeant. You're excused. And perk up. You're not sick. Be happy."

Clay nodded again, excusing himself, turning slowly, walking out of the orderly room into the heat. The sun was blistering hot. Clay glanced around, looking this way and that, aimlessly. His face was lined with sweat marks and dust, and his fatigue jacket was black at the armpits. He dropped his chin onto his chest and stood still, sadly shaking his head. No fan. No more. Priest had the fan now. He tried to remember the sound of the whirring blades. He couldn't. It was a beautiful sound, though; he remembered that much.

Stuffing his hands into his pockets, he scuffed his way slowly toward his barracks. There was no place else to go. The supply room was too hot, and it was still a little early for lunch, so he trudged to the barracks, walking inside, slowly moving up the stairs to his cadre room. Unlocking the door, he stepped over the pile of dirty sheets and stood quietly in the center. He began to undress. That was something he could do. Get out of his stinking clothes. He took off his pants and his fatigue jacket and his boots and his T-shirt and his socks and flopped on the bed, rolling around, trying to get dry.

Maybe he should take a shower. No. That meant moving. Later. His body ached and his arms were very stiff. A nap. That was better. Sneak in a little snooze before lunch. He rolled toward the wall. He would have to hurry. Get to sleep fast before the recruits came in for lunch and started their stomping around, making a racket, yelling and screaming and—

The recruits!

Clay groaned. Up at the I. & E. Building. He still had twenty bodies waiting up at the I. & E. Building. "Boy," he muttered. "Boy!" and he forced himself up into a sitting position. He looked at his watch. He was late. The recruits had to be back by lunchtime, and he was late. He grabbed for his T-shirt. It was sopping wet and he grimaced as he slipped it over his body, where it clung to his chest like wet skin. Standing, moving faster now, he put on his fatigue pants. They, too, were wet, and so was his fatigue jacket, cold and wet and clinging. He pulled his boots on over his wet socks and moved to the door, perspiring again, sweat pouring down his neck, down his face, down his chest.

Stumbling out of the room, he locked the door and hurried to the truck. His body ached worse than before, but he climbed in and started the motor. Yanking the gears into reverse, he backed out onto the company street and headed for C Road.

It was jammed. Thousands of trainees marching along, and he was forced to wait at the cross streets. The sound of the post flooded into the steaming cab—shouting voices, angry voices, marching boots, the sharp persistent rhythm of the drums. All around him a layer of dust was rising, and the distant horizon was covered by a faint gray haze.

Finally he reached Main Post and sped up, turning the corner onto Third Street, gunning for the I. & E. Building, then slowing as the building neared. Swerving into the driveway, he jumped from the truck and started toward the front door.

Slaughter met him on the porch. "You're late," he said. "I was about to call you. The lads are finished."

"I been busy. I forgot."

"What happened?"

"Priest got the fan," Clay muttered.

"Oh, Eustis, no." Slaughter shook his head. "Illegally?"

Clay shrugged. "He found out about the mattresses."

"I'm terribly sorry, Eustis. I really am."

Clay pulled at his fatigue jacket, flapping it. "Where are the bodies?"

"In the rear. Waiting." They walked around the building. "Fall in, gentlemen," Slaughter said then. They did. "The men are yours, Sergeant Clay. Thank you. They did an excellent job."

"Forward march and into the truck," Clay said. He watched as the men climbed into the back. Shaking his head, he pulled himself up on the running board, then ducked, and entered the cab. He turned on the ignition. The motor coughed. He pressed down harder on the gas pedal. Again, the motor coughed. Frantically he pumped his foot up and down on the gas pedal. The motor kept on coughing. Finally, he switched off the ignition and started pounding the steering wheel with his fists. "Tozzi is a dead man!" he shouted.

"You're having difficulties?" Slaughter asked from below.

Throwing the door open, Clay jumped to the ground and raced inside the building, down the corridor, into Slaughter's office. Grabbing the phone, he gave the number of the motor pool and sat down in the leather swivel chair, waiting. Finally the phone was picked up.

"Motor pool," Clay heard.

"Lemme speak to Tozzi."

"Tozzi's not here."

"He's got to be there!"

"He went to lunch a while ago. What do you want?"

"Gas," Clay said. "I'm out of gas."

"Well, you don't need Tozzi for that. The Lieutenant here can handle it for you. Lieutenant?"

"Shh," Clay said. "Forget it."

"Hello," the Lieutenant said. "Hello?"

Guiltily Clay dropped the receiver down into its cradle.

Slaughter appeared in the doorway. "No Tozzi?"

Clay nodded. "No Tozzi. No gas. No nothin'."

"And the troops are waiting in the truck," Slaughter went on. "And it's lunchtime." He sighed. "A most unpleasant situation. But I was thinking, Eustis. Come along." Slowly, Clay rose and followed Slaughter out of the building. "I was thinking that tonight we might have a dinner party. At my expense. In my office. Beer and sandwiches by the air conditioner. Would you like that?"

Clay shrugged, staring up at the blazing sun.

"I feel I owe it to you, Eustis. In a way, this has all been my fault. What do you say? Just you and Jerry and I. And then afterwards, we might go to the movies. There's a Randy Scott revival at the drive-in. Sound tempting?"

Clay wiped his forehead, shaking his head slowly. "It's two miles back to the company, Maxwell."

"Think of beer," Slaughter said. "Ice-cold, foaming beer."

"Everybody out and fall in," Clay shouted. The men got out of the truck. "Forward *harch*," Clay said, and they began to move.

Slaughter hurried alongside. "Beer, Eustis, beer."

"Beer," Clay nodded.

"Bon voyage," Slaughter waved.

"Column left *harch*," Clay ordered, and they started up Third Street, hugging the side of the road. Two miles. Two miles in the sun. And no fan. If you walked sixty paces a minute it would take . . . Two miles took two miles. "Your left," he said. "Your left. Your left, right, left." Up ahead was the Service Club. They moved on. Now they were passing divisional headquarters. A girl was looking at him from the sidewalk. "Hi, sweetie," she yelled. It was Frances McCoy. "Howdy, Frances," Clay said. "You gonna call me soon, sweetie? You ain't called me in a long time." He nodded. "Sure. Sure, Frances." Divisional headquarters lay behind them. Ahead was the turn for C Road. Clay sighed. Two miles to the company. Two miles through the dust. The sweat poured off him. Two miles. But Frances McCoy had a thirty-nine-inch bust. Thirty-nine inches. Not thirty-five. Not thirty-seven. Thirty-nine. 'Course, her face wasn't much. What was her face like? Blonde hair? Sort of blonde. "Column left *harch*," and they were on C Road. Some boobs. "Left, left, left," he shouted, and the men followed along. Beer. And Tozzi could fry before he got that field jacket. Main Post was ending now, and ahead of them the road trailed off into dust. "I got a girl who lives in the West," Clay sang suddenly. "She's got mountains on her chest." I'll say she's got mountains. Thirty-nine inches. Not thirty-five. Not thirty . . . Beer. Beer and sandwiches by the air conditioner. He wiped his forehead. Dust. Dust all around him, rising. He coughed. Beer. Ice-cold beer. Beer and sandwiches and Randy Scott. And then maybe he'd give Frances a call. Thirty-nine inches.

Woweeoboy!

V.

It was toward the end of lunch hour, and Sergeant Clay was in the supply room, playing broomball with Private Cronkite.

Clay had invented the game himself, years before in Germany, and had successfully transplanted it upon his return to the States. Basically, broomball was the same as baseball, except that a broom was used for a bat and the ball was made of paper. Clay made the balls himself, painstakingly. First he soaked the unused sections of Slaughter's *New York Times* in warm water for half an hour. Squeezing the sections into a soggy sphere, he then covered them with yards of packing tape, winding it carefully around and around until the finished product was approximately the size of a grapefruit. The result was surpisingly hard and durable. Swinging the broom took a lot of practice, and wind resistance was important for accuracy. Pitching was underhanded, and any missed pitch counted as an out. If the ball struck the floor in front of the batter, it was a single. If it reached the pile of blankets by the far wall, it was a double. Anything landing against the far wall was a triple, and a home run resulted when the ball struck the ceiling. The only problem with the game as far as Clay was concerned was that nobody wanted to play it with him more than once.

This particular July day, for example, the score was 78 to 6 and Clay was still at bat in the second inning.

"You got me on the ropes, Cronkite, old kid," he shouted, swinging the broom. "Keep pitching it in there."

Private Cronkite was tired. His T-shirt was transparent with perspiration and his face was lobster red. "I'm quittin', man," he said.

"You can't quit now. Not when you're doin' so good. Pitch it in there."

Private Cronkite lobbed the ball toward the folded shelter-half that served as home plate. Clay hesitated, then swung powerfully, and the ball careened against the ceiling. "That was a terrific pitch, Cronkite. You almost fooled me." He pulled at his lip. "Lemmesee. With two on, that makes it 81."

Cronkite muttered to himself and trudged after the ball. As he bent down, he groaned, shoved his right hand into his kidneys, and dropped onto a pile of blankets. "Let me quit," he said.

"You're only seventy-five runs behind and I got one out already; you're a cinch to make it up. I'm a terrible pitcher."

"My arm just fell off, man. Give me a break."

"Okay," Clay shrugged. "Game's over." He balanced the broom on the tip of his index finger. "But no deal."

"What do you mean, no deal?"

"No fatigue pants."

Private Cronkite pushed himself to his feet. "I got to have them fatigue pants, man. My old pairs keep running away from me. You said—"

"*You* said you'd play one whole game. Nine innings. You ain't even played two yet. So no deal."

Muttering to himself, Private Cronkite pitched again. Clay watched it sail up to him. Again he hesitated. But the pitch was just too good. He swung all he had and blasted the ball against the ceiling.

Private Cronkite looked at the ball rolling around in the far corner. Then he looked at Clay. Then he walked to the supply-room door, shaking his head. In the doorway he stopped, pointing a finger at Clay. "For your own safety, man, I'm warning you. Ride clear of the mess hall." Then he was gone.

Clay picked up the ball and dropped it back in his bottom desk drawer. Sprawling in his chair, he stretched out and tried balancing the broom from a sitting position. It was hard, but he did it. Nodding his head, he stared at his index finger. He had always been a terrific broom-balancer. Ever since he was a kid. But there wasn't any money in it. That was the trouble. If only he could think of something. He shook his head. People just didn't care about it. He shifted the broom along his hand until it was balanced on his little finger. Then he raised his eyes up the handle to the brush. Steady as a rock. If only there were broom-balancing contests. Something like that. He could clean up. Make a pile. Maybe become a celebrity. Have his own show on the TV. But people just didn't care. He closed his eyes. Whoops. He opened his eyes and saved the broom from falling with one deft motion of his hand.

In back of the supply room he heard the deep rich sound of Slaughter's car motor. Maxwell had the only touring car on post, a 1931 Packard. But what was he doing down here? At lunch hour? It was too early for him to be finished; Maxwell liked his lunch hours. The motor stopped and a car door slammed shut. Clay waited, staring up at the brush. Still steady. Fantastic. How did he do it? He shrugged. Just natural. A natural-born broom-balancer. Best in the West. He began humming the "Blue Danube" waltz, moving his little finger in time with the music. Back and forth. Back and forth. Maybe if he put light bulbs on the brush and did it in the dark, maybe that would work. But where was Maxwell? What was he waiting for? What rhymed with broom? He cocked his head. Lots of words. You could have fifty rhymes. It would be a cinch for the "Hit Parade." He sighed. "Whom breaks the gloom in my room? My broom." Not bad. Not bad a-tall. "Whom—"

Pfc. Meltzer dashed through the doorway. "I've been all over the company looking for you," Meltzer began, running around the counter up to the desk. "What are you doing in here?"

"Just working out a routine," Clay answered. "Hey, Jerry, look." He pointed to the broom. "Do you think if I put light bulbs on the brush that—"

"Something's the matter with Maxwell," Meltzer said.

Clay shifted the broom from one hand to the other, humming the "Blue Danube." "That's impossible," he answered.

"No. Really, Eustis. Something is."

Clay looked at him. "What?"

"I don't know exactly what. But he didn't eat lunch today."

The broom hit the floor. "He didn't eat nothin'?"

"He told me he wasn't hungry."

Clay stood quickly. "Woweeoboy," he whispered. "It must be bad." He turned to Meltzer. "What happened?"

"I think it was something he saw in the newspaper. Because we were taking coffee break and he was thumbing through the Capital City *Journal* and then he excused himself and went into his office and—"

"Let's go," Clay cut in, and they ran across the dusty ground to the orderly room. Grabbing a copy of the Capital City *Journal* from Booth's desk, Clay licked his thumb and started turning the pages.

Suddenly he stopped, shaking his head, staring down at a small headline. "It's worse than I thought," he muttered, dropping the paper, hurrying to the door.

"What is it?" Meltzer asked, following him outside.

"His girl friend died," Clay answered.

"What girl friend?"

Clay shook his head. "You know. That brunette chick he's got a picture of in his office."

"Maude Adams?"

Clay pulled at his lip, frowning. "I gotta think of something," he said.

"Maude Adams wasn't his girl friend, Eustis. She was an

old woman."

"You got the wrong Maude Adams," Clay muttered, turning around in the dust, fiddling with his fatigue cap.

"She was an actress, Eustis. She—"

"I don't know much about her," Clay cut in. "But he must be pretty upset. I gotta think of something. I just gotta think of something." He snapped his fingers, suddenly, breaking into a run toward the parking lot.

"She played Peter Pan fifty years ago," Meltzer called after him. "Eustis . . ."

"I'm off to cheer up Maxwell," Clay shouted over his shoulder. A moment later he was in his car and gone.

In fifteen minutes he reached the I. & E. Building. Getting out of his car, he walked quietly inside, creeping along the corridor, carrying a brown paper bag in one hand. When he got to Slaughter's office, he paused. Then he threw the door open and fired a barrage of shots with his index finger. "All right, Louie," he snarled. "Drop the gun."

Slaughter nodded to him. "Good afternoon, Eustis."

"Howdy, Maxwell." Clay closed the door, peering at Slaughter. He looked the same. That was good. "Here," he said, climbing on top of Slaughter's desk, sitting down cross-legged. "I brung you a present." He held out the brown paper bag.

"For me?"

"Yup. It's ice cream. Go on. Open it."

"I'm not really hungry, Eustis. But thank you. That was very thoughtful."

"Eat it, Maxwell. It's your favorite. It's butter brickle."

Slaughter shook his head. "You eat it, Eustis."

"You sure?" Slaughter nodded. Clay opened the bag, taking out the pint carton and a wooden spoon. He jabbed a wedge of ice cream loose and put it in his mouth. "Umm," he said. "Good."

"I'm sure it is."

"Try some," and he spooned another wedge, holding it out to Slaughter.

"No, thank you."

"Hey, come on, Maxwell. I know you're upset and all. But you gotta keep your strength up."

Slaughter sat deeper in his chair, his hands folded in his lap. "Perhaps later."

Clay pointed to the picture. "You going to the funeral?"

"No, Eustis."

"How come?"

"I never met the lady."

Clay peered at Slaughter for a moment, frowning. "You never met her?" He paused. "Jerry said she was a actress."

Slaughter nodded.

"You ever see her act?"

Slaughter shook his head.

Clay turned and stared at the picture on the wall. "How old was she, anyway?"

"Eighty," Slaughter said. "Eighty years old."

Clay put the ice cream down. "Maxwell," he said. "Just what the hell's going on?"

"Nothing, Eustis. Nothing's going on. And I'd rather not talk about it. I feel foolish enough as it is."

"I don't get it," Clay said, pulling his fatigue cap down over his eyes, blowing it back into place. "I mean, I just do not get it." He leaned forward. "You got a picture of a girl friend on the wall. Okay. You never talk about her. Okay. I don't have to know everything. She's a girl friend of yours. That's enough. But come on, Maxwell. Eighty is old. You can't ask for more than that."

"It's all very silly, Eustis. I know."

"Was she a friend of your mother's, or something? Was she—"

"I'd really rather not talk about it," Slaughter said.

"Well, you're gonna. This is me, Maxwell. Your buddy. Your partner. And I ain't leaving till you do." He cupped his chin in his hands, waiting.

Slaughter sighed.

"I'm waiting," Clay said.

"All right, Eustis," Slaughter muttered. "All right." He lit a cigarette and inhaled deeply, staring at the dark-eyed woman on the wall. "When I was nine years old," he began, speaking softly, "when I was nine, I saw her photograph in a picture book. That same photograph." He nodded toward the wall. "I was all by myself at the time, and I was turning the pages of a picture book, and I saw her. Staring out at me. With those incredibly beautiful eyes. So I stared back. We looked at each other for a long, long time, and I thought, I thought, There. There. That's what I want. More than anything else in the world, I want you. Looking just like that. More than anything. Now, I knew my chances were slim. She was a world-famous actress and I was nine, and besides, she'd never look like that again. But still, I wanted her. She was the most beautiful thing I'd ever seen. She still is. Look at her, Eustis. Isn't she lovely?"

Clay climbed down off the desk and walked over to the picture, examining it closely. "A-minus," he nodded.

"I collected pictures of her for a while," Slaughter went on. "But none of them compared with that one. So I settled for it. I've never been without it. But now she's dead and it's too bad."

"Come on, Maxwell. You said she was eighty."

"That doesn't matter. It's still a shame. It's a shame when anything dies. I've killed people, Eustis. In the Pacific during the war I blew up a man with a hand grenade. A little yellow man who was trying to kill me. And that was a shame, too. And so is this." He paused, inhaling deeply. "So in conclusion, Eustis, I would just like to say that I'm sorry, it's stupid, it's silly; I know all that. But in my own way, I am simply trying to show a little decent respect for the dead." He paused again. "There. Done."

Clay climbed back on the desk and started eating the ice cream. "Boy," he said. "This is good butter brickle. The best ever. Nice and soft and tasty. You better eat it, Maxwell. You better take it while you can, 'cause they don't serve no butter brickle in the loony-bin. And that's where they're gonna stick you if you keep on talking like that. Right smack in the middle of the loony-bin."

Slaughter smiled.

"Hey, Maxwell," Clay said then. "Ain't there nothin' I can do for you? Anything at all?"

"Nothing that comes to mind, Eustis."

Clay shook his head and finished the ice cream in silence, dropping the container into the wastebasket. "*Pkkooom.*" He moved to the door. "Well, I ain't giving up. Not yet." He doffed his fatigue cap. "See you later."

Slaughter nodded. "Until that time."

Clay closed the door.

The door stayed closed for more than four hours. It was well after five when Slaughter emerged, standing a moment in the quiet corridor. The building was empty; work was over for the day. Slowly, he walked to the back door and checked it; it was locked. He started down the corridor toward the front door. Taking the key from his pocket, he inserted it into the lock, gripped the knob, and stepped onto the front porch, closing the door behind him. He was turning the key when he heard a voice.

"Hi, fatty."

Slaughter looked around. A girl was sitting on the railing at the far end of the porch, swinging her legs. She smiled at him, jumped down and smoothed her skirt. She was wearing a yellow, candy-striped summer dress. Still smiling, she walked up to him.

"Hi, fatty," she said again.

Slaughter nodded. "Hello, little girl."

"Surprise!" Clay said suddenly, moving out from behind the corner of the building, giggling happily to himself as he jumped up the steps onto the porch. "Like to make an introduction," he began. "Maxwell Slaughter. This here is Bobby Jo Pepperdine. Bobby Jo, meet Maxwell."

"Hi," Bobby Jo said.

" 'Course, you met once already," Clay went on. "In the police station, remember?"

"Oh, I remember," Bobby Jo said. She pointed to Slaughter. "He was the man that was gonna put me in the Pit."

"That's right," Clay nodded. "Okay. Let's get going. I got to pick up Frances."

Slaughter turned and looked at him.

"Before we start," Bobby Jo said quietly, stepping forward, "I would like to say how sorry I am about your auntie dying of the measles, like that."

Slaughter turned and looked at her.

"I'm late," Clay said. "Let's get a move on."

Slaughter turned and bolted back inside the building.

"Oh, oh, oh," Bobby Jo said, staring after him. "Maybe I shouldn't have said nothing about his auntie dying of the measles. He looks kind of all upset."

Clay pulled at his lip.

"Maybe I ought to go in and tell him I didn't mean nothin'," Bobby Jo said, starting toward the door.

Clay grabbed her. "You just let me take care of it, Bobby Jo. I'll be out in a sec. You wait right here." He opened the door and walked inside. The corridor was empty. He ran down it to Slaughter's office. The door was closed. Clay opened it. Master Sergeant Slaughter was standing by the soft-drink machine, swallowing a cup of grape-ade. "Hey, Maxwell—" Clay began.

"Eustis," Slaughter cut in, "what have you done?"

"Just fixed us up with a little evening's entertainment is all. Ain't she cute? She's a living doll. You won't find no better in Hastingsville. You see, she had a date already, so I told her about your aunt dying of the measles. Bobby Jo's very sentimental. She broke her date. Wasn't that nice of her, Maxwell, doing a thing like that for you?"

"I'm not going," Slaughter said.

"You got to. And it'll be good for you." He stepped up to Slaughter and lowered his voice, confidingly. "You know, Maxwell, having a crush on a eighty-year-old woman, that ain't healthy. They'll put you in the funny farm. Besides," he went on, whispering now, "Bobby Joe is a very friendly type."

"I'm not going and that's final," Slaughter repeated. "Impossible."

"You'll like her, Maxwell. You will. Bobby Jo is known far and wide for her ladylike qualities. And everyone says about how sensitive she is. And on top of all that, she is very bright for her age."

"No, Eustis."

"But—"

"The girl is a moron!" Slaughter said. "And—"

"Shh."

"The girl is a moron," he whispered, "and the answer is no."

Clay sighed.

"I understand, Eustis. I appreciate it. But no."

"You're gonna get me in an awful lot of trouble."

"No, I won't. Look. I'll tell her myself. I'll simply explain that my aunt's dying of the measles came as such a shock that I'm not up to it." He walked past Clay to the door. "Come. The sooner the better." He moved down the corridor and onto the porch. "Little girl," Slaughter said, "little girl, come out."

"She's not here," Clay said.

"Little girl," Slaughter called.

"Where the hell is she?" Clay asked. He walked down the steps toward the street. Slaughter locked the building and joined him. "Beats me," Clay muttered, turning around. "I don't see . . ." He stopped, pointing. "Look! There she is."

Slaughter stared out at the small, candy-striped figure turning the corner onto Main Entrance Road.

"C'mon," Clay yelled, hurrying to his car. "Get in." They drove out of the driveway and down the street, turning at Main Entrance Road, closing the gap. When he was a few feet behind her, Clay slowed, shifting into first, moving up alongside.

"Hey, Bobby Jo," Clay said, "what's up?"

Bobby Jo stared straight ahead. "I ain't neither no moron," she mumbled. "I ain't neither no moron."

"Jesus," Clay said. He turned to Slaughter. "Didn't I tell you she was sensitive? Now look what you've gone and done."

Slaughter looked. Bobby Jo's eyes were red, and he could hear her sniffling. He sighed.

"Hey, Bobby Jo, stop," Clay called.

"I ain't neither no moron," Bobby Jo said again.

"Maxwell," Clay said, "do something."

"Little girl—" Slaughter began.

"Fatso!" Bobby Jo answered. "Blimp face!" She broke into a run.

"That's nice work, Maxwell," Clay said, shaking his head. He sped up, moving alongside her again.

"Little girl, I'm sorry," Slaughter went on.

"Balloon head!" Bobby Jo said. "Jelly belly!"

"You're winning her over, Maxwell. Just keep it up."

Slaughter shrugged helplessly. "What can I do?"

"You can lie," Clay told him. "That's what."

Slaughter nodded. "All right, Eustis. Cut her off."

Clay drove ahead and pulled onto the side of the road, blocking her. Slaughter stepped out of the car.

Bobby Jo backed away. "Don't you come near me, blubber mouth."

"Miss Pepperdine," Slaughter said, "there has been a terrible mistake. A grievous misunderstanding. Believe me." He took a step toward her.

She continued backing away. "I'm gonna scream for help, jelly belly."

"You got her now, Maxwell," Clay called. "She's repeating herself."

"It was not you that I was calling a moron," Slaughter said, talking very softly, staring at the ground. "Not you, Miss Pepperdine. It was my aunt that I was talking about. For she was a moron, Miss Pepperdine. A dear, sweet lovable creature, but a moron, nonetheless. Now, do you see?"

"I don't know," Bobby Jo said.

"It's the truth, Bobby Jo," Clay cut in. "There's a lot of morons in Slaughter's family. Half a dozen, ain't there, Maxwell?"

"I don't believe it," Bobby Jo said.

"I am truly sorry for the misunderstanding," Slaughter said.

"He wants very much to go out with you, Bobby Jo. He

told me so. Right, Maxwell?"

Slaughter sighed. "Right," he mumbled.

"I don't know," Bobby Jo said again.

"Please, Bobby Jo. For me. For Eustis."

Bobby Jo stuck her little finger in her ear and wiggled it. Then she marched by Slaughter and climbed into the back seat of the car. "Okay," she said. "For you, Eustis. But not for him."

Slaughter sat down at the other end of the back seat. Bobby Jo looked away, fumbling at a pocket for some gum. Taking two sticks, she folded them into her mouth.

"Everybody set?" Clay asked. "Everybody happy?"

There was no reply.

"We're off," Clay shouted, making the sound of an airplane. "*Thhhhoooooom.*" He drove forward out of Camp Scott, toward Hastingsville. "Sure is some night, huh, Maxwell?"

"Lovely," Slaughter muttered. "Wouldn't you say so, Miss Pepperdine?"

Bobby Jo cracked her gum, staring out the window.

"Yes, sir," Clay said again, softer now, his voice trailing off "Nothing . . ." He glanced into the back seat, shook his head and lapsed into silence. They drove to the edge of Hastingsville and turned left, then right, then left again. Finally he pulled up into a driveway, honking his horn. He lit a cigarette and waited. A minute passed. Another. The front door of the small house opened and a figure stepped out. Clay whistled loudly. "Thirty-nine," he muttered. "Fantastic."

Frances McCoy was seventeen years old. Her hair was dark blonde and hung straight down her back. She was tall, broad-shouldered, with large hands and feet, and was the only girl in Hastingsville who wore sweaters in the summertime.

She walked down the steps to the car. "Hi, sweetie," she said.

"Howdy, Frances," Clay answered, leaning over, pushing the door open. "Frances McCoy. This here is Maxwell Slaughter, my friend who is in mourning. We're gonna cheer him up."

"Sure we are," Frances said, getting into the front seat, moving across it, putting her arms around Clay's neck. "I'm so glad you called me, sweetie," she whispered, blowing in his ear. "And you look so cute, and—"

"Later," Clay muttered. "We got to cheer up Maxwell."

"Huh?" Frances said, her arms still around his neck.

"Okay," Clay said, rubbing his hands together. "We're all here. And we're all gonna have a great time. Yes, sir. So what'll we do? Who's got—"

Frances pulled hard on his neck and the two of them slid down the front seat out of sight.

"—any suggestions?" Clay finished.

"Sweetie," Frances whispered, "sweetie."

Slaughter sighed. He turned to Bobby Jo. "Miss Pepperdine," he began.

Bobby Jo turned away, cracking her gum.

"Dammit, Frances," Clay muttered, from below the front seat.

"Oh, it's all right, sweetie," she whispered. "No one's home but grandmaw, and she's busy watching the TV."

"Eustis," Slaughter said. "Eustis."

Clay fought his way up over the level of the seat. "That's enough," he said; "now come on." He straightened his shirt. "What'll we do tonight?"

Frances appeared again in the front seat. She looked sullenly at Clay. "You got any more gum, Bobby Jo?" she asked.

Bobby Jo nodded and handed a piece to Frances, who

unwrapped it and started to chew.

"Let's have some suggestions," Clay said.

Frances cracked her gum.

"Who's got any ideas?" Clay said.

Bobby Jo cracked her gum.

"Dammitall," Clay cried. "Let's do something."

"Is there a nice long double feature playing somewhere?" Slaughter said.

"I don't wanna go to the movies," Bobby Jo answered.

"Why don't we all go to the library and read," Slaughter said.

"Library!" Clay said.

"I don't wanna go to the library," Bobby Jo said.

"Well, we could—"

"I don't wanna do that either," Bobby Jo said.

Slaughter sighed.

"Hey, sweetie," Frances whispered. "You mad at me?" She started moving close to him again, her arms snaking around his neck.

Clay shook her off. "Hey," he said. "Hey, let's go play some pinball. And then after that maybe take in the carnival."

"I don't feel like playing pinball," Slaughter said.

"Let's play pinball," Bobby Jo said. "I wanna play pinball. Frances, do you?"

"Huh?"

"Frances says yes. We all say yes. That's three to one against you, fatty. Majority rules."

Clay looked at Slaughter. Slaughter sighed again. Finally he shrugged.

"And we're off," Clay shouted, jamming the car into reverse. "Pinball, here we come!"

* * *

The pinball parlor was located on the main street of Hastingsville, between a military store and a saloon. It was a long narrow room, with pinball machines set one flush against the other lining the walls, and just enough space down the center for a single narrow aisle. At the front the change man sat, jingling nickels.

"Five nickels, please," Slaughter said, and he handed the change man a quarter. Clay did the same, and the four of them began pushing their way down the center aisle. Three soldiers were gathered around one machine, swearing as the game progressed. Slaughter excused himself and edged past, leading the way. When he reached the far end of the parlor, he stopped.

"Here, Miss Pepperdine," he said, and he gave her two nickels. "Go play." Bobby Jo nodded and inserted a nickel into the machine closest to her. Slaughter stared from one machine to the next, studying them carefully. Clay found a machine he liked and inserted a nickel. Frances stood behind him, her arms around his waist.

Clay was an excellent player, with great imagination and daring, and marvelous flipper co-ordination. If he had a flaw, it was impetuosity.

"Fine play, Eustis," Slaughter said, watching as Clay executed a difficult reverse flip, saving the first ball.

"Thank you, Maxwell," Clay muttered, concentrating on the ball as it rolled back up into play. "I kinda liked it myself. You see that, Frances?"

"Huh?" Frances said, raising her arms to around his chest, blowing softly in his ear.

Clay shook her off. "Later," he said.

Finally, Slaughter chose a machine. Carefully he tested the plunger, gauging the resiliency of the spring. He hit the machine several times, sharp clean blows with the palm of his hand. The machine seemed sturdy. Leaning down on the glass, he gazed intently at the numbered lights. There were ten of them, and they needed to be struck in order. Slaughter nodded. When the ten lights were out, the silver bumper at the center of the machine turned red, and each time you touched it, you received a hundred thousand points. Slaughter nodded again. You needed five million for one free game. And six million for two free games. And when the silver bumper turned blue, you got a free game each time you hit it. When the silver bumper turned blue! Definitely worth remembering. Slaughter tested the flipper buttons; they reacted quickly to the pressure of his index fingers. Taking a deep breath, he inserted a nickel and began to play.

Bobby Jo walked over and stood watching him as he pulled the plunger back and delicately released it. The ball rocketed upward into the heart of the machine. Slaughter struck the machine once on the right side and the ball bounced cleanly into light number one, extinguishing it. The ball dropped down to the flipper and he let it bounce one time, twice, then, with a gentle flip, he sent it careening off at an angle into light number two. The ball rebounded as he had planned and struck the third light, grazed the fourth, and returned to the flipper. This time he flipped with quick force, sending the ball up into the top of the machine where the fifth light lay hidden behind a bumper. Slaughter slammed the machine twice on the right side and the ball touched the fifth light. The light went out.

The ball was dropping back toward the flipper when Bobby Jo kicked the machine on the leg. The machine grunted and went dark. A large green *TILT* appeared.

Slaughter stood frozen for a moment. Then he turned to Bobby Jo. She was giggling.

"That was hardly funny, Miss Pepperdine," Slaughter said, advancing toward her.

She backed away, not giggling any more. "Eustis," Bobby Jo called. "Eustis, he's gonna hit me."

Clay stepped between them. "What happened, Maxwell?" he said.

"She tilted my machine," Slaughter answered. "Intentionally."

Clay stepped out from between them. "Go ahead and plaster her."

Slaughter cornered Bobby Jo against the back wall of the parlor. "Now I'm warning you, Miss Pepperdine," he said softly. "Never do that again. And I'm not going to strike you, so stop cowering." He paused. "I gave you two nickels. Why don't you go play?"

"I used 'em up already."

"Have another quarter." He reached into his pocket.

"I don't wanna play pinball," Bobby Jo said.

"That's just too bad, Miss Pepperdine. We're here now." He turned, walking back to his machine, inserting another nickel.

Bobby Jo crept up beside him. "I'm sorry," she said.

"It's quite all right," Slaughter said, sending the first ball into play.

"Dammit, Frances," Clay muttered, a few machines away. "Quit pawin' me."

Slaughter extinguished seven lights with his first ball. With the second ball he touched the remaining three, and the silver bumper in the center turned red. "Now look, Miss Pepperdine," he said hurriedly, flipping the ball into the bumper. "Listen." The machine gave a dull *bonk*. "That's worth a hundred thousand."

Bobby Jo inched closer and stared at the moving ball. "That's good, fatty," she said.

"Thank you," Slaughter nodded, and he continued to play.

At the end of the third ball, he paused for a moment, checking his score. "Now see, Miss Pepperdine. I have four million, seven-hundred thousand. Three more hits and I win a free game." He pulled back the plunger, starting the fourth ball. It moved lazily back and forth across the top of the machine, then rolled down onto the red bumper. "Four million, eight," Slaughter said. He flipped once and the ball collided with the bumper again. "Four million, nine. One more hit to go."

The ball was dropping back onto the flipper when the machine grunted TILT again.

"Theft!" Slaughter roared.

Clay came running up. "What happened?"

"The bastard tilted on me," Slaughter answered, pointing to the machine. "I didn't even touch it."

"Same thing happened to me," Clay said.

Slaughter stepped up to the machine and inserted a third nickel. His face drained of color, his eyes riveted on the lights, he began to play, quickly, coldly, with great precision. He extinguished all the lights on the second ball and was well over the four-and-one-half-million mark before the machine grunted once more, TILT.

"Come, Eustis," Slaughter muttered. "We're leaving." He marched back down the aisle and approached the change man. "Your machines are rigged," he said. "I want two nickels back."

"Blow it out," the change man said.

Slaughter took a step backward, pointing a finger at the change man. "You are going to regret that," he said. "I promise you." Then he turned to Clay. "Have you your pocket knife?" Slaughter asked. Clay nodded. "Good. Stay here. Guard my machine with your life. I shall return."

Clay nodded again, watching as Slaughter left the pinball parlor.

"Where did he go?" Bobby Jo asked. "Where did fatty go?"

"To get a coat hanger," Clay answered. "He'll be right back."

"Hi, sweetie," Frances whispered, nuzzling up to Clay.

"Hi, Frances," Clay sighed, and he leaned against the machine. The parlor was half-filled now; a dozen or more soldiers were playing on the machines at the front, close to the change man.

"Do you like Maxwell?" Clay asked.

"He was gonna hit me," Bobby Jo said.

"Naw." Clay shook his head. "Maxwell's a real gentleman. You ought to be nice to him, Bobby Jo. You shouldn't have kicked his machine like that."

Bobby Jo stuck a finger in her ear and wiggled it back and forth.

Slaughter appeared again in the doorway to the parlor, shielding something under his shirt. With great dignity, he strode past the change man, hurrying up to Clay. "Gather round me," he said, taking the metal clothes hanger out from under his shirt, twisting it until it was one nearly straight piece of metal, three feet long. Wiping his forehead, he glanced around. It seemed safe enough. The change man was at the far end of the long room, with the other soldiers in between.

"Ready?" Clay asked.

Slaughter nodded. "Begin. Pocket knife." Clay handed it to him. Slaughter bent close to the machine. "Now start talking." Pulling out a blade on the knife, he set to work, unscrewing the front panel of the machine. It was hot, and his face was perspiring. "Talk," he muttered.

"What are you doing with that knife?" Frances asked, her voice very loud.

"Talk about something else," Slaughter snapped.

"Sure is a nice night," Clay said loudly.

"I just love your sweater, Frances," Bobby Jo said.

"It's my brand-new pink Angora, Bobby Jo. You want to feel?"

"How you coming, Maxwell?" Clay whispered.

"Almost there, Eustis." He twisted the knife a few more times and the front panel came loose in his hand. Clay reached out and took it. Then, carefully, gently, Slaughter took the metal wire and pushed it slowly up inside the machine under the glass. When it lay next to the silver bumper, he put a nickel into the machine and played the first ball.

"I do wish I knew what was happening," Frances said. "Ain't that illegal?"

"Not in this state," Clay told her.

"Oh," Frances said.

Slaughter let the first ball drop and played the second. It banged around at the top of the machine a moment, then fell out of play. Slaughter launched the third ball. "Change man watching?" Slaughter whispered.

Casually, Clay glanced toward the front of the store. "Nope. He's just jingling nickels is all."

The third ball was nearing the bottom of the machine when the silver bumper turned blue.

"Eustis," Slaughter said, "we're home," and he jammed the wire against the blue bumper. The machine made a wrenching sound and registered a free game. Slaughter touched the bumper again.

"Two free games," Bobby Jo said.

Slaughter continued pressing the metal wire against the bumper. "Keep talking," he said.

"If this is legal, why don't everybody do it?" Frances asked.

"Control her, Eustis," Slaughter said.

"Francis," Clay said, "hush up."

"I just don't understand a thing that's going on," Francis said, shaking her head.

"Twenty-five free games," Bobby Jo whispered, moving closer to Slaughter. "Isn't that something!"

"We got twenty-five free games," Frances said. "Hey, everybody, we got—"

Clay grabbed her and turned her around.

"Ask her what she learned in school today," Slaughter said.

"What did you learn in school today," Clay said.

"Donna Mae Parker's gonna have a baby," Frances answered.

Bobby Jo looked up. "That so, Frances? I thought she's been looking a little pudgy."

"Just three months away, Bobby Jo." Frances giggled. "That's why she's been wearing that raincoat all the time. Indoors and out, she's been wearing that raincoat."

"Who's the lucky guy?" Clay asked nervously, wiping his forehead.

"Oh, she ain't exactly sure," Frances said. "But me and a couple of the girls been helping her out and we got the list down to three."

"Eighty free games," Bobby Jo said, watching as Slaughter touched the bumper again and again. "Ain't that wonderful?"

"Which three?" Clay asked nervously.

"Oh, I forgot their names. But two of them is Catholic and the other is a second lieutenant."

Clay gave a sigh of relief.

"We're all hoping it's the second lieutenant," Frances continued. "On account of her big sister had to marry a Catholic and her mama ain't over it yet."

"I never knew she had a big sister," Clay said.

"Oh, yes. Name of Elly Sue Parker. She had sort of a gimpy leg. She couldn't walk too good. Well, no. She could walk okay but she didn't look too good. On account of she was always swaying over to one side. And she met this nice boy from the Army post, only—"

"Over and out," Slaughter said, pulling the wire from the machine. Clay handed him the front panel and Slaughter began screwing it back in place.

"A hundred and fifty free games," Bobby Jo said. "That's the most I ever saw."

Slaughter finished with the front panel and leaned against the machine, wiping his face. Then he started to walk down the aisle, stopping at the first group of players he came to. "Save your nickels," he whispered, gesturing with his thumb. "Free games." He continued on to the next group. "Free games," he repeated, gesturing. The men filed past him, hurrying to his old machine.

When he came to the front of the store, Slaughter stopped by the change man. "Here," he said, handing him the wire. "You'll find this excellent for clearing congested passages."

"What?" the change man said.

"Blow it out," Slaughter answered, and walked on by to the sidewalk.

"You fixed him good, fatty," Bobby Jo said, hurrying up to Slaughter.

"It was only just, Miss Pepperdine. Any man who would stoop to rigging a pinball machine deserves exactly what he gets."

Clay and Frances joined them. "Carnival?" Clay asked.

"I'm a trifle thirsty," Slaughter admitted. "I could use a grape."

Clay nodded and they began to walk to Crawford's drugstore in the middle of the block, Slaughter in the lead, Bobby Jo skipping alongside to keep up, Clay and Frances a few paces behind. The sidewalk was lined with the old people of Hastingsville, sitting in their folding chairs, fanning themselves, talking, muttering, staring at the people going by.

Crawford's was air-conditioned. Slaughter and Bobby Jo walked to a booth. Slaughter bowed slightly and Bobby Jo nodded back to him, then sat down, smoothing her skirt with her hands. Slaughter looked around for Clay.

"They're at the magazine rack by the door," Bobby Jo said. "Frances loves looking at the movie magazines. She's got a crush on John Derek."

"A lovely lad," Slaughter agreed.

A waitress appeared. "Can I have something?" Bobby Jo asked.

"Of course."

"Then I want a double chocolate ice-cream soda, but leave off the whip cream." She glanced at Slaughter's face. "Better leave on the whip cream."

"Thank you," Slaughter muttered. "And I would like two grape-ades, please. With as much ice as possible."

The waitress nodded and walked away. Slaughter stared for a moment at Clay and Frances by the magazine rack, then he turned to Bobby Jo.

"And what do you like, Miss Pepperdine?" he asked.

"How do you mean?"

Slaughter shrugged. "Well, you said that Miss McCoy likes movie magazines. I just wondered what you liked."

"Oh. Boys, I suppose."

Slaughter nodded. "Anything else?"

Bobby Jo cocked her head. "I guess," she began, "I guess that after boys I like crossword puzzles best."

Slaughter leaned forward across the table. "Crossword puzzles, Miss Pepperdine?"

"Um-hum. I just love crossword puzzles. Once you get started in doing 'em, you just can't stop. They're like . . ." and she cracked her gum, thinking.

"Please, Miss Pepperdine. Don't do that any more."

"I'm sorry," Bobby Jo said, taking the gum from her mouth, sticking it under the table. "Like eating peanuts," she finished.

"A sound image."

"You know what I mean? Once you start eating peanuts, you can't—"

"I understand," Slaughter told her. "As a matter of fact, I indulge in crossword puzzles myself. Tell me, have you ever tried the *Times* Sunday puzzle?"

"What's that?"

"A weekly battle to the death, Miss Pepperdine, that's what it is. A mortal conflict. My mind . . ."

The waitress returned and set down the drinks. Slaughter paid her and took a long swallow of grape.

"You just drunk half that glass," Bobby Jo said.

"I was thirsty," Slaughter admitted. He paused. "My mind against his. My—"

"Eat this," Bobby Jo said, and she spooned over the whipped cream.

Slaughter bent forward and took it in his mouth. "My rapier against his lance. That's very tasty whipped cream."

"Mrs. Crawford makes it herself. I just do the puzzles in the magazines."

"Makes it herself, you say?"

"Yup." She took a spoonful of ice cream. "I don't finish many."

"What magazines?" Slaughter said.

"The puzzle magazines," Bobby Jo answered. "They got 'em up there."

Slaughter excused himself and approached the magazine rack.

"I'm gonna marry John Derek someday," Frances was saying. "I'm gonna go to Hollywood—"

"Pardon me," Slaughter said, and he picked up a crossword puzzle magazine from the shelf.

"—and marry John Derek."

Slaughter paid for the magazine, purchased a pencil and returned to the table. "Here, Miss Pepperdine," he said. "A small token."

Bobby Jo grabbed the magazine and started turning the pages. "A new one," she said excitedly. "A brand-new one." She spread the magazine flat on the table and stared at a puzzle. Slaughter finished his first grape and started on the second. Bobby Jo licked the end of the pencil and wrote a word in the first space. She looked at the second space. Then she frowned.

"What's a young pig?" she asked.

"Shoat," Slaughter answered. "S-h-o-a-t."

Bobby Jo nodded and wrote the word in the space. "That's good, fatty."

"It was nothing," Slaughter told her.

Bobby Jo stared at the letters while she sipped her ice-cream soda. "I don't like this puzzle," she said, and she turned to the next page, staring at the first definition. "I don't like this puzzle, either," she muttered, turning the page again, staring at the new list of definitions. "I don't like any of these puzzles."

"You must learn patience, Miss Pepperdine," Slaughter said. "Patience is the first law of crossword puzzles. Read a number of the definitions before you begin. Try to gain an insight into your opponent's mind. What sort of man is he? Is he flamboyant? Is he secretive? Does he flaunt his erudition in your face or—"

"What are you talking about, fatty?"

"Just this, Miss Pepperdine. You must prepare yourself before you raise your pen. You must—"

"What pen?"

"A turn of phrase, Miss Pepperdine. It so happens that

I use a pen, but pencil means the same."

"Ink!" Bobby Jo said. "You do puzzles in ink?"

Slaughter shrugged. "I think best with a pen. And it adds a bit of zest to an often unequal struggle."

Clay hurried up to the table. "Can we get the hell out of here?" he said. "I'm goin' nuts with this John Derek."

"He does his puzzles in ink," Bobby Jo said.

Clay nodded. "Please?"

Slaughter finished his second grape and waited a moment. Then, when Bobby Jo was done, they stood and walked over to the magazine rack. "We're goin' to the carnival, Frances," Clay said. "Come on."

"He does his puzzles in ink," Bobby Jo whispered, pointing at Slaughter.

"Huh?" Frances said.

Reluctantly she put the magazine back and they moved out onto the sidewalk. The people in the folding chairs watched them, muttering, as they walked slowly toward Clay's car. Bobby Jo reopened her magazine and licked her pencil.

"I'm reading all these definitions," she said. "That right?"

Slaughter nodded.

"On account of I'm getting an insight."

Slaughter nodded again.

"Now I'm raising my pen," Bobby Jo said. She looked up at Slaughter. "What's a Siamese coin?"

"An att, Miss Pepperdine. A-t-t."

"And what's a palm leaf?"

"Olla. O-l-l-a."

They got into the car. Clay started to drive. "Carnival *ho!*" he shouted. Frances moved over and put her arms around his neck.

"We're doing good, fatty," Bobby Jo said. She looked

up from her puzzle. "But what's an insight?"

Slaughter smiled. "In how many letters, Miss Pepperdine?"

The carnival spread aimlessly across a large field past the edge of Hastingsville. It opened on the first day of July, running until Labor Day, drawing people from all the neighboring towns. An enormous, brightly lit Ferris wheel stood in the center of the field, and surrounding it were more than a dozen smaller rides, along with candy counters, hot-dog stands, strength tests, accuracy tests, bowling games, throwing games, two outhouses and a bingo parlor.

Clay pulled up in the far corner of the parking lot.

"Lookit the Ferris wheel," Bobby Jo said. "Boy, is that scary!"

Frances whispered into Clay's ear. Clay nodded and hopped out of the car, yanking at the roof, pulling it up and over, into place.

"Bye, Frances," Bobby Jo said.

"Bye, Bobby Jo, see you later."

Clay looked at Slaughter and shrugged. Slaughter nodded, saluted, and he and Bobby Jo commenced the walk through the dark parking lot toward the lights. As they grew near, they heard the dull, steady sound of voices, punctuated intermittently with the high shriek of childish laughter.

"What's a Berber?" Bobby Jo said.

Slaughter looked down at her. "Why did you bring that?"

"Someone might have stole it," she answered. "What's a Berber?"

They walked into the carnival. A group of children ran past them. "Riff," Slaughter said. "R-i-f-f. Now put the magazine away for a while, Miss Pepperdine. Look at the people."

"Can I have some cotton candy, please?" Bobby Jo asked.

"Of course," Slaughter answered, and they stopped at a candy counter. "Two, please," he said.

"I just love watching 'em make it, don't you?"

Slaughter nodded and paid. They began walking again, slowly, up one aisle and down the next. From the distance came the sound of a calliope.

"I don't like looking at the people," Bobby Jo said.

Slaughter took a mouthful of cotton candy. "Why not?"

" 'Cause they all look dead," Bobby Jo answered. "That's why. All the people around here look dead. You ever know that?"

Slaughter nodded.

"I'm gonna move into Capital City when I finish high school. And get me an apartment and a job and a twenty-one-inch TV set. And new clothes and new shoes. I'm gonna have me a ball in Capital City."

"I wish you joy, Miss Pepperdine," Slaughter said, and he finished his cotton candy, dropping the cone into a wire basket.

She giggled. "Boy, you don't talk like anyone else I ever knew." Bobby Jo lowered her voice. " 'I wish you joy, Miss Pepperdine.' " She giggled again. "Boy, is that dumb!"

A cry went up from their left, and they turned to see two skyrockets bursting into the sky above the Ferris wheel, flaming, fragmenting, dying away.

"I think that's sad," Bobby Jo muttered. "I think fireworks are the saddest things in the whole world. They disappear so fast. They ought to make 'em so they just hang up there all night long."

"You might mention that to Eustis. The two of you could go into business together."

They stopped, looking into the bingo parlor, a large

canvas tent filled with rows of wooden chairs. At the front, a tall, skinny woman read numbers from a wooden platform.

"I think bingo's dumb," Bobby Jo said.

"You're very opinionated, aren't you, Miss Pepperdine?"

"There you go again," Bobby Jo said. "Talking like that."

Slaughter put his hands in his pockets, walking on, past a souvenir stand, turning a corner, starting up another aisle.

"I didn't mean for you to be quiet altogether," Bobby Jo said then. "You can talk all you want to. I don't mind. You go ahead and say whatever you want. I'm a terrible kidder."

"Is that so?"

"Oh my, yes. In school, I'm always kidding everybody about everything."

"During recess?" Slaughter said.

"Oh, no. We don't have recess. I'm gonna be a sophomore in the fall. I'm gonna be the president of the sophomore class. I already been elected."

"Congratulations, Miss Pepperdine."

"I just hope I can do a good job," she said, nibbling at her cotton candy. "It's a terrible responsibility."

"I can see where it would be."

"Oh, it is. I've gotta look after all kinds of things. I've got to . . ." and she stopped, suddenly, as Corporal Lenahan grabbed her by the arm and spun her around.

"What the hell are you doing here?" Lenahan said.

"Hi, Freddy," she answered, backing away from him.

"What the hell are you doing here?" Lenahan repeated, louder. "You told me you were sick."

"I fibbed," Bobby Jo said. "I'm sorry." She pointed at Slaughter. "But his auntie died of the measles and he was all depressed and Eustis asked me would I help cheer him up and I told Eustis yes I would because I know how terrible

I'd feel if my auntie died of the measles, so I had to fib to you. Are you mad?"

"You're goddam right I'm mad," Lenahan said, grabbing her again. "You stood me up, you lying little . . . *Leggo!*"

Slaughter dug his fingers deeper into the back of Lenahan's neck, lifting Lenahan up onto tiptoe.

"She was just being kind," Slaughter said.

"Leggo!" Lenahan repeated.

"They're fighting over me!" Bobby Jo cried, pointing to the people gathering around. "Over me."

"And kindness must be repaid with kindness, mustn't it, Corporal?"

"Yes," Lenahan answered. "Yes."

"So tell her how happy you are that she did what she did."

"I'm happy," Lenahan shouted. "I'm happy as hell."

"And how sorry you are you misjudged her."

"I'm sorry. I'm sorry. I apologize."

Slaughter let him go. "We all make mistakes, Corporal," he said.

Lenahan glared at him, rubbing his bruised neck. Then he cut away sharply through the crowd. Clay and Frances came running up.

"What happened?" Clay asked.

"They had a fight over me," Bobby Jo told them.

"This is all terribly embarrassing," Slaughter muttered, breathing heavily, perspiring, his face pale. He turned abruptly and started walking away.

Bobby Jo ran after him. "Hey, fatty," she said, tugging at his shirt. "Where you going?"

Slaughter slowed. "No place in particular, Miss Pepperdine."

"Well, you just can't go and leave me now. I might need protecting again. And then you'd have to come to my rescue."

"Please," Slaughter said. "Talk about something else."

"You saved me from a fate worse than death, fatty. You—"

"I did not save you from anything of the sort, Miss Pepperdine. The lad had a perfect right to be angry. I shouldn't have interfered."

"But you did. You come to my rescue."

"A moment of weakness, Miss Pepperdine. Nothing more."

"And you lifted him up with one hand. And you shook him like he was a puppy dog. And you made him apologize like that. Freddy ain't never apologized to me before."

"I'm sorry it happened," Slaughter answered.

"Oh, I'm not," Bobby Jo said. "I found the whole thing very thrilling."

Slaughter plunged his hands into his pockets and walked on. Bobby Jo grabbed him by the arm, pulling him along. Slaughter let her lead, for a moment, but when they reached the edge of the parking lot, he stopped.

"Come ahead," Bobby Jo whispered, gesturing with her hand. "Come on." She moved quickly into the darkness, among the rows of silent cars.

Slaughter followed slowly, a few paces behind. When he reached Clay's convertible, she was standing on the running board. From behind him, he heard another sigh from the crowd, and he watched as Bobby Jo's eyes stared up, following the skyrockets. After a moment she looked back at him.

"Hey," she said then, jumping down from the running board. "You got any of them rubberjohnnies?"

"No," Slaughter said.

"That's bad," she muttered. "See, I don't usually like to have sexual intercourse with nobody unless they got a rubberjohnny, on account of I don't much want to get pregnant."

"Miss Pepperdine," Slaughter told her, "I shall treasure that sentence always."

Bobby Jo stuck her finger in her ear and wiggled it back and forth. "What the heck," she said. "Let's live dangerous."

"No, Miss Pepperdine. Let's not."

She looked at him. "What?"

"I said, let's not."

"Why?"

Slaughter shrugged, shifting his weight from one foot to the other. "Frankly, Miss Pepperdine," he said, "I don't find you attractive."

Bobby Jo's eyes grew bright. "You don't find me attractive," she snapped. "Well, I don't think you're such a beauty neither."

"Miss Pep—"

"Just where do you get off talking to a girl like that? Who do you think you are, fatty? Blimp—"

"Please, Miss Pepperdine. Lower your voice."

"Jelly belly!" Bobby Jo said. "Balloon head! Blubber—"

Slaughter grabbed her around the waist and lifted her, setting her on top of Clay's car. "Now just be quiet a moment, Miss Pepperdine. And listen. I didn't say that you weren't attractive. You are. I simply said I didn't find you attractive. There's a difference. After all, you've got to realize you're very young."

"I'm fifteen," Bobby Jo said.

"And I'm forty," Slaughter answered.

"Well, that shouldn't matter none," Bobby Jo said. "All my other boy friends, they just love having sexual intercourse with me."

"I'm sure they do."

She nodded. "Sometimes they just beg me and beg me and beg me."

"And you let them?"

Bobby Jo nodded again.

"Why?"

She shrugged. " 'Cause they want to so much, I guess. And 'cause it don't matter to me one way or the other. I never feel nothin'."

"I'm sorry," Slaughter said.

She looked at him a moment. "Me, too," she said.

Again there was the sigh from the crowd, and again Bobby Jo stared up into the darkness. Then she shook her head. "Lift me down now?"

Slaughter reached up and caught her, lifting her down. She smoothed her skirt with one hand.

"Shall we go back?" Slaughter said.

"I'm sorry for calling you blimp face," Bobby Jo told him, still smoothing her skirt. "But I thought you was insulting me again. When I was just trying to be nice."

They started walking slowly toward the carnival.

"Earlier," Bobby Jo said. "Before. It was me you was calling a moron, wasn't it?"

"Yes," Slaughter answered. "And I must apologize for that. I erred."

"Oh, I know that one," Bobby Jo said. "Err. To make a mistake in three letters."

"Correct," Slaughter told her. "Absolutely correct."

They entered the carnival again, moving slowly through the crowd. Bobby Jo opened her crossword puzzle magazine and, holding it in one hand, brought it close to her face. Slaughter took her other hand and led her along.

"I wonder, will I ever learn all these definitions?" she said.

"It takes time, Miss Pepperdine."

"Oh, I got plenty of that. As a matter of fact, I happen not to be doing anything all day tomorrow."

"There's Eustis," Slaughter said. He turned toward the Ferris wheel.

"I usually spend part of my time on the post," Bobby

Jo went on. "I wonder, will I happen to bump into you or not?"

"That depends, Miss Pepperdine. When are you going to be there?"

"All day if necessary," Bobby Jo said. "That's when."

"Over here," Clay called. "Where you been?"

"Chatting," Slaughter replied.

"We're gonna ride on the Ferris wheel," Frances said. "Do you wanna ride on the Ferris wheel, Bobby Jo?"

"That depends entirely on my escort," Bobby Jo answered.

"Do you wanna ride on the Ferris wheel, fatty?" Frances asked.

"Don't you go calling him fatty, Frances McCoy."

"Why not?"

"'Cause he ain't a fatty any more," Bobby Jo cried, throwing her arms around the front of Slaughter's middle. "He's my baby boy friend now . . ."

VI.

"It was a funny war," Slaughter mused quietly, shaking his head, taking a long drink from his beer can.

Bobby Jo looked up from her crossword-puzzle book. "Funny strange or funny ha-ha?"

"Funny strange, Miss Pepperdine," Slaughter answered. "Funny strange." Leaning forward, he reached into the dust and picked up a used cartridge shell. Turning it over slowly between his fingers, he studied it in silence.

It was almost seven o'clock in the evening, and they were sitting together on a blanket beneath the shadow of the officer's tower on K range, the last in an almost endless row of rifle and machine-gun ranges that lined the northern side of Camp Scott, forming a great bleak rectangle of flat, dying ground. Frances lay on a neighboring blanket, stretched out, her chin cupped in her hands, reading a movie magazine. Behind them, on the road, Clay's and Slaughter's cars were parked in a mild V, cradling a large garbage can filled with ice and beer. In front of them, in the center of the range, Clay and Meltzer were crawling toward each other along the dusty ground, in the midst of battle.

"Look at them—they're crazy," Bobby Jo said, pointing, as Clay made the sound of an M-1 rifle firing.

"Gotcha!" Clay cried.

"Missed! Missed! Missed!" Meltzer cried back.

Slaughter smiled. "It's only play therapy," he said, and when she looked at him questioningly, he spoke again. "They're both a trifle drunk," he added softly.

"Don't they know they're getting all dirty?"

"I don't think they care," Slaughter answered. "Remember. We're celebrating. It's a very special day." He stared at the cartridge shell again, bringing it close to his face. Then he sighed. "I'm off."

She looked at him quickly. "Where you going?"

"For another beer," he told her, and he stood slowly, starting the walk back toward the cars.

"Frances," Bobby Jo whispered.

"Huh?"

"You ought to stop that reading and listen to what my baby boy friend is saying. He knows absolutely everything."

"Oh, you keep saying that, Bobby Jo. But I'm busy now." She turned back to her magazine.

"Well, if you don't ever want to learn anything, Frances McCoy, then all right for you." She glanced backward over her shoulder. "Can I have another piece of ice, please?"

Slaughter nodded and reached down into the garbage can.

Bobby Jo watched him a moment, then turned, staring out onto the range, where Clay and Meltzer were crawling in circles, around and around. Suddenly Meltzer stood and made the sound of an M-1, but as he did, Clay rolled quickly up onto one knee and started firing a machine gun.

"Pkew, pkew, pkew, pkew, pkew, pkew, pkew, pkew, pkew, pkew, pkew, pkew, pkew, pkew!"

Meltzer grabbed his stomach and collapsed to his knees. Groaning, he hesitated for just a moment before slumping full length, face down in the dust. Clay crept up cautiously behind him, then lurched forward, using his bayonet.

"What are you doing that for?" Meltzer mumbled.

"I'm makin' sure you're dead."

Meltzer rolled over onto his back. "Boy, is that dumb!"

"No, it ain't. You might just have been faking."

"Hey," Meltzer said, sitting up. "Where did you get that machine gun anyway?"

"Never mind about that. You're dead."

Meltzer lay flat again. "Well, I just don't think it's fair, that's all, you having a machine gun."

Slaughter returned to the blanket and sat down, crossing his legs with difficulty. He handed Bobby Jo a piece of ice. She nodded and stuck it in her mouth.

"That's very good-tasting ice," she said.

Slaughter nodded. "For you, Miss Pepperdine, nothing but the finest."

She chewed on the ice for a while, looking around. "What are those things over there?" she asked, pointing to a distant row of wooden frames standing mutely at the far end of the range. "They're spooky."

"Those are where the targets go," Slaughter answered. "You fire at them from here."

"They sure are a long way away. I can't hardly even see 'em."

"It's about five hundred yards," Slaughter said.

"Can you hit 'em?"

"I think once, perhaps, I could."

"Well, ain't that somethin'," Bobby Jo muttered. "Oh, my, yes."

Now, in the center of the range, Clay and Meltzer were walking stiffly away from each other, strapping on their six-guns as they went.

Bobby Jo watched them a moment, then looked up at Slaughter again. "Why was it strange?" she asked.

"The war?" He lifted the cartridge shell to his lips, slowly, blowing on it softly, making a hollow, whistling sound. He blew again, and the sound repeated.

"That's spooky," Bobby Jo said.

Slaughter turned his head, staring down the endless line of silent ranges that stretched out for miles, narrowing, melding, dissolving into gray. "No heroes," he said then. "There weren't any heroes."

"Why not?"

Slaughter studied the shell for a long time. Finally he

shrugged. "Because it was an invisible war, I suppose. It didn't exist. More boys fought than in World War I, but it didn't exist. Not really. Nobody cared about it. It was a war without a cause, Miss Pepperdine. And you can't be a hero unless you have a cause. So no heroes."

"Oh," Bobby Jo said.

Clay and Meltzer started walking slowly toward one another. When they were twenty feet apart, they stopped.

"That's just about far enough, stranger," Clay drawled.

"Who says so?" Meltzer drawled back.

"Name's Scott," Clay answered. "Randy Scott. What's yores?"

"Call me Shane," Meltzer said.

"Dammit, Jerry," Clay shouted. "Be somebody else. I'm the good guy."

"Why do I always have to die, Eustis? You die for a change."

"Hell, no," Clay told him. "I'm a sergeant and you ain't nothin' but a measly Pfc. How about Boris Karloff? You can be him."

"I don't want to be Boris Karloff. You be Boris Karloff."

"I'm Randy Scott," Clay said, drawing suddenly, firing six quick shots into Meltzer's chest. "*Blam, blam, blam, blam, blam, blam.*"

"Blam yourself," Meltzer answered, and he turned, starting back toward the officer's tower.

Clay followed along behind him, throwing hand grenades. "*Kpoom. Kpoom.*"

"Boy, that Eustis," Meltzer said, squatting down in the dust in front of Slaughter's blanket. "He never lets anybody shoot him."

Bobby Jo pointed. "My baby boy friend can hit those targets 'way over there."

"Please," Slaughter muttered.

"Well, you can. You said so."

Clay flopped onto the blanket alongside Frances. "You having fun?" he asked.

Frances nodded. "I just love celebrations," and she turned a page in her magazine.

Clay looked at her. "You're all sweaty."

She nodded again. "I shouldn't have wore my cashmere."

Shrugging, Clay stood. "Who wants another beer?"

"Me," Meltzer answered, jumping into the air, clicking his heels. "I feel great," he shouted. "You know that, Maxwell? I've had eight cans of beer and I feel sensational. No kidding. I could run all night." He trotted around in a circle, chanting "eight, eight, eight" over and over.

"He's crazy," Bobby Jo said.

Clay came back with two beers and handed one to Meltzer.

"I would like to propose a toast," Meltzer said. "To Eustis Clay and Maxwell Slaughter, who are my buddies."

Slaughter blew softly into the cartridge shell.

"Do you want to know why they signed those truce papers today?" Meltzer went on, his voice getting louder. "I'll tell you why. As a present for me. Because I'm getting out in twelve days and old Mark Clark, he thought it would be a nice thing to do. No Meltzer, no Korea. It's as simple as that."

Clay sat down in the dust in front of Bobby Jo. "Hey, Bobby Jo," he said, "Maxwell tell you where we're getting shipped to?"

Bobby Jo shook her head.

"Paris, France. How about that?"

"No," Bobby Jo said.

"It's not definite," Slaughter told her gently. "I'm working on it. We won't know for a while yet."

"Well, I don't want to talk about it," Bobby Jo muttered. "I think it's sad."

"Nothing's sad today!" Meltzer cried. "Because I'm getting out and the war is over and I'm getting married and we're all sitting here together, so what the hell."

"What the hell," Clay echoed.

"Hey," Meltzer said then, jumping around. "Hey. You're all invited to my party."

"Oh, I just love parties," Bobby Jo said. "When is it gonna be? I got to wash my hair."

"Next week. In Capital City. The night I get out. All the liquor we can drink, and my mother's paying for it. She and Emmy are coming down, and we're going to drive back to New York and we're having a party to celebrate, and it won't cost us a cent."

"I'm going in training right now," Clay said.

"It's going to be a great party, Eustis. No kidding. We'll all get bombed out of our minds. Woweeoboy!"

"My baby boy friend never gets drunk," Bobby Jo said. "He just drinks and drinks, but he don't ever get drunk."

"The goddam war is over," Meltzer said.

"It was a funny war," Bobby Jo said. "Funny strange."

"Why?" Meltzer asked.

"No heroes," she answered. "On account of there wasn't any causes. And you can't be a hero unless you got a cause." She glanced up at Slaughter.

Slaughter nodded.

"Hey, that's good, Bobby Jo," Meltzer said. "You know, you're right. There weren't any heroes." He squatted down again. "At least, none I can think of."

Again, Slaughter blew into the cartridge shell, and they listened to the hollow sound. The sun was dropping rapidly now, the dark shadows from the range officer's tower covering them all. At the far end of the range, the wooden target frames stood in deep twilight.

"I can think of a hero," Meltzer said suddenly.

"Who?" Bobby Jo asked.

"Me, by god, I'm a hero. Because I lived through two years in the Army, and that makes me a hero, and I would like to propose a toast to Eustis Clay and Maxwell Slaughter, who are my buddies. Now come on, Maxwell. Put that damn thing down. The war is over."

Slaughter hesitated for a moment. Then he dropped the cartridge shell back into the dust.

"I'm the fastest guy in the world," Meltzer said. "Nobody can catch me."

"Nobody wants to," Clay answered.

Meltzer kicked some dust over Clay's shoes.

"I don't wanna chase you, dammit," Clay said.

Meltzer picked up a handful of dust and sprinkled it in Clay's hair.

"The aw-dassity," Clay mumbled.

Meltzer grabbed his beer can and started to pour beer onto Clay's hair, but Clay reached out, grabbing Meltzer's foot, diving on top of him, and the two of them rolled over and over in the dust.

"They're crazy," Bobby Jo said.

Meltzer sprang to his feet, bouncing up and down.

"Cut him off at the pass, Eustis," Slaughter shouted, and Clay took off in pursuit.

"Look at 'em go!" Bobby Jo cried, watching as they chased through the darkening range, running silhouettes, kicking up clouds of dust with every step. They ran and ran, and finally Clay pulled up as Meltzer changed direction, darting over the ground.

"I'm flying," Meltzer yelled. "I'm taking off."

Clay walked slowly back to Slaughter's blanket and flopped down, panting heavily. Meltzer continued to run, circling closer and closer to the target frames. Then he turned, suddenly, bolting back, driving forward with long strides, his arms moving rhythmically. "I'm a jet," he called, his voice nearer now, and the others watched as he increased his speed, racing through the twilight, vaulting up onto the officer's tower, climbing it quickly until he stood at the top.

"Now hear this!" he cried, cupping his hands around his mouth. "Now hear this. The war is over! The war is over!"

"What's he saying?" Frances asked.

"He's yelling that the war is over," Bobby Jo answered.

Frances shook her head. "What war is that?" she said.

VII.

It was the afternoon of Meltzer's separation, and Eustis Clay stood staring silently into his open wall locker. Cocking his head to one side, he pulled meditatively at his lower lip. What to wear? That was the problem. It was a miserably hot afternoon in early August, and his clean T-shirt was already soaked through. Clay wiped the back of his hand across his mouth. What to wear? Meltzer always dressed in the same, stupid way, dark pants and dark jackets and that silly black necktie. He looked at his own neckties. Which was the darkest? Nodding his head, he pulled out a red-and-blue job, one hundred per cent pure silk. Now which shirts matched? He pulled out his red-and-blue short-sleeve, and held it next to the tie. Almost the same. Good. But could you wear a necktie with a short-sleeved shirt? Meltzer never did. But what the hell, who would know, since a jacket would cover it anyway? Now pants. Ahh. He reached for his dark blue gabardine. Good deal. He put them on. Now for a jacket. What he needed was a blue jacket, and that was what he didn't have. What was close to blue? Brown? No. Green? Happily, he put on his green jacket and stood back, looking at himself in the mirror. It was good. It was damn good. Just like Meltzer.

He combed his hair, finally getting it to fall correctly across his forehead. Grabbing his wallet and cigarettes, he started to hum. "Rooty tooty tooty, dee toot, dee toot, dee toot." Going to the door, he opened it. "Bye, Donald," he said, and then he locked the door behind him. He started down the stairs two at a time, but slowed as perspiration began dripping around his eyes. Reaching for his handkerchief, he mopped his face, opened the front door and stepped out onto the barracks porch.

No one in sight. The entire area seemed deserted, and

only the few prisoners standing quietly in the yard of the stockade saw him as he crossed the company area and got into his car. He waved to them and one of them nodded back, and then he was driving out of the parking lot, turning toward C Road. The breeze felt almost cool as he drove along through the quiet post. And it was quiet. Something had happened in the past week. Suddenly. Almost overnight. There just weren't many trainees left. The bayonet field was empty and up ahead in Main Post only a few cars were parked in front of the Main PX. Clay started to sing again. "Cocktails. I'm going to cocktails." That fit nice to "Indian Summer," but it was a bitch to rhyme. Oh well, it was too hot for real songwriting anyway.

He parked behind the I. & E. Building and slowly mounted the back steps. Someone new was in Meltzer's office, and Clay glanced at him briefly before moving down the hall to Slaughter's door. Drawing his Buntline Special from his pocket, he threw the door open and jumped inside. "This here's a raid, so don't nobody move!" he yelled, kicking the door shut.

Master Sergeant Slaughter was sitting in his swivel chair, watching Bobby Jo, who stood quietly by the air conditioner, her back to him, staring out the window.

Clay walked to Slaughter's desk and sat down on top of it, cross-legged. "Maxwell," he said, "you're beautiful."

Slaughter wore a brown necktie and a brown suit with faint red vertical stripes. His white shirt was open at the neck, and his thinning hair was very carefully combed.

"Ain't Meltzer done yet?" Clay asked.

Slaughter ignored him, continuing to watch Bobby Jo, who had not moved. Clay looked at her. She was wearing her candy-striped dress with a tiny single strand of pearls around her neck.

"You look nice from the back, Bobby Jo," Clay said.

Bobby Jo continued to stare out the window. Finally she turned, pointing a finger at Slaughter. Her eyes were red.

"You are too," she mumbled.

"Please, Miss Pepperdine," Slaughter answered.

"You having a fight?" Clay asked.

"He's ashamed of me," Bobby Jo said. "He told me so."

"You misunderstood," Slaughter said. "I promise you. I am not ashamed."

"He don't want me to come," Bobby Jo said, hurrying to Clay.

"That is not true," Slaughter went on. "You've got to believe me. I merely wondered—"

"Jerry invited me," Bobby Jo interrupted. "He asked me to come."

"Why don't you want her, Maxwell?" Clay asked.

Slaughter threw up his hands and wheeled across the room to the soft-drink machine. Hitting it once, *Awwk,* he waited, than drank the glass of grape in two swallows. Pushing himself back to his desk, he took a deep breath. "I would like to change the subject," he said.

"Why did he say that to you, Bobby Jo?"

She shook her head.

Slaughter sighed. "Miss Pepperdine told me she was nervous, and all I suggested was that perhaps we both might not go. That's all I said. Nothing more. And if she chooses to interpret that as a personal affront, then there's nothing I can do about it."

"You see?" Bobby Jo said. "He's ashamed."

Clay hugged her and was about to speak when the door to the office opened and Meltzer walked in. He looked at them blankly.

"I'm out," he muttered.

"Bulldog, bulldog," Clay shouted.

Meltzer shook his head. "But I don't feel anything. No

different."

Bobby Jo walked over to him and stood on tiptoe, kissing him on the cheek. He grabbed her, swinging her high up into the air. Then he set her down. "Everybody ready?" he asked.

Slaughter stood and walked around the desk. "Congratulations," he said. They shook hands.

"I'm a civilian," Meltzer said dully. "I'm—"

"Let's go get drunk," Clay interrupted. "Let's go get plastered."

"We're going to Capital City," Bobby Jo said. "Just fancy that."

They walked along the hall and out the back door. Slaughter's touring car was parked in the driveway, loaded with a suitcase and a green duffel bag. Clay and Meltzer squeezed into the back seat. Slaughter opened the front door for Bobby Jo, then walked around and eased himself in behind the wheel.

"I'm out," Meltzer repeated, flatly. "I'm a civilian."

Slaughter started the car and they drove out of the driveway. Meltzer turned and looked back at the I. & E. Building. "So long," he said. Slaughter continued on, turning at Main Entrance Road.

"I'm a civilian," Meltzer said, louder now, as they sped along. Far off to their left, a single company was marching silently in silhouette, the dust rising as the men moved slowly through the heat. "So long," Meltzer shouted. "So long, you poor bastards." He looked at Clay. "Eustis," he said, "I'm a civilian." They came to the main entrance of Camp Scott, and Meltzer suddenly stood up in the back seat, staring at the post spreading out behind them. He cupped his hands around his mouth, ready to shout. After a moment he shook his head and dropped his hands and sat down again. "I couldn't think of anything to say," he muttered. Slaughter turned right, increasing speed, driving along the two-lane highway that led finally to Capital City. Alongside them, the outside fence of the post became a blur.

Then Camp Scott was behind them. A road sign indicated that Capital City was twenty-five miles away. Meltzer looked at his watch. "I told them we'd be there by five-thirty, Maxwell. Can we make it?"

Slaughter nodded.

"They'll have drinks and ice up in the room," Meltzer went on. "We won't have to waste any time ordering."

"I figure on being plastered by six-fifteen," Clay said.

"We'll decide on dinner later," Meltzer said. "We can either go out or have it sent up by room service. Depending on how we feel. How's that sound?"

"Oh, it sounds wonderful," Bobby Jo said, clapping her hands. She leaned over to Slaughter and whispered, "What's room service?"

Meltzer heard her. "It's a service of the hotel, Bobby Jo. You can order things from the restaurant and the bellboys bring it up. Food or drinks or anything else you want."

She clapped her hands again. "I'm gonna have a cheeseburger," she said. "With ketchup and pickle relish." She turned to Meltzer. "Can I have that?"

"You can have anything you want, Bobby Jo. I don't care. Mother's paying for it."

"She must be awful nice," Bobby Jo said.

"She's all right," Meltzer answered. "Of course, she still acts as if I was two years old. But otherwise she's fine."

"Docksail rhymes with cocktail, don't it, Maxwell?" Clay said.

"Beautifully, Eustis. But what does it mean?"

"Damn," Clay muttered, and he began pulling at his lip.

On either side of them now was farmland, flat and dry, filled with spindly stalks of corn, planted in endless parallel rows. There were no trees. Above, the sky was pale blue. Clay closed one eye and sighted down the rows of corn as the car hummed along.

"I hope you like Emmy," Meltzer said then.

"How come she's here?" Bobby Jo asked.

"We just thought it might be fun. Driving back to New York. She's never been down South before."

"How you going to get your mother out of the way?" Clay said.

Meltzer flushed. "We don't have to, Eustis. We're getting married next month. We can wait until then."

"I guess," Clay nodded.

"You wanted me to come along, didn't you, Jerry?" Bobby Jo said.

"Of course I did."

She leaned close to Slaughter again. "See?" she whispered. "He wanted me."

"Why are you so quiet, Maxwell?"

"No reason, Jerry."

Bobby Jo dropped her voice still further, talking into Slaughter's ear. "I won't embarrass you none," she told him. "I'll be good. I promise I'll be good."

Slaughter smiled, nodding his head.

"I hope you like Emmy," Meltzer said again. He looked at Clay. "She's not really what you'd call pretty, Eustis. You ought to know that now."

Clay shrugged.

"She's really kind of plain, Eustis. She's not pretty at all." He pounded one fist into the other. "She's very smart, though. And very nice. But she isn't pretty."

"Come on now, Jerry, will you?" Clay said. "We don't care none what she looks like."

"Anyway," Meltzer finished, "I hope you like her."

"Just fifteen miles more," Bobby Jo told them, pointing.

"That sign said so." She turned to Slaughter. "Me and my baby boy friend, we're going to a party."

"And we're gonna get smashed," Clay said. "Bombed. Fried. Plowed."

"You bet we are," Meltzer echoed. "You bet we are."

"Let's sing," Clay said, loosening his tie.

"Great idea," Meltzer said. "What?"

"How's this?" Clay answered, and he started on "Danny Boy," with Meltzer joining in, and when they came to the second line, Clay took the harmony. They moved closer to each other, eyes closed, singing in harmony at the top of their voices, and finally Slaughter began, and the three of them sang, Meltzer and Slaughter carrying the tune, Clay blasting away at the harmony, the sound carrying out, dying over the cornfields.

"The three musketeers!" Meltzer shouted. "Now and forever. One—"

"Don't stop!" Bobby Jo cried. "Go on, go on," and she closed her eyes too, listening as they sang the song again, even louder than before, racing on through the heat toward Capital City. . . .

Slaughter found a space across the street from Regency House and backed into it. Bobby Jo opened the front door and got out, stretching her arms up into the air. "Isn't this beautiful-looking?" she said. "I just love Capital City." She ran around the car and stared out at the large park, full of trees and blossoming flowers that spread from the street down to the green river below.

In the car, Meltzer struggled with his duffel bag. Slaughter reached over and took it, carrying it in front of him with both hands. "A small gesture," he said. "Eustis. Take the gentleman's suitcase." Clay nodded and stepped out, grabbing the suitcase in one hand.

"I never been inside Regency House before," Bobby Jo said. "Except for once. I walked through the front. They got the thickest rugs in there."

Meltzer led the way as they crossed the street, Clay following a step behind, Slaughter bringing up the rear with Bobby Jo hurrying alongside. Meltzer nodded to the doorman and continued on into the lobby. "You wait here a sec," he said, and he hurried over to the reservation desk.

Bobby Jo pushed her toe into the rug. "See?" she whispered. "Ain't they thick?"

Slaughter nodded.

"Some dump," Clay muttered. "Huh, Maxwell?"

"An excellent hotel," Slaughter agreed.

"It's the very best in the whole state," Bobby Jo told them. "And my mother had a friend who stayed here once and I forget what it cost, but it was a terrible lot of money."

"Hey, Maxwell," Clay asked. "Is Meltzer loaded?"

"Heavily," Slaughter answered.

Meltzer came back. "Okay," he said. "You want me to carry something?"

"Nope," Clay told him. "Just lead me to that booze."

They crossed the lobby quickly and entered the elevator. "Fourteen, please," Meltzer said.

"That's the very highest floor," Bobby Jo said, pointing to the flashing numbers above the elevator door. "We're going all the way to the top."

Slaughter nodded, and they waited quietly while the door opened again. Meltzer led them out of the elevator and down the hall. "It's that one, I think," he said, pointing to the room at the end of the corridor. Checking the number, he knocked once.

They waited. He was about to knock again when the door opened and a short, heavy, gray-haired woman stood in the foyer, staring out.

"Jay," the woman said, holding out her arms.

Meltzer kissed her quickly, then spun out of her embrace and moved inside.

Slaughter looked at the woman a moment, smiling at her. "Mrs. Meltzer?"

"Yes."

"I'm Maxwell Slaughter, Mrs. Meltzer." He stepped into the foyer. "And this is Miss Barbara Pepperdine. And Eustis Clay. We're very glad to meet you."

Mrs. Meltzer smiled, backing up a step, gesturing for them to follow. Slaughter set the duffel bag in the corner of the foyer and waited for Bobby Jo, who hung back.

"Come, Miss Pepperdine," he said.

Finally, Bobby Jo moved forward slowly, stopping beside Slaughter. Clay set the suitcase next to the duffel bag and closed the door. The room was very large, with windows facing the river. There was a long sofa set before the windows and two large chairs flanking the fireplace on another side of the room. Directly across the room from the fireplace was a serving table, laden with glasses, bottles and an ice bucket.

"A lovely room," Slaughter said to Mrs. Meltzer.

"Oh, it's beautiful," Bobby Jo cried, suddenly running past them across the room to the bank of windows on the far side. "Look, baby boy friend! You can see the park. And the river. And all the people. And the tops of the trees." She whirled. "You can see everything from up here. And look." She pointed to an open doorway. "There's more rooms in there."

"It's a suite," Mrs. Meltzer said to her.

"Oh, it sure is," Bobby Jo nodded. "It's—"

"Miss Pepperdine—" Slaughter began.

"It's just as sweet as can be," Bobby Jo finished.

"Yes," Mrs. Meltzer said. "Thank you very much."

"Oh, you're entirely welcome, ma'am."

They all stood smiling at one another in silence for a moment. Then Meltzer appeared in the doorway to the next room, leading a girl. Clay glanced at her from the foyer. No boobs. Bad legs. But nice dark hair and the complexion was okay. C. Solid C.

Meltzer and the girl moved into the center of the room. "This is Emmy," he said, perspiring lightly, wiping his hands across his forehead. "Maxwell. Eustis. Bobby Jo."

Slaughter walked up to her. "How do you do, Emmy?" he said, nodding and smiling.

She held out her hand. "I've heard so much about you," she began. Then she stopped, shaking her head. "That sounds terrible, I know. But I have. Jay has written so much about you, that . . ." She stopped again. "I'm just making it worse."

Meltzer stared at them a moment, then turned quickly toward the bar. "Who wants what?" he called. "Eustis?"

Clay walked out of the foyer to the bar. He looked down at the bottles. "You got any beer?"

"No, but we've got Scotch. And gin. How about a gin and tonic?"

"They any good?"

"Try it and see." He opened a bottle of quinine water, filling a glass with ice. "What do you think of Emmy?" he asked quietly.

"I haven't had a chance to talk to her yet, Jerry."

"Well, she's very nice and I hope you like her."

"I don't know if she's nice or not, but she's pretty."

Meltzer looked up. "You think so?"

"B or B-plus," Clay answered. "Depending."

Meltzer handed him the glass. "Well, how about that?" he said. He nodded his head several times, then called across the room. "Maxwell?"

Mrs. Meltzer turned from Bobby Jo. "Where are your manners?" she said. "Ladies first."

"Mother," Meltzer said.

"What would you like, dear," Mrs. Meltzer said to Bobby Jo.

Bobby Jo clasped her hands behind her back. "Could I have some root beer, please?"

"I'm afraid we have no root beer. But ginger ale we can give you."

"That would be fine," Bobby Jo said. "Thank you."

Meltzer poured her a glass of ginger ale and Clay took it over to her. They stared out the window at the park.

"Nice place," Clay said.

"Oh, it's just as sweet as can be," Bobby Jo told him. Clay nodded, and they continued staring out the window.

Emmy stood in front of the fireplace, talking with Slaughter. Smiling, she turned, looking across the room at Meltzer. "I think I'd like a Gibson," she said.

Meltzer stared back at her. "What's a Gibson?" he asked.

"They're very popular," Emmy answered.

"Since when?"

Emmy shrugged.

"I'm glad they're so popular. But what the hell are they?"

"Jay," Mrs. Meltzer said.

"Ask my baby boy friend," Bobby Jo called out. "He knows absolutely everything."

Emmy smiled.

"Well, he does. Just ask him."

"Miss Pepperdine—" Slaughter began.

"Tell what it is," Bobby Jo said.

Slaughter sighed. "It's a Martini. Five or six to one. With a cocktail onion."

"There," Bobby Jo said. "See?"

"Can you make it, Maxwell?" Meltzer asked.

"I can try," Slaughter said, and he crossed the room to the bar.

Bobby Jo turned to Clay. "Do you think he's mad at me?" she whispered. "Maybe I shouldn't have spoke up like that." Before Clay could reply, she hurried over to the bar and stood beside Slaughter, looking up at him.

Clay took a long swallow from his gin and tonic. Not bad. Not like beer, of course, but still not bad. Very tasty. Sort of a girl's drink. Bringing the glass to his lips, he drained it in three more swallows. Then he began walking back to the bar. On the way, he passed Mrs. Meltzer, who was standing alone in the center of the room.

"Howdy, Mrs. Meltzer," he said.

She nodded. "Are you sorry to see my Jay leaving?"

"Hell, yes," Clay told her. Then, "I mean, yes, ma'am."

She smiled and he continued on toward the bar, shaking his head. Have to watch that. Talk slow. Nice and easy. He handed his glass to Meltzer.

"Lemme have another of these things, huh, Jerry?"

Meltzer put some ice cubes in the glass. "Eustis," he whispered. "Don't mind anything my mother says. Okay?"

"She ain't said nothin' yet."

"Well, if she does, just don't pay any attention. She's really all right. But she's a mother, you know what I mean?"

"I guess." Clay took his glass and looked around the room. Slaughter and Bobby Jo were talking to Mrs. Meltzer now, over by the window. Emmy stood alone in front of the fireplace. Clay crossed to her.

"Howdy, Emmy," he said.

"Anybody need a drink?" Meltzer called from the bar. "We don't want any leftovers." He began pacing along the side of the room.

"Hello," Emmy said. She held her drink in one hand, a lit cigarette in the other.

Clay grinned at her. "How do you like Capital City?" he asked.

"I don't," Emmy said.

Clay nodded. "You really gonna marry him?" He gestured over his shoulder toward Meltzer.

"It looks that way."

" 'Course, you realize he's a goon."

Emmy nodded.

"I mean, we done all we could to shape him up. But we didn't have time enough to finish the job." He took a long swallow from his gin and tonic. "Hey. This stuff ain't bad a-tall. It's mighty tasty."

"Let's have some more glasses over here," Meltzer called. "Drink up."

"What do you do?" Emmy asked. "In the Army, I mean."

"As little as possible," Clay said. "I'm a supply man."

"Is that interesting?"

Clay shrugged and finished his drink. "Can I get you another of whatever-it-is?" He pointed to her glass.

"No, thank you. I'm fine."

"Don't go 'way," Clay told her, and he crossed the room back to Meltzer.

"Do you like her?" Meltzer asked.

"Oh, we're having a fine old time," Clay nodded, waiting while Meltzer opened another bottle of quinine water. "Why don't you come join in?"

"I will," Meltzer answered quickly. "As soon as business dies down here." He handed Clay the glass. "Okay," he called out. "Let's move this booze."

Mrs. Meltzer turned. "It won't spoil," she said.

"I know that," Meltzer said.

"Well, then?"

Meltzer began shifting the bottles around, setting them in parallel rows.

"You come join me and Emmy," Clay said.

"I will, Eustis, I'll be right over." He continued fiddling with the bottles.

Clay walked back to Emmy. "Your fiancé. He's a damn fine bartender."

Emmy shifted her weight from one foot to the other. "Jay wrote me that the post is closing," she said.

"Ain't it the truth."

"What does that mean? To you?" She looked across the room at Meltzer, who was leaning against the bar, his back to her.

"Not much. It means that we don't do nothin' except sit around. But I don't mind that."

"I meant what's going to happen to you? Where will you go?"

"Oh." Clay gestured with his glass. "Me and Maxwell. We're heading for Gay Paree."

"When?" She shifted her weight again.

"Well, we ain't got our orders yet. We're just sort of waiting around for 'em now. But we'll get 'em, all right."

"How do you know that?"

" 'Cause Maxwell's working on it. So we're as good as there. We'll probably ship from New York City or someplace around. We're gonna stop up and see you and Jerry. We're gonna paint the town."

"I hope we'll be there," Emmy said.

"Oh, we'll let you know in plenty of time," Clay told her. "Maxwell, he's good at making arrangements. We're a team. He's the brains, and I'm the idea man."

Emmy looked across at Meltzer again. He was pacing the side of the room, hitting one fist into the other. Emmy took a step forward, then stopped.

"Let's sit," Clay said. "Come on." He led her over to one of the easy chairs. Beside the chair was a triangular wooden table. Emmy sat down. Clay pushed on the table top with his hand, testing it.

"Bring that one over," Emmy said, pointing to the chair on the other side of the fireplace.

"I'm fine," Clay told her, and he sat on the table top, crossing his legs.

"So you're a team," Emmy began.

"Best in the West," Clay answered, grinning down at her. "Undefeated, untied and unscored on."

"And does he really know everything?"

"Course he does. But he needs me on account of I get the ideas."

"What sort of ideas?" Emmy asked.

"Come on," Meltzer called out. "I'm dying of loneliness."

"Then join the party," his mother said, from next to the window.

"Come over here with us," Emmy said.

"I will," Meltzer muttered. "In a while."

Emmy looked quickly away and up at Clay. "What sort of ideas?" she asked again.

"Well, now," Clay began, shifting the drink from his right hand to his left. "That takes some explaining. You see . . ." and he leaned back, gesturing grandly.

"Eustis," Slaughter called. "Watch it!"

"Damn!" Clay cried, and for a moment tried to lean forward, thrusting his arms out straight, grabbing for balance. There was a long pause. Then he fell backward, carrying the table over with him. He grunted loudly as he hit the floor, his drink spilling onto the rug.

"Are you all right?" Emmy asked quickly.

Mrs. Meltzer turned. "What happened?"

"The table fell over," Meltzer told her, running across to Clay. "That's all. The table just fell over."

Bobby Jo looked at Clay lying on the floor and giggled.

Meltzer pulled Clay to his feet. "You all right, Eustis?"

"The aw-dassity," Clay muttered.

"How did it happen?" Mrs. Meltzer said.

Bobby Jo giggled again. " 'Cause Eustis fell off."

Meltzer picked up the table and set it flush with the chair. "It's fine," he said. "No damage."

"A table isn't for sitting," Mrs. Meltzer said.

Meltzer turned on her. "Eustis sits on tables," he said, his voice rising. "It's all right." He dashed off into the bathroom for a towel.

Clay stared down at the wet spot on the rug. "I'm sorry," he muttered.

"It's all right," Mrs. Meltzer said, smiling at him. "No damage."

Meltzer dashed back and knelt, scraping the wet spot with a towel. Finally he stood. "Done," he said, and he reached for Clay's glass. "Here. Gimme. I'll get you a refill."

"Why don't we all sit down and talk together?" Mrs. Meltzer said.

"No," Meltzer answered. "Come on, Mother."

"I want to meet your friends, Jay. That's all." She walked to the sofa by the windows. "Bring up some chairs," she said. Slaughter and Clay each took a chair; they carried them to the sofa, forming a semicircle. Clay and Emmy sat in the chairs, while Bobby Jo and Slaughter joined Mrs. Meltzer on the sofa. "Come, Jay," she called. "You sit, too."

"I've been sitting for two years," Meltzer said, handing a new drink to Clay. "I'd just as soon stand." He moved behind the sofa.

"Suit yourself," his mother told him. She turned and

looked from Bobby Jo to Slaughter to Clay. "Now," she said, smiling at them, folding her hands in her lap, "tell me. How did you come to meet Jay?"

"It was rather difficult to avoid him," Slaughter answered quickly. "Our offices were in the same building."

"That's right," Meltzer agreed. "Everybody used to walk on tiptoe around Maxwell, and I wondered why, so I pestered him. Then he invited me to the Footlong for lunch one day and I—"

"What's a footlong?" Mrs. Meltzer said.

"A hot-dog stand. Anyway, from then on, we were what the Army calls buddies. Isn't that right, Maxwell?"

Slaughter nodded.

"Well, that ain't how we got to be friendly," Clay said.

Bobby Jo clapped her hands together. "Oh, tell about the accident," she said.

"It was nothing," Slaughter cut in.

"Well—" Clay began.

"No," Slaughter said. "Really, Mrs. Meltzer. It was nothing at all."

"I'd love to hear," she said. "Jay never wrote about it."

"Well," Clay began again, "Maxwell said that the post was gonna close and it was Tuesday, so he couldn't do nothin' in the way of a little celebrating, so—"

"He does it in ink," Bobby Jo said.

"So anyway, I was up at the Officers' Club, on account . . ."

Slaughter shook his head.

Clay paused. "I meditate up there," he said finally. "Every Tuesday they got a meditation hour alongside the Officers' Club, and—"

"This is very complicated," Mrs. Meltzer said.

"It gets worse," Clay laughed. He glanced at Emmy, who was staring up at Meltzer. "Well, you see, Maxwell sent

Jerry over and we went out to celebrate and we had a few, and your son, he got a little plastered, and—"

"Jay doesn't drink," Mrs. Meltzer said.

"We learned him how," Clay said. He started laughing again, louder. "So anyway, to get to the point, there we was, out on the highway, doing the four-minute mile, and I was in the car and old Meltzer, he was puffing along outside with me cheering him on, yelling at the top of my lungs for him to get a move on, because we was gonna rent the Rose Bowl and your son, he had guts to spare, because he'd already threw up once and we was zipping along, like I said, when all of a sudden from behind us this car comes zooming up out of nowhere, bigger'n shit, and—"

"It was really very funny, Mother," Meltzer interrupted. "It was, really."

"*Pkewkommbonkk!*" Clay shouted. "Crack-up!"

"I was in the other car," Bobby Jo said.

"And it was all straightened out in due time, Mrs. Meltzer," Slaughter said. "I'm afraid it just isn't very interesting." He mopped his face with his handkerchief.

"Yes," Meltzer agreed. "Maybe you had to be there." He turned and walked to the bar.

"It all sounds very exciting," Mrs. Meltzer said.

"At any rate," Slaughter finished, "that was how they met."

"Ain't you gonna tell about the Pit?" Bobby Jo said excitedly. "That was the best of all. My baby boy friend, he was gonna put me—"

"I don't think Mrs. Meltzer cares much about that," Slaughter cut in.

"Oh, I'm sorry," Bobby Jo whispered. "I didn't mean nothing."

Slaughter nodded, continuing to mop his face.

Meltzer came back from the bar, holding a glass. Clay

pointed to him. "See, ma'am? I told you we learned him how."

"What is that you're drinking?" Mrs. Meltzer wanted to know.

"It's my version of a Gibson," he answered. He stared at Emmy. "They're very popular."

"That wasn't necessary," Emmy said.

"Anyhow," Mrs. Meltzer said, smiling, "you all got to be friends."

"Yes, we did," Slaughter nodded. "And I think I can speak for Eustis in saying that we are genuinely fond of your son, Mrs. Meltzer. He's a wonderful lad; we'll miss him, and we wish him joy."

"Thank you," Meltzer said softly.

His mother looked up at him. "I like your friends, Jay," she said.

"So do I, Mother."

"What's the matter with you anyway?" Emmy asked. "She just said—"

"Nothing's the matter with me. Nothing."

"It's the strain of getting out, Emmy," Slaughter said. "It always tells on civilians. They go to pieces. They don't know where their next meal is coming from. Where they'll bed down for the night." He smiled. "It's a terrible thing."

Everybody laughed.

"Can I get anybody anything?" Meltzer asked. He drained his own glass. "Aside from myself."

"I think we're all taken care of," Slaughter said.

Clay gulped his drink and held it out. "Me," he said.

Meltzer took the glasses and moved slowly to the bar.

Outside, the sky was growing dark as the sun dropped slowly into a pocket of western clouds. Bobby Jo turned to Slaughter.

"Can I go look out the window?" she asked quietly.

"Of course you can," Slaughter nodded. Bobby Jo stood up and hurried to the window, her hands clasped behind her back, staring out.

"She's very sweet," Mrs. Meltzer said softly.

"Yes," Slaughter said. "She is."

"Look baby boy friend," Bobby Jo called. "It's the most beautiful thing. I never seen a sunset from up so high before." Slaughter rose and walked over to her. Meltzer came back, handing Clay his drink. "Doesn't everybody want to see the sunset?" Bobby Jo asked.

"How long have they been keeping company?" Mrs. Meltzer asked.

"Twenty-two days," Bobby Jo answered from the window.

"I introduced 'em," Clay said.

"No, you didn't either. We met in the station house."

Slaughter led Bobby Jo back to the sofa and they sat down.

"I love your dress, Emmy," Bobby Jo said. "It fits so nice and everything."

"Thank you," Emmy nodded.

"Yours is nice too, Bobby Jo," Meltzer said.

"Thank you, Jerry. It's my very best one."

They sat quietly then, staring out the window while the sun went down. Clay moved his drink lazily back and forth, listening to the clink of the ice cubes striking the glass. Just the upper edge of the sun was visible now, a distant fire, falling slowly into the darker haze of surrounding clouds. For a moment the clouds changed color, blazed red. Then they darkened again, and the sun was gone. Clay began to hum softly in time with the ice cubes, a blissful smile on his face. Slaughter moved in his seat. Bobby Jo waited until he was settled before pressing up close to him again. Meltzer finished his Gibson and headed for the bar. Slaughter turned, briefly, watching as Meltzer mixed the drink.

"Maxwell and Eustis are going to Paris," Meltzer said finally, coming back from the bar, standing rigidly behind the sofa.

"Really?" his mother said. "How wonderful."

"They're going to visit us in New York before they ship over. I told them we could put them up."

"Of course," Mrs. Meltzer said. "It would be a pleasure."

"We may not be there," Emmy said.

"What the hell do you mean by that?" Meltzer asked, his voice rising.

"Jay!" Mrs. Meltzer said.

"I don't mean anything," Emmy answered. "Except just exactly what I said. We-may-not-be-there. That's all I meant. We might be on our honeymoon. Wouldn't you say that was possible? And if they came then, why, we wouldn't be there. Isn't that right?"

Meltzer took a long swallow from his drink.

"When are you getting married?" Bobby Jo asked.

"Labor Day weekend," Emmy muttered.

"That's so exciting," Bobby Jo said. "Getting married, I mean."

"It's to be a small wedding," Mrs. Meltzer said. "Just the immediate families."

"I guess you'll be leaving here soon, then," Bobby Jo said.

"Not soon enough," Emmy told her.

"Why? Don't you like Capital City, Emmy? I just love Cap—"

"I think it's a dump."

"Oh, no," Bobby Jo said. "Oh, no. It's a wonderful place. There's fifty thousand people living here."

"You mean dying here," Emmy answered.

Slaughter looked quickly at Bobby Jo's face, then quickly

away. He sighed heavily, shaking his head. "It's really a very nice town," he said finally.

"What's nice about it?"

Slaughter leaned forward. "I'm not a member of the Chamber of Commerce, Emmy. But it's a lovely place to live."

"You're kidding."

"No. I'm serious. If I were thinking of a place to settle down, I couldn't do much better than Capital City. Of course, you're used to New York, and this isn't New York, but—"

"Hear, hear," Emmy said.

"What the hell do you know about it!" Meltzer shouted. "Just tell me that. What the hell do you know about it? You haven't even been here one day."

"You like it so much?"

"Maybe I do."

"Then why don't you stay here?"

"Maybe I should."

"What are you taking their side for!" Emmy yelled suddenly. "Why do you always take their side?" She spun from her chair, running to the window, staring out into the darkness.

"Jay," Mrs. Meltzer said. "Children. Children."

"Shut up!" Meltzer said, backing away. He stood stiffly for a moment, looking at each of them in turn. "Why don't you all just please, please, please shut up!" He waited a moment more.

Then he turned and fled into the bedroom.

Slaughter stood. "Gibsons are notoriously powerful," he said, smiling at Mrs. Meltzer. "But I may know a cure." Excusing himself, he started into the next room.

"Where's Maxwell going?" Clay asked, watching his ice cubes as they bounced around his glass.

"In there," Bobby Jo answered. "He's going in there."

Slaughter closed the door quietly. Meltzer stood next to the bedroom window, his glass in his hand, staring out.

"I'm not drunk," Meltzer began, his back still turned.

"I know," Slaughter said.

"And I wasn't taking your side."

"Of course you were."

Meltzer faced him. "So what if I was?"

"Don't argue with me, dammit!"

"Anyway," Meltzer muttered, "I'm not drunk."

Slaughter nodded. Meltzer looked at him a moment, then stared out the window again. Beyond, the river glistened faintly in the early moonlight.

"I'm sorry, Maxwell," Meltzer said.

Slaughter said nothing.

Meltzer turned, crossing to him. "I really am sorry. I am. You believe that, don't you?"

"I believe it."

"I don't know what happened to me in there, Maxwell."

"Of course you do. And so do I. And it's my fault for letting it happen. We shouldn't have come. We've got no business being here."

"I wanted you to come, though. I did. But I never dreamed it would work out this way."

"It always does, Jerry," Slaughter said. "It always does."

From the next room, they could hear Clay's voice, loud and fast, and then the sound of laughter.

"Eustis is having a marvelous time," Slaughter said.

Meltzer nodded.

"He generally manages to. The lad is uncanny." He stood and started moving to the door.

"Maxwell?"

Slaughter stopped.

"Will I see you in New York?"

"I doubt it."

"I'd like to. Really, I would."

Slaughter shrugged. "Well, then, perhaps we might arrange something. Just the three of us. We might meet for an hour or so. In some bar. Tell a few old stories, sing a few old songs. Something like that. But don't worry about it now. Go splash some water on your face."

He opened the door.

"Is everything all right?" Mrs. Meltzer asked.

Slaughter smiled, rubbing his hands together. "Everything is fine," he said. "You can keep your miracle drugs. With cold water and Ex-lax I can cure anything." He sat down beside Bobby Jo.

"Eustis was telling us about grading women," Emmy said. "I'm a B-plus."

Slaughter looked at Clay and nodded. "You should feel honored, Emmy."

"I do," she answered.

Meltzer appeared in the doorway, his face wet. "Apologies to one and all," he said.

"Accepted," Emmy said, and she stood, walking over to him.

"You know how children are," Mrs. Meltzer said to Slaughter. "Fight, fight, fight. It doesn't mean anything."

"No," Slaughter agreed. "But it whets the appetite." He stood, lifting Bobby Jo to her feet. "Which reminds me. You must be hungry." He snapped his fingers. "Come along, Eustis. We must be going."

"It was wonderful of you to come," Mrs. Meltzer said.

"And wonderful of you to have us," Slaughter answered. They all moved toward the front door.

"This place is just as sweet as can be," Bobby Jo said.

"You've put your finger on a truth, Miss Pepperdine."

"See you in New York," Clay said happily. "We're gonna paint the town."

Slaughter opened the door. "Good-bye," he said. "And thank you so much." They all shook hands briefly, saying good-bye, good-bye, good-bye, and then Clay and Bobby Jo followed Slaughter into the hall.

"Maxwell—" Meltzer began.

"I hate farewells," Slaughter said. " 'The words of Mercury are harsh after the songs of Apollo. You, that way: we, this way.' " He closed the door. They walked down the corridor to the elevator.

"I thought we was gonna stay for supper," Clay said, pushing the elevator button.

"You were mistaken, Eustis."

Clay shrugged. "Don't make no difference. I ain't hungry anyway."

They waited. The elevator door opened and they stepped inside, riding down in silence.

"That gin and tonic is very tasty," Clay said, crossing the lobby. "I'm plowed."

"That was the loveliest party I ever been to in my whole life," Bobby Jo said.

"I'm glad you enjoyed it, Miss Pepperdine. It was lovely."

They left the hotel and started across the street to the touring car. Slaughter took Bobby Jo by the hand.

"I'm really plowed," Clay repeated. He started to sing. "My head is bowed because I'm plowed. Don't laugh too loud, I'm plowed."

"You just make that up, Eustis?"

"Swear to god. Spur of the moment."

"It's very catchy."

"Why, thank you, Maxwell."

"The loveliest party," Bobby Jo said again. She stuck

her finger in her ear, wiggling it back and forth. Slaughter opened the front door for her. Clay scooted in first, and lay stretched out on the back seat, singing very loudly.

Bobby Jo turned to Slaughter. "Except for one thing, though."

"Which is?"

"Jerry Meltzer's gone away. For ever and ever. That's sad."

Slaughter smiled at her. "After all, Miss Pepperdine," he asked, "what isn't?"

VIII.

Sergeant Clay walked excitedly into the golf shop. "Service," he called. "Service."

"Don't let it slam," Corporal Monroe called back. "Grab it!"

Clay reached out toward the screen door and stopped it, closing it quietly. Then he looked across the room toward Corporal Monroe, who stood behind the counter, holding a test tube in one hand, an eye dropper in the other.

"What are you doing?" Clay asked.

"I'm makin' a aphrodisiac," Corporal Monroe answered.

"A what?"

"Aphrodisiac. You know. It's a love potion. It makes you feel sexy." Squinting, he squeezed the eye dropper, sending one drop of reddish fluid down into the test tube. Clay moved toward him, watching. Corporal Monroe was a big, suntanned draftee from California who generally spent his evenings drinking beer or bartending at the NCO Club. He had been golf pro at Camp Scott for more than a year—a job which consisted solely of tending the shop and giving occasional lessons to officers—and was universally considered to have the softest deal on post.

"Boy," he muttered, shaking his head. "This is tough work." He wiped the perspiration from his forehead and squinted again, sending another drop of fluid into the test tube. "Hey, Eustis," he said then. "You know much about chemistry?"

"Nope."

"That's a shame," Monroe said. "I just hope I'm doing this right."

"What's that red stuff?" Clay wanted to know.

"It's tabasco sauce."

Clay nodded.

"And this here in the tube is a combination aspirin and oyster powder."

"Oyster powder?"

"Took me three days to make it. Grinding them oyster shells is harder than you think."

"I guess," Clay said. He looked around the shop. "Anyway, I need me some equipment. Gimme a golf ball, Monroe." He dropped a fifty-cent piece on the counter.

"Can you get it yourself, Eustis? I can't stop now. Any of those in the box are okay."

Clay took a golf ball from a square box on the counter. "What else do I need?"

Corporal Monroe glanced at him. "Ever play before?"

"Nope. But I seen plenty of newsreels."

"Grab yourself some tees then. From over there." He gestured with his head.

Clay picked up a handful of tees and stuffed them in his pockets. Then he walked back and peered at the test tube.

"Eight . . . nine . . . ten . . ." Corporal Monroe muttered, counting the drops of tabasco sauce. Finished, he set the eye dropper on the counter and breathed deeply. "I'm way behind schedule," he said. "This stuff takes three whole days to dry and I've got a date with Minnie May Sandborn a week from last night. I'm gonna try it out on her."

"Where'd you learn how to make it?"

Corporal Monroe winked. "From a doctor."

"What doctor?"

Corporal Monroe winked again. "Wouldn't you like to know." He picked up the test tube and, placing his thumb over the top, shook it vigorously. "Guess what else goes in here?"

"I give up," Clay said.

"Imported English gin," Corporal Monroe whispered. "And a couple sleeping pills."

"You sure this guy was a doctor?"

"Course I'm sure. I met him last weekend in a bar in Capital City. He's a doctor and he specializes in aphrodisiacs. He told me so himself. You know, Eustis, nowadays they got specialists in everything."

"And he just up and told you how to make it?"

"Course he did. It cost me a couple of bucks for the license, but—"

"What license?"

"The doc's gonna send it to me. It's a aphrodisiac's license. They're very tough to get. That's why they cost so much. But it was worth it. You see, it's foolproof. All you do is dry it into a powder and stick it in a couple of cigarettes. Then, when the girl reaches for a smoke, you just whip 'em out and say, 'Try my brand.' " Corporal Monroe smiled suavely. "I been practicing saying that all week now. 'Try my brand. Try my brand.' "

"What if the girl don't smoke?" Clay said.

"Try my brand." Corporal Monroe went on. "Try . . ." He stopped suddenly, staring at Clay. "Son of a bitch," he said, and he pounded his fist on the counter. "She's just got to smoke. She's just got to. Eustis . . ."

"So long," Clay waved, and he walked out of the shop, banging the screen door shut behind him. Tossing the golf ball up into the air, he moved slowly toward the first tee. That Monroe. He was out of his head. Trying to make a love potion. No finesse. And besides, it wasn't fair. Getting them drunk on boilermakers was one thing, but using a love potion, that was cheating. He tossed the golf ball up again and caught it behind his back without breaking stride. Maybe there was a song in it, though. Love potion. Hmm. "Do you have a notion to try my love potion?" Nope. Not very good. But motion rhymed with it too. And ocean and lotion. So it was probably worth working on in his spare time.

Reaching the first tee, he flopped onto the grass and looked around. Everything was quiet. No one in sight. The whole post looked dead. He lay back and stared up at the sky. It was a perfect September day, warm, with blue skies and a few white clouds and a slight breeze blowing in from the north. Gorgeous. Beautiful. A day for dying. How could you get mad about dying in weather like this? "Let me die when the sky is blue. Let me whisper my love to you." What was the best way to die? At the age of a hundred and ten being shot by a jealous husband. That was it. Definitely.

Leaning on one elbow, he saw Slaughter and Bobby Jo rounding the corner of the golf shack. Bobby Jo was pulling a caddy cart with both hands while Slaughter walked briskly alongside, a tweed cap perched jauntily on his head. Clay waved to them and stood, watching them approach.

"I'm the caddy," Bobby Jo told him. "I get to pull the clubs."

"Good afternoon, Eustis," Slaughter said.

"Howdy, Maxwell."

Slaughter turned to the caddy cart. "Shall we begin?"

"Oh, lemme do it," Bobby Jo begged.

"Very well, Miss Pepperdine," Slaughter said. Quickly she reached into a pocket of the golf bag and pulled out a tee and a ball. Rushing between the markers, she pressed the tee into the ground, delicately balancing the ball on top. She wore a pair of yellow shorts and a white, sleeveless blouse, and her hair was pulled neatly back into a ponytail.

"You're lookin' good, Bobby Jo," Clay said.

She giggled. "Thank you."

"Score card, please," Slaughter said.

Bobby Jo reached into the pocket of her shorts and handed him the score card. Slaughter looked down the fairway to the flag. "Hmm," he mused. "Three hundred yards. Par four." He shook his head. "Impossible."

"I bought my baby boy friend that cap in Hastingsville," Bobby Jo said. "Don't he look adorable?"

"Mighty fetching," Clay agreed.

"Club, please," Slaughter said.

"Which kind?"

"The wooden kind."

Bobby Jo handed him a wood, and Slaughter strolled up to the tee, stretching his arms over his head. He looked toward the green, then at the ball. Taking his stance, he choked the club halfway down the shaft and, with a short, gentle swing, potched the ball out into the middle of the fairway, where it bounced happily along for fifty yards.

"Yea, baby. Rah, boy friend. Yea, rah, baby boy friend," Bobby Jo chanted.

Clay walked up to Slaughter. "You want to take that over, Maxwell?"

"Certainly not. I planned it that way."

"Okay. But you done it wrong. The whole thing is to really lay into the ball. Plaster it good. Look." He took the club from Slaughter and plunged his tee into the ground. Stepping back, he took a practice swing. "It's the same as baseball," he said. Taking a deep breath, holding it, Clay swung mightily and the ball rocketed out over the fairway. Smiling, Clay watched it for a moment.

"See?" he said.

"Why is it curving like that?" Bobby Jo wanted to know.

"Stop!" Clay shouted.

"Very interesting," Slaughter said.

"Why, it's practically going backwards," Bobby Jo said. "Isn't that amazing?"

Clay turned away.

Bobby Jo tugged at his shirt-sleeves. "How did you make it go backwards?" she asked.

"I suggest we regroup on the green," Slaughter said.

"Come, Miss Pepperdine."

"Bye, Eustis," she called, waving, as Clay began running at right angles to the fairway, traveling south.

Slaughter walked out onto the fairway, swinging his driver. "A beautiful day," he said.

"How did he make it go backwards like that?" Bobby Jo said.

"Eustis is a natural athlete," Slaughter answered.

They stopped by his ball and Slaughter selected an iron, choking it, half swinging, sending the ball into a soft curve for sixty yards.

"I just love being out here," Bobby Jo said, dragging the caddy cart. "We haven't done it before. Why haven't we?"

"Because the clubs only came into my possession yesterday."

"Did you buy 'em?"

"Not exactly. I was given them. Out of gratitude."

"That was very nice."

"Actually, the lad had little choice," Slaughter said, and he stroked the ball again, knocking it forty yards up the fairway.

"What's Eustis doing way over there?" Bobby Jo said, pointing.

Slaughter pulled his cap down over his forehead, peering out at the distant figure racing along on the far side of G Road. "I don't know, Miss Pepperdine. But he must have done something unbelievable."

They continued on down the fairway, chatting about this and that, Slaughter hitting the ball a few yards at a time. Finally they came to the green. Slaughter lagged the ball up near the cup.

"There," he said. "Now I think we ought to wait for Eustis. Come. Join me," and they strolled across to a small mound and sat down. "Seven strokes thus far," Slaughter counted. "I'm quite satisfied."

"Oh, you're a wonderful golfer," Bobby Jo said. "I knew you would be."

"Hardly, Miss Pepperdine."

She reached up and moved his cap slightly forward. "It fits you perfect."

"It was very sweet of you."

"I spent all morning looking. It's the only tweed cap in Hastingsville. I went to all the stores." She giggled. "You're just adorable." Suddenly, she jumped up and swung her arms out wide, turning around and around. "I'm so happy I want to scream," she said. "Do you know why?"

"Why?"

"Because it's only Thursday. It feels like Saturday, but it's only Thursday and that means that Saturday is still coming. And nobody's got nothing to do but just sit in the sunshine." She paused. "That's why."

Slaughter nodded.

"You ain't really going to Paris, France, are you?" she asked then.

"Not unless our orders come."

"Oh, I hope they never do. I hope they get lost somewhere. That's what I hope."

"Thank you very much," Slaughter answered quietly.

Bobby Jo came back and sat down beside him. "I wonder, where can Eustis be?"

"He's certainly overdue," Slaughter said. He looked at his watch. Half-past three. He turned. There was no one in sight. The entire course, patches of grass and dirt, lay quietly beneath the lowering sun. Standing, he climbed on top of the mound. "There he is, Miss Pepperdine."

Bobby Jo clambered up beside him. "Hooray, hooray," she clapped, as Clay came running toward them from a northerly direction.

"Where's the ball?" Slaughter shouted.

Clay sprawled at the base of the mound, panting heavily. "I'm done," he muttered.

"What happened?"

"I lost the damn ball down a sewer on G Road, that's what happened. I quit."

"You can't quit now," Bobby Jo said, jumping down beside him. "It's too beautiful out here. You can borrow another ball from my baby boy friend. He's got lots of them."

"It's a dumb game," Clay told her.

"But you can't quit," Bobby Jo repeated. "Not when we're having so much fun."

Clay laughed once, then grabbed her, pulling her down onto his chest, squeezing her. She yelled and giggled, and Slaughter stepped over them on his way to the green.

"I'll just putt out," he said. Putting three times, he managed to force the ball into the cup. Then, grunting, he bent down and retrieved it. Clay and Bobby Jo were still wrestling when he got back to them. "Shall we continue?" Slaughter asked.

Clay let her go and stood. "I guess."

"Whoopee," Bobby Jo cried.

They started toward the second tee. "My ball kept going in a damn semicircle," Clay muttered. "Every time."

"Why don't you change your stance, Eustis? Stand at right angles. See what happens. Miss Pepperdine, give Eustis a ball." She reached into the golf bag and handed one to Clay.

Clay looked down the fairway toward the second green. Then he executed a sharp left-face. Spreading his legs, he swung. The ball sailed out over the rough, then started to curve.

"See?" Slaughter said. "Perfect. Right on the fairway."

"Nothing to it," Clay grinned. "Nothin' . . ." He

stopped, cocking his head. "Hey. You hear anything?" They listened. From somewhere, the sound of a voice blew in toward them on the wind.

"I can't make it out, Eustis."

"Funny," Clay muttered. "I swear it's saying my name." He turned around. "Don't see nobody."

"Who knows you're here?"

"Just Cronkite back at the company. But he wouldn't tell nobody."

"Who's Cronkite?" Bobby Jo asked.

"He's first sergeant," Clay said. "He used to be a cook but now that Booth's shipped out they got him acting first sergeant." He cocked his head, listening again. The sound was gone. "Let's play."

Bobby Jo put Slaughter's tee into the ground. Slaughter potched the ball onto the fairway.

"Hooray, hooray," Bobby Jo cried.

"What's she so happy about?" Clay asked.

"It's only Thursday," Slaughter answered.

Clay nodded. "I guess that's a good enough reason," he said, and together they started walking down the fairway.

"I take it all back about this being a dumb game," Clay called, looking across the ninth fairway.

"Your shot," Slaughter called back

Clay addressed the ball. Then he made a left-face and swung. The ball took off in a beautiful curve, sliding in around the back of the ninth green.

Clay bowed low.

"Excellent," Slaughter acknowledged, swinging his own club, sending the ball bouncing up onto the front of the green. Grabbing the handle of the caddy cart, he started pulling it, beckoning to Bobby Jo, who sat on the grass, her chin cupped in her hands. "Come along, Miss Pepperdine. We're almost finished. You can make it."

She stood slowly. "I don't ever want to walk another step."

He waited and took her by the hand. "I shouldn't have let you pull the cart," Slaughter said. "I apologize."

They walked onto the green, and Clay took the putter. Getting down on all fours behind his ball, he sighted along the ground, one eye closed. "I wish to hell I knew what I was looking for," he muttered.

"It's excellent form, Eustis."

Clay nodded and stood again, stepping up to the ball.

"Clay!" Corporal Monroe was shouting from the doorway of the golf shop.

"What?"

"Phone call."

Clay tossed the club to Slaughter and dashed to the golf shop.

"I tried yelling for you before," Monroe said, "but you didn't hear me. It's long-distance. I wrote it down." He handed Clay a piece of paper.

Clay nodded. Hurrying behind the counter, he sat at Monroe's desk and picked up the telephone. When the operator answered, he spoke to her briefly. Then he waited, drumming his fingers on the desk. Slaughter and Bobby Jo entered the shop and stood watching him.

"It's from home," he told them. "From Mrs. Howard."

"Who's Mrs. Howard?" Bobby Jo asked.

"My aunt. The one who brung me up."

"Oh." She nodded.

Slaughter walked around the counter and stood behind Clay's chair. Bobby Jo leaned across the counter, staring down at the rows of white golf balls. Clay drummed his fingers on the desk, louder than before.

"Hello, Mrs. Howard?" he said then.

"Hello, Eustis?"

"Yes, Mrs. Howard."

"I tried calling you before, Eustis."

"I know. I just got the message."

"How are you, Eustis?"

"I'm fine, Mrs. Howard."

"Good. I'm glad to hear that. Mr. Howard and I, we've been worried about you, you haven't written in so long."

"I'm sorry. I didn't mean to worry you none."

"How are you, Eustis?"

"I'm fine, Mrs. Howard. I'm fine. But what did you call for?"

There was a long pause. Clay pressed the phone harder against his ear.

"I can't hear you, Mrs. Howard. You got to talk louder."

"I didn't say anything, Eustis."

"What is it, Mrs. Howard?"

"Well," she said finally. "It's about Donald."

"What about Donald?"

"Well, he's not acting so good."

"What's the matter with him?"

"He's awful old, Eustis."

"What's the matter with him?"

"Well, he's awful old, and—"

"Did you call the vet?"

"Yes. He's here now."

"Lemme talk to him."

"He can't come to the phone this minute, Eustis. He's—"

"Look, Mrs. Howard," Clay said. "I can't talk here. You just wait by the phone. I'm going back to the company now. I'll get me a pass. I'll drive right home. So you wait." He dropped the phone and dashed for the door.

"Eustis . . . ? Eustis . . . ?"

Slaughter looked down at the receiver dangling over the side of the desk.

"Eustis . . . ? Can you hear me . . . ?"

Slaughter picked up the phone. "He's not here any more, Mrs. Howard. He just left. But he'll call you back in a few minutes."

"Who is this?"

"I'm Maxwell Slaughter. I'm a friend of Eustis'."

"Oh." She paused. "Well, tell him not to bother calling back. The dog's dead. So there's no reason for calling back. Tell him not to bother."

"I think you'd better do that," Slaughter said, and he hung up. Sitting down in the chair, he stared silently out the window, shaking his head. Bobby Jo came around and sat on his lap.

"Where did Eustis go?" she asked.

"To see a man about a dog."

She giggled. "That's funny," she said, pulling the tweed cap over his face. Then, when his arms went tightly around her, she laughed even louder, and it was difficult to tell whether she was more pleased than surprised or surprised than pleased.

Clay jammed his foot down on the gas pedal, gripping the wheel with both hands, staring straight ahead as C Road blurred past him on either side. As he passed the stockade, he started into a long turn, brakes screaming as he rounded the corner of the company street and shot into the parking lot. Throwing the car door open, he bolted across the ground, stumbling once, regaining his balance, jumping onto the orderly-room steps, running inside.

"Where's Magee?" he yelled.

Private Cronkite looked up from his copy of *Downbeat.* "He blew, man. Half an hour ago."

"Well, get him on the phone. Tell him I need a three-day pass or a leave or something. But get him on the phone. I'll be right back," and he pushed out of the orderly room and ran toward his barracks.

Racing up the steps, unlocking the door, he kicked at the pile of sheets in the middle of the room and grabbed his overnight bag. Stuffing his toilet-article kit inside, he pulled a shirt from his wall locker and jammed it in on top of the toilet-article kit. What else? Nothing. He had taken two steps toward the door when he remembered the photograph. Dropping the bag, he sat on his bed and reached out for the picture frame, staring at the golden dog lying asleep in deep shadow. "You ain't gonna die on me, are you?" he said. "No, you ain't gonna die." But he was awful old, Donald was awful old. Clay stared harder at the picture, bringing it closer to his face, fixating now. Sixteen. That was a lot for a dog. A hundred years. You couldn't ask for more than a hundred years. Clay looked at the ceiling. "Hey, up there," he said. "Hey, this is me. Eustis Clay. And I'll give up beer and I'll give up women and I'll give up anything else you want, but don't let him die till I get there. Just don't let him die till then."

He stood up and carefully placed the picture in the overnight bag. Then he was out the door, turning quickly to lock it, and down the steps and out of the barracks and running like hell to the orderly room.

"I couldn't find Magee," Cronkite said.

Clay jumped up on the desk and grabbed the phone, talking briefly to the operator. "It's okay," he muttered to Cronkite. "After I'm gone you get ahold of Maxwell Slaughter and tell him to clear it with Magee. He'll do it."

"You going A.W.O.L.?"

Clay nodded, waiting. Then he leaned forward. "Hello? Mrs. Howard?"

"Yes."

"Listen. I'm taking off now. I'll drive all night and I should get there tomorrow sometime. Now let me talk to the vet."

"He's gone, Eustis."

"Gone? Why?"

"Because Donald was dead, Eustis, and there wasn't any sense in him waiting around. So he took Donald away. Do you understand? Eustis?"

"Sure," Clay said, finally.

"He was awful old, Eustis. And he was bumping into things."

"Sure."

"So I called the vet. And by then Donald was bumping into everything, and then he got up the stairs and climbed on your bed and he died. Do you understand?"

"Sure."

"I'm sorry, Eustis. But the vet said he'd take care of everything and I thought it best that way. Eustis? Are you still there?"

"I'm still here, Mrs. Howard."

"Will you be coming home soon, Eustis? Do you think?"

"Oh, sure, Mrs. Howard. I'll be coming home soon. You can bet on that. Good-bye, Mrs. Howard."

He hung up the phone.

"You really going A.W.O.L.?" Cronkite asked.

Clay grinned at him. "Change of plan," he said, and he vaulted off the desk and fled from the orderly room. Outside, he tripped on the steps, sprawling in the dust, but in a minute he was up again, running hard. Into his barracks and up the stairs to his room, but he couldn't get the goddam key in the lock. The goddam key wouldn't fit in the lock no matter how hard he tried, so he stepped back and kicked at the door, again and again, until the wood splintered and the door flew open. Stepping inside, he slammed the door shut and leaned against it. Then he opened his overnight bag and took out the picture. Throwing the bag aside, he lay down on his bed and propped the picture on his chest. He stared at it, waiting for the tears to come.

They didn't.

He blinked several times to start the flow, but his eyes remained dry. Clay shook his head. "Cry, you bastard!" he yelled out loud.

Nothing happened.

He waited. One minute, five minutes, staring at the picture, his body rigid. Finally he set the picture on the bed table and rolled onto the floor, starting a series of push-ups. Ten. Fifteen. Faster and faster. Twenty. Twenty-five, and his arms ached, but he kept on. Thirty-five. Forty. He stopped. Standing up, he slapped his arms around his body. Then he fell back on the bed and stared at the ceiling.

There was a knock on the door.

Clay did not answer.

Slaughter pushed the door open. "Miss Pepperdine and I are thinking of going into Capital City. Would you care to join us?"

Clay shook his head.

"I'll treat."

"No."

"What would appeal to you?"

Clay rose up on one elbow. "Something's happened," he began.

"I know," Slaughter told him.

Clay lay flat again.

Slaughter sat on the edge of the bed. "You are looking

at a bundle of cheer," he said. "At your service."

Clay stared at the ceiling.

"Come," Slaughter said. He stood. Clay lay quietly on the bed. Slaughter reached down and took him by the hand.

Clay jerked free.

"I'm going to be very persistent, Eustis. So you may as well come along now."

"I didn't even cry," Clay said softly. "I didn't even cry."

"Wait until you're drunk. You'll bawl like a baby."

"I've got to do something, Maxwell," Clay whispered. "I've got to do something. But I don't know what. So you tell me."

"I'll work on it."

"No. You don't understand. I've got to do something. Something . . ." He gestured helplessly.

"Well, you can't, Eustis. I've told you before. There just aren't any causes left. So forget about it. Now, come on." He pulled at Clay's shirt.

"Oh, you're so goddam smart all the time!" Clay shouted suddenly. "Don't you ever get tired of it? Get the hell away from me."

Slaughter moved toward him.

"Goddamit, Maxwell!" Clay cried, and he shoved Slaughter in the chest.

Slaughter looked at him a moment. "As you wish," he nodded, and he left the room. Clay listened to his heavy footsteps retreating down the stairs.

"Maxwell, I'm sorry," he called. "I'm sorry."

The front door of the barracks banged shut.

Clay started pacing up and down. What a thing to do! On top of everything else, talking like that to Maxwell. What a stupid thing to do! What a dumb, stupid . . . He shook his head. It had to be done, though. It had to be done. Tonight was a night for being alone.

He looked at his watch. After six. How had it gotten that late? Where had the time gone? He stared at the second hand. It was flying. Flying around and around, and he had to get going. He didn't have a minute to waste. Not a minute. Closing the door to his room, he raced down the stairs.

Outside, he stopped for a moment, turning around. It was a beautiful evening. Nice and warm, but not hot. Just a beautiful evening, that's all. He looked at his watch again. Then he started to run, past the orderly room, past the supply room, into the parking lot to his car. Backing out onto the company street, he headed toward C Road. There wasn't any time to lose. No time to lose. He raced up C Road, gunning the motor, not slowing until he came to Main Post. Then he pulled up sharply, braking at a side street.

Which way now? Right? Left? Straight ahead? That depended on where you were going. Well, where? Maxwell would have known. Maxwell would have told him. Clay slammed his hands against the steering wheel. He never should have pushed Maxwell like that. Never. He honked his horn. Again. That was dumb. What a dumb thing to do! Shoving Maxwell and honking the horn when there wasn't anybody to honk at. Stupid. Just plain stupid. He switched on his headlights, then switched them off, then on again. Which way? Well, one thing was sure. What he needed was somebody to talk to.

He parked in front of the NCO Club and looked around, but Slaughter's car wasn't there. A lot of other cars were there, but not Slaughter's. Hurrying inside, he half-ran through the front room into the bar. He blinked, getting used to the darkness. The bar was packed, jammed full, but the tables were empty.

Clay shoved his way up to the bar and ordered a boilermaker. The noise was terrible, and he had to shout to be heard. Behind him, four men were talking about the New

York Yankees. Corporal Monroe was on duty at the far end of the bar, and Clay waved to him. Corporal Monroe walked over.

"You want something?" he shouted.

Clay shook his head.

"That phone call get straightened out okay?"

Clay nodded. Then, "It was bad news."

"What?"

"I said it was bad news."

"I can't hear you," Monroe said. "Who's what?"

"Nothin'," Clay muttered, waving him away. "Never mind." The men behind him were talking about the Chicago White Sox now, arguing, talking louder and louder, and Clay shouted, "Shut up!" but nobody heard him. Grabbing his glass, he bulled his way past them and away from the bar. Soldiers! God, what was worse than soldiers? Nothing in the world. He moved to a corner table and stared up at the bar. Stupid, drunken lushes. That's all they were. Just standing there, drinking their lives away and yelling about the Chicago White Sox. Who cared? Who gave a damn? He looked around at all the tables, but Slaughter wasn't there. Maybe if he waited a while . . . No . . . No use. Maxwell was probably in Capital City by now.

Leaving his drink unfinished, he walked out of the bar. Why had he yelled at Maxwell like that? What was the point? What a terrible thing to do! He left the NCO Club and hurried back to his car. If he never saw another soldier again, it would be too soon. Driving swiftly, he turned onto Main Entrance Road, and in a few minutes the post lay behind him. Hastingsville. That was the place to go. Pushing his foot to the floor, he watched as the speedometer climbed from forty to fifty to sixty-five. Up ahead was the Footlong. Paulie. Clay slowed.

The Footlong was crowded for the dinner hour, and he

hesitated a moment on the highway. Finally, he turned off and found a parking place. The flies attacked him at once, but he ignored them, walking across the gravel to the counter. It was filled, all the way along, with people waiting, standing two and three deep. More soldiers. And high-school kids.

"Hi, Sergeant Clay," Paulie called, looking out at him. "Some day, huh?"

Clay nodded.

"It was seventy-six degrees at five o'clock," Paulie went on. "That's the last I've heard. Where's Mr. Slaughter?"

"Capital City."

Paulie went back to work, and Clay took a place in line. He waited impatiently, glancing at his watch. After seven. More people came and stood behind him, wedging him in. Paulie was running around behind the counter, sweating terribly, piling pickle relish onto a row of footlongs.

"Paulie?" Clay called.

"I'll be with you as soon as I can," Paulie answered, flailing out at the flies buzzing around the frankfurters.

Clay stepped out of line, moving slowly across the gravel to his car. Getting in, he sat back and closed his eyes, trying to rest, but the flies kept buzzing at his face, so finally he drove onto the road, turning toward Hastingsville.

It still looked the same. The lights still flickered over the military stores and the old men and women still sat in their stiff-backed wooden folding chairs, lining the sidewalk, staring as the people walked by. Clay found a parking place across from the city hall and got out. He looked along the sidewalk. A few paces away, he saw a skinny, balding old woman talking and nodding to herself. The chair beside her was empty. Clay walked over to her and sat down.

"Hello," he said.

"That's not your place," she told him.

"I know, but—"

"You can't sit there. You get out of that seat."

"Yes, ma'am," he mumbled, and he stood, moving quickly along the sidewalk, conscious of the people staring at him, hearing their *buzz, buzz, buzz* as he hurried on.

Turning in to the first tavern he came to, he sat down at the bar. The bartender was a great fat woman with a deep voice. He ordered a boilermaker, paid her, then looked around.

It was a townie bar, full of old men and women, chattering to each other across scarred wooden tables. Clay listened to the sound a moment. Down at the other end, sitting in a corner, he saw the Hastingsville chief of police, talking with three other men. The tables were filled, but at least the stools were empty. He took a long swallow from his boilermaker and stared up at the mirror over the bar, watching the people, his eyes wandering from table to table.

A hand touched his shoulder. Clay turned, looking up into the face of a wrinkled old man.

"Ain't you the guy was in that accident about six months ago?" the man asked.

Clay studied him. "I guess."

"Zowee!" the man said. "I thought so." He laughed, his mouth open, and Clay saw that he had no teeth. "That was the best night so far this year," the toothless man said.

Clay nodded.

The toothless man pushed himself up onto the neighboring stool. "I knew I recognized you. Second you walked in here. I remember the whole thing like it was yesterday. That blimp in them blue pajamas. Zowee!" and he laughed loudly. "You remember me, don't you?"

"Sure."

The toothless man put his arm around Clay's shoulder. "How you been?"

Clay looked at him a moment. "Not so good," he answered finally.

"What's been the trouble?"

"Well . . ."

"You haven't got an extra dime, have you? I could use a beer."

Clay waved to the fat woman. She came walking over slowly, wiping the sweat from her forehead.

"Beer," Clay said.

"He bothering you?" the fat woman asked.

"We're pals," the toothless man told her. "He's buying me a beer."

Clay put a dime on the bar and she set a beer in front of the toothless man. Behind them, the buzzing of the old people seemed to be growing louder.

"You ever have a dog?" Clay asked softly.

"Course. I had hundreds. Why? You wanna sell one?"

"No."

"I know a fella who's buying. Lives out on a farm. What kind you got?"

"Golden retriever," Clay said. "A thoroughbred golden retriever. But I don't want—"

"How old is he?"

"Sixteen," Clay answered, "but—"

"Zowee!" the toothless man laughed. "Who wants to buy a dog sixteen years old? Hell . . ."

Clay grabbed him, pulling him close. "I said I wasn't looking to sell him."

"Okay, okay," the toothless man said. "Keep him."

"He's dead," Clay muttered.

"Well, hell, why didn't you say so in the first place?" He finished his beer and signaled to the fat woman. "Two more. For my friend and me."

Clay put a quarter on the bar and pocketed the nickel.

"What was his name?" the toothless man asked.

"Donald," Clay said.

"Funny name for a dog."

"I didn't give it to him. He had it when I got him. See, some rich people on the other side of town, they owned him. Trained him to be a hunter. But he fooled them. He was gun shy. So my father bought him for me. Donald and me, we grew up together."

"That's very interesting," the toothless man said, finishing his beer, reaching across, starting on Clay's. "Was he smart?"

Clay nodded, staring ahead. "He was smarter than people. He understood me. Whenever I was unhappy, he was unhappy. I couldn't keep nothing from him. We grew up together. See, my folks came from Tennessee, but things wasn't so good there, so when I was a kid, they decided to go to California. But they didn't want to take me. Not until they was settled down. So we drove to Virginia. My aunt and uncle live in Virginia. Mr. and Mrs. Howard. And my father bought me Donald as a present to keep me company while he and my mother drove to California to get settled. But they never got there. They was killed on the way. Car crash. Both of 'em. So me and Donald, all we had was each other. And Mr. and Mrs. Howard, of course, but mostly it was me and Donald. Just the two of us."

"That's really interesting," the toothless man said. "Go on. Go on."

"Well." Clay shook his head. "Donald just died today and I—"

"Don't mean to interrupt you," the toothless man said, "but I'd like you to meet some friends of mine."

Clay turned and saw two more old men standing behind him, nodding.

"Go on," the toothless man said. "Listen to what he's saying," he told the other two. "It's very interesting." He snapped his fingers toward the fat woman. "Three," he gestured.

Clay froze.

"Go on, now. He died and what?"

Clay looked from one old face to the next. Then he jumped down off the stool, running from the bar, across the street to his convertible. Jamming it into gear, gunning the motor, he roared past the police station out of town. "Fool!" he shouted, and his mind echoed the word. Fool! Fool! He didn't care! He didn't care! You shouldn't have told him about Donald!

It was dark now and he was doing eighty, the car shaking terribly under the strain. He pumped the gas pedal and stared as the needle moved even higher. Eighty-one. Eighty-four. How much could the car take? Not much. Not much more anyway. Eighty-six. The car veered across the road, bucking and jerking. Clay swung it back onto the right side of the road, leaning all his weight on the gas pedal. The motor roared and the bucking increased and his calf muscle started to knot. Ninety. Ninety-one. The pain in his leg grew, but he still pumped at the gas pedal, trying to push it through the floor. Ninety-two. Ninety-three. Ninety . . .

It was then that he saw the Rainbow.

A square, dark log cabin, set half a mile in from the road. On the roof, a dim red neon sign flickered on and off, spelling out "Rainbow." "Rainbow." Clay slowed the car and peered through the darkness. What was the story on the Rainbow? Slaughter had told him something once, but he couldn't remember. But it wasn't just a bar. Maybe it was a bookie parlor, too. Or something. He couldn't remember. Turning off the main road, he followed the dusty, rutted lane leading in. At the end, the lane widened and two cars were parked. Just two.

Clay nodded. A quiet place. No people. A quiet, lonely bar where you could sit by yourself and drink and maybe have a conversation with the bartender. No soldiers, no high-school kids, no toothless men. He parked, got out of the car and bent down, massaging the calf muscle in his right leg, digging his fingers into the flesh. It felt fine. The cramp was gone.

Clay walked to the front door and stepped inside. It was a small room with the bar at the far end, booths lining the two side walls, square wooden tables filling the center. High above the bar was a bright light, and set directly in front of it, a large turning wheel, divided into a dozen pie-shaped sections. Each of the sections was a different color, and as the wheel turned slowly around and around, the color of the room changed from red to orange to yellow to green to blue, over and over.

Clay waited in the doorway a moment. The bartender stood at the far corner of the room, talking to some men who sat hidden in a booth. Clay chose the booth nearest the door and sat, with his back to the rest of the room, looking down at the table. Old and wooden, it was scarred with hundreds of deeply cut initials. Clay waited, watching the wall change color, from red to orange to yellow to green to blue.

The bartender appeared, a thick, crew-cutted man of thirty. He wore a brightly colored sports shirt with the sleeves rolled up.

"Boilermaker," Clay said, and the bartender nodded and disappeared. Clay took a dollar bill from his wallet and set it on the table. Across the room, he could hear the low mumbling of the other men.

The bartender came back with a beer and a shot glass full of whiskey. Taking the dollar, he dropped some change on the table. Clay took a sip of beer, then poured the whiskey into the larger glass, stirring it with his index finger. Bringing it to his lips, he chug-a-lugged it and raised his hand again for the bartender, who was sitting at the other booth, talking. The bartender crossed the room. Clay gave him another dollar and the bartender went away, returning a while later with another boilermaker.

"Keep the change," Clay told him.

The bartender shrugged.

Clay gestured to the bench across from him, but the bartender shook his head, walking away.

Another friendly one, Clay thought. That was the thing about the South. Everyone was so damn friendly. He mixed his boilermaker and stared down into the dark liquid. Boilermakers weren't much on taste, but they did the job. Nothing worked as fast as a boilermaker. What was it Meltzer had said once? That Martinis were worse? Ridiculous. Anyway, what did Meltzer know about drinking? He was a nice kid, but he didn't know for beans about liquor. Maybe they could have a contest in New York. Clay would take Martinis and let Meltzer try boilermakers. See who passed out first. No, that wouldn't be fair. Meltzer passed out on soda water. Maybe Slaughter would try it, though. Maybe Slaughter . . . How could he have done that to Maxwell? And the toothless man. Telling him. Clay took another sip of his boilermaker. Didn't feel a thing. Sober as a judge. He breathed deeply, trying to get his stomach to relax. No good. Maybe he should write a song about boilermakers. Sell it to some beer company. Make a pile. But nothing much rhymed with boilermaker. And Schlitz wasn't any better. Neither was Pabst. Budweiser! That was the one. He nodded again. Sure. Make up a song and sell it to Mr. Budweiser. Miser. Henry Kaiser. Hell, it'd be a snap. Slaughter could close the deal. Make the arrangements. "Hello, Mr. Budweiser? This is Maxwell Slaughter. Listen." And then Clay would sing the song. "The lad also balances brooms, Mr. Budweiser." That was how Slaughter would say it. And they'd split fifty-fifty. Maxwell could go live on his island in real style. None of them grass huts. A nifty house with a spare room or two for emergencies. And he'd fly down after his TV programs. Bring a couple of

Hollywood starlets along. Big blondes with nice boobs. Sensational! But everything depended on the song. He had to have the song ready for Maxwell. First he needed a rhythm, so he started drumming his fingers on the carved wooden initials of the table top but something was wrong and when he looked he was amazed to see that his hands were white fists and they were pounding down and he tried to unclench them but he couldn't and his fingernails were digging deeper and deeper into the soft flesh of his palm. Wrenching his left arm up, Clay stared blankly at his watch.

It was half-past eight.

And Donald was dead.

And he started to cry.

He fell forward, his arms locking around his stomach, the side of his face pressing onto the cold wood as the tears flooded from his eyes, falling into the wedged-out initials, filling them. He tried to stop, tried to hold his breath, but the contractions deep inside kept forcing his mouth open, making him gasp. He bit into his lower lip, but still the tears came and his gasps grew louder, and then somebody was grabbing at his shoulder.

"Let's pick it up," the bartender said.

Clay pulled loose, opening his mouth, trying to form words.

"Come on, buddy," the bartender said.

Clay shook his head.

The bartender grabbed him again, starting to drag him from the booth. "Out, buddy. Come on. You've had enough."

Clay fought him off.

"You've had enough," the bartender said again.

"I'm not drunk," Clay muttered. "I'm not drunk. My dog died."

The bartender stared at him a moment, hesitating. Then he turned quickly and walked to the far side of the room.

Clay rubbed his palms against his eyes, sniffling. He blinked. The room was changing colors again, and the colors reflected in the tiny pools of water in the table top. Little tiny pools of water, changing color before his swollen eyes. Little laughing pools of water, laughing . . . laughing . . .

Now Clay heard it plainly. Laughter. Coming from the far side of the room. He stared across, saw the bartender and the tops of the heads of the other men in the booth. The laughter grew, and he knew they were laughing at him. Brushing his arm over his eyes, he stood, moving to the center of the room.

"Stop it!" he yelled.

The laughter continued. Clay moved further forward, until he could see their faces. Then he stopped.

"You got troubles, Clay?" Sfc. Priest said, laughing out at him from the booth.

Clay took a step backward. Priest. Is that what Slaughter had told him? Was that it? That Priest came here? He shook his head. He couldn't remember. They were laughing louder, and he watched.

"Cut that out," he told them.

"Heard your mother died, Clay," Priest said. "You stupid son of a bitch."

Clay moved slowly up to the table, looking at their open mouths. He hesitated for just a moment. Then he picked up a glass of beer and threw it in Priest's face.

The laughter died.

Priest lashed out with his foot, but Clay moved in closer and slapped him across the mouth with the back of his hand.

"Get the door, Johnny," Priest ordered, and the bartender ran across the room, slamming the door shut, pulling down the shade.

Clay backed off into the middle of the room, watching as Priest stood, then Corporal Lenahan, finally the third man, a tall, thin blond. The bartender waited by the door, and Clay was conscious of the sound of his own breathing as he continued edging toward the center of the room, his arms hanging loosely at his sides. He counted them. One. Two. Three. Would the bartender do anything? Clay shot a glance toward the bartender. Four. Four, but none of them looked to be very fast. The thing to do was just keep on moving and don't let them get behind you. He started backing toward the bar. The other three spread out around him, Lenahan closest, Priest circling to the other side of the room, the blond following along behind. The bartender took a step away from the door. Clay felt his shoulder blades graze the bar. Now there was no place left to go. He waited. The bartender took another step away from the door.

And right then he saw it.

A path. Big as a highway, leading straight to the door. It was as clear as it was ever going to be, and he could make it to the door easy, open it wide and then take off, running like hell for his car before they knew what had happened. He could be long gone and they'd still be standing there, and he'd be free and laughing like a bastard and zipping back along the road that led to Hastingsville.

"I'm not running, Donald!" Clay cried.

The bartender took a step backward toward the door, and the highway closed.

Clay charged.

He pushed off from the bar and sailed into Lenahan, and Lenahan went down to one knee. Priest was behind him now, and Clay ducked, whirling out of range, moving in between the tables, knocking over chairs, his breath coming easily. Priest waited, and the blond was chicken, but Lenahan came in among the tables after him. Clay backed away again, keeping a lookout for the bartender, who still waited by the door. Clay moved fast, but Lenahan kept following him, and then

Priest was circling, trying to get behind him.

Lenahan ran forward, bringing his right leg back, kicking for Clay's stomach, but Clay moved out of the way just a fraction, then lunged forward, grabbing Lenahan's foot as it sailed by and jerking it upward with all he had, twisting the foot high into the air. Lenahan left the floor for one moment, then crashed down, his head slamming against the wooden floor. Grunting once, Lenahan lay still. Three. Three to go. "I'm not running, Donald," Clay shouted again, and his voice sounded harsh, strange, terrible.

"Get behind him, Johnny," Priest cried, and the bartender moved in, but Clay dashed by him, racing for the bar, planting one foot against it, waiting. He was sweating heavily now, and his entire body felt loose. He swung his arms in the air, gasping for breath, pulling it down into his lungs. The blond. The chicken. Get the chicken. Clay moved forward a step, but the blond jumped backward, edging close to Priest. Clay reached blindly behind him onto the bar, and his hand closed around a glass, and he threw it all he had, but just then the bartender jumped him from the side, and the glass shattered against the far wall. Clay pounded down with his elbow on the bartender's neck, jabbing it in, and when the bartender's grip loosened, he moved away down the bar, his hand still reaching blindly hehind him, looking for something to throw. Then Priest had a chair and was moving in toward him, but the chair was heavy and when Priest raised it, Clay waited, and when the chair started down, he jumped to one side and the chair splintered on the bar. Clay raced forward toward the blond, leaping on top of him, both of them going down in a tangle, kicking and yelling but the blond was faster than he thought and Clay could only hit him once high on the head before the blond was up and backing toward Priest. Clay pushed himself to his feet, moving in among the tables again, shoving them out of his way, knocking them over with a swipe of his hand. The bartender was up now, screaming at him, and Priest was screaming, too: "You son of a bitch! You son of a bitch! I'll kill you, you son of a bitch!" But this time it was Clay's turn to laugh. He snorted away, pulling at a ripped portion of his shirt-sleeve, tossing it behind him to the floor. Still three to go. Priest. Priest was the one to get. Once you got Priest, the others would be easy. Clay moved quickly away from the tables into the center of the room. Then he paused a moment, not caring about the bartender, who was creeping up behind him.

Clay ran forward, and when he was close to Priest, he jumped into the air, feet first, legs bent. He kicked out with his feet because it was a terrific thing to do, and the wrestlers always did it on the TV. But Priest took a step backward. Clay's legs lashed out against thin air, and then he crashed down full length onto the wooden floor, helpless, the breath knocked out of him. The bartender sprawled over him, pinning his arms, while the blond grabbed his legs and he tried to struggle, but he couldn't breathe.

Priest bent down and hit him in the mouth.

Clay blanked out for just a moment and everything went white as his head slammed into the floor. He blinked, the taste of blood strong in his mouth. His mouth was ripped open at one side and blood was pouring out and he tried pressing his tongue onto the cut, but Priest was lifting him now, like a rag doll, shoving him at the blond, who hit him, spinning him onto the bartender, who kneed him in the back, and then he was on the floor again, face down, watching the blood drip from the side of his mouth. Clay pushed his legs under his body and raised himself into a kneeling position, wiping his hand across his bloody mouth. If only he could get his breath back. If only he could breathe, then he could do something. The bartender lifted him roughly and dragged him across to the bar. The blond grabbed one arm and the bartender took the other, pulling the arms out and back, spread-eagling him across the bar, pushing his shoulder blades into the wood.

Clay raised his head. Priest was moving out from hehind the bar, a roll of quarters in his hand. Clay watched as Priest stood in front of him, his big hand opening and closing on the roll of quarters. Priest spread his feet wide, planting himself, getting ready. Then, without warning, his arm lashed forward and his fist ripped viciously into the pit of Clay's stomach. Clay went limp, gagging, falling to the floor. Priest was breathing heavily now and Clay could hear him talking in gasps, giving orders. Then they were lifting him again, pulling his arms, spread-eagling him, forcing his shoulder blades back against the wooden bar.

Priest's hand was white around the roll of quarters as he squeezed it tighter. Clay looked at the hand. He knew what was going to happen. This one wasn't going to the stomach. This one was going to the face. Clay dropped his head, staring at the floor.

The bartender grabbed Clay by the hair, jerking his head back up. Clay stared as Priest's hand began slowly drawing back.

"You ugly bastard," Clay muttered, and he closed his eyes, waiting, waiting. There was a sound and a cry, and then he opened his eyes.

Master Sergeant Slaughter was standing behind Priest, his hands locked around Priest's pulled-back wrist. Throwing all his weight into Priest's body, Slaughter pivoted sharply, pulling Priest off balance. Slaughter snapped his arms around and Priest careened across the room, falling backward over a table, slamming into the floor.

"Howdy, Maxwell," Clay mumbled.

Slaughter slipped a moment, losing his balance, but he recovered it quickly and lumbered forward toward the other two. The blond stepped away, letting Clay fall to the floor. The room was green, turning blue, and Slaughter was starting to perspire when the bartender dove at him. Slaughter shoved the bartender away and grabbed at the blond's wrist. The blond kicked out but Slaughter had him by the wrist and, throwing his weight one way, he pivoted again and the blond spun screaming into the wall head first, crumpling to the floor. Slaughter was breathing more heavily now, and his face started to drain of color as the room turned yellow, and perspiration momentarily blinded him, so he stopped, shielding his face with one arm, wiping the sweat away with the other. That was when the bartender hit him from the side, tackling him, knocking Slaughter to his knees. They rolled around on the floor with the bartender scrambling on top, but then Slaughter grabbed his arms, pushing him off. Moving to his feet, Slaughter clamped both of his hands around the bartender's wrists, starting to swing him toward the wall. The bartender was big, but Slaughter kept turning, faster and faster, snapping the bartender off his hands, slamming him flush against the wall. The bartender grunted and slid to the floor.

Slaughter stood in the center of the red room, his hands pushing at his chest, gasping terribly, his face dead white, his clothes soaked through.

"Look out, Maxwell!" Clay yelled, and Slaughter started to turn, but not fast enough, and Priest had him around the neck. They both went down, Slaughter moving slowly, trying to push him off. Clay started to pull himself to his feet, but his hands slipped and he fell again, watching as Slaughter rolled over onto his stomach, Priest lying on top of him. Slaughter's breathing thundered through the room and his face was a hideous color against the blue walls. Now the walls were red again and Slaughter had him! One hand at Priest's throat, the other at his belt, Slaughter struggled to his knees, holding Priest across his chest like a bar bell. Slaughter staggered to his feet, spreading them wide apart. With one final, terrible effort, he began to lift Priest up over his head. Priest struggled, but slowly Slaughter straightened his arms, lifting Priest higher, higher, higher still.

Then Slaughter fell.

He crumpled to the floor, the fingers of his right hand crawling over his body toward his heart. The fingers stopped. The hand fell back. Slaughter lay still. Next to him, Priest stirred. Slaughter made no sound. Frantically, Clay grabbed the edge of the bar and forced himself up onto his feet. Across the room, Priest stood. Clay started running forward. Slowly, Priest brought back his boot, aiming for Slaughter's face.

With a scream, Clay landed high on his back, his legs locking around Priest's stomach, his arms locking around his throat. Staggering, Priest tried to throw him off. He lurched forward, turning, spinning, jerking, bucking.

But Clay rode him down. Priest went to his knees, and Clay pushed his face into the floor. Priest tried to rise, but Clay was on him again, driving his fist into Priest's kidney. Priest buckled. Clay brought his knee up flush into Priest's face and the blood started to flow. Crying openly, Clay dragged the bigger man down and knelt across him, pounding with his fists at the bloody face. Priest's eyes were swelling shut and his mouth hung open, but Clay kept on hitting down, first one fist, then the other, the right, then the left, setting up a steady rhythm. "What did you do to Maxwell?" Clay sobbed. "What did you do to Maxwell?"

There was no answer. Priest lay still.

Coughing, Clay rolled off onto the floor and knelt there for a moment, his body shaking, out of control. Eyes tightly closed, he waited, not wanting to turn. But slowly, deliberately, he looked across the room toward Slaughter. Slaughter's eyes were open. Thank Jesus for that! Slaughter's eyes were open. Clay crawled over the floor and looked down into

Slaughter's face.

"Walk . . ." Slaughter whispered, gasping for breath, his face still terribly pale. "Walk . . ."

Gently, Clay helped him into a sitting position, then half-lifted him onto his feet. Slaughter's left arm hung limply at his side, and with his right hand he pushed at his chest, mouth open, trying to swallow. Clay led him to the door and out into the starry September evening. The cool air covered them and they stopped a moment, resting. Then Slaughter pushed loose and started walking, walking aimlessly around and around the parking lot, slowly walking around and around, his left arm still hanging at his side, useless, while with his right he pounded feebly at his heart.

"Eustis!"

It was Bobby Jo calling, and he turned, saw her waving to him from the window of the touring car. His eyes still on Slaughter, he moved through the cool darkness toward her. Slaughter was walking faster now, pounding harder at his chest, and his left arm was beginning to move again.

"What's my baby boy friend doing that for?" Bobby Jo asked.

Clay shook his head.

She looked at him. "Boy! You been in a fight. You should see yourself."

Clay nodded.

"We been following you all night long, Eustis. Every place you went. I'll bet you didn't know. I'll bet—"

"Hush up," Clay said.

She peered at him from the window. "What's the matter? Didn't you win?"

"I guess," Clay muttered.

"Oh, I knew you would," Bobby Jo cried, clapping her hands. "I just knew you would. On account of my baby boy friend," and she pointed through the darkness. "He can do anything."

IX.

Sergeant Clay sat rigidly in Slaughter's swivel chair, chain smoking, staring across the room toward the door. His throat felt dry and his head ached and his mouth tasted worse than he could ever remember, but he inhaled deeply, pulling the hot smoke down into his lungs. The air conditioner hummed steadily in the window and he listened to it for a while. Then, stiffly, he reached for a fresh cigarette and, using both hands, lit it off the burning end of the butt and mashed the butt flat in the ash tray.

It was the Tuesday following the fight at the Rainbow and Slaughter had been in Capital City since Sunday night. Maxwell had been gone for thirty-six hours and . . . *Ow!* Clay jerked his hand out of the ash try, blowing at the particles of burning ash that clung to his index finger. Sticking the finger in his mouth, he sucked on it, staring at the thin string of smoke rising from the ash tray.

With a quick swipe of his hand he knocked the ash tray across the room, watching as the butts scattered on the floor. Shaking his head, he got out of the chair and dropped to his knees, crawling around, picking up the butts, dropping them into the wastebasket.

The telephone rang.

Clay leaped to his feet and dove across the desk, grabbing the receiver.

"This is Miss Barbara Jo Pepperdine," he heard. "And I would like to speak to my baby boy friend."

"He ain't back yet, Bobby Jo. There's no point calling up here every ten minutes."

"Well, what in the world is taking him so long?"

"I told you. He's visiting the hair doctor in Capital City."

"That just don't make sense, Eustis."

"It's a new kind of treatment, Bobby Jo. It takes time.

But he'll be back soon. I expect him any sec now."

"Well, I got gym class next hour so he won't be able to reach me."

"He'll call you at lunch."

"I just don't understand what in the world is going on," Bobby Jo muttered. "Good-bye, Eustis."

"Bye, Bobby Jo." He hung up.

Where the hell was Maxwell? Clay looked at his watch. Eleven o'clock. Outside, the sun beamed steadily down. What was keeping Maxwell? Maybe he ought to make up a waiting song. No. What was the point? Who cared? He slumped down in the chair and dropped his chin onto his chest. "Come on, Maxwell," he said out loud. "Please. Come on." No sound from the corridor. Nothing but the goddam humming from that stupid air conditioner.

The back door slammed. Clay sat up, listening. Footsteps in the corridor. Vaulting across the desk, he planted himself in front of the doorway, starting to hop up and down, his head tilted to one side, his right hand gently striking his temple. When the footsteps were very close, he began to imitate the sound of trumpets blaring out a fanfare, all the time hopping as fast as he could.

The door opened and Slaughter walked in.

"I'm doin' an imitation," Clay yelled. "Guess who?"

Slaughter shook his head and walked to his desk, sitting down in his swivel chair.

"Esther Williams, you goon. Look. Don't you get it? I'm knocking the water out of my ears," and he hopped even higher, hitting harder at his temple.

Slaughter smiled. "That's wonderful, Eustis."

Clay slid back onto the desk and crossed his legs. "I just thunk it up."

Slaughter nodded.

"And Bobby Jo's been calling in. I told her you went

visiting the hair doctor."

Slaughter nodded again.

Clay leaned forward. "Well, what happened? What did they tell you? What did they say?"

"Nothing I didn't know already, Eustis. I'm going to die."

Clay reached out for a cigarette and slowly lit it, inhaling deeply. Then he glanced around the room, at Maude Adams, at the air conditioner, at the soft-drink machine. Finally, he looked at Slaughter.

"Bullshit," Clay said.

"No," Slaughter answered quietly. "It's true."

"Bullshit."

"It's true, Eustis."

"Come off it, Maxwell. You ain't gonna die. I refuse to—"

"God damn you!" Slaughter shouted. "Will you shut up. It's the truth."

"I'm sorry," Clay said, jamming his cigarette into the ash tray. He looked at his empty hands a moment, fidgeting, finally bringing them up close to his face, staring at the lines crisscrossing on his palms. "How do you know?"

"The doctor told me."

"Well, hell, Maxwell, come on. You can't go around believing what some pimpleheaded birdbrain in Capital City says. He probably couldn't tell the clap from the chicken pox. And that's the truth."

Slaughter shook his head.

"Now I know what I'm saying, Maxwell. Them Capital City doctors is all morons. Look. Let's go over to the post hospital. They'll tell you I'm right. You'll see."

"I can't go near an Army doctor, Eustis. Don't you understand? They'd discharge me in two seconds."

"But . . ."

"I've got a bad heart, Eustis. A bad heart. That's all there is to it."

"Well, you're sure as hell givin' up awful easy. You're sure as hell taking it awful calm."

"Calm!" Slaughter shouted, his voice suddenly filling the room. "Calm!" He shoved himself up out of the chair and began pacing. "Don't tell me calm. I've never been so angry in my life! Christ, Eustis. I mean that. All the way back from Capital City I've been thinking about it." He grabbed Clay by the shoulders. "It's so unfair, Eustis! So damned unfair. I'm a decent man. I've led a decent life. I haven't robbed and I haven't cheated and it's so unfair. All the way back from Capital City I kept thinking the same thing over and over. Not me. You don't mean me. Someone's made a mistake up there. You don't want me. You've picked the wrong man."

"And they ain't gonna get you either, Maxwell. 'Cause you know why? You know what we're gonna do? We're gonna go to New York City. We're gonna go see one of them fancy doctors in New York City. And he'll give you a pill or something and zingo, we'll be back in business. You'll see, Maxwell. We'll drive right to New York City and you'll see. Hell, we won't drive. We'll fly."

Slaughter shook his head. "It wouldn't do any good, Eustis."

"Come on now, Maxwell. Please. There's gotta be something we can do. There's just gotta be."

"We can prolong things," Slaughter said. "For a while. But that's all."

"How? How?"

Slaughter looked down at his middle. "I'm a trifle overweight," he muttered.

"How much you gotta lose?"

Slaughter shook his head. "Perhaps a hundred pounds."

Clay whistled. Then, quickly, he smiled. "Well, hell, that ain't so much. We can do that easy enough."

"But I don't want to," Slaughter said, his voice rising. "Don't you understand? I don't want to! I don't want to! I just want to stay like I am. I like things the way they are. I've spent a long time getting them there and I want to keep them that way. That's why it's so unfair. I'm an ugly man, Eustis. I'm ugly now and I've always been ugly and food has always been the one great pleasure in my life and it's so unfair that—"

"Easy, Maxwell," Clay cautioned. "Take it easy. Don't excite yourself like that."

Raging now, Slaughter grabbed him again, shaking him. "SEE? SEE? That's just what I mean. That's what's so terrible. No matter what happens I am condemned to a life of timidity! Timidity, Eustis, and I hate it and it's killing me." He turned suddenly and walked to the window, staring out.

Clay listened to the sound of his heavy breathing. "You ain't gonna die, Maxwell. I won't let you."

"Leave me alone, Eustis," Slaughter said softly. "Please."

Clay hesitated.

"Please."

"It's all on account of Donald," Clay said. "It's my fault."

"No," Slaughter answered, still staring out the window. "I knew what I was doing when I went into that bar. I knew the possibilities."

Clay nodded slowly, slowly turning, heading for the door. He put his hand on the knob, then stopped. "Hey, Maxwell," he said. "Will you have lunch with me? Huh? Will you?"

Slaughter shrugged. "Yes. If you like. But leave me alone now."

Clay opened the door.

"Eustis?"

"What, Maxwell?"

Slaughter turned and looked at him. "That goddam dog of yours. You loved it, didn't you?"

"Yes."

Slaughter nodded. "Good."

"See you later."

"Until that time."

Clay closed the door quietly behind him.

It was a little after twelve when he whipped his convertible into the I. & E. driveway and started honking his horn. Presently Slaughter appeared in the front door and slowly descended the steps. He crossed to the car and got in.

"Howdy, Maxwell," Clay said.

"Eustis," Slaughter said.

Clay began to drive. He drove out of the driveway and took a left, then another left, then a right.

"Where are we going?" Slaughter asked him.

"Never you mind," Clay answered, and they drove on a minute more. When they reached the parade ground, Clay stopped the car, pulling it half off the road. "We're gonna have a health meal," he said then. "Right out in the sunshine."

"What about food?"

Clay giggled and reached over to the floor of the back seat, pulling out a medium-sized paper bag. They left the car and wandered slowly onto the parade ground. The grass needed cutting and patches of dirt were more evident than before. The wind blew softly, but the sun was warm.

"Beautiful day," Slaughter said, as they walked along.

Clay nodded. "I been thinkin'," he began, "about what you said before. And it's kinda been bothering me."

"What's that?"

They walked on, drawing closer to the center of the field. Clay pulled up his shirt. "Hey, Maxwell," he said. "Look," and he pinched at some flesh below his ribs. "Feel that."

"I'd rather not, Eustis, if you don't mind."

"You don't have to. But look, Maxwell. It's a whole handful of flab. Right here. And I got one on the other side, too. I'm getting awful fat."

"I hadn't noticed."

"Well, I am. And so I got to thinking." He stopped, pointing at the grass. "This spot okay?"

Slaughter nodded.

Clay sat down quickly and crossed his legs. Slowly, Slaughter did the same.

"You were thinking," Slaughter said.

"That's right. And here's the thing. You see, I need to lose me a little weight. But it's awful tough doin' that all alone. And you need maybe to lose a little, too. So what I figured is that we ought to go on a diet together."

Slaughter did not reply.

"And with that in mind," Clay finished, "I bought us lunch," and he emptied the contents of the paper bag onto the grass. "Yogurt."

"Yogurt?"

Clay nodded. "Absolutely. I went and had me a little chitchat with the man at the commissary and he said that there's nothing like yogurt for taking off a few pounds. So here's what I got." He turned the four half-pint containers upright on the paper bag. "Two for you and two for me." They sat for a moment, facing each other, sitting cross-legged on the ground as the wind blew by. "See?" Clay went on. "Four flavors. Altogether different. Pineapple, strawberry, prune whip and orange. Ain't they pretty?"

"Lovely," Slaughter agreed.

"Okay," Clay said. "Let's dig in. Here," and he reached into a pocket, pulling out two wooden spoons, handing one to Slaughter. "You pick first."

"They're all so tempting, Eustis. I don't know which to choose."

"Well, go on anyway. Go on."

Slaughter sighed. "All right. I'll take the pineapple and the prune whip. You take the strawberry and the orange."

"Over and out," Clay nodded, picking up a container, pulling off the lid. "You're supposed to stir it up good first. Commissary men said so. The flavor's all at the bottom."

They started stirring their yogurt.

"Looks mighty good," Clay said, mixing his strawberry.

"Indeed yes," Slaughter said.

"Stir it up real good, Maxwell. Get that flavor all through. Woweeoboy!" He licked his lips. "Hey, you call Bobby Jo?"

"We chatted. She's very pleased about my hair."

Clay lifted a spoonful of strawberry, shoving it into his mouth, swallowing quickly. "Mighty tasty," he said.

"The prune whip is excellent, too," Slaughter said.

"Do tell? I'm big on prune whip."

"Care for a taste?"

Clay hesitated.

"It's all right, Eustis," Slaughter said quietly. "I'm not contagious."

Clay dug out a spoonful of Slaughter's prune whip. "Dee-licious," he said.

Slaughter nodded.

"I can just feel the pounds drippin' away, can't you?"

"Oh, absolutely."

They started in on their second containers. Clay stirred his orange, Slaughter his pineapple. "What a magnificent afternoon," Slaughter said, looking up at the sky.

"It sure is pretty," Clay said. "It sure is a pretty day."

They began to eat again, spooning the yogurt into their mouths. All around them, the post lay quietly under the distant sun.

"This was a lovely idea of yours, Eustis."

Clay grinned happily.

"Superb yogurt."

"Yup. It's so good I think I'm even gonna give up ice cream."

Slaughter smiled sadly at him and fell silent. Clay watched him a moment. Then, when Slaughter began to shake his head, Clay leaned forward suddenly.

"Hey, Maxwell," he said. "Hey, listen," and he banged down on the top of his head with the knuckles of his right hand, continually changing the shape of his mouth.

"What are you doing?"

"Well, listen." He continued pounding down. "I'm playing a tune."

Slaughter smiled. "That's wonderful, Eustis. I never knew you could do that."

Clay shrugged. "I ain't done it much since high school. It's hard on the head."

"Well, then, stop."

"Oh, no. It don't hurt now. What do you want me to play?"

"What do you know?"

"Well," Clay mused, "I used to be pretty good on 'Nearer My God to Thee.' "

Slaughter smiled again. "Somehow that's just too apt, Eustis. I'm sorry."

"Oh, Jesus," Clay muttered. "I didn't mean nothin'."

"I know."

"Don't die," Clay said suddenly. "Please. I don't want you to die."

"Thank you, Eustis."

"So don't. Okay?"

"All right, Eustis. We'll live forever. Does that suit you?"

"Suits me fine," Clay said. "Just fine."

"Can you play 'Danny Boy'?"

Clay nodded. " 'Course I can. Get close now. Listen." He started pounding at his head with both hands, his mouth open. "You hear it?"

"Yes," Slaughter said. "I hear it," and he gestured for Clay to go on.

So Clay went on. And they sat there, alone on the vast parade ground, sitting close together, Slaughter quietly watching, listening, as Clay's fists pounded down in rhythm, while the sun warmed them, and the wind cooled them, and all in all, as Slaughter remarked afterward, it was one of the more pleasant meals.

When it was over, Clay stopped in front of the I. & E. Building and Slaughter got out. "I'll call you later, Maxwell. See what's new? Okay?"

"Fine," Slaughter said, waving.

Clay waved back and then started the drive down to the company. The streets were quiet, with only an occasional platoon marching along, serving to break the monotony of the flat gray barracks and the flat gray ground. He pulled into the parking lot of the Transient Company a few minutes later and got out of the car, glancing for a moment toward the stockade. One lone prisoner stood in the compound, a single guard standing behind him.

Walking into the supply room, Clay sat down at his desk and picked up a broom, balancing it on his palm. The supply room was practically empty. The blankets were gone, the mattresses, the shelter-halves. Nothing but a few odds and ends left. He shifted the broom from one hand to the other. His head hurt him so he put the broom across his knees and began massaging his skull. Maybe you could do it with gloves on and still get the same sound. Or put a piece of foam rubber on your head. He continued rubbing, digging in with his fingers as best he could. Then he picked up the broom again. Putting his feet up on the desk, he sat back, staring at the brush.

Maybe the thing to do was call Meltzer. Meltzer was from New York. Probably knew a lot of doctors. Then they'd fly to the big town and pay a visit. Some office on Park Avenue. A penthouse, with a real gorgeous nurse. And she'd look at him and he'd give her the smile, and maybe they'd get acquainted good while Maxwell was in seeing the doctor. And then the doctor would come out. Old guy with gray hair, and he'd have his arm around Maxwell's shoulder and he'd say, "Glad you brought him in, Sergeant Clay. He's as healthy as a dime. Them pimpleheaded birdbrains in Capital City are nothing but a bunch of morons. Couldn't tell the clap from the chicken pox," and then they'd all say goodbye and zip on off to Paris, France.

Clay shifted the broom onto his little finger. Boy, that yogurt tasted awful. Really bad. But hell, they must have lost a lot of weight. Pounds. Lose that much every day, and Maxwell would be skinny by the time they hit Gay Paree. Skinny as a rail. Sure. Sure.

Grabbing the broom handle, Clay slammed it viciously across his desk top. Running out of the supply room, he looked at the sky. What a beautiful day. What a really beautiful day. He walked slowly to the orderly room, scuffing his feet in the dust.

Private Cronkite was sitting at the First Sergeant's desk, looking at a girlie magazine. Clay climbed on Booth's desk and picked up the phone. "Two-nine-two," he said. Then, "Maxwell?"

"Yes, Eustis."

"How are things?"

"Fine, Eustis."

"How you feeling?"

"Fine."

"What's new?"

"Not much."

"Just figured I'd call to say hello."

"Thank you, Eustis. Good-bye."

"Bye, Maxwell." He hung up. Cronkite was still looking at the girlie magazine. Clay jumped off the desk, moving outside, back to the supply room. Maxwell sounded okay. Just the same as always. But it was hard to tell. Idly, he picked up the broom and stuck it between his legs, galloping around the room, clucking his tongue. Maybe he should go call Maxwell again. Pass the time of day a while. It was probably too soon, though. Maxwell might get mad at him for pestering. And that would be bad. What if he had another of them fits? No. He'd never have another. Not with the yogurt slimming him down. He wouldn't die. Not Maxwell. "Jesus!" Clay yelled suddenly. There wasn't anything to do. Not a blessed thing. Just wait around with nothing to do but think. Maybe he could call Maxwell again now. He shook his head. No. Still too soon. He looked at the floor. It was clean. Spotless. No dirt. No nothing. Taking the broom, Clay walked to the farthest corner and slowly, with great care, concentrating on nothing at all except the broom, he started to sweep.

It was three o'clock when he emerged from the supply room, brushing his hands against his fatigue pants. The sun was already far across the sky, and it was cooler. Opening the door to the orderly room, he walked inside. Private Cronkite still sat at the First Sergeant's desk, his chin in his hands, studying the girlie magazine upside down. Clay picked up the phone. "Two-nine-two," he said, and waited. The phone buzzed once. Twice. Again. Clay listened. The buzzing continued. No answer. That was funny. He squinted. Now where the hell could Maxwell be?

Master Sergeant Slaughter stood in the center of the post commissary, looking down at the ice-cream freezer.

His stomach rumbled once. Slaughter sighed. It was three o'clock and he was ravenous. His stomach rumbled again. Frowning, he put the tip of his thumb between his teeth and began to gnaw. Ice cream. Hundreds of pints of ice cream. Chocolate, strawberry, tutti-frutti, vanilla, raspberry ice. He moved along the freezer, reading the labels. Orange ice, lemon ice, lime ice, chocolate again. Now chocolate chip and chocolate ripple and raspberry ripple, and there it was.

Butter brickle.

Reaching down, he picked up a pint and turned it over in his hand. Butter brickle ice cream. What could compare to butter brickle ice cream? Not many things. Not in his experience, at any rate. One of the great taste thrills. The ice cream supreme. He nodded. Perhaps Eustis might compose a song about it. Again his stomach rumbled, louder than before, and he glanced around, embarrassed. Had anyone heard? No. No one was watching. He brought the pint package to eye level. Butter brickle. Oh, the French had their baked Alaska and the Viennese their *Indianertorte*, and a delicate mousse was certainly tasty. But not superior. Pocketing the package, he took a step toward the cashier.

He stopped. No. He was being stupid. Sighing again, he replaced the butter brickle. Then, hurriedly, he purchased a head of lettuce, had the clerk conceal it in a brown paper bag, paid for it and left. Slowly, he ambled along the street to Headquarters Company. His stomach kept grumbling. "All right," Slaughter muttered. "All right." Lettuce. He shrugged. Lettuce was roughage and roughage was good for you. Crossing the deserted street, he headed for his barracks.

A young private dashed out of the mail room. "Here's your *New York Times,* Sergeant Slaughter," he said.

"Thank you, lad," Slaughter answered, and he tucked the paper under his arm. It felt heavier than usual. A good issue. Shall I compare thee to the *New York Times?* he thought. Nothing compared to the *New York Times.* It was the butter brickle of newspapers. Opening the door to his barracks, he paused at the bottom of the stairs. Then, very slowly, one step at a time, he trudged up to his room. Unlocking the door, he set the paper on his bed, the bag of lettuce on his table, and started to undress. He took off his shirt, stepped out of his trousers and hung everything in its ordered place.

Finished, he bent over his bed, rearranging the half-dozen large pillows, fluffing them with his finger tips. When they were in their correct position, he sat down, untied his shoes and lay back. His stomach grumbled, echoing in the small room. Slaughter reached for the paper bag and took out the head of lettuce. Removing the outside leaf, he folded it, stuffing it into his mouth. He bit down. The crackling sound filled the room. Terrible. Vile. It tasted as bad as it sounded. Chewing slowly, he swallowed. His stomach grumbled on, so he picked off another leaf and folded it into his mouth, chewing more quickly now, getting it down as fast as posisble. Temporarily, at least, his stomach was silent.

He lifted the *New York Times* and plopped it across his chest. He was perspiring slightly, so he wiped his forehead with the back of his hand. He opened the paper. The front section, the want-ad section, the real-estate section, the amusement section, the sports section, the News of the Week in Review, the book section, and finally, folded away in the middle, the Magazine. Licking his thumb, he turned to the table of contents. Page sixty-eight. Games and puzzles were on page sixty-eight. Licking his thumb again, he slowly turned the pages, one at a time, coming closer and closer and . . .

His heart thumped terribly against his ribs.

He hesitated, feeling the uneven beat. The palms of his hands were wet, and perspiration stood out on his forehead. He could hear the rasp of his own breathing in the quiet room. He turned another page. Another.

His heart thumped again. Trembling, Slaughter stopped. Not even the puzzle? Couldn't he even do the puzzle? No puzzle and no pinball, nothing to eat, cut down the drinking, and above all, don't excite yourself. Don't excite yourself. "Easy," Slaughter said out loud. "Easy." There just wasn't much left. Living. Living was left. But that was all.

"All right," he muttered, and he dropped the magazine, picking up the News of the Week in Review. Herblock had a drawing of McCarthy, and Syngman Rhee was complaining again, but with Oriental honor. Selecting an article at random, Slaughter started to read, but the words blurred before his eyes, made no sense at all. He was aware of the sound from his stomach, and he reached out, ripping off several leaves of lettuce, jamming them into his mouth. Viciously, he chewed. What was it that he had said to Eustis? A life of timidity? Well put. Good word, timidity.

Perhaps he could just look quickly at the puzzle, find out who the author was. Grabbing the magazine section, he flipped to page sixty-eight and stared at the name. He did not know it. So it was a new antagonist! Probably nervous, anxious to show off. Foreign phrases and archaic forms. Midden, dor, cholla. The words filed across his mind, passing in review. Lettuce. The lettuce eater, an autobiography. Butter brickle was better than lettuce. But lettuce was better than nothing.

His heart thumped again, making him gasp. Steady. Steady. Everyone's heart thumps when they get excited. Nothing wrong with that. But careful now. No chances. Don't excite yourself. Under no conditions should you excite yourself, and you'll have to lose some weight, Mr. Slaughter. A great deal of weight. He gazed down at the tire of fat hanging over the tops of his drawers, cotton. Grabbing a handful, he pulled at it angrily until the pain became unpleasant. Then he let go.

Lying back on the pillows, he crossed his arms on his stomach and stared at the ceiling. It was so unfair. So miserably unfair, but Eustis did love that stupid animal. That was something. Not a cause, but at least it was something. He closed his eyes, pulling a gray curtain down across his mind. Nothing. Nothing at all. Dropping his hands to his sides, Slaughter slept . . .

He was awakened by the sound of "Danny Boy" and Eustis was playing it on his head. But something was wrong. Eustis was hitting his head, but it sounded like a bagpipe. Lovely, Eustis. Lovely. Slaughter blinked. Now it was a bugle, and "Danny Boy" was gone. It was dark outside and he lurched to the window, throwing it open.

Retreat. Retreat was coming in over the loud-speakers, high and clear. Slaughter listened. Beautiful. The sound poured from the loud-speakers, drifting out, gently covering the dying post. Retreat, the autumn of the day. Lovely. Lovely.

The record ended. Slaughter turned, staring down at the plump head of lettuce sitting on his bed table. "Retreat, hell!" he muttered, picking up the lettuce, drawing his arm back, getting set to heave it out the window. He stopped. Grabbing his blue ball-point pen, he jammed it between his teeth and hurried to his wall locker. He took his can of lighter fluid and sat on the edge of the bed, opening the magazine section to the puzzle page. Humming happily, he put the lettuce between his knees and turned the can of lighter fluid upside down, squeezing it onto the lettuce. At the same time, he scanned the definitions. Hmm. They weren't bad. Twenty-four down was a lovely stroke, and nineteen across was excellent. Setting the empty fluid can on the table, he put the lettuce on the floor.

Then he set it on fire and watched it burn.

Clay found them at seven o'clock. They were sitting at Slaughter's table in the NCO Club, and as he entered the dark room, Bobby Jo stood up and yelled at him.

"Here we are, Eustis. Over here."

Clay approached. "I been looking all over for you, Maxwell. I called this afternoon but you didn't answer."

"I took a nap, Eustis."

"Good," Clay said. He sat down.

The juke box blared as usual and the room was dark as usual. But it was empty. Just a few couples sitting around the dance floor and half a dozen men standing at the bar.

"We're having a party," Bobby Jo said happily. She stood up. "And lookit what I got on." She turned around. "You can't see it so good in here but it's black and I bought it in Capital City."

"You look real pretty," Clay said.

"Doesn't she, though," Slaughter agreed.

"It's a cocktail dress," she went on. "And guess what? I'm drinking cocktails." She held up her glass. "It's got gin in it."

"You're just growing up like crazy, Bobby Jo. You stick with us."

"We're having a celebration," Bobby Jo cried. "We're having a super celebration."

"Why?"

"Because my baby boy friend ain't never gonna get bald. That's why."

Clay nodded.

Bobby Jo giggled. "And we had supper at the Footlong and my baby boy friend, he ate forty-eight inches of hot dog."

"No!" Clay said.

"Yes he did too. We figured it all out and it come to exactly forty-eight inches of—"

"No!" Clay said again, his voice rising.

Slaughter nodded.

Clay grabbed him. "What do you think you're doing?"

Slaughter said nothing.

"You're gonna answer me!" Clay cried, standing now, shouting, pulling at Slaughter's shirt. "Goddamit, you're gonna answer me!"

"Don't you dare speak to my baby boy friend like that," Bobby Jo said. "You apologize."

"It's all right, Miss Pepperdine," Slaughter said. He turned slowly to Clay. "I warned you, Eustis. I warned you. I told you I'd fail you sometime."

There was a pause.

"Where's Eustis going?" Bobby Jo asked then, staring as Clay turned from the table, bolting for the bar.

"Perhaps to get a beer, Miss Pepperdine."

"He sure is acting funny."

"It's the strain of waiting for orders. Nothing more."

"We're having a celebration," Bobby Jo said. She stared through the darkness toward the bar. "Is Eustis coming back? I hope so. I made a basket in gym class today."

"Did you really?"

She nodded. "It was my very first one." Bobby Jo watched Slaughter a moment, then stuck her finger in her ear and wiggled it back and forth. "Is anything wrong or anything?" she asked.

Slaughter smiled at her. "No. Nothing."

"Good." Bobby Jo nodded. She glanced toward the bar again. "Eustis is taking an awful long time getting that beer. I wonder, is he mad at me?"

"No, Miss Pepperdine."

She took a small sip from her drink. "Do you wanna hear how I made the basket?"

"Yes. Please tell me."

"Well, I just closed my eyes and the ball went through the hoop. You could have knocked me over with a feather." She clapped her hands suddenly. "Look. Here comes Eustis."

Clay slowly approached the table.

Slaughter looked up at him. "Will you celebrate with us, Eustis?" he asked, gesturing to the empty chair.

Clay made no move.

"Come," Slaughter said. "Join the party." He gestured again.

Clay sat down.

"I made a basket in gym class today, Eustis. I just closed my eyes and the ball went through the hoop."

"You could have knocked her over with a feather," Slaughter said.

"And that's the truth," Bobby Jo nodded.

They drank quietly then, and while they were drinking, the record changed. Suddenly the room was filled with violins and Clay jerked his head toward the machine.

"Remarkable," Slaughter said. " 'The Blue Danube' in the NCO Club."

Bobby Jo began humming. "That's the prettiest song, I think."

"It's lovely," Slaughter nodded, listening as the violins grew louder.

"Let's dance," Bobby Jo said suddenly.

"I don't know that I remember how, Miss Pepperdine."

She grabbed his hand and started pulling. "Come on. Come on quick before it changes," and she led Slaughter out onto the floor. "Now, it's simple. Look. Just one, two, three. That's all there is to it." Slaughter put an arm around her, took her hand, and they began to move.

"See?" Bobby Jo cried. "It's easy."

"Hey," someone at the bar yelled. "Slaughter's dancing."

"You shut your mouth," Bobby Jo yelled back.

"Oops," Slaughter said.

"Ow," Bobby Jo said.

"I'm sorry, Miss Pepperdine. My feet."

"It's all right, I don't . . . Ow."

"My apologies again."

The music was reaching a peak, and suddenly Slaughter grabbed her, lifting her off the ground. "This is much the best way," he said, hugging her, turning around and around, faster and faster, spinning across the floor.

"Look at us," Bobby Jo cried. "Hey, everybody. Look at us."

Slaughter held her tighter, turning, turning, the sweat starting to pour down his face. He was breathing heavily now, and the pressure was back in his chest. But not severe. Not this time.

"You'll get tired," Bobby Jo said. "You better put me down."

Clay watched as the color drained from Slaughter's face. Still they turned, Bobby Jo yelling and laughing, Slaughter spinning around and around.

The record ended. The saxophones began again.

"You take her, Eustis," Slaughter said. "I need some air."

Clay ran onto the floor, grabbing Bobby Jo, commencing a wild dance, jumping up and down, spinning, whirling, clapping his hands, snapping his fingers in time with the blaring of the saxophones. Bobby Jo stepped back, watching as Clay's dance grew more feverish, more frantic, his arms whipping around his rigid body, his mouth open, his eyes half-closed. Then Slaughter shouted from the doorway.

"Miss Pepperdine. Miss Pepperdine."

She turned.

"The next waltz, Miss Pepperdine," Slaughter roared. "The next waltz is mine . . ."

X.

It was too hot for October.

Clay struggled with his duffel bag, moving slowly, trudging across the dusty company area toward his car. The air was muggy, and above, great black clouds were gathering on the horizon. Dropping the duffel bag onto the gravel of the parking lot, he wiped his forehead with the back of his hand. He opened the trunk of the car and, inhaling, he bent down, lifted the duffel bag and shoved it inside. Slamming the trunk shut, he sagged against the car for a moment, resting.

Then, slowly, he retraced his steps, returning to the barracks, climbing the stairs, fanning his hand in front of his face. He entered his room, took an armful of civilian clothes, smoothed them as best he could and turned, descending the stairs again, moving out of the muggy barracks into the muggy air. He deposited the clothes on the hood of the car and stood on the running board and tugged at the roof, straining, finally managing to pull it back and down. One article at a time, he carefully spread his clothes across the back seat of the car. Turning once more, he started the slow walk to the barracks, scuffing his feet, silently shaking his head, staring down at the small pools of dust surrounding his shoes. Into the barracks again for another armload of clothes, then out, crossing slowly to the car.

Half a dozen trips later, he was finished. Sitting behind the wheel, he slumped back, closing his eyes. Then, for the last time, he stood and returned to his barracks. It was four o'clock, and from somewhere the echoing of a hammer came to him. He listened a moment, staring at the other buildings. They were closed, shut, boarded up, doors and windows both. Walking into his barracks, he glanced briefly into the shower room of the latrine, then proceeded up the stairs. At the doorway to his room, he stopped. There wasn't any reason to go further; the room was empty. Nothing was left. No sign of life. Nothing. He continued to stare inside for a moment. Turning, he closed the door behind him, and for the last time walked heavily down the stairs, listening to the sound of his shoes echoing hollowly in the empty barracks.

The company was deserted. Staring straight ahead, Clay walked past the mess hall, past the orderly room. When he reached the supply room, he stopped by a window. Standing on tiptoe, he peered in over the crossed boards. Empty. No sign of life. Nothing. He turned away, moving onto the gravel parking lot. Across from him, the stockade compound was empty. No guards. No prisoners.

Clay got into his car and backed out onto the company street, heading for C Road. Turning left, he drove away from the Transient Company, past the stockade, past MP Headquarters, past the deserted bayonet field, heading toward Main Post.

There were still a few cars left. Two were parked by the empty commissary, and three stood before the empty PX. The hammering sounds were louder, and here and there, an occasional soldier in fatigues moved slowly along the sidewalk. Taking a right at Main Entrance Road, Clay picked up speed. The air was cooler now and he wiped his face, still staring straight ahead. He drove faster, the sound of the motor increasing, and then he was at the main exit.

Clay stopped the car, letting the motor idle. Turning his head, he looked back. The entire post spread out behind him, great and flat, motionless and still, growing darker as the dark clouds started moving in from the horizon. This was it. This was good-bye and there ought to be something to say. Something. But what? Slaughter would know, of course, but Slaughter was dead. Biting down on his lower lip, Clay drove forward, turning left at the highway, heading toward Hastingsville.

The Footlong was open, and he saw Paulie leaning across the counter, his chin resting in his hands, staring around the deserted parking area. Clay hesitated a moment, then pulled off the road and drove up to the stand.

"Hi, Sergeant Clay," Paulie said.

Clay nodded to him from inside the car. "Hi, Paulie. Just thought I'd say good-bye. I'm leaving now."

"You ain't the only one," Paulie said, gesturing around the empty lot. "Hardly anyone been in all day. Haven't seen you much lately, either. I thought you'd gone. Whatsamatter? Been sick?"

Clay shook his head.

"You don't look so good. Little pale, maybe."

Clay shrugged.

"So where they sending you, Sergeant Clay?"

"Alabama."

"Aw, that's too bad. I hear it's a real pistol down there."

"I guess."

Paulie swatted at a fly buzzing around his ear. "Well, I'm pulling out, too. Thinking about going to California. Or Florida, maybe. They both got a beautiful climate. Hot weather's good for selling franks. No sense staying around here." He shook his head. "Hey. Come to think of it, where's Mr. Slaughter? I ain't seen him much either."

Clay stared at him. "Didn't you know? Maxwell's dead."

"Aw, that's a damn shame," Paulie said, swatting at the fly again. "Well, no wonder I ain't seen him. Who'd have thought that Mr. Slaughter—"

"Bye, Paulie," Clay said, backing the car around.

"Bye, Sergeant Clay. Thanks for stopping in. Good luck."

Clay continued on toward Hastingsville. The air was muggier than before as the clouds rolled on, blotting out the sun. In the semidarkness, Hastingsville looked dead. The streets were deserted, the military stores were gone, their windows empty, *For Sale or Rent* soaped across the glass. Ahead of him Clay saw two old men, bent over, walking slowly, going home, carrying their wooden stiff-backed chairs. "Wait for me," he shouted at them, the words bursting from his throat. But they paid no attention, didn't even turn to see who spoke.

He parked the car, got out and slowly crossed the deserted street, stepping up onto the sidewalk, walking inside Crawford's drugstore. He looked around. An old woman with hands that trembled was buying a pack of cigarettes, but otherwise the store was empty. Clay looked at his watch. Five minutes before five. Five minutes early. He approached the magazine rack and started looking at the titles. He reached out and took a crossword puzzle magazine and flipped it open, studying the diagram a moment. Shaking his head, he put it back. Movie stars smiled out at him, dozens of them, President Eisenhower frowned, and there was McCarthy scowling and it was five o'clock. One minute after. Two minutes.

The front door opened and Bobby Jo slipped in. "Eustis," she said, running over to him. "Eustis," and she threw her arms around him.

He stood still, eyes closed, his arms at his sides.

"I'm sorry if I'm late," she whispered. "But I had to leave my date down at the saloon. I fibbed to him. He thinks I got the loose bowels." She stepped away. "He's awful jealous. I can't stay but a second."

"I just wanted to tell you good-bye, Bobby Jo. That's why I called you."

"But why ain't you called me sooner, Eustis?" She moved close to him again, staring up at his face. "You been sick? You look awful."

Clay shrugged.

"You goin' to Paris, France, Eustis?"

"Alabama," he muttered. "South Alabama."

"Oh, that's a terrible place. That's even hotter than here. What happened?"

Clay said nothing.

Bobby Jo continued to stare at him. "Why ain't you called me, Eustis?"

Clay stared back at her. "Why didn't you come to the funeral?"

Bobby Jo turned, moving to the magazine rack, studying the titles.

"Why didn't you come to the funeral?"

"Because," Bobby Jo said, "because if I didn't go to the funeral, then he didn't die."

"You should have come to the funeral," Clay said.

She faced him. "I just couldn't, Eustis," she began. "I just . . ." She stopped as the front door opened and a squat, dark-haired man walked in. "Oh, oh," she whispered.

"What the hell are you doing here?" the squat man said, walking over.

"I want you to meet a friend of mine," Bobby Jo said. "Albert Blodgett. This is my friend Eustis Clay. Albert's from Capital City, Eustis. He's in the construction business."

"What the hell are you doing here?" Blodgett repeated. "You told me you were going to the head."

"I just come up here for some bowel tightener, Albert. And I happened to run into my friend Eustis. We was just saying good-bye."

Blodgett looked at Clay a moment. Then he gestured with his thumb. "Okay," he said. "Blow."

"Don't you dare talk to Eustis like that."

"Blow," Blodgett said again.

Clay started walking slowly toward the door. "Bye, Bobby Jo," he said.

"Eustis," she called, "Eustis. What's the matter? What's the matter with you? What's the matter with you? Eustis? Eustis?"

He closed the door behind him and moved across the street to his car. It was hotter than ever now, muggier, but as soon as the car started moving, the air rushed in over the windshield and dried the perspiration on his face. Turning around in front of the city hall, Clay drove slowly through Hastingsville, back toward the post, toward Capital City. He drove past the pinball parlor and past the saloons, the empty military stores, the deserted sidewalks that stretched ahead of him on either side. Then it ended, abruptly, and Hastingsville lay behind him. On his right now, the metal fence began, marking the outer boundary of the post. To his left was the Footlong, but he did not wave as he drove by. He glanced at his watch. Quarter after five. He ought to make Capital City in an hour or so. Looking up ahead of him now was the main entrance of the post, a wide gateway, with a wooden sign spanning it, CAMP SCOTT spelled out in dark letters. Increasing his speed, Clay stared straight ahead, driving past.

He had gone a quarter of a mile before he stopped.

Pulling off on the side of the road, he let the motor run. Sitting back, he stared at his hands as they opened and closed around the steering wheel. A car drove by, honking its horn at him. He waited. Another car. Then, gripping the wheel tightly, he turned the convertible around, going back, driving in the main entrance. Ahead of him, a figure stepped out of the shadows, blocking his path. Clay stopped the car. The figure moved around to the side. A young MP.

"Sorry, mister, but the post is closed."

Clay said nothing.

"The post is closed, mister. You can't go in any further."

"I got to," Clay said.

"Well, I'm sorry, but you can't."

"It's okay. See, I was stationed here. I just left. But I got to get back."

"Why?"

"I forgot something. I left something behind."

"What?"

Clay did not reply.

"What?" the boy said again.

"Me!" Clay cried suddenly, blurting it out. "Me! Now lemme alone!" and he pushed down hard on the gas pedal. The car jerked forward with a roar. He drove on, listening to the boy yelling, "Stop, hey mister, stop," from behind him, the voice growing fainter.

At the first road, Clay took a right and began the long drive around the perimeter of the post. He drove slowly, looking out, turning his head from one side to the other. There was nothing to see here, nothing but flat, dark ground. But then the companies began. He drove past several, and when he came to the end of the road, he turned left, starting up one side of the post. There were hundreds of barracks now, orderly rooms, supply rooms, hundreds of squat dark buildings, all boarded up. E Company, then F Company. C Battery. D Battery. He drove on, glancing around occasionally, looking to see if anyone was following him. There was no one. Not yet, anyway. Sooner or later there would be an MP car. He shrugged. Maybe not. Maybe the kid wouldn't call in about it. Either way, what difference did it make?

The companies stopped as the practice fields began, machine gun, rifle, bazooka. The road ended and he turned left again, traveling along slowly. The new road was dusty, curving in and out, up over small hills, down again. This was the bivouac area, huge and quiet, black beneath the blackening sky. Clay leaned forward, squinting out as the headlights cut through the heavy darkness. Dust particles dangled helplessly, trapped in the yellow glare. The windshield was covered with the bodies of bugs and flies, smashing softly against the sudden glass. The heat was worse than ever, and he increased his speed, drying the perspiration on his face. Then the road flattened out, the bivouac area ended, so he took another left.

And suddenly K Range spread out before him.

K Range. Clay stopped the car and got out. K. Range . . . The war is over. . . . The war is over. . . . He shoved his hands into his pockets and left the road, scuffing across the dusty range. The officer's tower was gone. Where had it been? Here? No, here, and he took a few steps sideways. Yes. And Meltzer had been yelling from the top, and Slaughter had been sitting in the shadow, blowing on that cartridge shell. When did it happen? How long ago? He shook his head and started walking again, very slowly, away from the road, crossing into the center of the range. Three months? Only three months? That was the last time they had been together. Really together. The war is over. . . . That party in Capital City, it really didn't count. Not with the strangers there. The mother and the girl. What was her name? Milly? No, Emmy. That was it. Her name was Emmy and she was a C. He walked on, kicking at the dust, shoving his hands deeper in his pockets. Up ahead was where the target frames had been. But they were gone, too. Nothing left. Just a hole in the ground. He peered down into the blackness of the pits. Just a big long hole in the ground. Was it really just three months? It couldn't be. The war is over. . . . The war is over. . . . Clay squatted, his arms around his knees. Just three months ago and now Slaughter was gone and Donald was gone and he was off to Alabama. Sweat poured from his face, stinging his eyes. Everything was gone. His eyes hurt, so he closed them, listening. The range was deadly quiet. Dropping his chin onto his chest, he took a deep breath and held it, a tiny dark figure, motionless between the black earth and the black sky.

The first crash of thunder knocked him off balance. He looked up. The thunder died away. Silence. Then a titanic bolt of lightning tore the sky apart. Clay stood up, blinded by its brilliance. He blinked. Again. Again.

Then the rain started. It was a deluge, a flash flood, a tidal wave of water slanting down, cutting down, huge drops that stung at his face, filling the air, wave after wave, harder now than ever, a murderous rain. Clay shrugged. At least it would be cooler. At least it would be easier to drive when the weather was . . .

CHRIST!

The convertible was open, his clothes on the back seat.

With a cry, he started to run, the rain stinging his neck. Already the top layer of dirt was turning to mud. He ran faster and faster and was almost halfway across the range before he tripped, falling headlong in the mud, face down. Breathless, momentarily stunned, he lay still, covered with mud. Shielding his face from the rain, he rolled over onto his stomach, gasping, forcing himself into a kneeling position. One final surge and he was up again, running again, as fast as he could. His feet were wet and the mud seeped in over the tops of his shoes, but he kept on, blindly peering ahead, looking for the car. His shirt was cold and wet and his pants gripped his legs tightly, scraping the skin. Panting, winded, he slowed as the car appeared before him.

The back seat was a shambles. Clothes were strewn all over, on the seat, on the floor. Dashing to the rear of the car, he grabbed the roof and started to lift, but his hands were wet and slippery and he couldn't catch hold. Rubbing his hands on his pants, he gripped it again, pulling.

But the roof wouldn't move.

He pulled harder, straining his entire body, but it wouldn't move. He gripped the edge more tightly and pulled again, but this time his hand slipped, jamming into a sharp piece of metal and his palm began to bleed. Shaking his hand, he brought his palm to his mouth and licked the cut with his tongue. The taste of cold mud on his tongue made him want to vomit and his stomach contracted. He spit the taste into the road, nursing his bleeding hand. With the other hand now he grabbed the roof and tried lifting it one final time. No use. He couldn't budge it. It was stuck. The rain raked away at him, and lightning crashed down again and again, cutting the sky to ribbons, and the thunder crashes hurt his ears.

Clay sagged against the car.

Wearily, he glanced into the back again. Ruined. All his civilian clothes, ruined. He picked up a handful and looked at them sadly. Then he let them drop. Slowly, he walked around the car and stared down into the back seat. "No," he said aloud. "No, please."

The back seat was filling with water.

Clay watched as the water level rose up from the floor. Turning away, he tried not to listen as the rain splashed inside his car. Slaughter wasn't enough and Donald wasn't enough and Alabama wasn't enough. He opened the front door of the car and some water cascaded out. He got in, closed the door, and sat still. His hand was throbbing terribly now, and his neck hurt from where he had fallen. The splashing from the back seat grew louder, and he turned around, leaning over the cushion, gaping, as his clothes floated aimlessly from one side of the car to the other. Everything was ruined. Clothes, car, everything. He stared as one of his white shirts glided along the floor.

"I give," he mumbled. "I give."

The rain increased in tempo.

A great bolt of lightning slashed down onto the range, and he shivered as the crash of thunder exploded. His white shirt was by the door now, and he reached across, opening the door, watching as the shirt skidded out of the car, falling into the muddy road. Mud still dripped from his face, and his hand was worse, and the water level was rising again, and you could take a swim in the back seat if you wanted to. You could strip off all your clothes and paddle around like a kid if you wanted to. You could . . .

Hey-hey-hey-hey-hey! What about that! What about that! Clay knelt on the front seat and looked down at the water. A pool! A goddam swimming pool in your own car. For kids. You could fit a piece of plastic over the seat and fill it with water so that your kids could have something to do when you went driving. Sure. Sure. And you could put water on the floor and sand on the seat and you'd have your own goddam private beach. Right in your own car. THE EUSTIS CLAY KIDDIE POOL! Fantastic. What a name! What a fantastic name! THE EUSTIS CLAY KIDDIE POOL! Catchy as hell. And the rhymes! Just a piece of colorless plastic. Carry it in the trunk when you weren't using it. Then, when you wanted it, just fit in over the seat. Let the kids play all they damn pleased. Hell, adults could use it, too. Everybody could use it. He reached down and splashed at the water with his hand. Felt good. Felt damn good. Get to a phone right off. Get to a phone and call Dee-troit.

He stopped. No. Wait a minute. Not yet. Too early. You had to patent it first. So those bastards in Dee-troit couldn't steal it from you. And they would, too. Hell, it would triple car sales. THE EUSTIS CLAY KIDDIE POOL! But before you patented it, you had to experiment around with it first. Take a month or two in Alabama getting it perfect, and then patent it. Figure it all out. All the angles. Use the old brains. He wasn't just the idea man any more. Now he was both, the ideas and the brains, so he had to take his time before he went to Dee-troit. Then let the bastards bid for it. Sell to the highest bidder.

He'd take the biggest hotel room in town and he'd be smoking a dollar see-gar and he'd flick a big fat ash on the rug, and he'd let 'em start.

"I bid two hundred thousand dollars," Mr. Ford would say. And then Mr. Chrysler would say, "I bid three hundred thousand dollars," and Mr. Ford would say, "Four hundred thousand," and Mr. Chrysler would say, "I bid half a million." And Mr. Ford was angry now. "I started the goddam car racket and I'm going to have THE EUSTIS CLAY KIDDIE POOL if it's the last thing I do, and I bid seven hundred and fifty thousand dollars." "One million," Mr. Chrysler shouted.

And the door to the hotel opened and old General Motors walked in. "Two million," the General said. He was with a girl. Maybe twenty years old, sun-tanned, with long blonde hair and a great body and sensational boobs. An A-plus. "Mr. Clay," the General said, "I'd like you to meet my granddaughter, Miss Louisa May Motors."

"Howdy," Clay said, and Louisa May blushed.

"Are you really Eustis Clay?" she whispered. "The famous inventor and song writer?"

"I guess."

"And can you really play tunes on your head?"

"Why, sure," and he started pounding down.

"Five million," General Motors said.

"Hush up, everybody," Louisa May cried. "Listen. He's playing 'Danny Boy.' Ain't it beautiful?" She walked close to him and smiled. "Go on," she whispered. "It's just lovely." She lay down beside him on the bed. "I live in South Alabama," she said softly. "Do you ever get down that way? I got a big plantation right near an Army post."

"Ten million," the General said.

"Twenty," Mr. Ford said.

"Goddamit, Henry. Twenty-five."

"To hell with you, General. I bid fifty million dollars. THE EUSTIS CLAY KIDDIE POOL belongs to me . . ."

Clay turned the ignition on. The motor started. Shifting into first, he began to drive. The rain was reaching a peak now, and up ahead a bolt of lightning ripped down across the sky. For a moment, far, far in the distance, the low, squat buildings of the post came to life. Then the lightning faded; the buildings vanished.

"Oh Danny Boy," Clay sang suddenly at the top of his lungs, battling the thunder. "The pipes, the pipes are calling. From glen to glen . . ." The thunder rumbled in, but he sang on, driving faster now, swerving from one side of the road to the other in time with the music, listening happily, triumphantly, as the water sloshed around in the back seat.

Lightning spit all around him; rain cut in at his face; thunder crashed against his eardrums. Another bolt of lightning, closer. Then another, closer still.

Clay looked up, straight up, right up into the sky.

"Fuck you," he said.

WILLIAM GOLDMAN was born in Chicago, Illinois, on August 12, 1931. He attended elementary and high schools in Highland Park, Illinois, received his A.B. degree in 1952 from Oberlin College in Oberlin, Ohio, and his M.A. degree from Columbia University in 1956. Beginning in September, 1952, he served for two years with the United States Army as an enlisted man. Mr. Goldman is an editor of the newly published magazine, *The Transatlantic Review*, and the author of two previous novels, THE TEMPLE OF GOLD, and YOUR TURN TO CURTSY, MY TURN TO BOW. He lives in New York City.

BOOKS BY

WILLIAM GOLDMAN

SOLDIER IN THE RAIN

1960

YOUR TURN TO CURTSY MY TURN TO BOW

1959

THE TEMPLE OF GOLD

1957